Wishing Will

H. E. McCarthy

ISBN: 978-1-9196098-1-2

Cover design by bespokebookcovers.com

For those who'd still be with us

if wishes came true.

Chapter One: Will and a Wot

Will Morgan grabbed his remote control and pointed it at the small television by the foot of his bed. The volume bar ran across the bottom of the screen, a wobbly, green blur through Will's raw eyes. Louder, louder, louder, until people in the next street were probably wondering where *SpongeBob's* voice was coming from. The crazy cartoon merriment clashed with the gloomy rock music already blaring from Will's CD-player, but neither could compete with his parents screaming bloody murder at each other in the room below. Apparently nothing could do that.

Another string of expletives rang their furious way through the house, followed by an explosion of smashing glass that made Will physically jump. The tears he'd been fighting back for the last hour fell so fast they barely grazed his cheeks. He nearly smacked himself in the face in his rush to wipe his eyes, and he yanked the peak of his baseball cap lower to hide them, prickling from head to toe with red hot embarrassment. It didn't matter that he was alone in his room; he couldn't shift the strange, nagging paranoia that, somehow, someone was watching him. Figment or not, the fact they'd just seen him cry was beyond mortifying.

Right then he hated his parents, he hated himself, he hated everything and everyone, and more than anything he hated the stinking basketball that sat on the bed next to him, half in and half out of its crumpled wrapping paper. Will had never hated an inanimate object before, but he definitely hated that one. His parents had given it to him when he'd ventured downstairs for breakfast. He supposed he should have been grateful that they'd put their fight on hold long enough to hand a gift over to him at all. But he wasn't. It was a basketball, for crying out loud. Why would they give him a basketball? They knew his game was football. Everyone knew his game was football.

But fine. If they wanted him to play basketball, so be it. He would play basketball.

He slid off the bed, shook the ball free from its torn wrapping and bounced it, again and again, harder each time, aiming to splinter the floorboards with it. Maybe the ceiling falling in on his parents' heads would shut them up.

Will had endured their madness without complaint for weeks, not once losing faith that, no matter how bad things got, everything would turn out okay. It would all be okay, he had told himself, because today had been on its way to fix everything. His mum and dad would put their animosity on hold to celebrate their son's special day, and they would have so much fun and eat so much birthday cake they'd forget all about being angry and remember how much they loved each other. Will hadn't just hoped this, he had known it. He had known it the same way he knew the sky was up and the ground was down.

And the world had gone and flipped upside down on him.

Today had fixed nothing. His birthday meant nothing. All its long-awaited arrival had done was make things worse, because now Will knew the truth: His mum and dad hadn't just fallen out of love with each other – they'd fallen out of love with Will too. The concept hadn't even crossed his mind until now.

He had never felt so alone.

He had never felt so stupid.

On a final, vicious bounce, he kicked the ball speeding across the room. It crashed into his floor lamp, which teetered before hitting the floor with a bang and a pop.

"Will!" his mother shouted from the bottom of the stairs.

Will stumbled around the bed, switched off the television with one hand and gave the top of the CD-player a hard smack with the other. Its lid lifted slowly, the disc rattling to a clumsy stop.

Ringing silence fell.

Maybe they hadn't forgotten him. Maybe he would get the fun day out they had promised him after all.

"Yeah, mum?"

"Stop that bloody racket!"

"Don't take it out on *him*," his father retorted, and the shouting flared up again at once.

A rush of anger froze Will to the spot. Stop that bloody racket? After weeks on end living with their shouting and swearing and random plate-throwing, stop that bloody racket? After they'd let him down so badly - *on his birthday* - stop that bloody racket?

Way past crying now, he gave his eyes one last painful rub with his knuckles, snatched up the basketball, and charged downstairs, making sure to stamp on every step before bursting through the front door and slamming it shut behind him. He hurled his birthday present at the car in the driveway. The ball clunked the windscreen, dropped off the shiny silver bonnet without leaving so much as a smudge, and bounced away, making smaller and smaller jumps until it was rolling pathetically over the garden path. Incensed that the car remained unscathed when he'd fully intended to shatter the glass to smithereens, set off its alarm, perhaps even trigger it to explode like cars always did on television, Will kicked its bumper, twice, and ran to the street, limping a little but trying not to show it. The ever-present figment didn't need to know the car had hurt his foot.

Wind roared in his ears and stole his breath away. It nearly stole his cap too, so he thrust that into the back pocket of his jeans – his 'going out' jeans, as his mother called them. They weren't as comfortable as his everyday ones, and he wished he hadn't bothered. It was a fight to move against the gales at any decent speed, but a fight Will was more than prepared to take on. The air cut through his flapping shirt and chilled him to the bone, but he didn't go back for a coat. He'd rather be cold than go back into that house with those people. He'd rather freeze.

Will's after-school football club had a nine a.m. match scheduled at Wynne Park today. Will usually played in weekend matches, but he'd opted out this time to spend his birthday with his parents. What a waste. Still, even if he wasn't part of the game, it was somewhere to go. At least he would be welcome there, with people who weren't crazy.

It took a good ten or fifteen minutes to reach the park on a normal day. This morning, even with the wind against him, he made it in five.

Something was different about today's match, which was already well underway. Both teams chased the out-of-control ball as one anarchic mob, rules and rivalry forgotten or ignored in the excitement of battling to keep from being blown over. Even the goalkeepers had left their posts.

Will perched on the metal gate at the park's entrance and let the wind swing him back and forth while he watched the mayhem, trying not to resent the laughter and cheers that reached him through the gusts. It didn't seem fair that he was the only one not having any fun. If they weren't taking it seriously, maybe they wouldn't mind an extra player with no kit joining in. He should ask them.

But the more he considered it, the more he realised that wasn't what he wanted. That was not why he had come.

Why had he come?

Golden yellow leaves on the trees bordering the opposite end of the park glinted and swayed in the wind like swarms of shiny bees playing chase around the tossing branches.

Why was he looking at boring trees?

He tried to keep his attention on the farcical match, but his eyes would only stay there for a second or two before flicking back to the dancing treetops. They were waving at him. Calling to him.

The woods were off-limits. All the local children knew that. Last Halloween, Will and his friends had spent a group sleepover scaring each other silly with various horror stories about Wynne Wood. It was haunted. People went missing in there. A serial killer had buried countless bodies under the trees. Child-eating witches resided in the shadows. Nobody who went into Wynne Wood lived to tell the tale. (Except, presumably, the serial killers and witches.)

But right now, Will felt defiant, and his defiance gave him courage, and his courage fuelled the sudden determination that overcame him to see just how far he could disappear into those woods before his parents stopped screaming at each other long enough to miss him.

Chin raised, pulse pounding, Will hopped down from the gate, marched around the edge of the field, and slipped unnoticed into the shadows beyond the first line of trees, where other children feared to tread.

Branches and trunks creaked. Leaves rustled. Falling twigs and tree debris scattered all around him and shadows danced. But there was nothing more. No ghosts, no zombies, no witches jumping out at him. No murderers, no mutilated bodies, no random long-lost people searching for a way out. Nothing to fear at all.

Mid-morning sunlight streamed through the canopy of intertwining branches overhead and lit everything it touched with a glow of gold. The farther Will walked, the bigger and better the trees grew: Real trees with thick knotted trunks and roots that disjointed the grassy ground below. By the time he found the perfect one to climb, he and the wind had both lost their ferocity. All fell quiet and still. Will appreciated the peace, the beauty of the leaves, ferns, untouched weeds and wildflowers, and, best of all, the absence of mad parents. Even the gentle, trickling background noise that he could hear now the wind had dropped was pretty nice, pretty relaxing, like the fountain in his next-door neighbour's garden. He abandoned his climbing-tree to follow the sound and came to a river banked by knee-high reeds. Silvery water rippled, flowing softly, glittering in the sunlight and bubbling where it gushed around several clusters of speckled grey and brown rocks.

A smile almost made it to Will's face - but faded before it got there. A dark shape bobbed ominously on the water. It looked like a person. He squinted and moved closer. It was a person.

Will waited for the man to get up.

He continued to wait.

Was the man drowning?

"Mister?"

No reaction. No movement. No sign of life.

He raised his voice and tried again. "Mister?"

Nothing.

It struck him then, like a swift, sharp slap to the face, that this man wasn't about to get up. Without thinking twice, he tore through the reeds and hit the water at a sprint. It sloshed over his chest, painfully cold and alarmingly solid as he part-waded, part-swam to the body. With an almighty push that sank him ankle-deep into the riverbed, he flipped the man face up, then struggled to pull himself free without losing his trainers.

"Hey," he said, breathless. "Are you okay?" He patted one of the limp arms. "Mister?"

The expressionless face was too white, the lips and sunken eyelids a sickly shade of blue. Dark hair waved silklike in the clear water. He only looked young, for a grown-up. Too young to be dead, anyway. Will felt sorry for him.

His numb fingers curled around the man's coat collar as he cast his mind back to the first aid lesson his class had been given last year, in which they'd practised mouth-to-mouth resuscitation on ugly plastic dummies that left a revolting antiseptic taste on the lips. His mother had joined the group to offer her expertise as an accident and emergency nurse. Her presence, Will recalled now, had not helped him in the least. Jesting taunts from his classmates had embarrassed him into holding his breath and staring at the window for most of the lesson. Could he even remember what to do? He had to at least try.

He hooked his arms under the man's armpits and eased him through the water, back to dry land, the thick, slimy bed trying to swallow his feet every step of the way. Once they'd run out of water the body got drastically heavier, and it took everything Will had to heave it just halfway onto the bank, where he slipped on wet mud and landed face-first in a clumsy, breathless heap on the sopping body. He recoiled in horror, overbalanced, and fell again.

Scolding himself for being a wimp, he hobbled on his knees to the man's side.

"I can do this, don't worry," he said, more to himself than to the stranger. He positioned his hands over the unmoving chest and took a deep breath. Arms straight, he pressed down a few times, trying to find a rhythm. There. He was doing it. Push, one-two-three, push, one-two-three... But how many pushes was he meant to do? Probably ten. Ten sounded right. Or was it more? No, probably less. Five, maybe. Or eight. One of those. Why hadn't he paid more attention?

He lost count while debating the number, concluded he must have pushed too many times, and made a mental note to do fewer the next time to compensate. He locked his lips against the silent stranger's startlingly cold mouth and blew. After he'd run out of breath, he remembered he should have been pinching the man's nose and gave it a quick token nip.

"You'll be okay, mister," he said, pounding hard on the sternum. "A, B, C: Airplanes, Bleeding, Circle-ation." He couldn't recall the relevance of these words but hoped that letting the stranger know that he knew them might speed the process along.

Time ticked by and Will kept going, convinced he could bring the unfortunate fellow back to life. Even when his spindly, goosepimpled arms tired and his muscles started to ache, he didn't change his mind. Even when something inside him demanded it was time to stop, he refused to listen.

"Come on," he panted impatiently when he felt himself flagging. "Come on, mister, wake up. You've got to. You've got to wake up. Wake up. Wake up!"

A vigorous shudder under Will's hands sent him falling backwards into the long grass.

The stranger rolled onto his hands and knees and proceeded to hack up a lungful of river water.

Will jumped back onto his feet, laughing out loud and punching the air, victorious. "Yes! Yes! I knew you'd be okay. I told you so!"

"What happened?" The stranger's panicked voice sounded sore and rasping, every strained gulp of air harsh and manic in his frantic efforts to catch his breath. His bloodshot eyes darted about in all directions like he couldn't get them to focus on any one specific thing.

"I saved you with the magic kiss." The enormous grin Will bore was the first genuine smile to grace his face in weeks.

The stranger reached shaky hands for his heaving chest and his neck, fingers spreading and curling and grasping all over his upper body as though searching for the right spot to hold that would ease his discomfort. Eventually his chest steadied, and he planted his hands on the ground to prop himself up.

Will watched his every movement, fascinated by the busyness of this living, pulsing, respiring body that only minutes before had been a literal dead weight - a suit of cold, heavy flesh over limp bones and nothing more.

"Are you okay?"

The man wiped his chin with his cuff and coughed. "Fine, just fine, thanks," he croaked, returning Will's smile out of politeness. Then he looked confused. "Who are you?"

"I'm..." Will hesitated. Until that moment, he'd had no qualm whatsoever with being in this person's company, nor with touching lips and all but straddling the man - but on this one simple question, Will suddenly became very aware of the fact he was all alone with a complete stranger, in a place he was in no uncertain terms not allowed to be, and his parents had no idea where he was. "I'm not supposed to give my name to strangers," he said, and immediately felt ridiculous.

The man's charming smile grew on one side. "We don't count as strangers anymore." He offered his hand to shake. "I'm Blue."

"No, you're not," Will assured him. "You're just a bit pale now." He pulled his dripping wet cap out of his pocket and slapped it over his spiked hair.

The man, still holding out a hand, appeared amused. "No," he said. "My name's Blue." He took Will's hand and shook it roughly. Wet muck squelched between their palms.

Will noticed Blue's outfit was drying at a remarkable speed. He also noticed for the first time what an unusual outfit it was. The bottoms of Blue's trouser legs were ragged around the heels of his boots, as though they'd once been too long for him and had been walked on until they'd torn. His knee-length coat hung loose around his lean physique, slightly fitted at the waist, slightly flared at the cuffs, an old-fashioned piece, like something from the period dramas Will's mother enjoyed watching on her nights off. If he'd been wearing a frilly shirt under it, Will might have assumed he was in fancy dress. The shirt he wore, however, a plain black cotton one that was in just as bad a condition as his trousers, somehow brought the tatty ensemble into the twenty-first century.

He was staring expectantly at Will through large eyes, awaiting reciprocation.

"Oh. I'm Will."

"Excellent." Blue dropped Will's hand. "I've never met a will before." He paused. "What's a will?"

"Me. I'm a Will. Will Morgan." It occurred to Will that Blue probably ought to see a doctor. His mother would have taken Blue straight to her hospital had she been with them. "Are you sure you're okay? What happened to you? How'd you end up in the river like that?"

Blue rubbed his head, dishevelling his sopping hair into a tangled mess. "I'm not sure what happened. Last thing I remember is... Foosay. She said some really awful things to me, and then I don't know. I can't remember. No, I think... I couldn't move. I think she put a spell on me. Why would she do that?"

Will realised his mouth had dropped open and clacked it shut.

Blue patted at his pockets. "Oh no. Oh no, she took my gem. Karson's going to have my guts, for real this time, for really real."

"What are you talking about? She put a spell on you? What do you mean? Like a witch?"

"Yes, exactly like a witch," Blue said, checking he wasn't sitting on whatever he was looking for. "Because she is a witch." He flinched and for a second looked nauseated. "She paralysed me and held me under the water until I drowned."

Will was pretty sure that Blue was delirious. He most likely needed a brain scan. "You're saying an actual witch put a magic spell on you?"

"Yes, an actual witch," Blue said. "An actual friend, actually. Obviously not anymore," he added under his breath. "Foosay Hoo. Do you know her?"

A giddy little laugh rattled through Will. "I don't know any witches. Witches aren't real."

Blue sat up straighter. He appeared to have recovered from his ordeal already, physically. His voice had lost its scratch and a healthier colour had returned to his skin. But he looked confused again. "Why would you say that?"

"Because they're not. Are they?" Though excited by the prospect of witches and magic being a reality, sense and reason insisted to Will that Blue must be making fun of him.

Of course witches weren't real.

"Of course witches are real," Blue said, with such matter-of-factness that Will's sense and reason were happily sent packing. "As real as me and you."

"No way. That is so cool."

"Please. Witches aren't cool. Wots are cool. I'm a wot."

"A what?"

"That's right," Blue said. "Listen, Foosay's got my gem, so there's not a lot I can do for you right now." His eyes lit up, an idea apparently dawning. "But you could help me. If you help me get it back, I'll be your wot for a whole four… no, five wishes."

"What?" Blue couldn't have said what Will thought he'd said, surely.

"Yes, your very own." Blue nodded. "We're only supposed to give out one wish really, but I think saving my life earned you extra." He gave Will a sharp pat on the arm. "My friend Cesar will help us. He's a ware."

"Aware of what?"

"No," Blue said, a little higher. "Just a ware."

Baffled, Will decided to say no more and simply smiled, hoping to appear intelligent.

"You'll like Cesar," Blue went on, glancing at the slimy sediment between his fingers and rubbing it on his shirt. "Well, he's not really a people-person, so you might not like him straight away. You might not see him straight away, actually. He has a propensity for going invisible around people he doesn't know."

"Invisible?" Will repeated loudly. "I wish I could go invisible."

Blue squirmed. "Oh. Sorry. You really need to wait until I get my gem back before you make any wishes."

Will wanted to tell Blue that he hadn't meant to make a serious wish, that it was just a throwaway comment, but for some reason he felt tongue-tied. His mother often said be careful what you wish for. He hoped he would remember these words of wisdom when Blue got his gem back.

A strong gust of wind knocked the breeze aside in its hurry. Will's wet jeans felt like they'd iced over and frozen the blood in his legs. He couldn't keep a limb still for shivering.

"Come on." Blue staggered to his feet, sidestepping a few paces before he found his balance. "You need a towel, is what you need. Cesar will have one." He took off walking, at speed, the damp frock coat swaying about his legs. "I know what you little people are like for catching your death."

The word 'little' hit Will like a punch. He'd always been that bit smaller than most boys his age, and he had a prettier face than a lot of the girls, but he couldn't stand people noticing.

He had to run to keep up with the wot, which was difficult in his cold, clingy jeans. "My mum says that whenever I go out with my hair wet, but I never catch any death."

"*There's a first time for everything,*" Blue said in a high-pitched trill.

Going by the way he then beamed proudly over his shoulder like someone who'd just done an uncannily good impression of someone else, Will could only assume that the person he'd impersonated sounded exactly like a man putting on a silly high voice.

"Cesar will help us," Blue said again. "He always does. He has a good heart. And a strange infatuation with kites."

"I had a kite once," Will said, solely because he didn't know how else to respond to such an odd, irrelevant remark.

"Excellent. Tell him that. It'll be a good way to acquaint the two of you."

Will couldn't tell if twenty minutes or an hour passed while he continued to rush after Blue, tripping over roots and stumbling in animal holes left and right while Blue glided along with all the easy dignity of a monarch on a red carpet. Busy watching where he put his feet, he didn't notice Blue had come to a stop until he was crashing into the wot's back.

"Sorry," he said, his automatic response to any unexpected collision. "Wow." The tree in front of them boasted the broadest trunk Will had ever seen. It was the width of a double-decker bus, with deep scoured ridges and thick, twisted knots. Short planks of well-varnished hardwood had been nailed up one side to act as a makeshift ladder leading up to a rickety treehouse that someone had built, badly, between the stupendous branches. A child might have put it together. Will imagined even he could have done a better job.

"This is where Cesar lives." Blue gestured to the treehouse. "Get yourself up there."

The request stumped Will. While he generally enjoyed nothing more than risking life and limb swinging about at great heights and was itching to have a go at climbing this monster of a tree, it felt wrong in front of Blue. Adults didn't normally encourage children to do anything potentially dangerous.

"Up there?" he said, to check he'd heard right.

"Yes, come on." Blue waved his arms, hurrying him. "Up, up, up."

That was good enough for Will. He launched himself at the tree and scrambled up the steps, the *Spider-Man* theme blasting in his head all the way.

"Hello?" he called into the shack.

"Go on in," Blue shouted.

Will pushed open the broken door. Inside was empty, save for a few splintered planks of wood jutting in from poorly constructed walls.

"Go on in," Blue shouted again, impatient this time. "What's the delay?"

There didn't seem any point in going inside. The barely-there walls and hole-ridden roof would provide zero shelter from the weather, and Cesar clearly wasn't home. Nor were the towels that Blue had promised.

Even so, Will did as he was told and heaved himself onto the musty baseboards to crawl in through the doorway.

In the blink of an eye, he was no longer in an old treehouse, in danger of being pronged by a rusty nail, but in a palace. Or the closest thing to a palace Will would ever step foot in, at least. A kingly red sofa stood invitingly in the centre of the colossal room, adorned with elegant ivory cushions and velvet throws. Embroidered ruby curtains draped at intervals over the windowless white walls, between each of which were antique-framed paintings of unicorns and dragons. The luxuriously thick, milky carpet felt so soft and springy under his hands and knees that he would have happily kept crawling if he hadn't been so eager to get a better view of everything. In the farthest corner a glass display cabinet exhibited an array of unusual ornaments, a giant glass-like marble presumably Cesar's favourite piece, for it took centre spot. But the most appealing trait of the place had to be the warm aroma of freshly baked shortbread that lingered heavily in the delicious air.

Blue waved a piece of green towel at Will until he stopped sniffing and took it. "Here, dry yourself off."

Will held up the rag between his finger and thumb and stared at it. It was only the size of a flannel. Was Blue trying to be funny?

Squinting, Blue mouthed, "What?"

"Thanks," Will said, not bothering to tone down the sarcasm. He patted the rag over his damp legs and jumped when the tiny towel lurched and sucked at the denim with the force of an industrial vacuum cleaner. He laughed in delight once the shock passed. "That's brilliant."

For quite a long moment Blue stared at Will. Then he shrugged his shoulders like he'd given up trying to work the child out and turned his attention to the room. "Cesar?" He wandered closer to the sofa. "Are you here? I need to talk to you."

A hazy flicker of movement in the air was replaced by a spry, jockey-sized man with a lock of wavy brown hair, who was surveying Will with the beginnings of a sneer that had not quite manifested. Something about his face reminded Will of a squirrel, or some other nervous rodent.

"What's this?" he demanded. The sleeves of his dazzling white shirt were rolled up to his elbows, exposing arms covered in scrapes, scratches, and odd bruises. A bright green grass stain marred one small patch of his otherwise immaculate stone trousers.

"This is Will," Blue said. "He's going to help me get my gem back. Foosay took it."

"Good grief, that's a bit over the top. What did you do to her this time?" The ware stretched his arms out to his left, like he was reaching into an invisible cupboard, and pulled a tray of fine gold-rimmed white porcelain teacups and matching teapot from thin air. "Tea?"

Will and Blue both shook their heads courteously, then frowned at each other when they thought Cesar wasn't looking, to express their mutual dislike of tea.

"I haven't done anything to her," Blue insisted. "I promise. She just went crazy and attacked me."

Cesar shrugged at their response to his offer, saying, "I really can't believe Foosay would do that." To Will's surprise, he then dropped the tea tray onto the carpet. Its contents clattered and splashed but somehow stayed in place. "Are you certain it was her?"

"Yes, I'm certain it was her. I got a good long look at her stupid face while she was dunking my head like a morning coffee."

"Are you being serious? She seriously took your gem?"

"Yes, I'm being serious. I'm being seriously serious. She seriously took my gem. My gem is seriously gone. I'm going to get seriously killed by Karson."

After a short contemplative silence, Cesar asked, "Are you okay?"

"No, not really," Blue said. "Imagine how you'd feel if someone took your Agulga sphere. Then imagine feeling a hundred times worse than that."

Cesar shushed him and glared at Will.

Feeling the need to defend himself, Will opened his mouth to speak, but Cesar cut in first.

"I can't believe Foosay would ever hurt you. The two of you used to be so close."

"She's an old lady now, you know. She must have done that going-senile thing. People do that, you know, they go mad." Blue added to Will, "I hope that never happens to me."

Cesar paced in front of his sofa for a few seconds before sitting down. Still glancing at Will every now and then to make sure he hadn't moved, he said, "I did hear a rumour amongst the forest animals that a local witch discovered the secrets to eternal youth. That was a few years back. Perhaps Foosay's the one they were speaking of."

"Really?" Blue asked, interested. "And what would those secrets be?"

"I don't know, Blue, they're secret." Cesar stroked two fingers down the side of his chin, a faraway look on his face. "But if I'm putting two together with two, your gem must have a role to play. Why else would she have taken it?"

"Why *my* gem?"

Cesar shook his head.

Blue scoffed. "I'm so cross with Foosay. I'm tempted to take something precious of hers when we get my gem back. See how she likes it." He took a deep, shaky breath. "I'd have been dead forever if not for Will. He deserves his wishes, don't you think? You know what it takes for a dead wot to be brought back to the land of the living, don't you?"

Cesar nodded, eyes on the tea tray. Then his brow furrowed at Blue, the nod becoming a headshake. "Actually, no, I don't. What does it take?"

Blue grunted. "Really? Have you not read that mystic's transcript?"

"Pah. There are so many of those ridiculous things floating about, prophecies of imminent doom everywhere you look. Who wants to waste their life reading them? I'm surprised you do. Although you do have more life to waste, I suppose."

"Karson made me."

"Oh," Cesar said, as if the world made sense again.

There was another short silence.

Will took the opportunity to get a word in. "What happened to you?" he asked, pointing to Cesar's cuts and bruises.

Cesar shrank back like Will's voice had startled him. "I fall out of my tree sometimes," he said, his cheeks burning so red he looked like a gnome.

"Wait, this is still at the top of that tree?"

"Of course."

"It's enchanted," Blue said in way of explanation.

"Of course," Cesar said again, picking at a scab on his elbow.

Will aimed a confused eye at the solid wooden door closed securely behind him. "How do you fall out?"

"Pah. The wind catches me sometimes when I'm watching my kites."

Will remembered the earlier conversation with Blue and wondered if he should try to connect with the odd little man. "I had a kite," he said.

The remark instantly softened Cesar. "You did? They're amazing, aren't they?"

"It was okay. I didn't even know grown-ups liked kites."

"What a thing to say. I love my kites. They're wonderful listeners."

"You talk to them?" Will wondered if Cesar was mentally deficient.

Blue answered for his friend. "Cesar talks to all animals. Did I not mention that?"

"Kites aren't animals." Will forced a laugh, sure that they were trying to fool him so they could accuse him of being gullible. Several people at school had done that to him lately, and it was getting old.

"No, they're so much more than animals." Cesar gazed at the chandelier above his head. "I just adore watching those magnificent angels fly. Don't you think they're the most perfect of birds?"

"Kites?" Will repeated slowly, to make sure he hadn't misheard the topic of their discussion.

Cesar's dreamy expression disappeared, and the glare returned. "Why are you even here? Why is he even here, Blue? Isn't it about time you were both leaving?"

Will worried that Blue would be upset, but his new friend didn't so much as bat an eyelid. He must have been accustomed to Cesar's blatant rudeness.

"I need to find Foosay Hoo," he said, as if Cesar had said nothing at all. "I really need my gem back."

Will wondered what it would be like to meet the witch. Would she have green hair and mouldy warts all over her haggard witch face? A broomstick and a pointy hat? "Hey, she won't have a cat, will she?" he asked. "I'm allergic to cats. If one goes near me, I could die."

"Is that so?" Cesar hummed in a manner that implied he would make a mental note of this potentially useful piece of information.

"She doesn't have a cat," Blue said.

"Right." With a face on him that Will's mother would have described as looking like a slapped bottom, Cesar jumped to his feet and wafted Blue and Will towards the exit. "I've told you a hundred times I don't want strangers in my home. Not with you-know-what here."

It felt odd to Will, being referred to as a stranger. And mildly insulting. They were the strange ones, not him.

The door swung open before they got to it, and a barn owl soared through. It landed in an undignified heap on Cesar's carpet, wings sprawled out to each side and talons in the air.

"Oh, look," Will said, amused, and the owl hopped onto its feet. "Where did your friend go?"

"He's a bit skittish," Blue said. He raised his voice. "It's okay, Cesar. It's just a bird."

"What bird?" Cesar reappeared and examined the creature by his door. "What are you doing here?" He listened to its awful, incessant screeching, nodding along. Finally, he lost patience and interrupted. "All right, I heard you the first time. Tell you what, why don't you go back the way you came and... go away."

The owl, unmoving, stared at Cesar through deep-set black eyes.

"I'm not the mouse-minder. I don't know where they are, do I? Go and look." Cesar gave Blue an exasperated look. "Why does everyone come to *me?*" He turned back to the bird. "What do you want me to do, go out there and find your dinner for you? Pathetic. You're a bird of prey. Go prey."

The disgruntled owl tugged a couple of stuck claws free from the carpet and flew on its way, quiet as a ghost.

Cesar made a strange, angry noise through his nose. "Look what that godforsaken beast did to my floor."

"What was all that about?" Will asked.

"Pah. He says all the mice are disappearing. What am I supposed to do about it?"

"I thought owls only came out at night."

"Well, you know what thought did."

"You're not going to tell us where Foosay is, then?" Blue asked.

"You're as bad as that owl," Cesar snapped. "I'll tell you what I told him: Go look!"

"Blue said you were a good friend, you know." Will folded his arms over his chest. "But you're not."

"Oh no, he is really, Will," Blue said. "I think he's just upset because I promised I wouldn't bring anyone here again. Not after…"

"Oh, you remember making that promise, do you? Yet you decided to break it anyway."

"It was an emergency. Promises don't count in emergencies."

"Why, though?" Will asked. "What happened that was so bad?"

"I brought a wenn up here," Blue admitted. "I didn't know she was a bad one. I thought she was nice. She asked if I knew a ware. She said she needed one to help her with a grasshopper she was having trouble with."

"So you brought her into my home…"

"What else was I supposed to do?"

"…and she stole from me."

"How many times do I have to say I'm sorry?"

"All I asked was that you not bring strangers into my home ever again. And what's this?" Again, he looked Will up and down. "A stranger. In my home."

"But Will's no wenn," Blue said with a nervous laugh.

"Don't think I'm getting involved with any of this, Blue, because I'm not. I'm sorry you're having trouble with Foosay, I really am, but I'm doing nothing for you until I find out what happened to my egg. I mean it." Cesar turned his back to Blue. "But I'm sure you're going to go off on your own and find her, so don't let yourself forget she's dangerous. Especially now you don't have your gem. So, mind your manners and be careful." He glanced over his shoulder at his friend before remembering to make a point of his anger and turning up his nose.

"Fine." Blue passed by Will. "Come on, Will. We've got a gem to find. Preferably before Karson finds out it's gone." He pushed the door open and stooped to find his footing just as an unexpected blast of wind blew. Caught off-balance, Blue fell.

On hearing the solid thud that followed, Will rushed to the door, in time to see Blue hop back onto his feet and pat stray leaves and acorn shells off his clothes. "Are you all right?"

"Get yourself down here, Will. Down, down, down."

Will swung himself through the doorframe, flabbergasted by the transformation of the glorious palatial abode into the shabby broken treehouse that was apparent from the outside.

"Finally," Blue said when he got to the bottom step. "How long does it take? Little kid like you."

Will wished people would stop calling him little. "Sorry if I'm not as good at falling down as you are."

Suddenly serious, Blue raised a hand to hush Will and crouched by the base of the tree. He pointed out a patch of soil.

"What?"

Blue's finger pointed lower.

Will stared closer, leaning forward until his nose was just inches from the ground. He could just about make out some tiny pointy-toed footprints in the grainy soil. "Wow. Are those footprints?"

"Yes, they are. Looks like Little Miss Pants-on-Fire has been back here."

"How big are wenns?"

Blue dithered and waved a hand about six inches over the other.

"They're so little!" Will wondered if they hated being called little as much as he did.

"Well, yeah. Where have you been all your life?" Blue peered around as if he might spot the wenn. "If we could get her to give Cesar his egg back, he'd tell us where Foosay is."

Will pulled a face behind Blue's back, not relishing the idea of spending any more time in the ware's distrusting presence. "Why don't we just go and find her ourselves?"

"Oh, yeah? And do you have the first idea of where to start looking?"

Will nodded. "She'll probably be in some creepy old cottage in the middle of the forest. That's where witches always live." He just hoped it wasn't made of gingerbread.

Blue fiddled with a button on his cuff. "I don't know about going to her home. It'd be safer to approach her somewhere more, you know, neutral."

"But we have to go to her house. That's where she'll have her spell books, and her cauldron, and her broomsticks. And you know what else will be there, don't you?"

Blue looked like he didn't.

"Your gemmy thing."

Gaping at Will like he'd sprouted wings, Blue said, "How is it that you know so much about witches when you know nothing of wenns?"

"Everybody knows about witches," Will said with half a smile.

"Except for the fact they exist, you mean." Blue set off walking, muttering, "Like witches are so special anyway."

Will followed, watching grass kick up from Blue's frayed boots. This time he managed to stop himself from bumping into the wot when Blue stopped without warning.

"Hey, I just thought, you'll still be living with your parents, right? Don't you have to let them know you'll be late home?"

"They don't care. They're too busy yelling at each other." Will's shoulders tensed as he waited for the inevitable grown-up lecture: Don't be silly, Will, your parents always care about you, you can't just run away and not tell them where you are, blah, blah, blah.

It didn't come.

"Oh, right," Blue said, and walked on, long strides covering the ground quickly for another minute or two until he suddenly took cover behind a patch of brambles and nettles. "Can you hear that?" he asked quietly. "I think I hear a witch spelling."

Will strained to hear, moving closer. "You mean there's a witch casting spells?" he whispered, the rapid influx of excitement making him tremble. Was he really about to meet a real live witch? "Through here?" A thorn caught in his shirt, and he had to hang back to pull himself free.

"What? No. I mean spelling-spelling."

Side by side behind the nettles, they peered out at an open patch of land amidst the trees.

A woman in a deep burgundy satin dress that draped delicately over her slim figure wandered barefoot over the mossy ground in front of Will and Blue, talking away to herself. Her dark hair shimmered mahogany red in the sunlight, pinned up on her head, several curled strands bouncing by the sides of her sun-kissed face.

"Those are A's, not E's! S-A-L-A, not S-E-L-E. Salamanders! Can't you read?"

Blue grinned at her through the weeds.

"That's not a witch," Will said, disappointed. "That's just a lady."

"That's my friend Dante Simms, and I can assure you she is most definitely a witch. She is one of four sisters from quite a powerful bloodline, actually."

The words sent a crawling-spider sensation across the back of Will's neck. His friends had told stories of the wicked witches of Wynne Wood. They had painted a less attractive picture of them in Will's head, but the fact that she wasn't a hag wouldn't make him any less dead if the witch fancied snacking on the nearest eleven-year-old.

"Are they… wicked witches?"

Blue's laughter settled Will's nerves straight away. "No, they're not wicked. How absurd."

The witch shouted long and hard, "No! I'd have written geckos if she wanted geckos. She wants salamanders. Just take the list and go before I snap your stupid neck!"

"Oh yeah," Will said, with a sideward nod at Blue. "There's no way she could be a wicked witch."

"And tell them it better be ready when I come for it!" she called out, as if whoever she'd been shouting at had already left.

Blue crawled out from behind the foliage and stood upright to wave at the witch. "Dante," he called.

A bright smile broke out across her face. "Oh, thank Chika, Blue. You're okay."

From their stances Will expected the two adults to hug, but neither of them made the step forward to do so. They merely stood opposite each other, smiling stupidly, and gradually lowered their arms.

"We're looking for Foosay," Blue said. "Have you seen her? She killed me and stole my gem. I have to get it back."

"She did what?" Dante made a grab for Blue's wrists. "What happened? Are you all right?"

"I'm fine." He squirmed and freed himself from her grasp like a child pulling away from his worried mother. "Will here brought me back to life," he said, taking Will's shoulders and aiming him at the witch. "I need to get my gem back quickly so I can give him a few wishes before he goes home."

Dante beamed at Will and blew him a kiss. He blushed and turned away, embarrassed and flattered at the same time.

"I'm just so relieved you're okay. I was on my way to find you, to warn you."

"Warn me about what?"

"You've heard about the other wots, right?"

Blue's grip on Will's shoulders tightened. "No. What about them?"

"Three are missing."

"What do you mean? Who?" Blue let go of Will. "Are they okay?"

"I'm sure they're fine," Dante said, sounding like she was trying to be comforting while knowing she wasn't being.

"Who's missing?"

"Come on, Blue, you know I'm bad with names." She wiggled her feet into some open-toed shoes that, like Cesar's tea tray, appeared from nowhere. A breeze rippled her dress and she shivered, looking accusingly around her. With a flick of her arm the breeze stopped, as though she'd switched off an electric fan. "I love all you wots, but your name's easier to remember than most of the others."

"Because my name's the colour of my gem."

"No, because you're my friend," Dante reminded him. "It's the yellow gem..."

"Henry," Blue said helpfully.

"Yes, and the green..."

"Popset."

"Of course. And the purple. Adrian."

"Adrian." Blue said the name with her, sounding more worried now.

"They're the ones that are missing, Adrian the most recently. I was about to start trying to track you all down, but I had to get this order off first. Molina would have been mad if I'd left it too late."

Blue looked at Will, aghast. "We have to warn Foyer and the others they're in danger."

"Oh, no, don't worry," Dante said. "She wouldn't have been mad with you guys." She hid a smile behind flawless fingernails that were the exact same shade of burgundy as her dress. "Oh. You meant from Foosay. Sorry. Yes, we should warn them."

"You don't have to come with us if you'd rather go home," Blue said to Will. "You can always come back for your wishes later."

"No, I'd rather stay and help you," he said, and Blue smiled like he was touched until Will added an unintentionally blunt, "I'd rather drown myself than go home."

"Drowning's not fun," Blue said grimly. "I hope the others are okay. We'll find them, won't we, Dante? They'll be okay, won't they? They won't be *dead*." Saying the D-word aloud seemed to ruffle him. "What if they're dead? What if she killed them like she killed me?" He sat down on the grass, face in his hands. "I don't know if I could go on living without Adrian and Popset."

Dante stared at the top of his head, blinking like she was trying to remember something. "When was the last time you even saw them? Wasn't it something like seven years ago, before you moved out here?"

Blue peered up at her from behind his hands like she'd asked him what the square root of a bongo was.

"Oh, come on." Dante crouched delicately beside him. "I'm sure they're fine." She gave his arm a tender stroke, rolling her eyes at Will. "He's a bit of a drama queen at times," she whispered.

Will had never seen a grown-up act this way before. Blue appeared to have thrown himself into a full-blown sulk.

"Cesar would know what to do," Blue muttered.

"Which one's Cesar again?" Dante asked.

"A ware who lives in a magic treehouse," Will said.

"Oh, him. He's an idiot."

"Yeah," Will agreed. "His house smells nice, though," he added, remembering the blissful warmth of freshly baked biscuits.

"I have no sense of smell, myself," Dante said. "It doesn't matter to me what the little freak smells like. Listen, Blue, I'll tell you what to do." She twirled around so they were face to face and raised herself to her feet in one effortless motion. "First, you're going to forget about that stupid ware. Then you're going to pull yourself together, and the three of us will go and see Foyer and Karson. We'll explain the situation. They'll know what to do. I need to see Foyer anyway. I could have sworn I caught him stalking me the other day." She scowled at the memory. "I wouldn't mind having a word with him about that."

"Karson's going to be so mad."

"Gosh, you'll be telling me water's wet next."

"Who are Karson and Foyer?" Will asked.

"They're wots, like Blue," Dante said. "Foyer's the black gem and Karson's the white." She smiled at Blue. "I'm really glad you're here," she told him, and leaned to rest her cheek against the top of his head. Before she quite got there, he stood up and sent her skipping sidewards to avoid a collision.

"Okay then," he said, straightening his coat. "You're right. Karson probably already knows what's going on anyway. He always knows everything. And it's not just me that Foosay tricked, is it, so he can't blame me for losing my gem, can he?"

"You didn't lose it. It was stolen from you. It's not your fault."

The glaring adoration on Dante's face as she gazed at the oblivious Blue tickled Will. He smiled at her when she turned his way, hoping she couldn't read minds.

"You see, Will, each of the eight wots have a gem that's kind of their power source. They live in their gems. So, without them, wots are pretty much homeless."

"And powerless?" Will guessed.

"I don't know about that," Dante said with another admiring glance at the wot. "I imagine he just can't grant wishes until he gets it back."

They granted wishes. They lived in their gems and granted wishes. Will's mind ticked over. "So, wots are genies?"

"Wots are what?" Blue asked.

Will expected Dante to understand, but her face was as blank as Blue's. "Genies. You know. With the magic lamps."

She tilted her head to one side. "Lamps?"

"Genies!"

They both stared at him in confused silence, and then shook their heads at each other.

"Wots are blessed with the gift of eternal life," Dante said. "My sister told me that Foosay Hoo, as she has aged, has become obsessed with learning their secret. Word is she's had a much anticipated eureka moment."

"Yes," Blue said. "That's what Cesar said. Only, he put it differently and didn't babble like a lunatic."

Dante tossed her head at the mention of Cesar's name. "My point is, perhaps Foosay intends to use your gems for some kind of spell that will keep her here forever."

"I don't want her around forever. Not this version of her anyway, she's horrible."

"I imagine you won't have to worry about that either way."

Blue's brow buckled. "What do you mean?"

"If she made a spell to receive eternal life, she'd have to take it. From you. From all of you. Wots would no longer exist."

"How would we no longer exist?"

"Because you'd all be dead."

Dante's frankness surprised Will.

"But wots don't die," Blue said.

"You do if Foosay kills you."

"She can't kill us all though. Wots are immortal." His nervous expression had not changed, large eyes fixed on the witch like he was waiting for her to admit she was pulling his leg.

"Not if they're killed off, they're not. Are you forgetting she killed you once already?"

"Yes, but we can't die."

"Wow, this really isn't getting through, is it?"

"I don't want Blue to die," Will said. Through all this talk of death and killing, he realised just how fond he'd grown of his strange new friend in the short time they'd spent together, and how protective he felt of the life he'd saved. That an evil witch wanted to murder Blue was unthinkable.

"Nor do I," Dante said.

"And I don't either," Blue agreed. "I've been dead already, and I really didn't care for it. And what would the world be without wots? Without wishes?"

"I'm sure it wouldn't be a world without wishes," Dante said. "Just a world without granted wishes."

Blue groaned, not in the least consoled. "That's even worse."

Will tutted. If he'd wanted to listen to a couple of adults moaning at each other, he could have stayed home. "Shouldn't we get going?" he asked, swinging his arms.

"No bother," Dante said. "I've got my brew stick. I'll take you."

Will squeaked and bobbed up and down on the spot, excitement bubbling. "You're going to fly us on your broomstick?"

Dante flashed a grin at Blue. "Broomstick? What a strange child you are. I said brew stick." She reached into one of her flared sleeves and pulled out a twisted, twig-like wand. It was knobbly but smooth, like it had been sanded and polished. She waved it through the air and brought it downwards in a firm swipe, creating a floating wisp of silvery yellow light, as though she had cut through the very air surrounding them to reveal something beyond it. Another quick draw of the wand opened a gaping hole of this heavenly glow.

"Thanks, Dante," Blue muttered, unfazed - as if it were a completely normal everyday occurrence for someone to cut a hole of twinkling light in the air. "That's nice of you." Then he stepped into the light and, to Will's astonishment, disappeared.

"Where'd he go?" he whispered, cold with fear and hot with excitement all at once.

"To Karson. You next. I have to go last to close the door behind us."

"That's a door?"

"Yes, and I can't keep it open all day."

Both hesitant and eager, Will neared the light, feeling the buzzing sensation of every one of his hairs standing on end at its touch. Adrenaline pumped so hard through him at such a remarkable rate that he felt he could have jumped to the moon, were it required of him.

With a deep breath, he pushed himself forward through the bristle of static shocks, and followed Blue into the scary, brilliant unknown.

Chapter Two: The Heart

One woodland tree was much the same as another in Will's eyes. *Christmas trees*, however, were special; too special to blend into forgettable obscurity with the rest. So, even if he had until now somehow failed to notice the unusual network of pastel-coloured woodchip pathways meandering between those everyday trees, there was no way he could have missed the gigantic Christmas trees growing amongst them.

It was irrefutable: He had stepped into Dante's doorway in one place and stepped out in another. Like magic.

Glancing down at the powder pink path to his right, he dragged his feet a few steps to stand with Blue, who was staring at the nearest Christmas tree. They'd need a fireman's ladder to put a star on top of that one. It was taller than Will's house. It was taller than Will's house giving the neighbours' house a piggy-back. He joined Blue in staring at it, waiting for something to happen. Nothing did.

Dante slipped into view from between a pair of invisible curtains and swiped her twiggy wand in an upwards motion, closing reality around the light like she was zipping up a tent.

"Where are we?" Will asked.

"Near the very middle of Wynne," Blue murmured, sounding distracted. "The Heart, they call it."

"So where are the wots?" Will had half-expected to see them straight away, all lined up ready to be introduced.

"There's one of them." Dante pointed a finger at an oval shaped, stone-like jewel nestled in some long grass at the base of the tree that Blue was staring at. It was pure white, about the size of Will's palm and smooth as a pearl. And it looked comfortable - or as comfortable as an inanimate object could look - in its lush resting place.

A wary breath rattled in Blue's chest, and he ducked under the spiny branches to give the gem a quick nudge with the toe of his right boot.

Smoky white mist burst from the stone like steam from a kettle and floated around a ghostly figure that materialised within. The figure coughed and waved the fog away with both hands.

The smoke cleared, revealing a man shorter than Blue but taller than Cesar, donned in a smart black suit, a pristine white shirt, and shining black shoes. He tutted when he saw Blue, his initial look of pleasure at receiving unexpected company gone in a blink.

"Good grief, look at the state of you." A disapproving scowl pinched his features. "Do you never bother with your appearance? You have a job to do. The least you could do is dress accordingly."

"Since when was there a dress code?" Blue pulled a face. "Since when was it a job?"

"Don't argue with me," came the fast reply. Karson did not raise his voice, but the sharp authoritativeness behind his words intimidated Will into unwittingly shrinking closer to Dante.

The witch pushed her way in between the two wots. "He was essentially murdered this morning. You can't expect him to be in perfect condition."

Karson fiddled with a cufflink. "Ha. Even days he's spent one hundred percent murder-free he looks this way, my dear witch," he said. "Anyhow, do explain. To what do I owe the displeasure?" Cufflink secured, he held his hands neatly behind his back and puffed out his chest.

"Karson." Blue bowed his head and fell quiet. At first Will thought this was a mark of respect while addressing his boss, his leader, his king, or whoever Karson actually was, but quickly understood when Dante put a comforting hand on her friend's back that Blue was merely upset.

"Come, come, lad. Spit it out."

"It's Foosay Hoo. She drowned me." He mumbled a few words about his stolen gem that would have been impossible for Karson to put together with no context even if he had managed to catch any of them, and then spoke clearly again to add, "I'm worried she's hurt Adrian and Popset. They're missing."

"No great loss," Karson said.

"How can you say that? They're my best friends."

"I'm well aware of that, Blue, and they're about as insufferable as you are too." He waved a hand dismissively. "I'm sure they'll turn up. So, off you go. Run along and grant some nice wishes, lad."

"I can't," Blue said through his teeth. "The witch has my gem."

Karson gave Dante an I'm-bored-of-this-now look. "Give him back his gem."

"Not her." Blue clapped a hand to his forehead. "Foosay Hoo. Aren't you listening to me? This is serious. I'm not joking, I promise. She tried to kill me. No, she did kill me, and she stole my gem while I was dead, just like she's going to steal all our gems so she can use them for some stupid spell." He glanced at Dante. "That's right, right?"

Karson squeezed a finger and thumb over the bridge of his nose as if to relieve a forming headache. "For pity's sake, Blue, what have you done this time? You had better find that witch, apologise to her, get your gem back and sort this mess out before you see me again, or I swear you will wish you'd never been born." The creases on his forehead deepened in yet another scowl. "Get gone, the lot of you."

With that, he disappeared into a puff of white smoke that retreated into the gem at the foot of the tree.

Will sneered at the gem, finding its inhabitant repugnant. The white-gemmed wot was worse than Cesar. At least the ware had offered them tea before rudely sending them on their way.

"He never listens to me," Blue said. "Foyer will help us."

Dante led the way. The three of them crossed over a dusty yellow pathway, a baby blue one shortly after, and through ankle-deep grass for a few more minutes after that.

Will wondered about the paths as they left them behind. Where did they lead? Who had made them? Why were they such stupid colours? Just as he took a breath to ask, Blue and Dante stopped by another tree – not a Christmas tree, Will noted – under which sat a pebble-like gem of similar size and shape to Karson's. This one was a gleaming coal black and glittered where it caught the sun's rays.

Blue pushed it gently with his foot. It rocked and settled. Nothing happened so he gave it a sharp kick.

This time a sooty black burst of cloud gusted up from the gem and swirled around the man-shaped shadow that gradually emerged.

"Behold, the great Foyer Naxlar, granter of thy deepest desires, creator of—" The booming voice stopped short when the black mist dispersed enough for Foyer to see Blue. "Oh, it's you," he said, disappointed but not unkind. "I thought it might be… Oh, never mind. What's the matter?" His eyebrows shot up when he spotted Dante, and he swung a hand to his head to scrape his thick mop of black hair away from his face and pat it behind his ears. "Dante," he said, a bashful smile creasing his cheeks. "Hello. How are you?"

Dante shrugged and brushed something off the back of Blue's shoulder.

"Lovely."

Will snorted. Adults.

"We're in trouble, Foyer," Blue said. "Big, big trouble. And Karson's not interested, so you have to help."

"You had a problem, and you went to Karson for help?" Foyer let out a low laugh that petered quickly. "When will you ever learn?" He noticed Will. "Hello there. Who's this?"

"Will." Blue shoved Will on the back.

Foyer's right eye half closed. "What's a will?"

"It's my name," Will replied, feeling jarred by Blue's shove. "It's short for William."

Blue repeated the name slowly, enunciating each syllable. Then he did it again, with particular emphasis on the 'yam' sound.

Foyer interrupted his third try. "All right, I got it, thanks. What's the trouble? What do you need help with? Because help you I will, if you so wish." He backtracked as though the words hadn't come out the way he'd intended. "Or even if you don't wish it. I'll help you anyway. Because I want to." His chest deflated along with his pride, and he gave a long, dejected sigh. Neither Blue nor Dante seemed to notice his miserable discomfort.

"That's good, thanks," Blue said. "Because you have to find Foosay Hoo and get her to give me my gem back, okay?"

"Whoa, whoa, whoa, hold up, what did I miss?" Foyer was suddenly the epitome of seriousness. "What is Foosay doing with your gem?"

"She stole it." Will slapped his hands down over the peak of his cap. They were going around in circles now, explaining their situation to everyone they came across but never doing anything about it. If they hadn't kept stopping to repeat themselves every five minutes, he and Blue would probably have been having fun playing with Blue's gem by now. "So why don't we just go and get it back off her?"

Foyer paced a few steps. "We'd need a ware to help us find Foosay. We should talk to Cesar."

Dante chuntered something under her breath, sounding as bugged as Will felt, and she swiped at her dress to shake off some yellow woodchips that had stuck to the hem. "You're all as bad as each other, you lot. I'll go and hunt Foosay down myself if you're so incapable."

Will wished she would.

"Dante, no." Blue touched her arm. "You can't go like this."

She gazed fondly at his face. "I can't? Why not?"

"Look at you, all pretty," Blue said, to the witch's delight. "You're dressed all wrong for a showdown with that rotten hag. She'll ruin that dress. Go put on some old trousers or something first, in case she tries to drown you. She does that."

Will could not stifle a giggle at Dante's embittered face.

"No, Dan, come on," Foyer said. "You can't face her alone, it's too dangerous. Forgive Blue," he added, reprimanding him with a pointed glare that Blue failed to notice.

"Forgive him for what? Knowing I'm not the feeble little princess you take me for?"

"Feeble little princess? I don't think that of you at all. You don't honestly think I think that?"

"I wouldn't let her go *alone*," Blue said, putting another hopeful smile on Dante's face. "Foosay killed me once already, and she may have killed my best friends. I have to be there to see her get what's coming to her."

"What do you mean?" Foyer asked sharply. "What friends?"

"Adrian and Popset."

"And Henry," Will added, wondering why Blue didn't seem to care about Henry's fate as much as the other two. Poor Henry, whoever Henry was.

"And she took their gems too?" Foyer resumed his pacing. "Do you happen to know which one she took first?"

Dante adjusted the wand in her sleeve, which must have shifted while she'd been shaking woodchips off her dress, with a jiggle of her arm that made Foyer and Blue edge back. "Yellow, I think," she said. "Henry, right?"

"And the last?"

Blue raised a hand. "Mine."

"No," Dante said. "The purple must have been the last. It happened shortly before I bumped into you two."

"How could you possibly know that?" Blue asked.

Dante flicked her hair casually before answering. "A witch happened to pass my sister Elmer in a bit of a state because something snatched Adrian from under her nose when she'd been trying to get a wish out of him. Elmer told me right away, bless her. She knew I'd want to help you as soon as I sorted out that order for Molina." For Will's benefit she added, "That's my other sister." She noticed Blue's strained face. "I did say he went missing recently."

"So... Did you know *I'd* been attacked?"

"Not until you told me. Nobody had really noticed you were gone yet."

"Oh, wonderful." He turned away, offended.

Dante grimaced at Will. "So sensitive," she mouthed.

"Okay," Foyer said. "It's likely she'll be after the red one next. So, I suggest we find Maik and wait for Foosay to come to us."

"That's brilliant, Foyer," Blue said.

Foyer glanced over to Dante, Will assumed in the hope of a similar acknowledgement.

Dante, however, kept her gaze firmly in Blue's direction. "You're so quick to praise people," she said, and Will was certain she was actively trying to wind Foyer up now. "I really admire that in a man."

"It's very admirable," Foyer said awkwardly.

Will felt embarrassed by the pathetic display. He wouldn't have been surprised if Foyer next started cartwheeling and shouting, 'Look at me, look at me,' in a bid for her attention.

"Well, yes." Dante looked pointedly at Foyer. "I do admire people who don't lurk in bushes spying on me."

Foyer stiffened, startled by her words, and his fringe flopped back into his eyes.

Dante pulled Will away from the large white flower he'd been dismantling. "And this boy," she said, beaming. "He brought Blue back to us."

"Not that anyone would have noticed if I'd never come back at all." Blue guided Will to his other side, away from Dante and Foyer, in the manner of someone being possessive over their favourite item without wanting anyone to notice.

"I wasn't spying," Foyer said in a shocked, loud whisper.

Will tugged at Blue's sleeve. "Are we going now?"

"Of course we would have noticed!" Dante exploded, having taken a moment to find her voice through her dismay. "You know how much you wots mean to me, I love you all, but Blue, you're…"

"All of us?" Foyer said.

Dante glowered at him.

Foyer cleared his throat. "Maik shouldn't be far. He tends to stay close to Karson. God only knows why."

"Because," Blue replied in a tone of surprise as the group began, finally, to walk, "he's the oldest and wisest of us."

"Blue, the man's unreasonable." Foyer stooped to pick up his gem as he passed. "You get on his nerves just by being within sight of him. You know that."

"What a horrid thing to say," Dante said. "Don't listen to him, Blue."

"It's fine, I know he hates me. He always has. I don't know what I ever did to upset him so much though."

"I've told you a thousand times before," Foyer said. "You did nothing. Trust me. It's not your fault."

They trudged across the blue woodchip pathway to the grass at the other side. Will had expected to arrive back at Karson's gem, but there were no Christmas trees in sight now. His three companions seemed to know exactly where they were going, but Will was completely lost. It crossed his mind, after they walked a while longer, that he would never be able to find his way back to where they'd started from on his own. He'd never be able to get back to the park. He'd never be able to go home.

He didn't have chance to worry about that. A motionless, man-shaped heap came into view under a distant tree.

"Look." Will stopped and pointed. "Over there. What's that?"

"That's Maik." Foyer sped to his crumpled friend, the others running with him. "Maik, talk to me, are you okay?" Foyer and Blue took an arm each and sat the lifeless man up between them. "Are you okay?"

Drawn and pale, Maik struggled to wake at the sound of Foyer's voice.

Dante's silky soft hand clasped around Will's, as though she sensed his unease.

"Where's my gem?" Maik murmured, without opening his eyes.

Blue winced. "She's got five."

"She'll be after Dyelann's next." Foyer got to his feet, leaving Maik lolled against Blue.

In his hurry to stand, Blue dropped Maik, and the semi-conscious wot collapsed back to the ground like a sack of potatoes.

"You'll have to go and warn him, Blue," Foyer said. "Find him before Foosay does."

"I suppose." Blue shifted about and gnawed on a fingernail, watching Foyer lift Maik back into a sitting position.

Foyer looked up at him. "What are you waiting for?"

"Do I have to?"

Dante slid her crooked wand out of her sleeve and got to work with it again, slicing that silvery yellow portal, this time in a zigzag.

"Fine," Blue said, sounding very much like it was not fine. He marched Will through the light with him, leaving Foyer to take care of Maik without so much as a goodbye.

Static crackled in Will's ears, and he patted his cap. The sensation reminded him of balloons being rubbed against his hair, which reminded him that it was his birthday. No balloons this year. No party. No celebration. But who needed any of those things when they had a witch closing a magic door behind them?

Smiling to himself, Will took a quick look around, at more trees, more bushes, more grass, and pinpointed the gem with minimal effort. This gem was a fraction larger than the black and white ones.

It was an interesting shade of orange, deep and shiny, not unlike an egg yolk.

In his relieved enthusiasm Blue kicked the gem a little too hard, and it was an angry creature that came out of the subsequent orange mist, with a swift and hard thump in the face for Blue. Knuckle clunked jawbone like a bat hitting a baseball. The impact sent Blue flat on his back.

"Dyelann!" Dante bellowed, furious.

Once he saw that Blue wasn't seriously hurt, Will grinned at Dyelann. The punch had been pretty impressive.

Dyelann, like Foyer, looked a few years older than Blue. He wore a black shirt and boots that were identical to Blue's except in better condition, dark trousers, and an expression of uncertainty as he stared down at the person he'd struck.

"Blue? You never come here. What's going on?"

"What did you hit me for?" Blue asked, allowing Dante to help him up.

"I didn't know it was you."

"I could have been a helpless child, for all you knew. Or a stinking great rhino, then you'd have been sorry."

"I'd have hit harder if I'd known it was you." Dyelann smirked. "Come on. What are you doing here?" His stare flicked to Dante. "And what are *you* doing here?"

"As a matter of fact," she said, "we're here to protect you."

Dyelann leaned against the nearest tree, a twinkle in his eye. "Oh, yeah? From…?"

"A witch. Foosay Hoo, to be specific."

Dyelann noticed Will for the first time then, and he moved away from the tree to crouch before him. "Do you want me to be your wot, kidlet?" he asked. "I love kids' wishes," he added to Blue and Dante. "Go on. What do you want?"

"Don't you worry about Will," Blue said.

"Will?" Dyelann acquired the same confused look that everyone around here wore when they first heard Will's name. He stood up straight. "Never heard of them."

"Worry about the fact Foosay's going to steal your gem," Blue went on. "She's going to do some kind of spell with it to give herself eternal life."

Dyelann reacted as if he'd been asked to lance a boil. "Foosay living forever? What a depressing thought. I was looking forward to dancing at her funeral."

Blue clicked his tongue. "You only don't like her because she blew up your big hair that time."

"It took a lot of patience to grow my hair out long enough to do that style, I'll have you know."

"If you ask me, she did you a favour. You looked ridiculous with all that hair." Blue took a quick stride back when it seemed Dyelann might take another swing at him. "Picture a Highland cow," he told Will. "But hairier. And stupider."

Dyelann twisted his mouth to disguise a smile.

Will gazed up at him, still awestruck by the speed of the man's right hook. He'd never seen anyone punch someone in real life before. "How long have you and Blue known each other?" he asked.

"Oh, a long time," Dyelann said. "Ages. What do you call them? Years. Years upon years."

"How many years?" Will pressed.

"Many. Many of the years." Dyelann nodded. "I've known him his whole life. He's the youngest wot. With the second oldest gem, funnily enough."

"Wow." Will took a moment to act like that piece of information meant anything to him. "So, how long?"

"A long time, Will," Dante said. "They're both super old. Anyway, how about we come up with a plan? Foosay could be here any time now."

Dyelann bit his knuckles in mock terror. "Oh, but no! How will we ever defeat a little old lady?"

"If she gets your gem, you're dead, Dyelann."

He laughed. "Wots don't die."

Dante shook her head at Will, and he took it to mean that she would imminently give up trying to explain this concept to the wots. "Fine, you just stand there and be useless, and I'll deal with her. Maybe you don't care about what she did to Blue, but I do. Maybe I'll stab her right through her vicious little head!" She brandished her wand, curling her lip. It was abundantly clear to Will that this witch would not hold with anyone harming her favourite wot.

Her favourite wot who was not paying a blind bit of attention to her. He was focused on something the others hadn't noticed.

"What did she do to…?"

"I don't believe it," Blue shouted over Dyelann's question. He started to run. "Come on, Will," he called, and scrambled down a steep bank that ran between two rows of small trees not twenty strides away from the spot where they'd found the orange gem. A shrill scream rang out, and Will rushed to the edge of the bank to see what was happening.

Dirty water sprayed up from Blue's thrashing legs and arms as he struggled to run and grab at something in the boggy ditch below. After a final determined lurch, he stood straight, both hands latched around a tiny, winged person with long white hair. She had small piggy eyes and dainty black butterfly lips that could have belonged to a china doll. Writhing and wriggling, she strained and pushed against Blue's fingers, then sank her teeth into his thumb. He shook her hard to make her stop.

"What did you do with Cesar's egg, Reese?" he demanded, voice edged with pain.

Her dangling legs, in a pair of white tights, kicked out at him. It was to no avail, so she gave up and screamed in frustration, with surprising power for so small a person. Her long wings twinkled in the light. They looked delicate enough to tear with rough handling, and Will was on the verge of worrying for her when Blue gave her another shake.

"You're really asking for it, Blue," she shouted. "The egg's safe. Let go of me."

"Why did you take it?"

"I wanted it. Why else?"

"How could you do that to Cesar when he was going to help you? You knew how proud he was of that egg." He released his grip and her wings hummed into action, a silver blur at her back as she bobbed in the air before him.

"I can't help it. If I give it back, will you leave me alone?"

"Cesar will kill you dead if he sees you." Blue glanced to the heavens in exasperation. "Take me to the egg and I'll return it to him. Then we'll forget all about it. How about that?"

The wenn pouted. "It's not fair, you know. That ware always has more than he needs. I need a bird. To fly me about."

"You can fly yourself about. You're flying yourself about right now."

"Flying is tiring. Not that you'd have any clue what it's like." Her chest rose and she drew a deep, long breath, only for Blue to snatch her back into his hand and shake her again in panic.

"Don't you dare, lady!"

"Let go of me!"

Reality wobbled. Everything dulled. Blue and Reese's bickering voices muffled, and the temperature plummeted, like Will had been plunged underwater. For the next few seconds, his own short, sharp breaths were all he heard.

He had to duck. He had to get down. Something was warning him. He had to get out of its way. He had to...

Will dropped to the spiky grass below. Sound whirred back up to its normal volume just in time for him to hear the roaring, shimmering stream of air blasting full throttle through the spot where his head had just been and thundering its way towards Dante and Dyelann.

He pushed himself off the ground and spun to see what had happened. Dante and Dyelann were both down.

"Blue," he yelled hoarsely, and ran as fast as his legs could carry him. Blue stumbled up the bank, quick to catch up.

"What happened?" the wot asked his fallen friends, inappropriately blasé considering the situation. "Was she here already?" He allowed Dante to lean against him while he helped her to stand.

"I didn't see anything," she said, savouring their closeness. "That can't have been Foosay. Can it? It was too fast. It was too strong."

"Tell me about it. You're talking to the wot she killed already. Did she get the gem?"

Dyelann rubbed the back of his neck and flinched like it hurt to touch. "Yes, she got my bloody gem. Some protectors you lot turned out to be. Now, if you don't mind, you can all get lost." His face was fierce. "And don't come back."

Dante glared right back. "You have to help us."

"Help you?" He scoffed like he couldn't understand why she'd ever suggest anything so ludicrous. "You brought that witch here. This is your fault."

Blue walked away a few paces, muttering, "Why does everyone always blame me for everything? Everything's always my fault. I didn't even do anything."

Dante cuffed Dyelann on the arm. "Dyelann, she's making plans to kill you all. Stop being so pig-headed for once. Come help us get your gems back."

"Don't be a silly witch," he said with a patronising smirk. "Wots are immortal. She can't kill us."

"Why isn't this sinking into your thick skull? She killed Blue already."

"Yes, he certainly looks dead. The good kind of dead, though. The walking around perfectly healthy kind of dead."

"Don't you want your gem back?"

"Oh, don't you worry, I'll get it back."

Blue's expression was grave as he asked Dante, "Do you think she'll need the black and white gems for her spell too?"

"She'll be going for the black one next," Will said, and then wondered why he'd opened his mouth.

"Oh, yeah?" Dyelann said. "And what would you know about it, half-pint?"

Will's heartbeat quickened under Dyelann and Dante's increasingly suspicious stares, and he wished he could think of something clever to say. "It was just the first thing that popped into my head when Blue asked."

Blue made a strange growling noise, hands clasping his hair, elbows high.

"What's up?" Will asked, glad for the attention to be diverted from him.

"Reese got away."

"How many times?" Dante said. "You don't need the ware's help, Blue. You've got me. You've got my sisters. You know the four of us together are more than a match for any one witch." She patted at her hair, a modest but not-so-modest smile on her face. "The four of us draw power from each corner of the earth, you see, Will. I am the sister for the south. Our family has powerful allies in the otherworld, who can be summoned across the divide should we ever need their guidance or their protection."

Although Will wanted to act suitably impressed, only one thing came to mind. "I didn't know the earth had corners."

Dante's smile grew. "I suppose they're more like points than corners."

"I wish I was a witch," he said, causing Dyelann and Blue to flinch and grimace in unison. "Then I'd be able to help too."

"You can help."

"I'll probably just get in the way."

"That's crazy. Never think that. You saved Blue's life." Dante planted a firm kiss on his cheek and chuckled when he wiped it off. "But I do think you'd make a great witch," she said, and gave his cap a playful twang.

Squirming at the sentiment, Will nudged his cap back to its proper position. He hoped she hadn't left any lipstick on his face.

"But I should get Cesar's egg back for him," Blue said. "It's my fault it got taken. Won't you help me find the wenn again, Dante?" The expression that Blue put on for the request - the sad smile, the longing eyes and crooked brow - reminded Will of the ones he always put on himself when he was trying to get his mother to agree to anything he said.

It seemed to work. Dante waned. But then she found her resolve, stood tall to face him, and said, "No."

"I don't think I like Cesar very much anyway," Will admitted. Now that Dante had made it so clear she detested Blue's friend, Will didn't feel so guilty for disliking him too. "He was so mean to you," he added in explanation after Blue shot him a wounded look. "And he didn't like me very much either, did he?"

"Of course he liked you. Why wouldn't he like you?"

"Who cares what a ware thinks anyway?" Dyelann said.

Blue patted Will away from Dyelann. He obviously did not want to share his new friend with anyone else, and especially not someone with a tendency to aim a punch his way on occasion.

"Oi," he said to Will, quietly so Dyelann wouldn't overhear. "You don't like him better than me, do you? Because I'd grant you any wish better than he would." He didn't give Will chance to respond. "Dyelann may seem all fun and generosity. And I suppose he is. But he's not my friend. I mean, it's not that I don't like him. I do. But I've known him all my life, Will. I know what he's like. And I *don't* like him."

Unsure of the correct response, Will said, "Okay." This word was often useful to get adults to stop lecturing him. He had found this not only with his parents but with teachers at school too. It also seemed to work on wots.

"Good," Blue said. "Thanks." Then he shoved Will away, nearly knocking him over.

A confused expression replaced Will's smile as soon as the wot turned his back, and he stared aimlessly into space until the conversation caught his ear again.

"You'd best go find your sisters, Dante," Blue said. "We're going to need them. Dyelann, you find Maik and Foyer. Get everybody to meet at Karson's. Will and I will meet you there."

A strange look came over Dyelann that made Will fear an argument was about to break out. But nothing came of it. Dyelann contained himself, and the dangerous tension in his face softened into his usual smirk.

"I can do that," he said coolly. There was a flicker of arrogance in his step as he trudged on his way.

"Wouldn't you prefer me to stay close?" Dante moved towards Blue. "What if you should need me?"

He stepped sidewards, widening the distance between them. "We'd be better off if you were with your sisters."

Will watched, intrigued, as Dante exhaled loudly with a mix of frustration and disappointment, whipped out her twisted wand and swung it to cut open her passageway. Before she stepped into the beaming glow of light, she smiled sweetly at Blue. "I'll see you soon?"

He smiled back. "You're such a good friend to me, Dante."

"Yes, yes, I know I am." She wanted to be more than a friend to him, any fool could see that. Any fool except Blue, apparently. She stepped into the light, melted into it like a shadow, and was gone. The tip of her wand could just be seen rising through the ray of light to zip the portal up behind her, and when it got to the top it disappeared with a spark.

"How does she do that?" Will asked.

Blue shrugged, unimpressed. "Anyone could do it if they had a decent brewer and a vein of magic in them." He headed back to the ditch he'd caught Reese in. "Let's have a quick look for the wenn before we do anything else. Don't mention it to Dante. You know how she gets."

"I won't," he promised. He kept a sharp eye out for the little winged lady, keen to spot her before Blue did. "I'm sorry you lost her. The wenn, I mean, not Dante."

Blue laughed. "I could never lose Dante. I can't get rid of the witch. She pops up everywhere."

"Because she's in love with you."

"What?" Blue swung around, coat spinning with him and spraying the remnants of filthy ditch water over Will's face.

Will wiped it out of his eyes.

"What are you talking about? Dante's not in love with me. Don't be crazy." He laughed again, awkward this time.

"She is. I'm eleven and I can see it, that's how obvious it is."

Blue continued to walk alongside the ditch, rubbing his forehead. "No, that's too weird. She's not in love with me, that's disgusting."

"Why?" Will failed to see the problem.

"Because she's my friend. You're seeing too much into things that aren't even there." He raised a hand at Will and stopped walking. "Let's just drop it, okay?"

"Fine, I just thought…"

"Drop." To ensure Will couldn't finish his sentence even if he'd wanted to, Blue shouted, "Reese, where are you? Reese!" He let out a disheartened sigh. "We're never going to find her, are we?"

"We've only been looking for two seconds."

"Oh, wo-ot," a singsong voice chirped from the other side of the ditch. Reese stood atop a disfigured yellow toadstool that was bowing under her weight, wings laid delicately over her back.

Blue approached her with caution, like a dog preparing to set chase.

She held up her hands in surrender. "If I give you the egg, will you do something for me in return?"

"Do what?" Will asked before Blue could agree, which he could tell the wot had been about to do.

"Find the wye with the claret vita and get it to return our pear tree to us. The wye took our tree away, which means we now have to travel three times as far to the next one. It's absolutely horrendous. Some of us are thinking of packing up and moving."

"You have to travel? Three times as far?" Blue turned up his lip. "Wenns have to be the laziest creatures that ever existed. I am not going to approach a wye and demand he put back an uprooted pear tree just so you don't have to fly a bit further than usual to pick up dessert."

"Why, are wyes scary?" Will asked.

"Not at all. They're kind and generous people. A little slow, yes, but I will not take away their only pleasure in life for the likes of a thieving, lazy, evil little creature like you."

"They'll have that poor tree stripped to nothing if we don't act fast. What would last us a century would last a wye five minutes, you know that. I promise you, wot: Give us the tree, we'll give you the egg." The wenn planted her hands on her hips. "That's the deal. Otherwise, I'm keeping the kite."

"Yeah, well, I hope it eats you. Come on, Will."

"Is that it?" Will felt let down by Blue's quick defeat. "Aren't you going to yell at her and force her to give you the egg? You're bigger than her. Yell a bit."

"No, I don't like yelling at people. Besides, there's no point with wenns anyway. She'd just start singing and disappear on us."

"What do you mean?"

"Oh, a little thing about wenns, for your information: They sing to you, you lose consciousness. Yeah, they can knock you out cold if they want to. They use that ability to steal, mostly, or to make quick getaways."

"Really? That's amazing."

"I wouldn't say amazing. Anyway, let's go and find the wye she was talking about and see if we can't come to some sort of arrangement."

"But you said we were going to meet Dante and the others at Karson's, remember?"

"I know, but the thing you have to understand is, Cesar's a ware, Will, okay? If we get him the egg, he'll tell us exactly where Foosay is, and we can go and explain to her what she's doing is wrong, and then everything can get back to the way it should be."

"That's stupid."

"Beg your pardon?"

"You think you're just going to talk to her, and she'll stop trying to kill you? I'm eleven and I can see that's not going to happen. She wants to kill you, Blue."

Blue stared at Will, as though trying to work something out. "Why do you keep pointing out your age?"

"I don't."

Blue waited a while longer before he spoke again. "There's no problem that can't be solved with patience and understanding," he said carefully. "Foyer taught me that."

"Where do we look for a wye, then?"

"They're really quite hard to miss. Don't worry. This shouldn't take long."

Will braced himself for trouble and rushed to keep up with the wot. He wondered what on earth a wye was – and if Blue really was stupid enough to confront a killer witch, armed with nothing more than his patience and understanding.

Chapter Three: Finding Foosay

After spending what felt like a year of his life walking between endless rows of identical trees, Will lost all faith in Blue's sense of direction. Just when he was about to complain that they were walking in circles, a raised piece of grassy ground came into view and proved otherwise.

There were no trees about the immediate area, just many heaps of discarded seeds, pips, and nuts, alive with buzzing flies. The sickly-sweet stench of rotted fruit went straight to the back of Will's throat and made him gag. He covered his mouth and nose with both hands.

"It stinks. It really, really stinks."

"It does a bit." Blue skulked around the small hill.

Hidden behind it, a gigantic man slept on his back. His upright feet were almost as tall as Will. He looked like a beached whale. A beached whale in desperate need of a bath and a shave. The trail of pink drool dangling from his open mouth vibrated with each noisy breath.

"Esko." Blue slammed both hands on the giant arm. "Wake up."

"Is this the one who took the tree?" Will asked. Without intending to, he'd spoken barely above a whisper.

"We'll find out, if he'll ever *wake up!"* Blue shoved and pushed on the arm, but the motion only triggered the giant's snoring: a grating, rasping sound on the breath out and the trumpeting of an angry elephant on the breath in.

Will's hands quickly went from covering his mouth to covering his ears. It didn't seem possible that wyes could have remained a secret. Surely his mum and dad could hear these snores from wherever they were now?

Blue gave Will an apologetic little grimace. Then he kicked the wye in the chest.

The snoring stopped. The giant roused, sat up slowly, yawned, and blinked unseeingly at Blue. Long, unpreened hair fell over his pronounced forehead into wiry black eyebrows.

Will let go of his ears.

"Blue?" The wye smacked his lips together. His stale breath held to it the same off-fruit smell that surrounded the piles of pips and nuts on the other side of the hill, and it made Will's stomach turn.

"Yeah, it's me. Have you taken a pear tree from the wenns by any chance?"

The question didn't register straight away. For a while Esko just stared blankly in Blue's direction. "Oh!" he said, finally awake. He coughed and spluttered. A spray of fruity saliva just missed Will.

"Gross!" Will leapt away from it.

"A pear tree, you say?" the wye asked in a low, wavering voice.

"Yes, a pear tree," Blue said patiently. "Have you taken one?"

The wye continued to stare at Blue. "Did you know there's a witch around these parts screaming to the heavens that she is about to end the time of the wots and see the start of a grander world?" His unkempt eyebrows darted about as he spoke. "Don't you think you should be worrying less about the whereabouts of a pear tree and more about the threat to your kind?"

Will and Blue gesticulated to one another with their heads and shoulders, each trying to urge the other to step up and speak to the wye.

"Fine," Blue snapped. "We need you to give the pear tree back, is the thing. The wenns won't return Cesar's egg until you give them their tree, and Cesar won't help us find the witch you just mentioned until he gets his egg. You understand? We need the tree."

The wye shook his head several times, scratched at an eyelid with his impossibly large fingers, and then pulled himself up. Blue and Will had to strain their necks to see his face. Will's mouth gaped a little in his uncertainty. Esko was twice Blue's height at least, and four or five times wider. Will found himself inadvertently edging behind Blue, and he could tell that the wot was very much enjoying the fact that Will sought safety there.

"Why won't Cesar help you without the egg?" Esko asked.

"Because it was my fault the egg got stolen in the first place."

Esko rubbed his bristly chin. "I would say it was the thief's fault it was stolen in the first place. Not yours."

"That's what I said," Will exclaimed, and promptly ducked back behind Blue.

"I think, if the ware were a real friend to you, he would not have blamed you at all."

"It's not as simple as that," Blue said.

"I think he's right." Will's fear was giving way to respect, and he didn't feel the need to hide anymore.

"You people don't understand," Blue tried to say again, but he was cut off before he could finish.

"Oh, we understand," the wye said. "That's one of the reasons wares are the only creatures I can't abide in my face." He picked at the sticky fruit remains on his beard. "Also because you can't trust anything that turns invisible every time something makes it jump."

"Nobody understands what true and loyal friends wares are," Blue insisted. "I would trust Cesar with my life."

"Indeed, you would," Esko said. "That's in your nature, and you wouldn't be Blue otherwise. I'm sorry, though. I'm afraid I was not the one who took the pear tree you speak of. It was Alley."

Blue threw Will a look that he could only translate as 'duh.' "Of course it was. The wenn even told me it was the one with the claret vita. Come on, Will, keep up. You should have reminded me of that small detail."

Will scowled at Blue, but the wot was talking to Esko again and didn't see.

"Can you ask her to give them their tree back, please?"

"The tree's gone, Blue. You're going to have to let go."

"Let go of what?"

The giant shrugged his boulder-like shoulders. "Hope, I suppose. Isn't that just what one says when another one's ranting on a bit too much about something that no longer exists?"

"Well, that's it then, isn't it?" Blue flapped his arms. "The wenns won't get what they want, so Cesar won't get what he wants, so he won't tell us where to find Foosay Hoo, and we're all going to just go ahead and be murdered to death."

"Says a lot for the person he says he would trust with his life, doesn't it?" the giant said, and Will just nodded, entirely agreeing with him and deciding he liked the wye after all. Despite his beastly exterior, this giant had made more sense to him than anyone else he'd spoken to all day.

"I'll help you find your witch," Esko offered.

"How?" Blue asked dramatically. "How can you possibly help? Are you going to get the egg from the wenns?" He stopped to think. "Actually, that's not a bad idea. I'll do what Will suggested I do earlier."

Will didn't remember suggesting anything.

"I'll yell at them."

Oh, yes. Now he remembered.

"I'll bully the wenn into giving me the egg. I saw how threatened you were when you saw the size of Esko, Will, and I'm so much bigger than Reese. That's how she will look at me." He nodded resolutely and made as if to walk away.

"That's a great idea if you fancy a nap," Esko said, stopping Blue before he'd even reached mid-stride. "I told you, I'll help you find Foosay. I know where her house is."

Blue slumped with relief. "Oh, good. Where?"

Esko indicated to a gap in the trees past the hill. "There's a track through those trees there. Follow it until you reach a well. Turn right at that well. There's no track there, but there are lots of purple flowers. Keep your eye on them. If there are no purple flowers, you've gone off course. Follow the flowers and you will reach a clearing. Her cottage was there, last I looked."

"Wait, why are you giving us directions? You're not going with us?"

"I can't go with you."

"Why not?"

"Because I don't want to," the wye said, as though it was a solid reason not to help a friend in need.

Blue surprised Will by responding in kind. "Fair enough. Thanks for putting us on track. Come on, Will." He straightened his coat and strode to the pathway that Esko had pointed out.

"What about the others?" Will imagined that Dante and Dyelann would have rounded up their people by now. They'd all be waiting on Blue, perhaps fearing for his safety. It didn't seem fair to leave them hanging. "We were supposed to meet up with them. You're the one who told them to, remember? Shouldn't we go get them? They could come with us." He trotted after Blue, annoyed when his questions went ignored. "Blue? Wouldn't we be safer all together?"

"Stop fretting." Blue glanced back at him but kept walking. "There's no hurry. And I have absolutely no desire in my heart to hear Molina Simms lecturing me right now. Anyway, you heard what Karson said to me. He said I can't go back to him until I've sorted out this mess."

"But it's not even your fault."

"If Karson says it's my fault, then it's my fault, and that's the end of it." Blue picked up his speed. "He's our leader, Will. You don't argue with your leader, or anarchy ensues. Did no one ever tell you that?"

"Even when your leader's wrong?"

Blue slowed back down for a few steps, and then came to a stop. "You shouldn't say things like that."

"But he is wrong."

"No. No, Will, he's not. It *is* my fault. I could have stopped all this before it started. When Foosay attacked me, she caught me off guard obviously, but I had the upper hand at first. I could have beaten her. I took her brew stick. I had it. But I couldn't do anything. I couldn't hurt her. I just stood there like an idiot, doing nothing. And as soon as she knew I wasn't going to do anything, she took it back and used it to drown me." He took another pained glance up to the sky. "Just before she held me under the water, she told me I'm worthless and my very existence is a waste of good oxygen, because if I can't even protect myself then how could I ever be any use to anyone else?" His gaze dropped to his boots, and he twisted a heel into the soil. "She called me futile."

Will, who had until that last remark been listening with a sympathetic ear, felt a prickle of irritation when it crossed his mind how ridiculous it was that Blue had let the witch's words upset him. "So what?" he said loudly. "Who cares what she thinks?" He was cold, thirsty, and sick of everyone being so serious. It was his birthday. Why couldn't everyone cheer up and let him enjoy it? "She's the baddie, Blue, remember? She's bound to tell lies and say nasty things to you. That's what baddies do. You just have to ignore her."

"I suppose."

"Because you're the goodie. And that's what goodies do."

Being the goodie seemed to appeal to Blue. A proud little smile grew on his face. "You're right," he said. "Let's go get my gem back."

By the time they reached the well that Esko had spoken of, the wye caught up with them, having decided to offer his assistance after all. He carried in his massive hand a branch of an apple tree that he held and picked at like a big bunch of grapes.

"Although I still have no interest in the matter," he said, scratching noisily at his beard, "I have a proposition for you."

Will grinned, very much supportive of the wye's presence. "That's nice of you." He glanced around, assuming that a proposition must be some kind of weapon they could use against the evil witch. "Where is it?"

"My proposition is this." Esko bit an apple in half with a loud crunch. Juice spurted from his mouth. "I shall give you my help in finding the dwelling of Foosay Hoo..."

"You already told us where it is," Blue said dismissively.

Esko's face fell. He grunted. "Very well. My proposition is this: I shall help you retrieve what is yours from the wenns…"

"Actually, it's Cesar's, not ours," Will said, trying to be helpful.

The wye grunted again.

"No, go on," Blue said, interested now. "You'll help us get the egg, if…?"

"When you find the witch's book, you shall grow me a superior pear tree for my Alley, so she and I may never again run out of such a glorious foodstuff."

A brief silence fell upon the three of them as this was contemplated.

Esko held out his branch. "Apple?"

Disturbed by the unidentifiable gel-like substance on several of the otherwise tasty-looking plump, green apples, Will declined.

"Would she even have a spell to make a tree?" Blue pushed the branch out of his face.

The wye lifted the branch back. "Who wouldn't?"

"Witches aren't like wyes."

"No, they're smaller," Will said. "And they don't smell as ba-ah." He caught himself. "Bananary." The wye wasn't paying attention anyway. From the look of it he was considering his own proposition.

"Very well," he said. "I shall help you. As long as you promise to grow me the tree if it is at all possible for you to do so."

"Deal." Blue motioned for Will to walk on. "See how rubbish wyes are at bargaining? That's how they get taken advantage of so much."

Esko ambled along behind, happily picking at his apples.

"That's mean," Will said. "It's not their fault if they're stupid."

Blue put his hands on Will's shoulders and drove him forward, following the dotted purple daisy-like flowers. Most of them were wilted and looking quite sorry for themselves.

He pulled Will to a stop, then released him to rush a few paces ahead. "Does this look like a clearing to you?"

Will traipsed to where Blue stood. The trees ended at a grassy open area, in the middle of which was a stone cottage with a thatched roof. A large block of orange cheese had been left on a breadboard out on the porch.

The wye leaned forward. "I'm sorry," he said. "I promise, her house was here not two days ago."

This confused Will. The cottage sat right there in front of their noses. Could they not see it?

"Yes, I'm sure it was," Blue said. "Just the same as I'm sure there's a bunch of bicycle-obsessed chimpanzees living around the corner from here dressed in matching dungarees." He stared in the direction of the cottage. "Never mind, it was worth a try. Come on, Will."

"What are you guys going on about? There's a house right there." Will pointed at the cottage. "There's some cheese on the doorstep."

"Cheese," Blue repeated quietly, frowning.

"Cheese?" Esko asked loudly, drooling.

"Yeah, lots of it."

"I can't see anything," Blue said, still quiet.

"I can't see any cheese," Esko said, still loud.

"Not just cheese. There's a whole house." Will pointed again, more vigorous this time, in case they simply weren't looking in the right place. "It's right there. Can't you see it?"

Blue stepped into the clearing, shading his eyes with a hand as if that would magically improve his vision.

Something wet and heavy hit Will's head and sent him scuttling forward, removing his cap. "Esko!" He flicked off as much of the saliva as he could. "Seriously. Gross."

The wye lifted his shovel of a hand to wipe his lips.

Blue walked on, arms out like he was playing Blind Man's Buff. "It must be cloaked. Or maybe she just put an invisibility spell on it."

"But it's not invisible." Will replaced his cap firmly on his head, satisfied that it was clear of goop. "I can see it." He approached it at a run and hopped onto the porch.

Esko tossed the now stripped branch aside. "The boy's floating. Wot, do you see?"

"I can't see anything." Will peered through the glass pane of the front door. "The curtains are closed." He stared nervously at the doorknob, wondering if he had the guts to try it.

"Go in and find her book," Blue said. He lifted his foot to step up to where Will was and toppled straight down through the porch.

Will laughed, astonished. "You've gone right through the floor!"

Blue stood in the porch, half in and half out, like a ghost.

"You're walking right through the wood like it's not even there." Will leaned over and pressed the planks that surrounded Blue's legs. Then he shoved Blue's knee.

"Ow. Pack it in. Just get in there and find the book. In, in, in. The book."

Slowly, cautiously, Will pushed open the door and ventured into the house. It was dark inside with all the curtains drawn. Tiptoeing, afraid to make a sound, he slipped into a room at the end of the hallway. A black iron cauldron hung from chains over the cold fireplace. Before the hearth sat an enormous book, bound in midnight-blue leather. The golden symbol on the front cover resembled an upside-down Christmas tree, if the tree had no trunk. Forgetting, in his delight at having found the book so quickly, to mind his footsteps, Will charged across the room to pick it up before it could disappear on him.

Its incredible weight caught him off guard. It was like trying to pick up a breeze block. He rocked his body back and forth a few times to gather the momentum he needed to hoist it into his arms.

When he turned to leave he noticed, lined up in a neat row on top of a solid antique oak dressing table next to the door, the wots' gems.

Will stared at the blue one, heart skipping. There they were, right there in front of him, exactly what his new friends wanted. And he could return them. He could end all their worries, right now. He'd be a hero.

Struggling to balance the book over one arm, he reached out. His hand hovered over the blue gem. He touched a finger on it, lowered his palm over it, felt the stony coldness on his skin – and paused. He pulled his arm back in, clasped the book and backed away.

The witch wouldn't have left them unguarded.

But he couldn't return to Blue without it. Not when it was right there. He couldn't miss this chance.

He snatched the gem from the table and made a clumsy dash for the exit, staggering under the book's bulk. He ran for the front door, feet clattering on the floorboards, and leapt over the doorstep into the brightness of the day. The breadboard caught under his foot, and he tripped, sending the book flying over the porch and landing with a tremendous thud near the wot and the wye, causing Blue to jump back from the object that, to him, had appeared from nowhere, with a somewhat girlish shriek.

"Oh," he said, with a gruff cough to compose himself. "Well done, Will, good work."

"So, you'll find the spell now?" Esko asked. "That was the deal, was it not?"

Lifting the book in one hand like it weighed nothing, Blue used a thumb to flip through all the pages in quick succession. "Sorry. Nothing about pear trees in here," he said, although he couldn't possibly have seen anything but an inky blur.

Will corrected himself from his twisted stumble and called out to Blue, the gem cupped tightly in his hand.

"Hang on a beat, Will. I'm going to summon Foosay to us."

"But, Blue," Will said giddily.

"Things might get nasty, but don't worry, I promise I shan't let her get near you."

"Just look." He waved the gem, but Blue's attention was fixed on a page in the book.

Esko crouched to get a closer look. "Are you certain there's nothing you can do for me?"

"You haven't carried out your end of the bargain yet either, remember, so don't try to imply you've been wronged somehow," Blue said flatly, running his index finger over some handwritten words. "I think I've found the spell that will bring her to us."

"Blue, look. Blue. Blue." Will slapped the gem down on the page in front of him, and then gawped stupidly at it, realising he'd picked up the wrong one. This one was a stunning translucent purple.

Blue whipped the gem up in both hands, dropping the book. "Where did you get this?"

"From the house." Will pointed back at the cottage that Blue could not see. "I meant to get yours. I thought if I got it back to you before the witch found out, we'd be safe." His heart slammed into his ribs. "I'll go back in and get it." Slipping in his hurry, he threw himself back towards the porch, only to come to an immediate stop.

A woman stood in front of the doorway. She was a small lady, not as old as Will had imagined the witch would be, but inarguably old, nonetheless. Her silver hair was fluffy and wild like an Old English Sheepdog's. She wore a black skirt, black boots, and a bright rainbow-coloured poncho.

"May I help you?" she asked, her voice soft as a hum.

Apparently able to perceive the house's existence now, Blue marched to the porch, a fierce glower on his face. "Give me my gem back, Foosay."

Two chimpanzees scampered by the side of the witch's cottage, both dressed in blue and white striped dungarees. Another three chimps followed close behind the first two, in the same outfits. One of them pushed a child's bicycle along with it, giggling like a human.

"Someone made a wish one time," Blue said in answer to Will's bafflement.

"Listen to me." Foosay clip-clopped down the steps of the porch and neared Blue in such a way the wot retreated a few paces. "All the *gems* in my possession belong to me. *Me.* I want you to leave, right now. Don't make me do anything in front of the boy."

Will smacked a palm to his forehead. How could he have picked up the wrong gem? Was he really so useless?

"What have you done to Adrian?" Blue demanded, holding up the purple gem. "What did you do to his gem?"

Foosay snatched the gem from him, too fast for him to object. He looked at his empty hand, aghast, as the witch hunched her shoulders and returned to her front door.

Will jabbed Blue. "You can't just let her go." Seeing that Blue was at a loss for words, Will jumped onto the porch and caught the door before Foosay could close it. "You can't just take things that don't belong to you, Mrs Hoo."

Her crooked smile bared perfectly formed teeth and she sniggered like a naughty schoolgirl. "You can take whatever you want from the world. How do you think people claimed what they wanted as theirs in the first place?"

Will was stumped.

"Yet I may take and take and take, from part of earth to part of lake, and thief of me they cannot make, for what is mine is mine for mine's sake." Still smiling, she took a step closer to Will and whispered, "That rhyme belongs to an aunt of mine. She told it to me, a few months after her funeral."

Will didn't move a muscle.

"Speaking of my aunt, you don't happen to know a colour-mixer, do you, my dear?"

Will was sure her eyes were turning more and more grey the longer he looked into them.

"Just ignore her, Will." Blue dragged him down from the porch so harshly he made Will lose his footing.

"Oh, there was no need for that," Foosay said, the purple gem clutched in her spindly hand. "I only asked the boy a simple question." She tried again to enter her house, but Blue lunged for the gem, closed his hand around it and tried to yank it from Foosay's grasp. She resisted and pulled against him until the two of them were tussling, rather pathetically, in their attempts to keep hold of the gem.

Foosay squealed and gave one last almighty tug, the gem hers again.

Blue groaned, exasperated, and glared at Will. "You could have helped."

"Don't be so lame. She's just an old lady, Blue. Go in and get your gem back."

This time the witch stopped herself from closing the door. She marched back to Will, her pointy heels tapping on the wooden porch. "What exactly do you think is going on here?" Her eyes widened when she spotted her book open in the grass. She almost dropped the gem in shock but caught it back up again and lifted her book from the ground by merely raising a finger. The pages snapped shut and it floated straight to her. She caught it and hugged it to her chest.

"What on earth did you boys think you were doing? This book is very, very dangerous for the likes of children to be pawing through! Who do you think you are? How dare you?"

"Sorry," Blue said at once.

Will couldn't believe his ears. "Sorry? No. We're not sorry. You can't have it both ways, you know." He was quoting his mother with that last part.

"Both ways?" the witch asked.

"Yes. Either it's wrong to steal or it isn't."

"This is hardly the same thing now, is it?" Foosay bustled back to her door and stopped dead when she noticed something was wrong. "Well, now. Where on earth is my cheese?"

Will's eyes panned to the breadboard. Sure enough, the big lump of cheese was gone, not a single crumb left behind.

The witch turned to Blue. "You took my cheese? Why, this is beyond the pale. It's one thing to take a witch's powerful, dangerous item of property, but to take someone's food? What is wrong with you?"

"I didn't take it," he said, instantly on the defence. Then his face hardened. "Foosay, come on, I want my gem. Please give it back."

"I don't have your gem, as you well know. Now, off with you."

"It's in her house, Blue, I saw it."

"You most certainly saw no such thing," Foosay said, her hair wobbling like silver candyfloss. She stroked a hand protectively over her book. "You owe me some cheese, boy."

"Forget cheese, you mad old hag, you owe me a gem." Blue stood up for himself at last, and Will could have cheered. "What's the point in lying about it, when we, all three of us, know you have it? Just give it back."

"This isn't funny, Blue," Foosay said, shrill with stress.

"Why do you want to kill the wots, Mrs Hoo?" Will couldn't understand how this woman could possibly be the person that had been described to him all morning. He didn't believe she had it in her to hold Blue upside down in the river and watch him drown.

"I most certainly have no intention of killing anybody," she said through gritted teeth. "Though you're beginning to tempt me. Now, good day." She slammed her door shut in their faces.

Blue and Will stared at each other, both waiting for the other to suggest what they do next. Before either of them could speak, however, Foosay's house vanished.

And it would have taken only a moment for Blue to realise that Will had vanished along with it.

Chapter Four: Gart

Piercing screams rang in Will's ears like alarm bells. Fresh, damp air hit him in the face and penetrated his lungs. One moment Blue had been at his side, and the next the wot had gone, the trees and the grass with him, and now Will was standing on the rocky edge of a cliff overlooking an expansive, glittering sea, surrounded by seagulls that really loved the sound of their own voices.

Waves whooshed and crashed against the rocks below. It was a long way down. Will backed away from the edge.

He shuffled to Foosay's front door, clinging to the porch rail. Reluctantly, and only because he didn't know what else to do, he knocked.

It opened. The witch's fingers appeared first, followed by her forehead. She curled her body around the door.

"The boy?" she whispered to herself, casting her eyes behind him to see if he was alone. A few seconds ticked by before she decided to address Will. "What are you doing here?"

"I don't know. What am I doing here? Where are we? Where's Blue?"

"Oh, for heaven's sake." She grabbed Will by the shirt and dragged him into her house.

He pulled away from her, worried that she wanted to use him in one of her spells, or something worse. Witches didn't really eat children, did they? Surely not. "Please don't eat me," he said in panic before he could stop himself.

Foosay nearly laughed but changed her mind at the last second. Her smile drooped. "I can't seem to get a moment's peace lately. And I don't blame you, my dear child." She slipped her poncho over her head, revealing a bright yellow cardigan with fluorescent green buttons the size of milk bottle tops. "I blame that godforsaken wot you brought along with you." At Will's crestfallen expression, she added, "I'm not saying he does it deliberately, of course. He's only young, still sees life with the gusto of a child. But he thinks I still do too, and that's the problem. I can no longer cope with practical jokes being sprung on me out of nowhere. I wish he could see that." She hung the poncho on a hook behind the door.

Will stood still, quiet, confused. As was so often the case in this place, his confusion went unnoticed.

"I had to get away from him. I certainly had no intention of bringing you along with me. But never fear, I shall return you safe and sound. As soon as I've remade my potion, that is. I just used the last of it on the trip here. What a waste." She beckoned him into the back room in which he had found the gems, and she patted the side of her cauldron. "It may take a bit of time to heat up," she said. She lifted her wand from a shelf by the fire and pointed it at the blackened wood. It set alight with a blast of flames that only just missed her face. One inch closer and she'd have been missing her eyebrows.

Will stared at Foosay, his back against her wall. He glanced down at the row of gems on the dressing table. The purple one had been returned to the exact spot he had taken it from.

"I don't get it," he said. His throat felt scratched, too dry to speak comfortably. "You said Blue's like a child, but Dante said he was old. Super old, she said."

Foosay looked at Will in surprise. "He has been around a lot of years, yes. But wots, they live forever, and Blue is barely two hundred. That makes him, by all accounts, the equivalent of an eight-year-old witch."

Amused by this piece of information, Will broke into an involuntary burst of laughter.

"Wots age too fast for themselves at first," Foosay went on, "then slower as time goes on. Physically, that is. Unfortunately, their brains aren't quite so keen to grow up." A smile brightened her face and Will saw warmth in her grey eyes. "Once they reach the physical appearance of a thirty-year-old witch, they won't age any further for many centuries. And once they reach the appearance of a fifty-year-old witch, they'll age no further at all. Ever. They're fascinating, really. And only eight of them in existence."

"If you like them so much," Will said, feeling braver now, "why would you want to kill them?"

Foosay immediately seemed irritated again and Will's discomfort came back just as quickly. "Who has put it in your head that I want to kill anybody, boy?"

"You killed Blue this morning. You drowned him and stole his gem."

"Don't speak nonsense." Foosay poured a bucket of green liquid into the baking hot cauldron. It hissed as it hit the sides. Bottle green smoke surged from the cauldron in an enormous ball that dispersed slowly.

"I'm not," Will said when the noise relented. "I'm just telling you what Blue said happened. Somebody killed him this morning, and he thought it was you."

"Oh, he thought now, did he?" She scooped some ash-like substance from a bowl that she had raked out from under her armchair and threw it into the cauldron, hard, clearly trying to speed the process along to be rid of her uninvited guest. "Don't speak such nonsense," she said again. "Blue did not die this morning, let alone by my hands."

"He did die. I saw him."

"Don't be ridiculous." The witch peeled a strip of her dreadful blue and green striped wallpaper from the wall and dropped it into the mixture. Bubbles glugged and popped as the liquid engulfed the paper. She gathered some jars from a cupboard behind her chair, glass clinking against glass.

"I'm not, I saw him dead. I brought him back to life. That's how we met in the first place." He had to shout over the crackling when Foosay tossed one of the jars into the potion without even taking off the lid first. On hearing his words, Foosay stopped what she was doing and stared at Will long and hard.

"You're saying you brought a wot back to the land of the living?" she said, as though a memory had returned to her that she had long since misplaced. She let out a long, loud 'hmm', and then another as she paced back to her cupboards. The next thing she pulled out of there was a clear plastic bag chock-full of black, sooty powder, which she chucked into the cauldron, bag and all. A small packet of self-raising flour followed.

Will wondered if she was making the recipe up as she went along.

"I can't understand why Blue would think such a terrible thing of me." She emptied the contents of a salt tin into her potion. "But it does sound terribly worrying, if someone really has taken his gem."

"Yes," Will said. "You." He pointed at the blue gem displayed on her dressing table.

Realisation struck Foosay. "Oh, no, no, that's nonsense," she said, with a tight-lipped smile. "Those gems aren't real, my dear child." She tip-tapped nearer and gave him a reassuring pat on the head before dashing back to add more jars to her concoction, each one producing a different bang, slap or popping sound on hitting the frothing, now stinking brew.

It smelt worse, if that were possible, than the sickening rotted fruit smell of Esko's breath. It was when the witch added the final jar that the stink waved mercilessly in Will's direction, a hot wind of sour milk and bad eggs. Will covered his face with his hands and tried to breathe through his mouth, which didn't help. He could practically taste the stench.

Foosay seemed oblivious to it. Either she was so used to the smell that it no longer bothered her, or Dante wasn't the only witch in Wynne whose nose didn't work.

"They're a collection I've put together over the last thirty years or so. I found a rock one time while out walking on the beach. That one on the far right there. You can see, it looks exactly like a wot gem. It was already that perfect black, that perfect shape. I thought it was the real deal at first. I expected a wot to pop out when I touched it. That obviously didn't happen. So, I kept it. It took a long time to make the complete set, but I've had the lot of them for years. They're certainly nothing more than rocks, dear."

Will took in the row of colourful rocks. Now that he looked closer, he saw that these gems were all identical in size and shape, and he'd been certain Dyelann's orange one had been that bit bigger than Karson and Foyer's white and black ones. Foosay was telling the truth. They were replicas, nothing more.

"I wish I knew why Blue accused me of killing him." She took a deep breath and stared into space. She didn't seem confused, nor did she seem sad, just on the cusp of a daydream, deep in private thought and with a quiet air of peacefulness as she tossed the last ingredient into her cauldron: A clump of carpet she'd hacked from the space under her chair using the end of her wand.

The potion calmed down then, no longer bubbling or crackling, and the smell faded, although Will expected he would taste it in the back of his throat for a long while to come.

"House," Foosay said, still sounding like her mind was elsewhere. "Get back to our spot in the asters, please. Oh, and be sure to bring the roof along this time, will you?" She dipped a tarnished ladle into the cauldron and stirred. "You be a good lad and explain the situation to Blue," she said, presumably not talking to the house anymore. "Tell him I have absolutely no desire to see any harm come to him. I never have and I never will. I'll always be his friend. You tell him that."

Will believed her, but none of this added up yet, and he couldn't bring himself to leave without at least trying to find out more. "But Dante said you wanted to live forever. She said you'd figured out how to make a spell with the gems."

Foosay let go of the ladle and watched it sink. "I think your friend may have me confused with another witch. An old friend of mine,

Scilla Simms, once thought she'd discovered the key to eternal life. But, like I've said to Blue many a time, acceptance is the key to a happy life. Nobody can be happy if they don't accept that eventually they will die, they will move on, and there's nothing can be done about it. Even the wots, one day, with the burning out of the sun and the end of all life, even they will cease to be."

She rushed to a window and tugged open the curtain, darting her head about like a nervous hen. "We're here. You can leave. I'm going to go back to where we came from. Hopefully, I'll have some potion to spare this time. It takes a lot of juice to move a whole house, you know, so try to keep well away this time, won't you? I don't want you coming along with me again. I hate waste. I'll give you a minute."

Will didn't need telling twice. He hurried along the hallway to the front door, only stopping once to shout a goodbye to the witch. Then he ran. He burst out of the cottage and sprinted to the trees like his life depended on it, scared that something would spring out and stop him at the last second. When he looked back, the house had already gone.

"Blue?" Will scanned the area for his friend. "Blue?" Nothing. Will screamed the name at the top of his lungs, now worried he had been abandoned in the middle of a magical forest with absolutely no idea of how to make his way back to the real world. Even more worrying than that, he wouldn't be able to warn Blue that it was another witch, and not Foosay Hoo, that posed the danger.

There was no response to his desperate bellow.

Casting his eyes over the trees, grass, scattered purple daisies, and birds flittering in the branches above, Will listened hopefully. Still nothing. "Blue?" he tried again, quieter, and he peered behind each tree trunk he passed, holding onto the vain hope that Blue had decided to play hide and seek without letting him know about it.

After his tenth attempt to jump around a tree and catch Blue in hiding, Will gave up and walked on with no purpose in his stride, in no specific direction, shoulders slouched miserably. The sun had died down and, although the wind had dropped, there was a fresh chill in the air that bit through Will's shirt. He stuffed his hands under his armpits, trying to warm his fingers.

It didn't matter anyway, he tried to convince himself. It didn't matter that he was lost. It wasn't like he wanted to go home. And Blue had Dante and the others to help him. They didn't need a child getting in the way. Will had nothing to offer anyone.

Except information, he reminded himself. What if Blue needed that? What if that information was important? What if it were all that would save Blue and the rest of the wots, to find out in time that they were after the wrong witch?

Why couldn't Blue have just waited for him to get back? There was no way he was going to be able to find the wot now. He'd just have to live in the forest all by himself with weird monkeys in dungarees. His friends could add him to their stories of people who ventured into Wynne Wood and were never seen again. He stopped dead to stamp his foot. "It's not fair!"

A head appeared from behind the tree closest to Will, startling him. He shot back so fast he nearly tripped over his own feet.

The head belonged to a man with a weirdly square jaw and only a few tufts of ginger hair sprouting from his otherwise bald cranium. At first Will thought he didn't have any eyebrows either, but on closer inspection saw they were just very fair. His yellow left eye refused to stay in one place. It swung back and forth in its socket, up and down, right to left, like somebody had spun it with such ferocity that it had not yet lost momentum. The right eye, however, was dark, steady, and fixed on Will.

Will scuttled back from the stranger, hoping this man was one of Blue's harmless wot friends and not some evil lunatic that had escaped from prison to seek refuge in the forest, ready to feast on an eleven-year-old's brain at the first opportunity.

"Please don't eat my brain," he said, near closing his eyes, face crumpling as he waited for a reaction.

The man, cautious in his step, shifted around the thick trunk so that he faced Will, his back pressed up against it. "Gart," he said, belting his torso with a fist.

Will jumped.

"Gart," he said again, not punching himself this time but standing up straighter.

Will pushed the peak of his cap up so he could see better. "Oh. That's your name?"

The man let out a goofy laugh.

"I'm Will." He held out his right hand, believing this to be the proper thing to do when you introduced yourself to someone, but Gart gazed down on the extended hand as though he'd never seen such a thing.

There fell upon the two of them an awkward silence, where Will found that he could not keep himself from staring at Gart's dancing yellow eye despite being all too aware of what his mother would have to say to that. *Rude to stare, rude to stare, rude to stare...* He forced his eyes away from Gart's and stared down at the man's feet, which were bound in tight, old, grey shoes that both big toes protruded from, the nails of which were overgrown, chipped, and as yellow as his eye. *Rude to stare, rude to stare, rude to stare...*

Will found a place on Gart's face where he could rest his gaze without focusing on the ridiculously square jaw, strange hair or lack thereof, or his madly bouncing eyeball and asked, "Do you know a wot called Blue?"

"Gart witch." Gart slapped his thigh.

"Do you know where I can find Dante, then? Please, you've got to help me. I'm a bit lost, and I need to find a wot or one of those four good witches."

"*Gart witch.*" Gart spoke the words with such vigour that his body quivered and the several tufts of hair sticking from his head wobbled along with it. His left eye proceeded to roll uncontrollably. "Witch, Gart, Gart, witch. Gart good."

"Yeah, I know, but I mean four 'pecific witches. They're sisters of the four points of the earth corners, or something like that. One of them's called Dante."

"Yes," Gart barked, raising his head higher. "Yes."

"Yes?" Will took a discreet step back.

"Yes."

"Okay. Good."

"Good." Gart waved a triumphant arm. "Gart you help."

"You know where they are?"

"Gart know." He clicked his fingers. "Come." Gart twisted jerkily around and staggered away from the tree as though inebriated. The man seemed to find it impossible to walk a straight line, his knees swinging upward much higher than necessary, then flailing to each side every time he put his foot down. Watching him struggle along made walking seem a much more difficult task than it ought.

Will followed hesitantly, transfixed by the stranger's extravagant leg action. "Are you sure you know where you're going?"

He received only a pained grunt in reply, and the sound of Gart's fist connecting with another part of his body. Will wasn't sure which, as he'd not been watching at the time, more concerned with something squishy underfoot. He had stepped in a pile of discarded fruit innards. Maybe Esko was nearby. It would be good to see a familiar face. Will was not at all convinced that Gart was sound of mind and would have appreciated someone there to assure him that the man-witch wasn't dangerous.

"Is it far?" he asked, hopping along on one foot, trying to fling some of the fruit gunk from his trainer on the other.

"Far, far, no, no, yes. Try. Try."

That was helpful. Will's shoulders rounded again in a silent sulk. He missed Blue's company. At least Blue could answer questions properly. And so many questions Will had for him now, not the least of which regarding the wot's age. No wonder Blue acted so childishly at times if what Foosay had said was true. And yet at other times he spoke and behaved more like Will's grandfather than an eight-year-old. Blue or Dante would tell Will the truth, he was sure. If only he could find them.

"If Blue had just waited for, like, five stupid minutes, we wouldn't have split up in the first place," Will explained to Gart, although he was sure that the odd man wasn't paying attention to him. "Thanks for helping me. We won't be long now, will we? Gart?"

"Gart," Gart shouted.

"Gart," Will agreed, copying Gart's exuberant tone.

"Gart witch. Gart… witch. Will. Will?"

Will gritted his teeth. "It's just my name. It doesn't mean anything."

Gart gave him a backwards nod, striding on, his spidery legs dragging the far less energetic body along with them. His left shoulder struck a tree, and the blow knocked him off course for several paces until he managed to get back into the swing of putting one foot in front of the other.

"Are you okay?"

Will took Gart's silence to mean that he was and continued to follow, staring at the back of Gart's head.

A high, singsong voice called out for Gart from a place Will could not pinpoint, shouting the name over and over. Sometimes it sounded like it came from ahead of them, sometimes from behind. Gart didn't seem interested, for he did not break pace.

"Gart, I think someone wants you," Will said stupidly, wondering if the witch had not heard the call.

"No." Gart walked faster. "No. Move. Move."

Will fell quiet again.

"Gart, are you deaf?" the now aggravated voice asked.

Gart tripped and fell headlong onto the leaf-covered ground between a pair of crooked oaks. Will saw then that the voice belonged to a wenn – and that she had caused Gart to fall on purpose. She was the same height as Reese, with the same piggy black eyes and china doll lips, but she was slimmer and darker skinned.

"Who's this you're with?" She put on a sweet face and fluttered noiselessly upward to meet the boy's eye. "How did you get here, dear child? What are you doing all alone – with Gart?" She glared at the fallen man, who appeared to be losing a fight with the ground.

"I was with a wot, but I lost..." Will started to say, but he cut himself short when he saw the intrigue that crossed her little face.

"Really, really, is that so? And your name is?"

"Will. It's short for…"

"That's nice," she said before he could finish, and Will huffed through his nose at her. "Well, Will-it's-short-for, my name is Eve. Now do tell me, which wot is it that you've misplaced, where did you last see him, and how is it that you came to be parted?"

Gart flapped and squirmed like a fish pulled from water, rustling about in the crisp red and brown leaves.

"Aren't you going to help him up?" Will asked, avoiding the wenn's questions. Intending to hoist Gart up, he offered a hand, only for one of Gart's legs to kick it away.

"Gart doesn't accept help," Eve said, sticking close to Will, her dragonfly wings humming in a silvery blur behind her. "You were saying? About the wot?"

"That was mean of you to trip him over, if you knew he wouldn't be able to get back up again," he said. He watched Gart closely because he needed a reason not to look at Eve. And also because a full-grown man acting like an overturned tortoise wasn't something you saw every day. "Come on, Gart, you can do it. Put your hands on the floor and push yourself up."

Gart screamed out in fury.

"Gart doesn't accept help," Eve said again. "Forget him for now. Tell me about this wot of yours."

Will pretended not to hear. "I'm lost," he said. "Gart was going to help me find the witch sisters."

"Oh, he was, was he?" The wenn's voice changed from sweet as sugar to a dangerous hiss. "What have we said to you about going near those witches?" She spat in Gart's direction. It was barely a speck of saliva, but Will found himself utterly disgusted by her.

"Stop picking on him," he snapped, fully aware of the absurdity that Eve did not even reach the height of Gart's knees. Not when he was standing upright, anyway.

"He needs picking on. He needs some sense banging into him. The creature's positively thick-headed."

At last, Gart managed to sit up, and from that position swung out his arms to heave himself onto his feet, where he shook madly until he regained his balance. Chest heaving, exhausted, he lolled against one of the trees to catch his breath.

"Nice one." Will hoped he didn't sound patronising. "Are you okay now?"

"Of course he is. For now." Eve flew in front of Gart's good eye. "How dare you even think about seeking out those witches?"

Gart looked as furious with her as she did with him.

"What's it got to do with you, what he does?" Will said, hands on his hips, standing the way that his mother stood whenever she told him off. "He can go wherever he likes. It's a free country. Tell her, Gart."

"Gart witch."

"Gart stupid," Eve said. "Eve tell Gart time and time again not to see those witches. You know what I'll do to you, don't you?" She added with a growl, "You know what our dear friend will do to you."

"Don't threaten him," Will shouted, surprised by his own bravado.

Then the wenn, glaring at him with hatred that chilled his blood, took an almighty breath and opened wide her dainty mouth…

Chapter Five: Jonah Scrossly

The fat, bright moon loomed behind black branches that bent in a perfect circle around its light. Stars twinkled. Something creaked and groaned in the breeze.

Will was on his back, he realised. He sat up, startled by the darkness, and struggled to see something, anything, past the shadows of the two crooked oak trees. There was no sign of Gart or Eve or anyone else.

The leaves above rustled.

Will shuddered, partly because of the cold and partly because of the fear crawling up his spine. He kept catching movements from the corner of his eye, but whenever he tried to see what was there, there was nothing.

Tricks of your eyes: That's what his mother had always said to him when he'd been younger and had seen things in the dark. It would be nice to hear her say that now. He hated to admit it to himself, but he wanted to go home. However much his parents upset him lately, it had to be better at home with them than out here on his own. If only he had his duvet to hide under until daylight dawned.

"Is anyone there?" he whispered, as afraid of hearing an answer as he was of not hearing one. "Blue?" He would have given anything for his friend to come and find him then.

A shuffling, scuttling noise started up in a patch of blackness beneath a bank of foliage, where the moonlight couldn't reach. Will strained his unblinking eyes. "Hello?"

More scrabbling sounds followed.

Everything in him screamed to run the other way, but Will pushed the instinct away and took a few wary steps closer. Maybe Gart had fallen again. Maybe Eve had hurt him.

His vision adjusted enough to see a movement out of sync with everything else. Something grappled at the grass. It wasn't Gart. It was something smaller. Will leaned over and flattened a cluster of weeds to let the tiniest amount of light in. A wide-open eye glinted near the outline of a smooth head and the hook of a beak. A bird. It was just a bird. Will let out the breath he'd been holding and pawed clumsily at the weeds to free the trapped creature. It lashed out. Its beak scissored through the thin flesh on the back of his right hand, slicing open the soft spot between his thumb and index finger.

A scream echoed so loudly around him that Will jumped with shock before realising the awful sound had come from his own mouth.

The bird's wings thrashed in wild panic, but it went nowhere, still trapped.

Will pressed his bleeding hand under his left arm and tried to squeeze the stabbing pain away. He wanted to forget the bird, leave it there, the horrid, ungrateful creature. But he couldn't do that. The poor thing was frightened, all by itself in the dark with no means of escape. Feeling much the same way himself, Will took pity and tried again.

Shivering, teeth chattering, he kept his hand as far away from the bird's pointy end as possible and shook the clump of weeds until he heard a snap. The bird lurched past him, trailing the remainder of a branch along with it. After a hearty attempt to take flight, it crash-landed in a patch of moonlit grass, attacked its own leg and toppled over. But it wasn't its leg that the bird was biting, Will saw then. The spiny branch had caught in a large, luminous plastic leg-ring, inscribed with a distinct letter 'C'.

"I bet you belong to Cesar, don't you?" Will asked the bird, knowing full well that it couldn't reply. "You're a kite, aren't you?"

And he was right, the bird did not reply.

More of its unwanted load broke away, and the bird gave its feathers a vigorous ruffle and set off flying, free at last. It collided with the first tree in its path and spiralled to the ground, letting out a blast of angry whistles on its way down.

If the bird could lead him to Cesar, Will knew he had to follow it. At least Cesar might be able to help him find Blue, even if Will did hate the ware, and even if the ware did hate him in return.

He saw what people meant about Wynne Wood being spooky now. The moans and creaks of waving branches were enough to send his imagination into overdrive. Zombies and monsters lurked behind every tree, vampires and werewolves in every shadow. Trying his hardest to be brave, Will concentrated on not letting Cesar's kite out of his sight.

"Is everybody okay?" someone called out. "Hello? Does someone need help? Answer me! Lillian. Lillian, is it you?"

A frail old man not much taller than Will weaved around the trees ahead, a cane in one hand and a lantern in the other, dressed in a fluorescent yellow jacket with reflective straps that beamed out like beacons when they caught the light.

"Boy?" he pointed his lantern at Will and limped closer, carrying the cane rather than using it. "Boy, did you hear a lady scream?"

Glad of the darkness now, certain that his face had turned bright red with embarrassment, Will uttered a meek, "No."

"I heard a lady scream," the old man said. "I'm sure of it, ain't I? Are you positive you didn't hear it?"

"No. No screams." Will searched for the kite, finding it impossible to see anything beyond the brightness of the lantern. When he craned his neck and shielded his eyes from the old man's light, he could just about see it opening its wings. He tried to walk away, but the old man latched onto Will's wrist, an uncomfortably tight grip, and wrenched it up to see the oozing V-shaped wound on the back of his hand. "Ow!"

"You're bleeding. Were it you that screamed? Oh, thank the heavens. I thought it were my dear granddaughter Lillian, getting herself into trouble. She went out over a week ago with something on her mind and hasn't been home yet. I'm sick with worry for her, just sick."

Will yanked his arm back.

"Would you like that wound dressing, my lad?" the man offered, leaning on his canc.

"Not by you." Will feared the rough old man would tear off his fingers if he let him at them, even if only by accident. "I have to go. Look, the bird's getting back up. I can't lose it, or I won't be able to find Cesar's treehouse, and that's my only chance to get back to Blue."

"The wot? Dear old Blue, eh?" The man scratched at his jaw with the hand in which he held his lantern. The light so close to his face cast shadows under his baggy eyes and curved nose, dehumanising him. But Will was no longer afraid, only hopeful.

"You know him?"

"Why, I ain't heard that name in near sixty years."

"Sixty years? Wow. You must have a really good memory."

The old man lowered his lantern. "Sixty years passes by in the blink of an eye. You'll be my age before you know it, with some smart-arse whippersnapper making you feel old."

"But you are old." Will checked on the bird. "Do you know where Blue is? I hope he hasn't gone to bed. I need to find him."

"Nay, don't talk daft, lad." Noticing Will struggle to see the bird, the old man cast his light over it for him, revealing that it was still testing its wings. "Wots live on a different time cycle to the rest of us. They ain't due a sleep 'til Thursday or Friday."

"But it's Saturday."

"Nay, it's Sunday."

"No, it's Saturday," Will insisted.

"It's ten past four in the morning, lad. That means, it's Sunday. Pay attention."

Ten past four in the morning? Will had never been out of the house so late before. He should have been in bed hours ago. What would his parents be thinking? They must have noticed his absence by now. They'd be furious.

"Wots stay awake about nine or ten days, sleep for five," the old man said.

"That's weird. They just stay awake all night, even though everyone else is asleep?"

"They spend most o' their time in their gems anyway, so they ain't particular' aware that everyone else is sleeping." The lantern quivered as the old man's arm began to give under the weight, and he lowered it again. "They see in the dark just the same as they see in the day, so they don't barely notice the night-time at all."

The bird hopped.

"I have to go now." Will strode through the long grass and waved. "Bye."

"Hang fire, lad." The man waggled his cane.

Will waited out of politeness, but his attention was on the bird.

"Here, take this, won't you? Don't like the thought of a young lad out here alone in the dark."

Will took what was being offered to him from the gnarled old fingers. "Thanks. What is it?" It felt like a small, plastic tube.

The old man tapped it and torchlight shone.

"Really?" Will asked, moved by the stranger's generosity. "I can keep it?"

"O' course. Looks like your feathered friend's away."

Will searched for the bird with the circular light of his new torch. "Thank you!" he shouted, running. "I have to go."

"Take care now, lad. And when you see old Blue, you tell him, you tell him Jonah Scrossly sends his best tidings."

"Okay." As an afterthought he shouted over his shoulder, "I'll keep an eye out for Lillian for you!"

The bird had recovered its bearings and was already in flight, having gained some extra determination in its down time. No more collisions. No more falls. It soared high over the trees and onwards, only breaking pace to circle and whistle when Will fell too far behind.

Its willingness to be his guide was a comfort as he charged after it, stumbling in ditches, puddles, and random holes, avoiding trees, bushes and random bumps, tripping on roots, tree stumps and random rocks.

Finally, exhausted and overheated in the early morning chill, he reached Cesar's tree. The gargantuan trunk was unmistakable. He watched the kite shoot between two planks of wood in the unstable treehouse and disappear into thin air.

Yesterday, Will wouldn't have imagined being this thrilled to see the stroppy little ware's home again. Excitement fuelled his climb up the steps. When he reached the top, he fell through Cesar's door, breathing like an asthmatic bulldog.

"Will!" Blue leapt from Cesar's sofa, sprang across the glorious carpet, and squeezed Will against his chest. "You're not dead. I thought she was going to kill you. I came to get Cesar to tell me where she was so I could save you, but you're here. I'm so glad you're not dead."

Just when Will was beginning to panic that he couldn't breathe, Blue pushed him away, hard. He returned to the sofa and flopped down on it.

"I didn't need you to save me. I was only gone five minutes. You could have waited for me."

Blue's expression fell. "Well, excuse me. I thought you'd been kidnapped by a murderer. How was I supposed to know you'd just gone off for a jaunt?"

"I didn't go off for a jaunt." Will didn't know what a jaunt was but took offence all the same. "Mrs Hoo didn't kidnap me. Her house accidentally took me with it when it moved." Will was so relieved to be safe with Blue in the well-lit, cosy mansion that he could barely control the speed at which his words rolled out. "She was really nice and brought me back. And it wasn't her who killed you, by the way. Those gems she had weren't even real, they were just ornaments. And she said she doesn't even want to live forever."

"Will," Blue said, incredulous. "I was there when she was drowning me. It was her. I mean, I couldn't believe she could be so cruel, and she definitely wasn't acting like herself." He hesitated. "But it was her." He didn't sound so sure that time.

"I don't think so," Will said. "I really believed her. You would've too if you'd been there."

Blue put a finger to his lips to shush Will. "We'll have to keep it down. Cesar's asleep, and we don't want to wake him. Trust me. He sleeps a lot. But then he's awake like that." He clicked his fingers. "Strange."

The mention of strange sleep patterns reminded Will of his encounter with the old man. "Oh, and a man told me to send you his tidyings."

"Bit rude. What man?"

"He said his name was Jonas Crossly. He said you were his friend."

"Jonas Crossly?" Blue frowned, thinking. "Oh." He shifted to the edge of his seat and clapped his hands together. "You mean Jonah Scrossly?"

"That's what I said. He gave me this." Will showed Blue the small, black torch, which was still switched on. He couldn't find the button to turn it off.

"What is it?"

"A torch."

"What's it for?"

Will checked Blue's face, to see if he was being serious. "For, you know. Lighting."

Blue didn't seem to be listening anyway. "Jonah's great. How is he? I should meet up with him. I haven't seen him for a while." The wot smiled at a memory. "He used to mix a potion that would stun someone for a time of half a mint."

"Mint? You mean a minute?"

"Yeah, a mint. We used to throw the potion at someone then tie their laces together and take their hats off or swap their gloves over, things like that. Their faces when the potion wore off, so funny. They could never fathom what happened. We got a right telling off when Karson found out. I'll have to look out for him if he's around."

Will felt sorry for Blue then, clueless to the fact that the young friend he once had fun with was now a decrepit old man with a stoop that probably halved him from the height he'd once been. "He's got a granddaughter called Lillian."

"Yeah, I know. Crazy." Blue laughed. Then his face fell, and he understood what Will was saying. "Oh, yes. Of course." He stared at thin air for a short while, then sank back in the sofa. "He probably won't want me around anymore, same as Foosay. Never mind."

"I bumped into a wenn while I was looking for you," Will said, careful to keep his voice down. He sat on the arm of the sofa. "She kept asking me about you. I didn't tell her anything, but it was really weird, because she just disappeared, and it got dark."

Blue nodded. "Did you feel pleasantly rested?"

"I did until I had to chase that bird here."

"She must have sung to you. I warned you about that. Did she steal anything?"

Will patted his sides. "Nothing to steal."

"The last time a wenn sang to me was because Foyer paid her to. I'd been having these nightmares because of what a different wenn had been telling me, and I couldn't sleep at all. I was so tired. So, Foyer got the wenn to knock me out. Their song seduces you into dreamless slumber." He snorted. "They're horrible little creatures really. But they give you a good rest at least."

Cesar emerged from a door camouflaged so perfectly in the wall that Will hadn't been aware it was there at all until it had opened. His cotton pyjamas were dazzling white, his eyes pink and puffy, and his hair suffering from a bad case of bed head. "What are you doing here?" he asked, making no effort whatsoever to mask his displeasure. "I thought I got rid of you two earlier. Didn't I tell you to go away once already?"

"We did go away," Will said. "Then we came back."

"Do I have to tell you not to come back? Because I can, if that'll keep you away."

"Last time you offered tea."

Blue gave Will a quick warning headshake.

"You want tea?" Cesar dragged his tea tray out from its invisible space and pushed it into Will, making him drop the torch. The cups rattled and clinked against one another, dark, steaming hot tea sloshing from the teapot's spout. "Have tea! Then leave, and don't come back."

"I don't want any, I was just saying…" Will stopped himself when he noticed the flash of anger in Cesar's expression. For the first time in his life, he understood the phrase 'If looks could kill.'

Cesar's already pink ears turned a drastic shade of red. He took the tray from Will and thrust it back into nothingness with such ferocity they heard the smash even after it had vanished.

"You don't have to be so cranky," Will said. "I did save your kite."

"What?"

"That kite that just flew in. I unstuck it for you."

Blue waited, intrigued, for Cesar's response. There was a long moment where Cesar didn't react at all. Then he scuttled away, bright white fluffy slippers slapping his heels.

Will picked up the torch, regretting that the fall had put its light out. He fiddled about with it while they waited for Cesar to return, trying to figure out where the batteries went. It seemed to be a solid piece of plastic, with no space for batteries. There was no bulb in it either. In fact, where had the light even come from? Both ends of the tube were black. There were no buttons. It was a smooth piece of plastic, not a torch. He tapped it a few times before deciding, whatever it was and however it worked, it was broken.

The ware shuffled sedately back into the room and moved a cushion so he could sit between Blue and Will on the sofa.

"Thank you," he said to Will, without looking at him. "Dreyfus is very grateful to you. And so am I."

Blue grinned at Will behind Cesar's back.

"He had been trapped there quite some time, he says, and all because of my stupid ring." Cesar rested his head in his hands, distraught. "I could have killed him. My favourite kite, my beloved kite. So much potential in that one, you know. He's going to grow to be extraordinary. Barely out of fledglinghood and already one of the best flyers I've got."

Will thought back to the bird's haphazard journey home and said, "Really?"

Cesar did not seem to notice the remark, just continued to blubber into his hands. "I should remove the rings from all my birds. He could have died there, and I never would have known what happened to him."

"I thought the rings had spells on them to keep the birds protected," Blue said.

"Protected from other creatures and thieves, yes." Cesar sniffed and wiped his eyes, taking a deep, wet-sounding breath. "But not from *branches*."

"Blue's been trying really hard to get your egg back," Will said, hoping to cheer Cesar up.

The ware laughed sadly. "It was stolen months ago, Blue. It won't be an egg anymore."

Blue got to his feet. "We'll leave you alone."

Cesar's fingers caught the bottom of Blue's coat, causing the wot to stop and look down at him. He gazed back, beady eyes wide open and shiny. "If you still want my help to find Foosay," he said shakily, "just say the word, my friend."

"Thanks, Cesar. That means a lot. But we're not looking for her anymore. Thanks anyway, though." He tried to leave, but Cesar wouldn't release his hold.

"Why have you stopped looking for her?"

"Will thinks it wasn't her that took my gem after all."

"You said she killed you."

Blue shrugged. "It must have been someone who looked like her. Exactly like her. Evil-twin alike."

"She said it was another witch who found out how to live forever, not her," Will said. "A friend called…" He closed his eyes to think. "…Scilla Simms."

"Scilla Simms?" Blue repeated in a loud, mocking voice. "Sorry, but Foosay got that wrong."

"Perhaps she bewitched the boy." Cesar surveyed Will, cautiously, like he was a bomb that would detonate if they made one false move. "Did she make you drink anything while you were with her? Did she open any bottles?"

"No." Will started to feel self-conscious under his intense stare and slid off the sofa's arm.

"I can't believe she's throwing wild accusations around like this," Blue said.

Cesar let go of Blue and stood up. "Did she throw any powder or liquid in your direction, boy?"

"She didn't throw *anything*. All she said was it wasn't her who wanted to live forever, it was Scilla Simms who wanted that. She said they were friends. And she's your friend too. She'll always be your friend. She told me to tell you that." Will was speaking too fast again, but Cesar and Blue, unlike his parents, didn't seem to have any trouble keeping up.

Cesar folded his arms and paced the length of the room, his messy hair bouncing with each step, slippers flapping.

"Scilla Simms can't be the one taking our gems," Blue said. "She's a good witch. She's the Simms sisters' aunt. She raised Dante and the others like they were her own."

It hadn't crossed Will's mind that Scilla Simms was related to Dante when Foosay mentioned her. He'd forgotten that Dante was a Simms. "Scilla Simms is Dante's mum's sister?"

"No, she married Dante's uncle," Blue said. "But he died not long after Dante's parents died."

"They *all* died?" The prospect of losing so many loved ones horrified Will. "How?"

Blue took a breath to answer the question but stopped before any words came. "I never asked." He asked Cesar, "Do you know?"

"I know they were murdered. I don't know by whose hands."

Murdered. A shiver got stuck halfway up Will's back and he shuddered to dislodge it. "Poor Dante," he whispered. His mum and dad may have been causing him considerable anguish lately, but he'd be lost if anything ever happened to them. His anger towards them suddenly seemed trivial.

"Scilla took the five children in and loved them like they were her own," Cesar said, echoing Blue. "They never needed for anything. And surely, if Scilla Simms were indeed an evil witch, she would have raised the children evil too. As it is, the sisters are all wonderful examples of what a witch should be."

"Exactly," Blue said. "So, if it isn't Scilla, and it isn't Foosay, then who on earth is taking our gems?"

"Someone with a Foosay mask," Will said. "Hang on." He had been going over the conversation in his head and noticed a mistake. "You said five children."

"That's right." Cesar stopped pacing and sat on the arm of the sofa, crossing his legs tightly like he was about to start meditating.

"But you said there were only four sisters."

"Right. Four sisters and a brother."

"Dante's got a brother too?" Will inspected Cesar and Blue's faces. "How come you didn't say about him before?"

"Dante doesn't like talking about him," Blue said. "Don't bring him up in her presence, okay? She'll just get upset."

"Why?" Will pried.

"Nobody knows what happened to him." Blue spoke quietly, as if afraid that Dante might overhear him even though she was probably miles away.

"Why? What happened?"

"I just said, nobody knows."

"No, I know, but I mean, is he dead?"

"Nobody knows," Blue said again.

"Why? Did he go somewhere?"

"Will." Blue leaned slightly to face him. "Nobody knows what happened to him."

Will gave up.

Yawning, Cesar untwisted his legs and secured his small feet into his floppy slippers. "If you no longer require my assistance, I shall retire until a more reasonable hour. You can stay here for the night if you'd rather. I'm very grateful to you, young man. And Blue, I shall help you in any way I can. For now, though, I need my sleep. So, I bid you goodnight." His hand went straight to the hidden doorknob without needing to feel for it.

"See, I told you he's a good friend," Blue said when Cesar had gone. "Are you ready to go?"

Will rubbed his bare arms, reluctant to leave the comfort of indoors for the cold, dark night outside. "It's freezing out there."

"Here, put this on." Blue thrust a navy cotton jacket at Will, who had no idea where the wot had acquired it from. It was fleece lined and hooded, similar to one he had at home.

"How did you do that?" He pulled it on and wrapped it tight, leaving Jonah's broken torch on Cesar's coffee table.

"I may not have my gem but I'm still a wot. I know what you're looking for when you want something."

"That's amazing. Thanks."

"That's okay. I'm sure Cesar won't even notice it's gone."

Will suddenly felt awkward, not sure he wanted to wear stolen property.

Blue headed for the exit. "Let's go. I'll get you your wishes, I promise you that."

Wishes were the last thing on Will's mind. He was more concerned about what was going to happen to Blue and the other wots if they didn't get their gems back.

Blue stumbled through the door. He managed to stop himself from falling but slid all the way down the trunk, feet bumping against each one of the nailed-on steps, and he groaned when he reached the ground and held out his hands to examine his scraped palms.

Will climbed down with relative ease. "Where are we going?"

"To meet up with Karson and the rest. As arranged." Blue took a deep breath, gave his hands a quick rub, and began to walk at his exceptionally brisk pace in the same direction they had headed the last time they'd left Cesar's treehouse.

"How are we going to get there without Dante?"

"We'll have to use these things." Blue tapped his legs.

Walking with Blue was certainly quicker than walking with most people - more like running, in fact - but Will couldn't imagine they'd make it on foot before the others got tired of waiting. Still, it wasn't as if there were any buses running through the forest, so, unless a couple of the chimpanzees offered to lend them their bicycles, they didn't have much choice. He broke into a jog to catch up.

"Don't worry, Will," Blue said, as if he could sense what was bothering him. "We'll get there soon enough. Then we're really going to get started with finding out who the baddie is."

Chapter Six: One to Go

When the sun eventually showed its face and Will could see properly again, he initiated a game of I-Spy to pass the time on their way to Karson's Christmas tree. It proved to be a difficult game to play with Blue, for two reasons: One, Blue walked so fast that Will had to keep running to catch up, making it a real effort to talk at all, and two, Blue cheated. The wot couldn't come up with an answer even nearly right for something as obvious as G for Grass or T for Tree, and yet he expected Will to be able to guess that U stood for Unhappy-looking mushroom and H for Hiding slug - answers Will would never have guessed even if it had been possible to notice these things as anything more than a momentary blur at the pace they were speeding along. Worse still, Blue couldn't take the hint Will had grown bored of the game and wanted to stop. Even after Will said the words, "I'm bored of this and I don't want to play anymore," Blue just went on playing without him, spewing out letter after letter until they finally reached their destination.

Will counted eight people gathered by the Christmas tree, chatting amongst themselves. The four wots, Dyelann, Foyer, Maik, and Karson, stood with Dante and three other women who Will presumed were the witch's sisters.

"Blue," Dante called, waving her arms about as though he would have missed them otherwise. "I was worried about you." She embraced him in an eager hug. His arms dangled behind her in his reluctance to return it. No longer trailing her fancy burgundy dress, she had changed into a pair of flared, black trousers and a thin blouse that changed colour where the light touched, like the inside of a shell. Her fingernails had been repainted too, this time an exact match for the iridescent blouse. "Will." A wide, loving smile lit her face. "These are my sisters. Molina, Harrier and Elmer."

Harrier and Elmer were identical twins, indistinguishable from one another but for Harrier being dressed in black and Elmer in lighter colours. They shared the same dark hair as Dante that glinted mahogany red in the sunlight, and they were both aiming friendly smiles at Will. Molina, however, whose hair was hidden under a black and red headscarf, wore an expression of blatant disdain.

"Hello," Will said politely, trying not to pant too much. His lungs ached from exertion. He felt oddly grateful to Eve for knocking him out the day before, for there was no way he would have been able to stay awake all night and run all this way if she hadn't.

"Good to meet you," Molina said, though her flat tone suggested the contrary. "I gather you saved Blue's life. Well done, you."

Will forced a smile.

"Will. Is that short for something?"

"William."

"William," the witch repeated, and Will could see Blue mouthing the name along with her. "Well, hello, William. And Blue. Always wonderful to see you." The comment to the wot was just as deadpan.

Karson's intolerant voice quivered through the group like a pulled guitar string. "Look at the state of you, Blue." He appeared from behind the twins, a couple of inches shorter than them and still dressed as though he was attending a black tie only party for the highest class of royalty, and tugged Blue's lapels straight. "Try running a comb through your hair, you scruff."

Dante beamed a smile. "I think he looks just fine."

Blue's eyes shot to Will.

"See?" Will whispered, and mouthed, "She loves you."

"I told you to get this mess sorted out, and now there are people showing up left and right, telling me you sent them here. What do you think you're playing at? And stop slouching."

Blue stood with his shoulders sagging forward like one of Will's classmates being scolded by a teacher. It made Will uncomfortable.

"I tried to sort it out on my own, but I can't. I need help."

"Useless, good for nothing little..."

"All right, Karson." Foyer stepped up, managing to drag his attention from Dante at last. "That's enough. Leave the poor lad alone." He slapped Blue's arm. "Don't worry. Karson's just in a bad mood. It's not your fault. He woke up on the wrong side of his gem, so to speak."

"At least he's got a gem to wake up in," Blue muttered. "Some of us are sadly lacking."

Maik, now recovered from his brush with the gem thief, slunk to Foyer's side. "So how are we going to get them back? That's what we're all here for, right? You have a plan?"

Showing that he was listening to what was going on around him for the first time since Will had arrived, Dyelann said, "We have to find Henry."

Maik nodded. "And Adrian."

"Of course, and Popset too," Dyelann said. "When we get our gems back," he said to Will, "you just say the word, kidlet. Any wish you want. It's yours."

An icy blast of loathing surged Dyelann's way from Blue's glare.

Molina tapped a dainty foot. "We don't have all day, you know. Hurry up and decide what you're doing. Are we to confront Foosay Hoo, in force?"

"No," Will said. The old witch had been nice enough to him, and there had been no mistaking the compassion in her face while she'd been telling him all about the wots. It wasn't fair that all these people wanted to ambush her for something she hadn't done. "You can't do that. It wasn't her."

Karson loomed over Will. "And what would a child know of this matter?"

"Like I said." Blue moved in front of Will to shield him from Karson. "We tried to get my gem back, like you told us to. We found Foosay, and she…"

“Fed you a pack of lies that you swallowed like a pair of fools,” Karson finished.

Elmer and Harrier giggled. Thcy had wandered away a few steps, to have a private exchange about something that, Will hoped, had nothing to do with what the rest of the group were discussing.

Blue gazed helplessly at Karson. “Will spoke to her and…”

“Enough.”

“Enough yourself,” Foyer said. “Let them speak.” There was a strength to his tone that Will wouldn’t have expected from the black-gemmed wot.

Keeping his eye on Karson as if anticipating a backlash, Blue said, “Will had a word with Foosay, and it turns out she wasn’t the one who killed me after all.” He let out a breath of a laugh, embarrassed or nervous or a mixture of the two.

“She’s not going to admit it to you,” Karson all but shouted. “What do you expect she’s going to say? ‘Yes, I stole your gem, please go and tell everyone you know’?”

“No!” Will raised his voice enough to rival Karson’s unnecessary volume, the urge to defend Blue overriding his sense of decorum. “It wasn’t her. If it was her, why was she so nice to me? If it was her, she wouldn’t have bothered talking to me.”

“Not unless she wanted you to get everyone off her scent,” Dante said. “We’ve heard all about Foosay Hoo, Will. She’s a senile old witch who’ll stop at nothing to uncover the secrets to eternal life. And she’s discovered them. It has to be her. Blue said himself she was the one who drowned him and took his gem yesterday.”

“But she didn’t,” Will insisted, refusing to believe it. “She told me you were confusing her with someone else.”

Blue shook his head urgently at Will to stop him from saying any more, but Will couldn’t bring himself to back down.

“She said it was Scilla Simms.”

That was exactly what Blue must have been trying to stop him from saying, Will realised, too late. The four Simms sisters turned their heads in unison to stare directly at Will's face. Molina's eyes flashed with abhorrence, whereas Elmer and Harrier just appeared dumbfounded.

Dante held an expression of sad sympathy. "Oh, Will," she said, hand to her heart. "She really did get to you, didn't she? You poor little thing."

Molina pulled her sleeves up to her elbows like she was getting ready for a fistfight.

Blue put his hands up in surrender. "Keep your hair on. We all know it's not Scilla. But Will's adamant Foosay was sincere, and I believe him."

An uncomfortable silence fell upon the group while Karson grew steadily redder in the face and the others fished for words to express their own feelings on the matter. Only Dyelann remained indifferent to the rising tension, gazing into space with a level of nonchalance that Will found enviable.

Dante was the first to speak. "If Blue believes Will so strongly," she said, "then we should give him the benefit of the doubt."

"Benefit of the doubt?" Molina stiffened and swayed, looking on the verge of slapping her sister. "What doubt? There is no doubt. How dare she accuse Auntie Scilla of such things? How *dare* she?" She spun back around to step away from Dante, and Will was relieved. "Auntie Scilla knew Foosay would turn on her one day. Didn't I tell you?" She raised an arm to Elmer and Harrier, inviting them to join in. "Didn't I?"

"It's always the best of friends that make the worst of enemies, isn't that right, Mo-Mo?" Elmer said.

Maik scoffed at the comment. "Best of friends? That's a stretch. They were acquaintances, once upon a time, maybe."

"That just proves Foosay's lying," Molina said.

"No, it doesn't." Will was sick of arguing but too stubborn to give up. "She doesn't want to hurt anybody."

"That's just what she wants you to think," Harrier said, sounding and standing exactly like Elmer. "She's got you right where she wants you, advocating for her."

Blue said, "I know Foosay better than any of you do, and I know she's not a liar."

Molina glared at him. "Maybe *you're* lying."

"Why would Blue lie?" Dante returned her sister's glare on Blue's behalf. "We're talking about the destruction of his race here, let's not forget."

Molina was poised in the same about-to-attack position that had unnerved Will before. "You're always on his side, aren't you? You'll always stick up for this wot, even when he's clearly talking out of his backside."

"Which is most of the time," Karson said.

"Blue talks more sense than any of you lot do," Dante retorted.

"There you go again," Molina said. "You've had a crush on that wot since you were twelve years old. When are you going to wake up and accept that behind the fully-fledged good looks and big words is an ignorant brat of a child?"

"He's two hundred years old, Mo," Dante shot back. "He is not a child."

"Yes, he is. For pity's sake, Dante, when will this sink in? He doesn't even like girls yet. And he won't ever, not in your lifetime."

"That's crazy. You're a grown man, aren't you, Blue?" Dante nodded at Blue, urging him to stand up for himself.

Blue threw a cautious glance Karson's way. "That's right. Older than the four of you put together. Stupid witches. Dante agrees with me all the time because I'm *right* all the time, that's why."

Foyer clamped his eyes shut like he could bear to witness no more.

"And you like girls, don't you, Blue?" Dante asked, sneering at her older sister.

"Girls are lovely."

"And you like me, don't you?"

"Of course," Blue said, a little apprehensive. "Very much."

"There, you see," Dante shouted in triumph. "And I love him very much too!"

The declaration was followed by another bout of silence when Dante realised what she'd said and how many people she'd said it in front of.

A swift bat to the back of Blue's head could have popped his eyes right out of their sockets.

"Shh!" Will hissed to Dante, much too late.

The blood drained from Blue's face to the point it reminded Will how he'd looked floating in the river the morning previous.

"Told you," he said to the wot.

Karson gaped in revulsion. "A witch in love with a wot. Preposterous."

"Yeah, right." Dyelann laughed. "Unthinkable."

Dante kept glancing at Blue, and Will could tell all she wanted right now was for Blue to return the sentiment. He imagined how happy she would be if that happened, and a flutter of joy zipped through him. Blue, however, said nothing at all.

"You're a fool, Dante Simms," Molina said. "You're hanging on to a little girl's crush on a little boy and you know it. That's not love. That's an excuse to hide from real feelings, you coward."

For a split second, Dante and Foyer's eyes met.

"Pathetic," Molina said.

Dante approached her sister with dangerous speed but stopped short when Molina produced two knives from somewhere behind her back. "Oh, you're going to stab me now?"

Molina smiled. "Of course not. I'd never stab you. Defence mechanism."

"Put those horrible things away, Mo-Mo," Elmer said.

"Wow." Will edged as close to the knives as he dared. Their handles were made of silver skulls, the blades about the length of the hands that held them. "So cool."

"You like them?" Molina asked. "So do I. Magic is all well and good, but it's let me down a few too many times in a pinch. Knives, though. Knives you can count on." She flipped one around and offered the handle to Will.

He let his eyes feast on the beautiful silver skulls and noticed some ivy sculpted between them.

"Go ahead, feel the weight."

Dante pushed Molina's arm back. "Don't, Mo, he's too young to be playing with knives."

"You're right." Molina slipped the knives back out of sight. "Better keep them away from Blue too, in that case."

Seeing Dante's anger surfacing again, Foyer stepped in to take control of the situation. "All right, people. Let's sort this out, right now. Karson, take yourself and your gem somewhere safe, where nobody can find you, and preferably somewhere far away so we don't have to put up with you."

Karson's forehead became alive with pulsing veins. "How dare–"

"Get gone." Foyer clapped repeatedly to drown out Karson's retort. "Get gone. Now. Go fast, go far."

Seething, Karson bustled to retrieve his gem and vanished in a cloud of white smoke.

"Now," Foyer went on. "You, witches. If you're going to help, take yourselves off and make a locator potion. Find our gems for us. See if Foosay has them or not. Dyelann, Maik, you two go find Henry, Popset, and Adrian. They've got to be out there somewhere."

Dyelann opened his mouth to complain, but Foyer thrust a palm up to his face. "No. No arguing. Get gone. Get."

Dyelann and Maik did as they were told.

Will wondered if Foyer's demonstration of leadership was merely an effort to win Dante's affections. If so, it was for nothing. Still fuming at Molina, Dante wasn't paying any real attention to anything or anyone else.

Blue coughed and found his voice, though it came out softer than usual. "What should I do, Foyer?"

"Very important job for you, Blue," Foyer said. "I want you to find Scilla Simms and ask her, very politely, if she has any information that could prove useful. Maybe there's some truth to what Foosay told Will." He held up a hand to Molina, who had inhaled abruptly to voice her fury and reached for her knives again. "Not now," he snapped before she could speak. "Nobody thinks your aunt is behind this. Would I send Blue to her if I thought she wanted to kill him? Of course I wouldn't. But we need help. We need all the help we can get. Are you helping us, or aren't you?" He scraped his dark fringe away from his eyes to better glare at the witch.

"Fine," she said. "Come along, girls. Let's go and see if we can recover the gems for these imbeciles."

Dante dithered, torn between staying with the wots and leaving with her sisters. In the end, after one last glance at Blue's avoiding eyes, she seemed grateful for the opportunity to get away.

Blue's gaze remained on the grass, and Foyer thwacked him on the back of the head to snap him out of it.

"Oi," he said. "Don't worry about Dante. Nobody expects anything of you."

"Thanks, Foyer."

"Go on. Off you go."

Will didn't like the thought of Blue going near Scilla without backup. What if Scilla wasn't the nice lady everybody believed her to be? "Are you sure?" he asked. "Are you sure it's not her? I mean, are you sure?"

Foyer took a deep breath and released it as a long, weary sigh before answering Will. "As sure as I can be. I don't really know what to think right now, to be honest. All I know for certain is we wots are in very real danger. If whoever's behind this gets hold of Karson and me – if they get all the gems and release their power – well, that'll be it. End of story." Seeing the fear in Blue's face, he hastened to add, "Don't worry. Karson and I won't let it come to that. You two just find Scilla."

"What are you going to do?" Will asked, peering at Foyer from under the peak of his cap.

Foyer didn't get chance to reply.

There was no warning this time. The rippling sheet of solid air that had taken Dyelann's gem came from nowhere at an unstoppable speed and ploughed into the three of them. Will's injured hand slapped the ground hard, his arm buckled, and he rolled a few times until he hit a tree. Too frightened to worry about the pain, he looked up as quickly as he could and saw...

Foyer was flying.

Fist held out ahead, super-hero style, Foyer soared up into the sky, and Will nearly choked on a startled gasp. The wot twisted mid-air and came back down, fast, crashing headfirst back to earth. Then he was up again, flying, looping, until he landed harder still, this time on his shoulders.

Will realised his mistake when Foyer started scraping and bumping along the ground. He wasn't flying, he was being dragged. The living-air monster that had knocked them down was doing its all to shake Foyer off while he desperately held on to the gem it was trying to steal from him.

The air monster lifted and dropped him, over and over, the world behind it hazy and distorted.

Blue caught Foyer's legs and tried to anchor him.

Sparks spritzed from the black gem, and the air monster lost its grip, leaving Blue and Foyer to stumble backwards.

One blink later, something changed. The threat disappeared and the two wots were face down in the grass. It had happened like a stutter in a movie. A scene had been skipped.

Clutching his wounded hand, Will used the tree he'd bashed into to help push himself up and ran to the wots on unsteady legs.

The two of them sat swiftly upright on his approach.

"Are you okay?" Blue asked Foyer.

"This can't be happening," Foyer shouted at his empty hand, struggling to get up. Blue took him by the elbow and helped him. "This can't be happening. This can't be..." He made an impatient grunting noise at himself, apparently frustrated by his own denial and making a conscious effort to accept the truth. "I have to get back to Karson," he said. "We have to protect his gem. His is the only one we have left. If they get hold of it... No. There's no if. They're not getting it."

Blue was searching, staring around in all directions, breathing faster in panic. "I didn't see anyone. I don't know what just happened. I didn't see a thing."

"Nor did I. The witch must have been with a wenn or hit us with a stun potion or something. Wonder why she didn't just kill us and be done with it."

"What are we going to do? What are we going to do?"

Will wanted to panic too, to ask the thousand questions that were rattling around in his mind, but he refrained. Foyer and Blue were as bewildered as he was, if not more so, and he knew they had no answers.

"Listen, Blue," Foyer said, firm but kind. "Calm down. I need you to calm down, okay? Stick to the plan. Go with Will and find Scilla. Everything's going to be fine. I promise. We'll meet at No-go Ebb, okay? See you there." Visibly shaken despite his stoic effort to hide it, Foyer began to run.

Will watched him go until he could no longer be seen for trees.

"Okay, Will," Blue said, straightening up, slowly but surely reverting to the confident man Will had grown accustomed to over the past twenty-four hours. "Let's go and find Scilla."

"Do you know where she is?" Will asked, hating the idea of going on yet another wild goose chase when the wots were in such immediate danger.

"Yes, she lives in Itchen Hush. It's not too far from here. I first met Dante there. She used to live there with Scilla, and I used to keep my gem here with Karson and Foyer. I only moved away, Dante says, seven years ago. She tried teaching me about years, but I don't think I ever really understood them like she wanted me to." He walked on at his quick-march pace, striding out onto the pastel pink pathway that led away from Karson's Christmas tree. "Adrian and Popset moved away then too. I haven't seen them since." His composure weakened again. "Now I might never see them ever again. I just don't know what I'll do if they're dead."

"How come you're the only one who's bothered about those two?" Will winced when Blue glared at him. "I just mean everyone else seems to care more about that Henry person, except for you. Don't you like Henry?"

"Of course I do." Blue slowed down. "No, I know how to explain this. I'm naturally closer to Adrian and Popset because our gems are closer."

Will stared blankly at Blue until he elaborated.

"Adrian and Popset's gems are purple and green, direct cuts of my blue one. Maik will be as concerned for Adrian as I am, because they're connected by the red gem. But Maik won't be affected that way by Popset being missing, because they don't share that connection. Popset's gem was cut from mine and from Henry's. It's all to do with our gems. You see?"

"Yeah, I think I get it." Will was just glad Blue had slowed down to a steady amble he could keep up with. "It's like paints. If you had the yellow gem and not the blue one, you'd be stressing out less about Adrian, and more about Popset and... uh... Dyelann?"

"Ha!" Blue curled his lip. "I don't think even if I had the red and the yellow gems both that I'd ever give a flying fruitcake about Dyelann."

"Dyelann doesn't seem so bad." Will didn't want to confess he enjoyed Dyelann's company. "He's probably just pulling your leg."

"If Dyelann had his way he'd pull my leg off altogether and smack me over the head with it until my brains poured out of my ears." Blue grunted. "Let's not talk about him anyway. Let's concentrate on Scilla, before I change my mind and think it'd be a great idea to let the wots be wiped out after all, just because it's the only way I'll ever be rid of Dyelann."

"You don't mean that." Will rubbed his stomach. Aching pangs of hunger hit him, like his belly had only just managed to get a word in through the chaos currently residing in his brain. When was the last time he'd even eaten? Yesterday's breakfast? No wonder he felt queasy. "Blue?"

"All right already, Dyelann's fantastic, Dyelann's the greatest wot ever in the history of the world, and we should all bow down at his oversized feet and count our blessings for ever having shared space with such a superstar." Blue kicked out at the pathway and sent a spray of pink woodchips scattering.

"I was just going to ask if you had anything to eat."

It took a second or two for Will's request to sink in, but when it did Blue stopped pouting and dug through an inside pocket of his coat. "Here." He handed over a bar of milk chocolate.

Will had genuinely been expecting Blue to say there was only nasty tree-fruit to eat in Wynne and took the chocolate with glee. "Thank you." He gave Blue's arm a brief hug of gratitude. "Where do you get your stuff from?" he asked, ripping off the foil wrapper. "Do you have to go shopping like normal people? Where do you get your money? Do people pay you for wishes?"

"No, people don't pay us for wishes. What do you take us for? I get an allowance from Karson. He's the one who handles our finances."

"A what?"

"Yes, a wot. Wots know about finances too, you know."

Will sniggered at Blue's defensiveness, too busy enjoying the sensation of the chocolate melting on his tongue, clagging around his teeth and sliding down into his welcoming belly to care that his question went unanswered.

They continued to follow the path, which became narrower the farther they went, and the trees grew closer and closer together until there was barely space left for a path between them at all. Only when Will had finished eating and given his fingertip one last noisy suck did they begin to speak again.

"Are we nearly there yet?" Will thrust the chocolate bar's wrapper into his jacket pocket and slapped his hands together, energized and strangely full. The air was milder now the day was well into its stride, and Will felt much more content for having something in his stomach.

"Nearly."

"What's wrong?" Will asked, sensing glumness in his companion.

"Nothing. I'm just worrying about what to say. Foyer told us to be polite. Very polite. What am I supposed to say? Excuse me, Mrs Simms, but we have it on good authority you discovered the secrets to eternal life, and we're wondering if you possibly let the information slip to anyone?" He groaned, flustered.

"That sounded fine to me. I think— ah!" A flash of light scared the life out of Will, and he cried out in fright, arms shooting up to cover his face so fast he knocked himself over.

Blue laughed at him.

Embarrassed and annoyed, Will took long, firm blinks until his sight returned in blurry splotches. "What was that?"

"Sorry. I should have warned you. We just passed into Itchen Hush. There's a barrier around this part of Wynne that stops wyes getting through. That's what that light was. We stepped into the spell. Are you okay?"

Apart from feeling humiliated and being somewhat taken aback by the information that wyes were effectively banished from the spot in which he now stood, Will was fine. "Why can't wyes come here?"

"The witches from these parts don't like wyes. Dante says it was a thousand more whatever years ago they cast the spell." Seeing Will's repulsion, Blue added, "It's okay. Wyes don't like witches who don't like them anyway, so it's no skin off their noses. They're better off not coming here."

Will hummed cynically. If Scilla Simms lived in a place that kept out wyes, which were perfectly decent beings as far as Will knew, surely this was only confirmation the witch was not a good person? What if only evil witches lived here? Everything had darkened after that flash – maybe that wasn't to do with his blinded eyes after all.

"Don't worry," Blue said. "This isn't such a bad place. We're safe. If I can work out what I'm going to say to Scilla, that is." His grin failed to hide his nerves.

"Just tell her we need her help. Butter her up. Tell her how good she is. That's what works with my mum."

Blue gave an unconvinced nod of his head.

"Okay, tell her Foyer sent you. Then it's his fault." He touched the wot's arm and slowed to a stop, prompting Blue to stop too. "Blue," he said. "I really think she's the baddie."

"No, she's definitely not the baddie. No. If you knew her, you'd understand. Scilla's too by the book to be bad."

"What book?"

"I don't know, Will," Blue said with an impatient eye-roll. "The rulebook. She follows the rules. She lectures you if you do bad things. She's a goody-two-shoes, is what she is. If you don't wash your hands before you eat, she'll talk your ears off about hygiene and dinner table etiquette. That's the sort of person she is. She's not the sort of person who'd go around stealing and killing. Trust me."

Will allowed Blue to walk on and followed behind, dragging his feet, defeated. He hoped Blue was right. "I can't help it, Blue, she sounds-"

"Shh." Blue waved an arm at him. "Don't say anything bad about her."

"Why?" Will whispered.

"She might hear you. Her house is just past this last patch of trees. Come on." He took a deep, unsteady breath. "Let's go and get this over with."

Chapter Seven: Banter

Had the walls of Scilla Simms' cottage been off-white instead of brick red, and the roof thatched instead of tiled, it would have been identical to Foosay Hoo's, right down to the breadboard sat square in the centre of the wooden porch. There was no sign of any cheese here though.

"I suppose we should knock," Blue said, ushering Will forward.

Will stood fast. "Yes, you should." He spun away from Blue's hand and moved back so Blue was closest to the house. "She doesn't know me. And Foyer told you to do it."

"True, that's true, but you got on well with Foosay, didn't you? Maybe you'd like talking to Scilla too." Blue slipped behind Will again and forced him a few steps on.

"No," Will said, leaning back in protest.

"Please, Will, come on." Blue stopped pushing him. "You're good with people. I don't know what to say."

"You wouldn't make me do it if Karson was here." Already wary being in this particular witch's vicinity, Will didn't want to be dumped with the responsibility of wheedling information from her. "Dyelann would do it," he added, knowing this would give Blue the shove he needed.

He was right. Blue made an annoyed sound in his throat and trudged up Scilla Simms' steps to thump her door, probably imagining it was Dyelann.

Nobody answered.

"Try again."

"You're wrong, you know," Blue said, giving the door a quick series of sharp knocks. "Dyelann wouldn't do this. Dyelann Envetta doesn't do anything he doesn't want to do, especially if doing it would benefit someone else."

Will pulled a face. "Envetta? And I thought his first name was stupid."

This remark put the smile back on Blue's face.

Scilla's door creaked open an inch.

"Err… Mrs Simms?" Blue peered at the blackness through the crack in the door.

It slammed shut.

Blue dashed forward and knocked again. "Mrs Simms, can I talk to you, please?" He knocked harder. "Please, I really need to talk to you. It's important." He stopped knocking and pressed his ear against the door.

A curt reply came from inside the house: "There's a first time for everything. I heard you were dead. How are you alive?"

"Someone brought me back to life."

"And you're here because...?"

"Foyer sent me." Blue squeezed one eye shut at Will in an exaggerated wink. "He wants me to ask if you can help us fathom out who took our gems," he said, facing the door again. He stared at the door like he expected it to open. When it didn't, he looked at Will like it was somehow his fault and banged on it again with a fist. "Come on, Mrs Simms, why won't you open the door?"

"Mrs Simms isn't here."

Blue rattled the door handle. "Yes you –"

Will dragged himself up, shocked at having found himself flat on his face. He spat out some leafy mulch that had somehow got into his mouth. "What happened? Blue?"

The wot was sprawled over the porch, unmoving, and Will's heart gave a sickening lurch when he spotted him, for one horrible second thinking the wot was dead. He sank with relief when he saw the rise and fall of Blue's chest.

"Blue?" He scurried closer to shake Blue's limp arm. "Wake up." He shook harder. "Wake up."

Squinting in confusion, Will took a glance at the cottage and its surrounding trees, trying to remember what had happened to them. Scilla's door was open a crack, but there was no sign of activity from in or around the house. She must have done something to them. It was all he could think. She was an evil witch, just as he'd suspected, and she'd done something to them and run away with the gems.

"I bet she has a Foosay mask in there," he whispered.

"Blue!" a melodramatic voice wailed from afar. A man in an aqua green tank top, salmon pink shirt, and green and pink striped trousers to match came dashing in their direction, his hair flapping as he ran.

"Who are you?" Will's tone of disgust was aimed more at the man's outfit than anything else.

"Oh, my poor Blue." The stranger lifted Blue's head and shoulders, sobbing against him.

Will felt embarrassed for the stranger, awkward for the unconscious Blue, and just a little irritated too, and he wished the man would stop dripping gross face liquid all over Blue and go back to whichever circus he'd sprung from. "He's fine. Who are you?"

"I can't believe he got you too," the stranger wept, continuing to act as though Will didn't exist.

"Hello?" He waved a hand. "Who are you?"

The man finally looked at him through wet, red eyes, and sniffed. "Why don't you tell me who you are first? I can't go around inadvertently betraying my kind by engaging with some evil protégé of the mastermind responsible for all this heartache." The words were so mumbled through his tears Will only just understood.

"*What?* I just want to know who it is slobbering all over my friend."

The man laid Blue back down and sat up, swallowing, wiping his face dry on his sleeves. "I'm not slobbering." He sniffed. "You must have meant sobbing."

"Sobbing, slobbering, big diff. Listen, you, I want to know what's going on. Where did that witch go?"

"I don't know," the feathery-haired, badly dressed man said, taken aback by Will's bold demeanour. "I only came here to visit Mrs Simms. You can imagine my horror at finding one of my dearest friends lying dead on her front doorstep."

"He isn't dead," Will snapped, upset at the suggestion.

"Well, I know that now."

Blue sprang to life like someone had flicked his on-switch. He leapt up, glowered at the porch as if it had tripped him, and then swung back to the door. "Yes, you are!" He hit the door with both hands. It rocked on its hinges and Blue gaped at it, confused. "Will?" he yelled, much louder than necessary. "What happened? Did she leave?" He whirled around to look for Will and came face to face with the man standing behind him. "Popset!" Blue dragged the badly dressed man into an exuberant hug. "Will, look, it's Popset." He shoved the man down the steps. "He's not dead, hurray."

"And you're not dead either," Popset said, happy again once he'd caught his footing. "I thought he'd killed you."

"No, no, no, this is just Will," Blue said, pride in his tone. "He's helping us get our gems back. They only need one more before we're dead, Popset, this is urgent now, urgent. Serious. Not a joke. Serious. Will Morgan, meet Popset Harmianca."

"Huh." Will lowered his voice. "And I thought Dyelann's name was stupid."

Popset tried to speak, but Blue was too overexcited to listen.

"We came here looking for Scilla Simms. She answered the door but wouldn't talk to us, and she disappeared when you showed up. Popset, I'm so relieved to see you. I didn't think I was ever going to see you again. Do you know where Adrian is? Have you met Will?"

"He's a wot?" Will tutted. "You're such a bunch of cry-babies."

"Hey." Blue glared at him. His smile didn't leave his face for long. "Popset, I'm so glad you're okay. What are you doing here?"

"I came to see Scilla…"

"So, you think it's her too?" Blue cut in. "We thought Foosay at first, but Scilla was acting suspicious." He turned to Will purposefully. "You know what?" he said, quieter. "Did you wake up on the floor too?" On Will's nod, he shouted, "A wenn! A wenn did it. A wenn must have been posing as poor Scilla." He slapped a hand on his head. "And there I was, saying such things about her. That wenn's impression was spot on though. She must know her."

Popset held up his hands, gesturing for Blue to be quiet. "Blue, you have to calm down. Listen carefully. I need to find Scilla. It's important."

"Yes, so do we, we need to find Scilla too. It's important for us too."

"Listen to me, Blue. My gem was taken…"

"Mine too, that's what I'm saying."

"Blue, seriously, shut up, will you?" Popset informed Will, "He always gets hyperactive after he's been knocked out by a wenn." He grabbed Blue's shoulders. "Please try to listen to me. Are you listening? I have some unfortunate news. A wenn must have sung to me, knocked me out. When I woke, I came here to talk to Scilla because…" He swung his hands down by his sides. "I know who took my gem."

"Who?" Will asked.

"The wenns," Blue shouted. "The wenns are behind this!"

Popset sat on Scilla's porch and motioned for Will and Blue to do the same. "This will be hard for you to hear, Blue. I know he was always a good friend to you. But I saw him."

Blue gasped. "Cesar?"

"Cesar?" Popset struggled to get out his next words through his frustration. "No. No! It's someone much more dangerous than wares or wenns. It is a witch, Blue. It's Gartaspia Simms."

Blue stared vacantly at Popset.

"I saw him," Popset said again.

"But it can't be him. Nobody knows what happened to him."

"Dante's brother?" Will asked, remembering him as the one nobody knew what had happened to rather than recognising Dante's family name.

"Perhaps it's why he left in the first place," Popset said. "Perhaps he went away looking for a way to achieve eternal life and found out our gems are the answer. He's only come back to get what he needs. He always was an exceptionally attractive creature, and I'll admit I did used to think what a shame it would be to see him wither and die. But I never thought he would do something like this."

"He wouldn't," Blue said. "No. No. There is no way, no way on this earth Gartaspia is taking our gems. He had a heart of gold." Needlessly he added, "Not literally," for Will's benefit.

"Blue, the man went missing, hasn't been heard of since, and he just so happens to be there when my gem is stolen from me? He must have been out here, hiding, plotting to destroy us." He jabbed a finger into his cheek. "But that really doesn't sound like something he'd do, does it?"

"No." Blue lost all trace of his previous excitability.

Will made a loud noise with his tongue, annoyed. "Any time anyone suggests someone, someone says no. First Foosay, then Scilla, now Dante's brother. What if just more and more people might have done it and we never find out who?"

"It was Gartaspia," Popset said. "Don't worry." He smiled. "All we have to do is find Scilla and tell her what he's been up to. She'll give him a good telling off. He'll give us our gems back. I know he will. We'd be better trying to find him before his sisters find out. They'll be devastated if they learn what he's been doing while he's been gone. They hero-worshipped that boy."

"So did you, if I recall," Blue muttered.

"Sorry, what was that?" Popset didn't wait for an answer. "Anyway, I'm here to help you now. You'll be safe with me."

Will eyed the open door behind the two wots, tempted. Poking around Foosay's house had turned out okay, after all. Why not see what Scilla was hiding in hers? He stepped between Blue and Popset. The door creaked when he pushed it open. "I bet your gems are in there."

"You're barking up the wrong tree," Blue said. "Both of you are. I don't think any of the Simms have anything to do with the gem thief."

Blue continued talking, but Will didn't hear once he was through the door. He wiped his feet on the doormat, a habit instilled by his mother, and stepped onto the runner. Five closed doors were set equal distances apart along the hallway, two on the left, two on the right, and one straight ahead of him. This last door didn't match the other four. It was enormous, black, solid wood, with a heavy brass knocker and letterbox, like it belonged to a different house inside the house. Intrigued, Will approached it and stared. It dwarfed him.

Blue and Popset soon joined him.

"That wasn't there last I was here," Blue said.

"You've been here before?" Popset asked in surprise. "I was never allowed in."

Blue took a peek through the keyhole. "They used to invite me in to eat with them. But there was never a door here, just a cupboard." He straightened up. "Should we open it?"

"Absolutely not. I don't like the look of it. There could be anything behind it."

"Like your gems?" Something inside Will burned with curiosity, until it wasn't just that he wanted to open the door but that he needed to open it. He reached for the handle, only to have his elbow snatched roughly by Popset.

"Don't. Scilla might get mad if she ever found out. What if there's something behind there we really shouldn't see?"

Blue put himself between Popset and Will. "Come on, it's only a door. We can knock. Knocking at a door never did any harm."

Famous last words, Will's mother would have said to that. Her ever-guiding voice sprang to mind but he pushed it away, too hungry for even just the briefest glance behind that door. His fingers curled together in anticipation.

"In the words of our dear friend Mrs Simms, there's a first time for everything," Popset said. "I'm telling you no. I mean it." He put his hands on his hips and looked down his nose as if daring Blue to defy him, and Blue's face fell like he'd just had his wrists slapped.

Maybe Popset could treat Blue like a pushover, but Will wasn't about to stand back and be bossed around. Before anybody could stop him, he grabbed the knocker and slammed it twice against the massive black door. The loud, sharp knocks echoed along the hallway.

The door returned two solid thuds.

Alarm instantly replaced Will's cockiness.

"Knock again," Blue said.

Will obliged and pounded the knocker four times, slow and heavy.

The door responded with four dull thumps.

Will and Blue burst into giddy laughter.

"All right," Popset said, disgruntled. "That's enough now. Let's be on our way."

"Is someone there, please?" Blue called, nearing an ear to the door.

"Obviously someone's there." Will peered through the keyhole, blatantly ignoring Popset's disapproving scowl. "Who is it?" he shouted.

Blue swept his head away from the door, asking, "Isn't it customary for the person knocking to be asked that question, as opposed to the person being knocked for?"

"They knocked too."

"Yes, but it's their door."

Popset snapped, "For crying out loud, the two of you, let's just get out of here before Scilla Simms returns to find us all arguing about her most likely private door."

"Scilla Simms, is that you?" Will asked the door, and then added quietly to Blue, "Maybe we should open it."

Popset sighed to the ceiling. "It's like talking to a brick wall."

"You open it," Blue encouraged Will.

"*Two* brick walls."

Will turned the handle and pulled the door wide open.

Brightness scorched his retinas. A dark figure waited in the doorway, the overpowering light behind reducing it to a mere blur of a shadow. Will stumbled backwards in terrified awe.

Blue moved closer to Popset, who was still talking to the ceiling, something about how if only children would listen.

A hand stretched out slowly from the silhouette, growing visible as it did so, revealing itself a sickly shade of blue from the many veins that spread thick beneath its wafer-thin skin. Its three digits were long, flexing in motion, stretching out to Will, curling and reaching. Will continued to edge backwards, silently cursing himself for not leaving the door alone like he was told.

Just when he had gathered his senses together enough to decide this would be a good time to run for his life, the creature latched onto his arm and hauled him back to the doorway. It twisted his wrist forcefully to expose the jagged wound on the back of his hand, and he shrieked at the searing pain, trying in vain to pull free from the creature's mighty grip. The elongated fingers tightened. Claw-like nails nipped into his skin.

Mouth open but void of screams, Will pleaded wordlessly for Blue and Popset's help.

Blue tried to force the creature's fingers from Will, but its free arm swept forth and knocked the wot clean off his feet. His head hit the wall with a sharp clunk on the way down.

A face began to emerge from the blanket of light - vein blue and gaunt, with enormous bird-like black eyes and a gaping, salivating, lipless mouth baring its few chiselled teeth.

Popset punched pointlessly at its arm. This wot too was thrown to the ground with a paltry swipe.

Will stared into the deep, black eyes. Oval and bulging, no eyelashes, no colour at all, just two flared pupils, flickering as they stared right back at him. The creature reeled him in, momentarily lifting him up. It raised his hand to its orifice and sank its teeth into his wound, sending a surge of blinding pain tearing through Will the likes of which he had never known. He cried out, pulling and tugging with all his strength to escape, but to no avail. The creature didn't even notice his struggling. He was nothing more to it than a worm wriggling on a hook. Its suction drew the warmth from him as it swallowed mouthful after mouthful of his blood. A dribble rolled smoothly down his arm and disappeared under his sleeve. It tickled his armpit.

Blue and Popset writhed at the door, trying their all to shut it on the beast. It stopped feeding to bare its bloody teeth at them. They beat it back until only its arm remained through the crack, still gripping stubbornly onto Will, who was swaying, about to fall.

Popset slammed his body against the door. Blue copied him and the two of them combined their efforts, throwing all their weight at it. The three-fingered hand finally released its grip and the creature retreated. The heavy door slammed shut. Will dropped to his knees. The wots pressed themselves against the door, acting as a barricade until they were sure the creature was not attempting to open it.

Blue hurried to support Will, who was trembling in shock, eyes brimming with stinging tears he would not allow to fall.

Popset pointed a finger at the door, his arm the shape of a water bird. "Why on earth would a witch have that thing as a tenant?"

Blue held onto Will as if he expected him to collapse. "I thought banters were extinct. They're supposed to be extinct. Aren't they extinct?"

"Does it look like they're extinct, Blue?" Popset leaned against the black door. "Oh well, what can you do? These things happen when people don't listen to their elders. Don't they, children?"

"What do we do?" Blue gasped for breath. "What do we do, Popset?"

"Oh, now you're willing to listen."

"No, I know, it's okay." Blue swallowed and steadied himself. "It's okay," he said quietly. "It'll be all right."

"What's wrong?" Will clutched his injured hand, willing the pain away. "I'm okay. I just went a bit woozy then, for a bit. I'm okay now. Bit woozy." His head spun, and his spine felt like someone was using it as a climbing rope, but other than that he felt okay. Blue seemed more disturbed than him, which didn't make sense.

"Well, yeah." Blue forced out a laugh. "You're fine. Don't even worry. I'm not worried. There's nothing to worry about. We're worriless."

"Worriless?" Popset snipped. "Do you know nothing of banters at all?"

Blue twisted Will's cap around so he could look him in the eye. "It bit you because they're drawn to the scent of blood, that's all. You're going to be fine." He nodded again.

Will smiled, relieved, but the pain still throbbed where the banter's teeth had pierced.

"What about the fact the banter poisoned him, and he has only a small amount of time before the toxin consumes him from the inside out?" Popset said, as though helping Blue to remember something he'd forgotten.

"Yes, thanks for that, Popset. Thanks a bunch."

Will's heart missed several beats. "I'm going to die?" Determined not to lose his composure in front of the wots, he forced himself not to succumb to tears. "That's not fair. I'm only eleven, I can't die."

"You won't. I said, didn't I? You'll be fine. Because there's an antidote, isn't there?" Blue helped Will up.

"What's a 'nantidote'?" The pulse in his neck hammered.

"Medicine," Blue said. "A remedy. A cure. And you're lucky you didn't get bitten when I was little like you because that stuff was a lot harder to come by back then. Now you can get it from anywhere, practically. Honestly, there's no need to worry. We'll get to the shop with plenty of time to spare."

It was strange to think that Blue was going to buy some magical cure from a shop, rather than finding it growing out of a mouldy tree stump somewhere in the forest. "How much time have I got?"

Blue turned to Popset for the answer, having no real concept of time himself.

"Five to six hours, the witches say."

"There you go, five to six hours."

"Five to six hours," Will repeated. Now it felt like his heart was shuddering. "We can't get to the shops in that much time. It took us ages to walk all the way out here. Ages!"

"Trust me," Blue said. "I know all the shortcuts to shops. I travel out there a lot to pick up snacks to charm, you know." Seeing Will's questioning frown, he added, "I don't really like eating, so I hide big meals in snacks. You got full on that chocolate I gave you, right? That was down to me."

"Ahem," Popset said, to stop Blue from beckoning Will out of the house. "Are you forgetting we're on a witch hunt here? You can't just leave, Blue. We need you."

"I can't leave Will to find his cure all by himself, can I? We'll be back as soon as we can." He led Will a few steps closer to the exit. "Go and find Dante. See if her locator potion's located anything yet."

The motion of the door gusted fresh air in Will's face, and he closed his eyes to appreciate it. It didn't last long enough. A fan would have been nice right about now. Yesterday morning's wind would have been better still. His skin felt tacky, his mouth dry as dust, and the pain raged so mercilessly in his hand he considered asking Blue to chop it off.

"What is the cure, Blue?" He tried to bury the fear, ignore the pain, not think about his impending demise and focus only on Blue. He had to trust Blue. Blue knew what he was doing. Blue would take care of him. Blue wouldn't let anything bad happen to him.

"It's a pointy fruit from a faraway distant land. They squash it into thick, yellowy liquid and sell it in cartons. You've probably heard of it. It's called pineapple juice."

How could he have put so much faith in this clearly challenged man? Maybe he'd heard him wrong.

"Erm… Pineapple juice?"

"Pineapple juice," Blue said again, with his kind, lopsided smile. "Just one swig will see you right. All we've got to do is get to a shop before our sixth hour is up. Whatever that may be."

Chapter Eight: Shopping Trip

Will and Blue didn't speak or even acknowledge each other's presence for a long while, both too lost in their own separate thoughts. They walked side by side, further and further into a very dense part of the forest, and Will could only trust that Blue knew where he was going.

What would happen when he died? Was there really a heaven? Or did running away from home earn him a one-way trip to hell? Would it hurt?

He had to stop thinking.

"I get why Karson hates Popset," he said, dragging them both back to reality.

Blue watched his own boots move back and forth.

"Sorry. I know he's your friend." Will tried to swallow but his mouth was too dry. His tongue felt like carpet. "Am I really dying?"

"Not for long."

"Will pineapple juice really save me?"

"Yes. Promise."

"I'm sorry I opened that door, Blue, I'm really sorry."

"Yeah, well." Blue stuffed a hand into the inside pocket of his coat and ripped out a ragged strip of its lining. "I'm really sorry I asked you to do it," he said, still staring at his feet. "This is my fault more than yours."

Will didn't know why Blue was dangling the piece of fabric in front of him but took it anyway and held it up between a finger and thumb to inspect it.

"For your hand." Blue eyed the ugly wound. The banter's teeth had hacked the flesh even further apart than it had been already. Blood seeped. "How did that happen anyway?"

"Cesar's stupid bird bit me." No good deed goes unpunished, someone had told him once. In future he would have to bear that in mind. "Why does that banty thing poison you if it's just going to kill you anyway? I mean, it's not fair, is it? If you get away from it, but it's poisoned you too, that's not fair."

"They don't poison you to be mean. What happens is, they drink just enough of your blood to keep you from running away, wait for the poison to do its job, then sup up the rest. The poison turns your blood black and sweet-flavoured. Treacly."

"Gross, that's disgusting, yuck! How does pineapple juice make a difference?"

"It just does. It has something in it that breaks down the poison in your blood somehow, makes it harmless. Don't ask me, I don't know. Just be glad someone fathomed that out once upon a time." Blue stopped walking. "Come here." He took the frayed piece of coat from Will, who had been struggling to keep it in place. "Let me do it."

Will braced himself for another bout of manhandling, only to be surprised by Blue's tender touch. His injured hand could have been resting on cotton wool, the wot held and wrapped it so gently.

"There you go." He gave Will such a smack between the shoulder blades, Will nearly fell.

"Thanks," he said between coughs, partly sarcastic but mostly grateful.

"No problem. Let's get a move on." And off the wot went again.

"Are you sure we're going the right way?" Will asked, hoping to have his mind set to rest.

"Not really."

Will swayed a little and took off his cap to get some air to his burning head. His hair was damp with sweat. "Are you kidding? Blue… I'm going to die."

"You're not. I told you, I know a shortcut."

"But you don't even know where we are."

"Well, no. Not yet."

A painfully bright burst of light flashed like lightning. Will yelled out in terror and covered his strobing eyes with both hands, dropping his cap.

"There, that's what we were waiting for," Blue said. "Hey, it's all right. What's wrong? It was just the spell, remember?" He leaned over to pick Will's cap up for him. "I forgot to warn you again, didn't I? Sorry." He handed the cap to Will. Will didn't take it. "I'm sorry, Will," Blue said again, waiting to be told he was forgiven. He paused a few seconds before trying one more time. "Sorry?"

Will snatched his cap. "Whatever. I don't care. I'm fine." The thought of the banter out there somewhere on his trail, searching for its blood-treacle, turned his legs to jelly, but he could never admit it. He wrapped Cesar's jacket tighter around him, cold and unbearably hot at the same time.

"You're sure?"

"Please, let's just go, Blue."

"We're going. I know where we are now. Don't worry."

Easy for him to say, Will thought. "It won't find me, will it?" he asked, so quietly he didn't expect Blue to hear him.

"The banter? Oh, no. No. They're too slow. Did you see how slow it was, coming out of that door?" There was a big smile on Blue's face when he checked to see that Will was keeping up. Will was certain it wasn't sincere but appreciated his efforts to stay positive regardless. "Really, we had ample time to get ourselves out of its way, didn't we? And I would've made sure we did if I'd realised what it was, but I honestly thought they were extinct. Sorry about that. But I promise there's nothing to be afraid of. You are completely, without a doubt, one hundred percent safe from that banter." His smile tightened into a goofy grin, an attempt to amuse Will.

It worked a little.

"I can't guarantee you're safe from the witch who wants the wots dead, mind," Blue said, walking backwards, manoeuvring so nimbly around the next few trees and clusters of weeds that Will could have sworn the man had eyes in the back of his head. "But if that witch does happen to show up, you only have to make yourself scarce. It's me they're after, not you." Still smiling, he turned around and jumped with a start when he came face to face with an old woman.

An excessive amount of flame red hair stuck untidily from her head in thick, frizzy waves. Her lips were pursed, wrinkled and thin on her bony face, and her hands were set firmly on her hips.

"Mrs Simms!" Blue stumbled a few paces backwards. "Your hair…"

"Watch that cheek," Scilla cautioned, matching his steps.

"We looked for you in Itchen Hush. What are you doing here? And what happened to your hair?"

She patted self-consciously at her head and pushed Blue aside to get a better view of Will. "A wot and a child were seen loitering in front of my house. I take it that was the pair of you?"

Trying not to wobble on his jelly-legs, Will aimed his best menacing glare at Scilla. This was the bad witch, the gem-thief, he was certain of it, and he wanted her to know he knew.

Blue was rolling his eyes to the heavens again. "You're nowhere to be seen when we're looking for you and now you show up? Typical. We don't have time to talk to you right now."

The witch's brows arched so high that had she been a cartoon character they would have been drawn above her head. "You don't have *time*? Is that some sort of joke? You'll make time, boy." Her eyebrows plunged back down to the opposite extreme, squinting like she was trying to decipher a puzzle tattooed on Will's forehead.

"Which part of 'we don't have time to talk' is fettling you, here?" Blue asked.

"Less of the lip. Tell me what you were doing in my house, or so help me…"

"I don't care." Blue didn't let her finish her threat. "We have to go. I'm sorry. We could really use your help when we come back, so if you'd be so kind - which although unlikely isn't impossible, considering *there's a first time for everything*, right? - you'll let us find you later."

Scilla thrust herself onto her toes, positioning her face so close to Blue's that her nose almost brushed his chin. "How dare you?"

"Please, Mrs Simms. Just make yourself easy to find when we return."

"And what would you have me do, Blue?" Scilla said. "Would you like me to wear a beacon and fire flares into the sky? Or would you prefer smoke signals?"

"Come on, Will. We have to go."

Will peeked over his shoulder as Blue led him away and was disturbed to see that the witch had already gone. Guilt poked at him. The wots needed answers from Scilla Simms. Now she was out of reach again, because of him. Blue, Foyer, Dyelann and the rest, they didn't have time to be shopping for pineapple juice. If only he'd listened to Popset and not opened that door.

"Don't worry, Blue," he said, panting. "We'll find her again."

"That's what I'm worried about." Blue walked ahead, not noticing Will sway and lag without his support. His speed continued to increase while Will's continued to decrease. The distance between them widened. "Come on, Will, shake a leg."

"I'm trying." Will grasped his chest. It felt squashed, like someone was sitting on it. Everything hurt. "Blue," he said, trying to ignore it. "How did Mrs Simms disappear so fast? Is she a ghost?"

"She's a witch."

"She's a horrible witch. She could easily be a baddie."

Blue returned to Will's side and guided him straight again. "Being strict doesn't make her a baddie. She's just as strict with herself as she is with everyone else. You'd understand if you knew her."

"What if I understand better because I *don't* know her? What if I can see what you can't see because you know her, and I don't?" He knew he'd have to stop talking soon. There didn't seem to be enough room in his windpipes for air to get through.

"Why are you so set on me thinking badly of poor Mrs Simms?"

"I just can't help feeling..." His heart fluttered for no apparent reason. "Sick." He ended his sentence bleakly. "I feel really, really sick." His head felt light, light enough to float away from him, and the need to hold on to the top of it overrode his fear of looking foolish.

"What's the matter?"

"I don't know." Will wondered if this is what being on the point of fainting felt like. He'd never fainted before. He didn't want to start now. His legs wobbled more dramatically, and he stopped forcing them to go on. He leaned against the first tree he could reach. Blue hoisted him back up when his knees gave. "I don't feel... I don't..." The world was spinning, the trees weaving in and out, closing in on him then backing away.

The dizzy spell only lasted a minute or two. After several strained intakes of breath, the trees stopped circling, his head stopped floating, and he found his feet.

"You won't leave me, will you, Blue?" Will was afraid he would pass out and never wake up.

"I'm not going to let your blood congeal so a nasty old banter can imbibe you, if that's what you mean." Blue shot his charming smile at Will. "We need to be quick. Can you walk?"

"Yeah. I'll keep up. As long as you know where you're going."

"Oh, absolutely. No worries there, just follow, follow, follow."

They passed a few moss-covered boulders into an area with shorter, thinner trees that grew closer together than the larger ones. Will thought he was beginning to understand how poor Gart must feel. It was hard being so uncoordinated. If he ever got better, he'd try to appreciate being able to walk and breathe at the same time. He felt so ill it was hard to imagine he would ever feel normal again.

"You really don't think Mrs Simms took your gem, then?" he asked, mostly to distract himself.

"I'm certain she didn't. I don't believe any of the Simms family would do that to us. I'd have sworn it was Foosay who drowned me, you know. I never wanted to believe she could turn on me like that, but what are you supposed to think? You trust your eyes, Will, and you shouldn't. Eyes aren't reliable in Wynne. They can't always see the truth. Sometimes creatures play tricks with them." Something seemed to be occurring to him. The thought didn't have time to come to anything before Karson's angry voice snapped him out of it.

"Have you found Scilla Simms yet, as you were instructed?"

A puff of white smoke had appeared on their left, which Karson was wafting impatiently away with both hands.

"Yes, we found her."

"And what did she have to say for herself?"

Will wished Dyelann was there to thump Karson for him. "How did you know he was instructered to find her?" he asked abruptly, wheezing a breath. "You weren't there when he was instructered to do that."

"Instructed," Blue corrected him quietly.

Karson glared at Will, who, realising he had spoken out of turn, edged closer to Blue and gave a little bow.

"I don't appreciate that tone, young man," Karson said slowly, without his usual trace of harshness. That harshness was recovered during his next sentence, which was aimed at Blue. "Foyer explained what happened. I don't have long, boy, come on, spit it out. What did Scilla have to say for herself? How did she react when you told her what's been going on?" Karson rolled his hands around each other to urge Blue to answer quicker.

"Well…"

"Well? Well, what? Come along, Blue, this is important."

Blue glanced at Will. "She didn't say anything because I told her we were in a hurry and didn't have time to talk." He nodded decisively. "Which is what I'm going to have to say to you too. Sorry."

"I beg your pardon?"

"Sorry, Karson. We'll have to talk later."

"How dare you walk away from me?" Karson's question was asked out of genuine surprise rather than anger, and he leaned back to look Blue over, as if he couldn't quite believe that Blue really was Blue.

"If Will doesn't get some pineapple juice soon, he's going to turn into a walking tin of banter treacle, and I'm not having that, Karson, I'm just not. I'm sorry. The gems can wait."

"No, Blue, they cannot." Karson lowered his voice. "There is only mine left now, and the enemy shall reach me soon enough. Whoever is behind this will become stronger and more dangerous than you can possibly imagine. They cannot wait."

"They'll have to."

Guilt poked at Will again, more forcefully now.

"Go to Cesar. He can alert you if any witches approach. Then you'll have time to escape."

"How do we know Cesar's not the one behind all this? How do we know he can be trusted?"

"He's Cesar. He's our friend. I'll sort this mess out when I get back, Karson, I promise."

"It's beyond you now, Blue."

"I'll sort it!" Blue stooped over, face contorting in pain.

"What's the matter with you?" There was no callousness in Karson's tone at all now, only concern.

"Blue?" Will whimpered.

"It hurts." He gasped for breath. "What's happening?"

Karson put one hand on Blue's back and the other on his arm, peering down at the wot with the first genuine hint of compassion Will had seen on his face. "Just stay calm," he said. "Panicking won't help anything. You'll be all right."

As fast as his pain had come, it stopped, and it left Blue with a very different look in his eye. No longer confused or afraid, he was vacant and still. "My gem," he murmured. "Something's happening to it." He glanced at Karson. "Time's running out."

"Then let's get moving," came the cold reply.

Will's knees weakened again and, without intending to, he propped himself up against Blue.

"But Will's time is running out too." Blue didn't dare look at Karson as he said it.

"And this stranger is more important to you than your entire family?"

Will only just made out the words, Karson had spoken them so softly, but they upset him. He faced away, saddened.

"It's not a matter of importance. It's a matter of priority."

"Will," Karson said, rigid. "I am a wot, my son…" He stopped. Shaking his head, he gave up on whatever it was he'd been about to say. "No, you're quite right. Be on your way." His eyes found Will's. "Good luck. Wish it back for us."

Will blinked, so hot and clammy that even his eyelids felt sticky. "Okay."

Karson vanished into a burst of white smoke.

Will had no watch and no idea how much time they had left, but the further they walked the stronger the terrible feeling grew that time had never ticked away so fast. After what might have been hours but felt only minutes from leaving Karson, Will's throat clenched, blocking every wheezing breath. His vision kept blurring, distorting the world around him until it became nothing but a sea of green between tacky blinks. Then the green changed to grey, and the loud rhythmic whooshing of speeding traffic told him they weren't in the woods anymore. He forced his eyes to stay open long enough to focus. Long enough to see that they were getting dangerously close to a motorway.

"Are you ready for this?"

Will heaved another airless breath and blinked up at Blue. "For what?"

"To run."

"Run?" He clutched Blue's coat to keep from keeling over. "You can't run across a motorway. You can run into a motorway and get squished, but you can't run across a motorway!" Exhausted by all the talking, he closed his eyes and concentrated hard on his next breath.

"Oh, relax. I do it all the time. It's the fastest way to the shops. They're just over the road and a mile or two over a couple of fields."

Will's gasping grew hoarser. "Miles?"

"Goodness' sake, Will, you'll give yourself a heart attack if you're not careful. I promised you already, and I'm promising you again, we'll get to the shop before you're dead." Blue patted Will on the head, grimaced at the touch, and wiped his palm on his coat.

Will wiggled his fingers through his hair to fix the spikes Blue had flattened. "Where's my cap?"

Blue scanned the ground for it. "You must have dropped it."

Will slapped a hand over his brow. "Could today get any worse?"

"Considering all our lives are hanging in the balance right now, no, you losing your hat is the worst thing to ever have happened in the history of the world. When I get my gem back, I'll make you a thousand hats, okay? Let's get over the road."

"It's not a road, it's a mo…" He fell to his knees. "It's a mo…"

Blue hauled Will up and over his left shoulder.

"What are you d…?"

"What do you think I'm doing? Carrying you."

Without warning Will of what was about to happen, Blue hopped over the barrier and took off running at such a speed Will would have lost his cap had he been wearing it anyway. The wot somehow dodged a speeding, roaring vehicle in each of the three lanes to reach the central reservation unscathed.

"There, you see. I told you. I do it all the time."

"Great," Will said, finding it harder to breathe than ever with Blue's shoulder pressed into his stomach. "Now we're… Now we're stuck… in the middle of a motorway."

Blue shrugged to secure Will on his shoulder and dashed forth.

A horn blasted in his ears, wailing long and deafening, and a rush of sucking wind pulled at him as the rattly lorry zoomed by. He squeezed his arms around Blue to hold on, shivering, burying his face into the back of his coat.

"It's fine. It didn't hit us." Blue put Will down on the grass, then picked him back up again when it turned out he could no longer stand. "I told you I'd get us over, didn't I? We're over. Just two fields to go and we're there." After a few easy strides, he stumbled, dropping Will, who rolled from his open arms and landed on the humpy, molehill-ridden grass verge.

Will glowered at Blue, but Blue, crouched over with his forehead pressed in the long grass, didn't see.

"Oh no," he groaned. "This can't be good."

Straining with the effort of gasping air through his blocked throat, sweating and aching all over, Will forced himself up onto his knees and rested on his trembling arms. The world started to spin around him again. "Blue, help me."

"Someone, help me," Blue said at the same time as Will.

The two of them stayed that way for a couple of minutes, each having to bear their suffering alone, neither one capable of offering comfort to the other.

"What happened?" Will asked when Blue sat up.

"Nothing, I'm fine." He stood. "It's just my gem. If they kill my gem, I'm dead."

"Your gem's alive?"

"Sort of." He leaned over to help Will up. The next thing Will knew, Blue had scooped him up and set off running again. He raced across the next two fields like he had a rocket tied to his back.

"Why didn't you tell me you could run so fast?" Will asked between gasps. "You could have carried me earlier."

"What am I, a pack pony?" Blue slowed to a walk, not even breathing hard. The incredible sprint had been nothing to him. "We're here now, aren't we?" He froze mid-step, and Will looked around to see what had caused the sudden change in mood.

The shop was only a small building amid a row of equally small houses. And there was a bold printed 'Closed' sign on the glass door.

"Oh."

Blue tilted his head to see the sky. "This is ridiculous. The sun is hardly even out. Not enough to shut up shop over. One time I came all the way out here and it had been raining constantly, and then the sun was out for less than a heartbeat and that was that. Shop closed."

"What are you talking about?" Will said. "It's nothing to do with the sun. It's closed because it's Sunday."

Blue put Will down, leaning him against the wall. "That's what I'm saying, there's not enough sun to even call it a sun day."

Having neither the strength nor the will to explain the concept of the seven days of the week to Blue, Will slid down the wall and sat in a desolate heap on the concrete. The shop was closed. They couldn't get the pineapple juice. He was doomed. Game over.

"It's just as well," Blue said. "I don't have any money anyway." He untied the lace of his left boot and pulled his foot out of it, revealing a spotlessly clean white sock. He then picked up the boot and pitched it through the glass panel in the door. A spray of glittering shards scattered into the shop's entrance, the boot landing upright on the welcome mat. Blue stuck his hand through the jagged hole to unlock the door, marched on in, stepped his bootless foot into the glass with a yelp of pain, and promptly stumbled over his footless boot.

And Will smiled at the idiocy despite himself.

Blue scurried around the tiny shop for several seconds before thinking to check the refrigerator.

"Oh no," he called out. "I don't think they have any." Cartons of milk, blocks of cheese, and pots of yoghurt were flung in all directions in Blue's rush to get to the products behind.

Will's vision blurred. Certain he was about to die, he bowed his head and begged, to whoever might be listening, for his life.

Glass crunched, and Blue was back, handing him a litre carton. He placed it in Will's shaking hands. "Come on. Get this down your neck. Come on, quickly." He tore off the perforated corner for him and directed it to his face.

The first mouthful spilled down his front.

"That's the hard part, getting it down," Blue said with a false smile. "Come on." He signalled for Will to take another swig.

Will poured more juicc into his mouth and closed his lips to lock it in, cheeks inflated. His throat tightened. He choked and sucked some of the liquid up the back of his nose. The rest sprayed Blue's face.

Eyes closed, Blue slowly wiped the sticky droplets onto his sleeves. Again, he motioned for Will to keep trying.

Suffocating, drowning in pineapple juice, Will sat, clenching the carton in his hands just trying to steady himself. Finally, he managed to ingest the tiniest sip, and then another, and his hands stopped shaking. Swallowing gradually became easier. Once he'd finished the remains of the juice he could breathe effortlessly again. Air was wonderful, he decided, and he would never take it for granted ever again.

"You'll feel better in no time now. I told you, didn't I? I remember when I was bitten by a banter. One of the scariest things that ever happened to me." He laughed, as though he'd just shared an amusing anecdote.

Will stared at Blue's face, sure he must have misheard. "You've been bitten by one before? What happened?"

"I was walking to the witch market for Karson, minding my own business, when this little witch girl asked me to tell her what was lurking about behind her house. I went to take a look at it for her, and there was this banter. It bit me right on the kneecap."

"Why the kneecap?"

"I'd fallen over and skinned it. I was smaller then, like you are now. Anyway, it bit me, and this grown-up witch came to see what was happening. She set her stick on it and blew it into a thousand pieces. Blood and guts all over me." The grin on his face implied he was proud of that fact. "The witch told me it was the very last banter, so I didn't have to worry about ever seeing one again. I never saw her again either. Which is weird really because- ah!" Pain cut him off mid-sentence, and he doubled over.

Will clambered onto his feet, scared for his friend, wishing he knew how to help.

"Something's happening," Blue stuttered. "I'm in trouble."

Will tried to impersonate Blue and his earlier optimism. "But not for long. Right?"

"It'll have to be not for long. Else it'll be too late."

The words landed like a kick in Will's chest. Was Blue already regretting his decision to help Will instead of staying with Karson? If anything happened to the wots now, Will would never forgive himself. He should have listened to Popset. If he'd only listened to Popset, they never would have been waylaid. They would probably have spoken to Scilla and solved the mystery of who was behind the gem thefts by now.

Blue's face had lost its colour again. "We'd better get back," he said.

"Yeah. But do we really have to go back over the motorway? I really don't want to do that."

A woman said, "You won't have to."

He must have been growing accustomed to strange voices piping up from nowhere, as Will was barely startled this time.

A pleased smile grew on Dante's face once she had their attention, and she straightened the large sun hat that she'd put on during their time apart, despite there being no sun and therefore no need for it.

Blue stared at the shop's window, his pain and sense of imminent danger evidently undermined by the fear of uncomfortable eye contact.

"Dante." Will was glad to see her. "You've got your wand." He noticed it peeping from her sleeve and was glad to see that too. No more dodging motorway traffic for him.

"My brew stick, you mean?" Dante said. "Yes, of course. That's how I got here, through my portal. Straight to you both, first time." She poked the tip of the wand further into her sleeve and out of sight. "I always carry my stick in my sleeve. People call me strange, but still I do it anyway. The white-gemmed wot told me what happened." She cast her eyes over Will, inspecting him. "You're okay?"

"Yes." Will showed her the empty juice carton. "Blue got me here in time."

"What a relief." Dante glanced at Blue. "Anyhow, you'll be pleased to know the yellow-gemmed wot is still alive and kicking. Dyelann found him."

Blue scoffed so hard his entire body rose two inches. Then he stood hunched, arms folded, glaring at the ground, and muttered something derogatory about Dyelann under his breath.

"Karson's still got his gem?" Will asked, dropping his carton into the bin by the shop's door.

"For the time being."

"Good. That's good, isn't it, Blue? And you came to help us?"

"That's right. I came to get you back to the others. They're all waiting on you." Her wand slid into her hand, and she whipped it through the air to cut that familiar gap of brightness in one long slash. "There's your portal."

Will automatically looked to Blue for confirmation he could go on ahead. The wot was still aggravated, grinding his teeth, fingers gripping at his sleeves.

"Oh, and just so you know, Blue, pumpkin," Dante said, with a big smile. "It was a moment of madness that made me say what I said before. Of course nobody's in love with you. The very notion is ridiculous. You're a child."

That didn't sound right, coming from Dante. Even if she had just found out that Blue wasn't mentally mature enough to return any romantic feelings she may have had for him, Will couldn't imagine that would change the warm affection she always showed her favourite wot. Something sinister must have caused her change of heart.

A nervous half-smile appeared on Blue's face. "I'm not a child, Dante. I'm just not… I mean, I… It's not that I don't like you. It's not that…" Finishing a sentence seemed out of the question just now, and he looked hurt when Dante laughed at his attempts.

"Pull yourself together. It's fine. We're fine." The portal's light shimmered on the side of her face, highlighting the curve of her cheekbone. Her fingers tightened around her wand. "Come on, boys. We can't just stand around here forever."

There was a sharp swishing sound, and another bright wisp of light materialised in the air directly beside the existing one, the pointed tip of a wand protruding from it.

Will jolted out of its way. "That could have had someone's eye out, that could," he said, and then fell quiet when he saw who was stepping through the light after the wand. His mouth dropped open.

Blue took several clumsy steps back, dragging Will along with him.

Two Dantes were now standing side by side, equally surprised to see one another.

"What's going on?" the new Dante demanded after she'd sealed her portal, glaring at the first Dante. "Who the heck are you?"

"Me? You're the imposter here, witch." The first Dante waved for Blue and Will to join her, keeping her wand aimed at the portal as if to hold open the door. "Come along, boys. Let me get you back to safety."

The new Dante blocked them from the other witch, her back to them. "I don't think so," she said, quite calm. "Word is spreading in Wynne that young Will may be key to saving the wots," she said, talking to Blue without taking her eyes from the other Dante. "Karson told me what happened to you, Will, so I came to make sure you were okay. And look at that - you're not."

"How do we know which witch is which?" Blue whispered. His hand clutched his stomach, and he gasped a pained breath.

The new Dante twirled around to scc what was wrong. She stopped herself from touching him at the last second, forehead creased with worry.

"That's obvious," Will said. If Blue couldn't tell which witch was the real Dante after that, he was beyond ignorant. Her reaction to Blue's distress had been reflexive, whereas the first Dante was more interested in checking her hat was on properly.

Dante flicked her wand at the imposter, sending a zap of mist spiralling from its tip. It didn't get chance to reach its target, who hopped into her portal and disappeared.

Rage distorted Dante's pretty features into those of a deranged lunatic. When she calmed down, she took a quick glance Blue's way. "Are you both all right?" she asked, pretending to examine her wand.

"We're fine, aren't we, Blue?" Will said, unable to fight back the sullen feeling arising within. "Are you definitely you now?"

"Yes. Good job I came for you, isn't it? You could have gone along with that witch to your certain deaths. I loved that hat though. It quite suited me. Don't you think?"

Now Will understood why Blue had been sarcastic to him when he'd been upset about losing his cap earlier: It was inappropriate to be talking about hats when you should be talking about more important things. Another thing he'd have to remember.

"What were you saying about me?" he asked. "What do you mean, I'm a key? What key?"

Dante stopped fiddling with her wand and checked her reflection in the shop's window instead. "We'll find out more when we get back."

"Whoever that witch was knew you, Dante," Blue said glumly. "And he knew about you saying you loved me, too. He must have been watching us."

"Why on earth would you presume she was a man?" Dante asked, pretending to be offended, but Will could tell she was only trying to lighten the mood. "Are you implying I'm manly?"

Blue fell quiet.

"Blue." She lowered herself to catch his eye. "Do you know who it was?"

He didn't seem to want to answer, unable to meet her gaze straight away. Then he found the resolve to look right at her and said, "The one who drowned me said I was useless because I couldn't save anyone. When he was little, he fell into that enchanted well and couldn't get out, and I couldn't do anything. I had to find you and your sisters to save him, remember?" He paused, and Dante blinked worriedly while she tried to process what Blue was saying to her. "Popset told us he saw him," he said, and finished in a whisper, "I think it might have been him."

Dante's face hardened.

"I didn't want to believe it," Blue added, louder. "But this witch knew you, Dante."

"Wow," Dante said. "You're saying my brother is behind this. Really? My brother who has been missing for the last decade. You're accusing him?" She could hardly speak for her emotion. "How can you say that to me, Blue? How could you even think it?"

"I'm sorry, Dante. I don't want to think it."

"But you said there was no way it could be any of the Simms," Will said to Blue, hoping it would comfort Dante to hear. "You told Popset you'd never believe it was Dante's brother. You said he had a heart of gold. Why did you change your mind?"

"It was the…" Blue paused when Dante coiled around to watch him speak. "It was the other you, Dante. What she said about you keeping your stick up your sleeve."

His words must have hit a nerve in Dante, who faced away so they couldn't see her tears.

"What's wrong?" Will asked, searching for clues in the back of her head. "What does that mean?"

Dante wiped her face and sniffed sadly before she replied. "My family don't like me carrying my stick in my sleeve. They think it's dangerous. My brother copied me one time when we were little and nearly blew his hand off."

"Ouch," Will said, unable to think of anything more helpful.

"I don't believe it's him, Dante, not really," Blue said. "It just made me think, that's all. After what Popset said."

"Yes, well, you always did take Popset and Adrian's word over anybody else's. But there's no way my brother has anything to do with all this, Blue, so get that idea right out of your head."

"You're right." Blue nodded as if to say message received.

"We'd better get away from here," Will said.

"Why? What's the matter?" Blue asked.

"Nothing, it's just, we're standing right outside the shop we just broke in to. And there's a camera staring right at us." He pointed out the security camera at the left corner of the building.

Dante pointed her wand at the device. The camera made a loud popping sound and dispersed a dejected wisp of smoke. "Nothing to worry about now." She started to make a portal. "Let's be on our way, shall we?"

"Wait," Will said, stopping her.

"What now? What?"

Will pointed at the broken glass. "Can't you fix it?"

Dante rolled her eyes impatiently and flicked her wand. "Off the floor and in the door," she muttered.

The three of them watched as the pieces of glass clicked and clacked themselves together and thwacked back into place with a clunk and a slap.

"There. Happy now?"

Blue made as if to follow Dante.

"Wait."

This time it was Blue who responded with a bored, "Now what?"

"You forgot your boot."

Blue glanced at his feet and laughed at the sight of his immaculate sock. "Oh, yeah." He rushed back to the shop, shaking his head in amusement, and tried to push the door. It was locked again. Will stood beside him and peered through the now intact glass to see the boot.

Blue lifted his foot, pulled off his remaining boot, and swung it up.

"Hey, whoa." Dante caught his arm before he could throw it. "Let's not do that again. I just fixed it." She released him and touched the handle with the tip of her wand. The door creaked open.

"Thanks, Dante," Blue said, reaching in to grab the boot. As soon as he was out of the way, she swung her wand like a conductor waving a baton during a particularly exuberant piece of music and the door slammed shut.

"Is there anything else, Will?" she asked. "Or can we leave now?"

Blue winced. "Ow, it hurts again," he said, gasping. "Ow, ow, ow." He paused. "Okay, it's gone now."

Dante put a hand on his back when he bent to tie his laces. "You're worrying me. What's going on? Why do you keep hurting?"

"It's my gem. Something's happening to it."

"Why would that hurt you?" Will asked.

Dante answered for Blue. "Wots are very closely connected to their gems. Their gems are like their…"

"Homes," Will interrupted. "You already told me that."

"I was going to say soulmates," Dante said. "In a way. The gems created their own wots, from witches. Foyer told me a long while back that Blue's gem waited over a thousand years to choose its wot." She smiled at Blue. "He's very special." She turned her head in regret. "I'm sorry, Blue. I'm not trying to make you uncomfortable. I'm sorry for the way I've been acting. I'm so ashamed."

"Don't be silly," Blue said. "It doesn't matter."

"Come on." She remade her portal. "Let's get you home."

Chapter Nine: No-go Ebb

Will, the wot, and the witch emerged from Dante's portal in the midst of countless trees that were all bent over at the same sharp angle, as if there had once been a raging wind that had been too powerful for even one of them to withstand. It was a peculiar sight to behold. Will felt tilted just looking at them.

"Where are we?"

"No-go Ebb," Dante whispered.

"What's that?" Will asked, thinking Dante had spoken a foreign language.

She shushed Will urgently and listened for a few seconds before continuing to speak. "This is the end of the inhabited part of Wynne," she explained in the same hushed tone. "The banters used to reside past this point when they were thriving. That's why it became known as No-go Ebb."

"Why are we whispering?" Blue asked.

"Because I don't know who could be watching."

Will circled on the spot to check the gaps between the trees. "There aren't any banters here, are there?" he asked, fear affecting his ability to keep his voice down.

"No, they moved away from these parts a long time ago. It's highly unlikely we'll run into any."

"Why was that one living in your auntie's house? What was she doing with it?" The fact that the woman was keeping a nasty, blood-sucking monster in her cupboard only reinforced Will's certainty that she was the baddie. Knowing how strongly Blue and Dante believed otherwise, however, he decided against bringing this opinion up again.

"I haven't had chance to speak with Scilla yet," Dante whispered. "Please don't shout around here, William," she added, agitated. "There are more dangerous things than banters after you now."

Blue slapped a hand over Will's mouth to cut off his outburst before it began. "What do you mean?" he asked on Will's behalf, while Will pushed his hand away.

Dante didn't answer.

"What do you mean there are more dangerous things than banters after Will, Dante?" Blue asked again. "Why would anyone be after him?"

"Because!" Dante was no longer following her let's-be-quiet rule. She beckoned for them to follow and stormed ahead. Blue trailed after her, dragging Will again. Will was getting a bit sick and tired of being man-handled but held his tongue.

"The wots want to talk to you. That's why I came to find you, as well as to make sure you were all right, of course. They were going to send Molina to pick you up, but I volunteered. I thought it would be better for me to come and get you. She's no good with portals. She usually ends up two miles away from the destination she's aiming for, and that's true no matter how wonderful she claims to be."

Blue came to such a sudden stop that Will, who had still been hurtling forward at the same fast pace, was jerked backwards. The wot swayed, doubled over, and sucked in a deep, shaky breath.

"Dante, wait," Will called. "It's happening again."

"No, I'm okay." Blue let Will go and waved him away. "Don't know if I can say the same for my poor gem. But I'm okay." All the while his face paled ghostly white, eyes turning duller by the second.

Will glanced at Dante, who had rushed back to Blue holding her hands out ready to catch him if he fell, and asked, "If you were supposed to be taking us to the wots, why didn't you take us all the way there?" The question came out sharper than he'd meant it to.

"Because they're in a limited access area. Portals won't open in limited access areas. What's with the attitude, Will? Don't you think I'm trying my best?" She rubbed one of her eyes with a clenched fist, and Will was impressed to see her mascara remained perfectly intact.

"All I'm trying to do is help my friend, so please stop acting as though any of this is my fault."

"Sorry."

Dante put an arm around Blue. "It's not much farther," she said to Will, in a kind tone that made him feel forgiven. "Are you okay, Blue?" She shook him. "He's catatonic or something."

Will took two large strides away from the wot. "He's turning into a cat? But I'm allergic to cats."

"I just meant he's not answering me." She clicked her fingers before Blue's face, but he was gone. Blank, cloudy eyes gazed into nothing.

It didn't seem right for someone to be unconscious while still standing. Will pushed on Blue's back, wondering if he could urge him to take a step. The pressure tilted Blue further forward.

"Huh. That's quite something." Dante clapped her hands by Blue's ear. "Come on, Blue, don't do this to us. Snap out of it."

"What's wrong with him?"

"I don't know." The witch arched her neck. "Shh. Do you hear something?"

All Will heard was the familiar background birdsong and the rustling of leaves, but Dante had her wand at the ready. Will squeezed the sleeve of Blue's coat as if the inanimate wot could somehow protect him.

"What is it?" he asked.

"I don't know."

"Has it gone?"

"I don't know."

"Is it something bad?

"I don't know. Good grief, Will, be quiet!"

Convinced that the banter had caught up with him, thirsty for a nice drink of treacle, Will stared where Dante stared and tried not to speak, which was always hard when he was afraid.

Dante relaxed and jabbed Blue with her wand.

Blue blinked and came back to life again. "Ow," he said, prising Will's fingers from his sleeve. They had twisted tighter into his skin than Will had realised. "Why are you hurting me?" He rubbed his arm. "What's happening?"

"Nothing," Dante assured him. "We're just going to find Foyer and the others, remember?" She hooked his arm in hers. "Let's hurry. We don't have time to waste standing around fretting."

Will followed close behind, keeping a sharp eye in all directions, seeing shapes in every shadow and in every flicker of movement the breeze brought. Waving branches were flying monsters, every patch of darkness a banter in waiting.

He only noticed they'd reached the end of their journey when he heard Popset shout out: "Thank goodness you're all right."

They were at the front of a small, round hut of a building, as slanted as the trees surrounding it. Will angled his head, trying to figure out if it had been built wonky to match the trees or if it had been built upright and bent along with them.

"Everyone's waiting inside for you," Popset said, opening the door for Blue and Dante. He gave Will a swift smack on the back and let out a loud laugh mixed in with a choked sob. "You had a lucky escape there, young man."

Will kinked an eyebrow at him before stepping into the shack, which turned out to be much more spacious inside than he had expected from its outward appearance. A solid wood dining table took up most of the room, positioned central to a long, scruffy green settee that backed square against three of the walls.

A frazzled looking man in a fluffy navy sweater sat in the middle section, sandwiched between Dyelann and Maik. His dark hair stuck from his head in all directions like he'd been electrocuted. Will presumed this was Henry.

Foyer's head rested on the edge of the table, both arms dangling lifelessly in front of him. Karson and Cesar sat opposite him on the left section of the settee, along with an odd man picking fastidiously at a piece of iced cherry cake with a silver fork.

The stranger looked a bit out of place. He had short, neatly combed blonde hair, an equally neatly combed blonde moustache, and wore a properly buttoned and tucked in shirt and knotted black tie that even Karson couldn't have faulted.

Popset floated in to join them and took a seat beside Foyer, bouncing on the cushion and smiling down at his forlorn friend.

"Who's that?" Blue pointed a finger at the neat, blonde man, who continued to pick at his cake, ignoring Blue's rudeness even as the wot approached him, finger getting closer and closer to his face.

"This is Art," Popset said. It seemed Popset was the only one in the room that had retained any hope. The rest had slumped into a state of depression, judging by the look of them. "Be nice to Art. Art's a mystic."

"I'm a seer," Art corrected him in a low, gravelly voice.

"Yes," Foyer mumbled, not raising his head from the table, "but Blue trusts mystics. So, you're a mystic, okay?"

"I'm a mystic," Art said to keep the peace, a glimmer of irritation in his piercing blue eyes. He abandoned the cake, put down the fork and pushed the plate aside.

Blue lowered his pointing hand but kept his scrutinizing gaze on the neat man. "So, who's taken our gems?"

"As I've been explaining to your friends," Art said, returning Blue's stare with not a flicker of unease, "I cannot tell you who is behind this."

"Then what's the point of you?" He struggled a harsh, wheezing breath.

"It's getting worse," Dante said, guiding Blue closer to Foyer. "I had to put a spell on him just to get him here. He passed out on the way."

"Sit down, boy," Karson said, but Blue heard nothing. His eyes were blank again, head drooped, arms limp.

Popset helped Dante sit his friend down on the settee next to Foyer, and then sat close beside him. "Is he going to be all right?"

Will wanted to know the same thing. "Why's this only happening to him?" he demanded. "Why aren't the rest of you like that?"

Art interlocked his fingers and rested his hands on the table. "The witch is trying to break open the gems. The gems are resisting. The blue gem is fighting hard to draw its wot in." The seer's eyes flashed red, unnerving Will. They changed back to their natural ice blue as Art sat back regretfully and said, "It cannot resist much longer."

Dante gestured to Blue. "But look at him. He's not being drawn to anything."

Art's eyes glowed fiery red again. "When he comes to, he should be able to shed some more light on the whereabouts of his gem."

Will shrank behind Dante, and she stroked a reassuring hand down the back of his head.

"If you can see what the witch is doing, how can you not see who it is?" she asked.

"She cast a spell to block her face from the view of anyone who should look for her," Art explained. "It is why Cesar does not know who the witch is when I tell him her location. She changes her appearance when she is hiding in the physical realm also. Yesterday, Blue saw her as Foosay Hoo. Today, he saw her as you, Dante Simms. She is faceless to all who look for her." His eyes continued to flash from blue to red as he spoke. "I am not seeing everything I should be seeing. We have all forgotten things we should know. She is blocking something from us all."

"But it's definitely a she?" Dante asked, and she took a deep, relieved breath when Art nodded yes. "Right," she said softly. "At least we can be thankful for that."

Her words irked Dyelann. "What difference does it make if it's a he, she or it? This witch is planning to kill us and has left us blind so we can't even defend ourselves. What is it exactly that we're supposed to be thankful for?"

"Hey, don't talk to her like that." Foyer lifted his head at last. "This isn't her fault, and she's putting herself out to help us. You'd do well to remember who your friends are."

A grateful smile lit Dante's face and she looked away from Foyer bashfully.

Will was about to be pleased for Foyer, finally getting a positive reaction from Dante, but he caught sight of Blue and his heart dropped like a rock. Poor Blue, sitting among his friends, unable to take comfort from them. It wasn't fair.

"Dante," Henry said, shaking his scruffy head. "Why can we be thankful it's not a man behind this?" He sounded timid and jumpy, like someone who'd been drinking too much caffeine.

Dante urged Will to sit next to Popset, which he reluctantly did, and she sat beside him. She rested her elbows on the table and immediately instigated a flurry of nervous noises from most of the people sitting around it. They scooted back a couple of inches, all eyes on the tip of the wand that poked out from the witch's sleeve. Cesar vanished, startled not by the wand but by the reactions to it. Only Dyelann and Art appeared unfazed.

The group didn't take long to settle after their initial fright but remained on guard while they waited for Dante's answer to Henry's perfectly reasonable question.

"Did Blue tell you I saw your brother?" Popset asked when it became clear she had no intention of giving one. "Is that the reason?"

The rest of the wots, except for Dyelann who merely grinned in dark amusement, broke into a chorus of appalled gasps and groans.

"Yes, actually." Dante stroked a strand of hair from her eyes. "I was concerned for him, that's all. But now you all know he's got nothing to do with this, so, let's say no more about it."

"Art?" Will raised a hand as if addressing a teacher at school. When everyone looked at him, he felt foolish and pretended to scratch his head before tucking his hand away under the table. "You know things, don't you? Can't you tell Dante where her brother is?"

Dante smiled, misty-eyed. "That's okay, Will. We've already done everything you could possibly imagine, to find him. All of us have tried over the years. We've asked all the seers we know. All the wares. Even Cesar."

The ware reappeared at the sound of his name, beady eyes searching for the one who had spoken it.

"Wares can sense a witch's location," Dante said, "and he sensed nothing. Gart was just gone." Her voice cracked with sadness. She rubbed her forehead. Everybody flinched at the sight of her wand bobbing.

"I'm so sorry, Dan… Wait a minute." The name rang an enormous clanging bell in Will's mind. "Gart?" he repeated. "Gart the witch? Gart, witch, Gart, witch? That Gart?"

"There's only one Gart, Will," Popset said.

"But I met him yesterday."

"You met Gartaspia?" Dante asked, raising her voice to be heard over the various whats, oh my gods, and huhs from the wots.

"He said his name was Gart. He was going to help me find you, but a mean little wenn caught up with us and told him he wasn't allowed to leave. Then she did that singing thing, and when I woke up, they'd gone." He added to Cesar, "That's when I found your kite."

"Are you making this up, Will?" Dante asked in a shaky whisper, as though she dared not believe.

"I swear I'm not."

"Was he okay? Did he look well?"

Will cast his mind back to the brief time he'd spent with Gart and sneered a little, wondering. Did almost bald and barely able to walk constitute wellness?

"What did he say to you? Did he explain where he's been? Did he say why he hasn't been in touch with us?"

Every set of eyes in the room was fixed on Will now, and he cringed, afraid to say the wrong thing.

"We didn't talk long. He just tried to help me find you. But the wenn was mean to him. She wouldn't let him help me." He leaned closer to Dante and asked, "Did his eye always spin around?"

Judging from her look of horror, it had not, and Will wished he could take the question back. She buried her face in her hands and shuddered with suffocating sobs.

"Sorry," Will said.

"It's okay," she squeaked, flapping a hand in front of her eyes as if trying to wave her emotions away. "Other than the eye, is he okay?"

Not wanting to upset her further, Will stayed quiet.

Karson took advantage of the pause. "I'm sorry to interrupt this moment for you, Miss Simms. But I must. We have not yet reached the purpose for this little gathering, and I feel I should push the point forward so we can get on. We're running out of time and we've none left to waste."

His comment went ignored.

Dante asked Cesar, "Can you sense my brother now?"

Her question caught the ware off guard, and he responded with a headshake and a rabbit-in-the-headlights expression.

Dante clenched her fists on the table. "How can it be that I've been searching all these years, and Will comes along for one day and just happens to bump into him? It's not right. There must be a mistake. It couldn't have been Gart. Maybe you misheard, Will, and it was Bart or Dart or Garth, or anything."

"No," Will said firmly, offended by the implication his information was unreliable. "He said his name, like, a hundred times, Dante, and he said Gart. I'm not deaf."

"But how? Not one person has sighted him since the day of his disappearance. How could you have just happened upon him so quickly? How?"

"I don't think the boy 'just happened' upon anything," Karson said. "That's exactly my point. Let me ask you this: How did the boy get here in the first place?"

Will could answer that one. "I walked."

"Yes, but how did you walk into this place?"

"With my legs?"

Karson slid along the seat to get a bit nearer to Will and was about to speak when he was interrupted.

"You're right," Dyelann shouted, and Henry jumped in fright, crazed hair jolting on his head. "He waltzes right on into Wynne, saves Blue's life, and bumps straight into the missing Simms witch? There's no way that's a coincidence."

Karson nodded solemnly at Dyelann. "My thoughts exactly. Art's too."

The grating of porcelain across wood made everyone look. Popset had leaned over Blue's lifeless body to reach the piece of cake that Art had discarded and was pulling the plate closer. Once it was in front of him, he carefully picked off a cherry, rubbed the icing from the bottom of the sticky red fruit with a finger and wiped it onto the table, distracting everyone with their disgust in him.

Art cleared his throat to regain their focus. "I'm thinking the boy could be the descendant of the Maker," he said. "And just so we're clear, now the young wot is sleeping, I am in fact a seer."

"Seer, mystic, know-it-all, it's all the same to us," Dyelann said. "What's that supposed to mean, anyway? Descendant of the Maker. The maker of what?"

Karson took a deep breath and budged another inch closer to Will. "You may not remember, young man," he said, with an air of respect that took Will by surprise, "but I believe you to be the Maker."

"You think I'm... God?"

The air of respect was blown away by Karson's rampant huffing and puffing before he snorted out, "No, of course that's not what I mean! You're the Maker of the wots. Now that I look at you, you do look very much like him. He was just a boy like you. Scrawny little beggar he was, like yourself."

Will frowned, sensing an insult.

"If I were to say to you, boy," Karson said, quiet and steady now, "I am a wot, my son. I come from your heart. Your will be done..."

"I am your wishing will, you come from my heart, wish for me still." Will said the words but had no idea where they'd come from.

A fascinated smile grew on Karson's face. "It is you," he said eagerly. "Our Maker. You live again."

"No, no." Will stood up, laughing a little to hide his fear. All of a sudden, just like when he'd been alone in the dark last night, the thought of going home didn't seem so bad. He wanted nothing more than to get away from that table, away from all those staring eyes, and back to reality. "That wasn't me. I don't know who said that, but it wasn't me."

Dante clasped a hand around his. "It's okay, Will. It's all right."

"You've come to help us," Karson said. "You're the only one who can."

"I can't do anything." Will put his free hand to his chest. "I'm just me. It wasn't even me who said that then, it just came out."

"What's this all about, Karson?" Maik spoke up, causing the jittery Henry at his side to spill the cup of steaming hot tea he had somehow acquired in the last sixty seconds. Maik patted him consolingly on the back as he said, "You're seriously suggesting that this boy is the boy who supposedly created our gems from his sheer will?"

"Not suggesting," Karson said. "Sit down, son." There was a kindness in him that Will understood to be out of character for this naturally brisk man. "There's no reason to be upset."

"I'm fine." Will did not sit down.

Dyelann accidentally elbowed Henry as he shifted angrily closer to the table. "Wait just one stinking breath. This is getting stupid now. The story of the Maker is a myth. He didn't really exist."

After a long glare at Dyelann, Karson continued speaking to Will. "Listen to me, young man." He gently placed his pebble-like gem onto the table. It had once looked remarkably white to Will, but next to Cesar's whiter than white shirt it was practically dull. "This gem was once nothing more than a stone. A child picked it up over a thousand years ago and changed that. His family, his father, mother, brothers and sisters were all slaughtered. The boy was left all alone, with nowhere to go, no one to turn to, knowing only that his family's killers would kill him too if they ever found him. He was terrified, starving, and near death when he happened upon Wynne."

Interested in spite of himself, Will asked, "What happened?"

Karson pointed to the settee. This time, Will sat.

"The child cried for his family, praying out loud for them to come back to him. He vowed that though he was but worthless and small, his will was not, and that he would do great things if only he had the chance to get back what was his."

Dubiety pulled Will's face askew. "He really said all that?" It didn't sound like something a child would say.

"Yes. A witch overheard his cries. She approached him, wondering how he had found his way into her woodland, which was cloaked from sight and access."

This made Will think. Yesterday, Blue and Esko had been unable to see Foosay's cottage when he could. Was this the same thing Karson was talking about now?

"Seeing the boy's distress, she asked him who he was praying to. The boy replied that he had been praying to whoever would listen. She took him into her home. She fed him, clothed him, mothered him, and taught him the ways of Wynne, the ways of the witch. Still desperate to be reunited with his family, the boy searched through every book he could lay his hands on, looking for a way to recreate life."

Karson picked up his gem and rolled it between his finger and thumb, lost in his own story. "He took this stone, and he summoned the ancient powers, the forces of the old ones and the otherworld, the water, the air, the earth, the fire, to bring forth an almighty strength that would grant his wish."

Will watched the gem twirling in the wot's fingers. Karson looked up, and their eyes locked. Will thought he saw something there: Regret.

"It became a conduit for the supreme power the boy invoked that day. He didn't realise that the energy passed into the gem and stayed there, or that it had created life and spirit. He just wished upon it with all his will for his family to return. That was all he wanted. When nothing happened, he threw the gem away. When he told his witch mother what he had done, she sought it out. She understood how dangerous it would be in the wrong hands. I was just a baby at the time."

His voice dropped, like he was embarrassed to bring himself into a story that, from the look on Dyelann's face, the other wots did not necessarily believe to be true.

Will was having difficulty absorbing the information. How was this story even relevant to the predicament the wots were in now?

"The gem took me into its heart," Karson said. "We became one. Our spirits intertwined. It called me to it, just as all the wots were called to their gems. We were born witches. Our gems chose us to be their eternal keepers. They protect us from harm and death, and we do the same for them in return. They're alive, child. And they need us, just as much as we need them."

Dyelann grunted impatiently, and Karson responded with a scowl. Dyelann rolled his eyes at that, which aggravated Karson all the more.

"Your trouble is you never listen, Dyelann. If you ever did, you would already know everything I'm telling you now. You should know it. It's your history."

Dyelann only rolled his eyes again, and Karson turned his back on him to focus on Will.

"When the boy and the witch saw the gem was bearing life, they had to decide what to do with me. They couldn't find it in themselves to destroy me, but I had far too much power to be allowed to exist. So, the two decided they had no choice but to split the power. They first detached from it the energy summoned from water, which became Blue's gem. When they saw that wasn't enough, they worked their magic again to create the red and the yellow, splitting the forces four ways. But that still wasn't enough, so they split them until we were left with what we have now. The red and orange are of fire, the blue and purple water, the yellow and green earth, and the black and white retained the air. That's why our gems have different attributes. But they are all equally powerful, and all equally dangerous in the wrong hands."

A sharp clatter dragged Will's eyes away from Karson, and he saw that Foyer had slapped the table and made Henry drop his cup.

"Will, the energy our combined gems contain is beyond any of us. The Maker and his witch mother had to split it eight ways for it to even be able to exist without cataclysmic consequences."

"Do you mind?" Karson asked, appalled by Foyer's interruption. "I'm in the middle of a story here."

"I was just whipping you to the point," Foyer said, leaning back. "You seemed to be struggling to get there. Listen, Will. What Karson's - very slowly - getting at, is there are other forces at work here, forces much larger than Foosay Hoo or Scilla Simms or any other witch that could have taken our gems. This person, whoever she is, is trying to reunite the gems' energies, to bring them back to that state. The world doesn't want that. But there are creatures that do."

There was something to the way he said the word 'creatures' that prickled at the back of Will's neck.

"They're what are after me, aren't they?"

The question surprised Foyer. "How do you know that?"

"Dante said so. Why are they after me? What did I ever do to them?"

"These creatures," Karson said. "They were brought into existence because wots were brought into existence. Created by nature as an opposing force for the scales. Where wots grant wishes, these creatures grant nightmares." He lowered his voice. "They are the neethers: The bringers of misery."

"And we intend to keep you well away from them," Foyer said when he noticed Will freeze. "Nothing to be scared of."

Dyelann muttered something sarcastic under his breath.

"But why?" Will asked. "Why me?"

"Because," Art said in his gravelly voice, his eyes burning red, "they believe you are the descendant of the Maker. Only the Maker could rival the power of the wots and the neethers. The Maker was endowed with the power from the conduit he held in his hands when he summoned the four forces. It took someone of impossible strength to have called upon these powers in the first place. To this day he is the only one to have succeeded, although many have tried. There was something special in that child."

"Yeah. The fact he didn't exist, maybe." Dyelann kicked the solid table so hard its legs rattled. "This entire conversation is the stupidest thing I've heard in my life. The Maker, the four powers, it's all fantasy. Wots were created by a witch who liked pretty colours and the idea of granting wishes for all eternity."

Karson took his gem back from the table and slipped it into the inside pocket of his dinner jacket, smoothing it with a quick flick of his hand. "Is that so? And who, may I ask, told you this?"

"My mother." Dyelann's face dared Karson to argue.

"That wasn't your mother, Dyelann! That was a crazy old witch who thought she was everybody's mother for nearly a hundred and fifty years." He glanced at Art. "Yes, I know from years," he said, answering a question before giving it chance to be asked.

Will stood up again, frustrated. "What are you all going on about? What has any of this got to do with me? I keep telling you, I'm not the Maker. I'm not a disnendant."

"The neethers want you either way," Karson said. "They know you have the same unexplained power inside of you that the Maker had. You have his same will, and only you can stop the collision of the four powers."

Exchanging a sceptical frown with Dyelann, Maik said, "That doesn't even make sense. Why would the neethers want the powers to be put together? It'd kill us, right? If we died, they'd die too."

"On the contrary," Karson said. "If the four powers collide, their power too will increase beyond imagination."

Dyelann scoffed. "Then why wouldn't ours too? How can you be this stupid?"

"Watch that insolence, boy." Karson's face reddened in fury. "If our gems become one again, your life connections to them will die and so shall you all."

"Because you're all ancient," Art agreed. "Were you still the witches you were born as, you'd all be long dead by now anyway."

"Then how come the neethers wouldn't die too?" Maik asked. "I agree with Dyelann. This all sounds like hokum."

Dyelann thrust his arms approvingly at Maik, giving Henry another accidental wallop. "Thank you! Precisely. Neethers can't exist for the sole reason we exist if we don't exist, can they? And there was me thinking you had a brain inside your head, Mr Oh-So-Superior."

Foyer raised his hands to stop Karson from shouting. "Okay, that's enough. I'm about sick of this now. The purpose of this meeting was not to start some futile argument about what may or may not have happened in the past."

"Foyer's absolutely right," Dante said. "None of this is helping. What's important is getting your gems back. That's all."

Karson was raging. He grunted and snarled like a disgruntled wild pig, but again Foyer interjected before he could speak.

“Enough!”

Through force of habit, Will reached to pull his cap down before remembering he’d lost it. He groaned woefully and grasped his spikes.

“Let’s not fall out,” Popset agreed, still in unusually good spirits. His positivity led Will to wondering what had caused the previously stern wot’s new attitude.

“He was getting a bit beside himself earlier,” Foyer explained, correctly reading Will’s expression. “We made him take a pill.”

“This whole ugly business is very unsettling,” Popset said through a mouthful of cake, sputtering crumbs.

“There’s an understatement.” Art scratched his moustache and got to his feet. “Am I allowed to leave now?”

“No.” Foyer propped his head lazily on a hand, elbow on the table.

There was an alarmed look on Cesar’s face, more so even than usual. He kept taking deep breaths and opening his mouth, as if he wanted to speak but couldn’t help chickening out at the last second. Will wanted to shush everybody and ask the ware what he was trying to say, but Will couldn’t get a word in edgeways either.

Karson’s chest heaved higher with each breath. “I believe this meeting is over!”

“Stop sulking, Karson.” Foyer sounded ready to give up. There was no emotion in his words, just a tone of calm depression. “It’s very unbecoming in a person of your stature.”

“Someone fat, you mean?” Dyelann said.

Foyer lowered his hand so his eyes were free to glare at Dyelann. “Can you just shut up? Stop winding him up. Just stop. It’s bad enough we’re…”

Unable to contain himself any longer, Cesar yelled: “Listen!” His shout frightened Henry out of his skin for a third time and grabbed the undivided attention of every individual in the room, except for the unconscious Blue. “Just shut up and listen! Trying to speak to you people is like asking a cat to bark.”

"Maybe if you tried opening your mouth and making sounds..." Dyelann began.

"A witch is approaching," Cesar interrupted. "And if Dyelann says one more word to me, I'll be leaving."

"What witch?" Karson demanded.

Dyelann snarled at Cesar. "That's right, go running back to your hidey-hole."

Foyer scraped back his fringe with a strange grimace of despair. "Cesar, I'm sorry," he said, deflated. "You have to forgive Dyelann. You know what he's like."

Karson thumped the table in front of Cesar. "What witch, I asked you!"

"Why does everyone keep attacking the table?" Dante said in a high, irritated whine. "It's five hundred years old, could we not show it a little respect?"

Karson whacked the table-top three times with all his might, frightening the ware into another disappearing act. "Come back here, Cesar, you pathetic little weasel!"

The door clunked open.

The six conscious wots, the witch, the seer, and Will all stared in anxious anticipation, waiting to see who was behind it.

"Hello?" A woman with ash blonde plaited pigtails and a rosy young face stepped into the slanted hut. "Oh, there you all are." She hitched her khaki duffel bag more securely on her shoulder and smiled. "My name's Lillian Scrossly. I'm here to help."

Will recognised the name straight away, and it brought a grin to his face. This woman may have been a stranger, but her name was one he associated with a friend, which as far as Will was concerned automatically made her a friend too - and she'd come to help.

"You're Jonas Crossly's granddaughter," he said.

"I'm Jonah Scrossly's granddaughter," the fair-haired witch corrected him with a coy smile.

"That's what I said."

"You know my grandfather?" The large canvas bag over her shoulder weighed her down on one side, causing her to stand as slanted as everything else in No go Ebb. She shrugged it back up again and leaned further against its heft. The strap looked too wide for her delicate shoulders.

Karson rose from his seat and stood tall, or as tall as Karson could stand, to square up to Lillian. "What do you want, witch?" He pawed at the empty space beside him, where Cesar had just been. "Cesar, get back here, you useless cretin."

"Oh, it's okay." Lillian set the bag down. It made a heavy clanking sound when it touched the floor. "Like I said, I'm here to help."

"Cesar!" Karson ignored Lillian's attempts to explain herself. The ware reappeared at his command, nervous and jumpy, his beady eyes searching all around him for any sign of danger. Karson grabbed him by the arm and pointed him at Lillian. "Is this witch the witch she claims to be?"

Cesar tried to escape from the wot's fast grip. "Yes, it's Lillian Scrossly, yes," he yelped, and Karson let go of him. He fell back onto the settee, cradling his freed arm protectively with the other.

Foyer sat up, scowling his disapproval at Karson. "Forgive us," he said to the newcomer. "The tension's a little high in the wot fold at the moment."

"Absolutely understandable," Lillian said, holding up her petite hands, and Dante mimicked the words like a jealous child.

"But," Cesar added, "that doesn't mean she's not the one taking your gems."

"Oh, no." Lillian hooked her thumbs under her dungaree straps. "I promise you, I'm here only with your best interests at heart." Her gaze set on Blue, and she jerked her head at him. "What's wrong with him?"

"Nothing, he's fine." Popset threw an arm around Blue's shoulders, only for the lifeless wot to fall forward and bang his head on the table, causing Dante to shriek, Henry to jump, and Dyelann to laugh wickedly.

Foyer dragged Blue back up. "Popset, keep away from the poor lad, would you?"

"Is he all right?" Will asked, just as Blue began to lift a limp arm. "Is he waking up?"

Blue slowly put a hand to his head, eyes still closed, and moaned dolefully.

"Are you okay, Blue?" Will asked, in unison with Foyer and Dante.

Blue leaned against the table, finger and thumb pinching his forehead. "What happened?"

"Popset dropped you on the table." Will glared at the accused.

"My head."

Never had Will been so grateful for someone banging their head. "Are you okay?"

"*No*," Blue retorted, as if it were the most stupid question he'd ever been asked. "I feel terrible."

"You'll feel better soon enough," Art said.

Blue aimed a scowl the seer's way. He sat straight up when he spotted Lillian by the doorway, any pain and discomfort overcome or forgotten. "Tamzin?"

Shock froze her face for a second, but she shook herself out of it, blinked a few times and smiled. "No, I'm Lillian. Lillian Scrossly.

Tamzin Rickrack was my grandmother. She died when I was just a child."

"You're her absolute spitting image." Blue glanced over her baggy denim dungarees and the red and black striped sweater under them. "She never would have dressed that way though."

Karson hadn't stopped staring at her, watching her every move and holding on to his gem like she might have leapt forward and taken it from him at any second. "What are you doing here?" he asked again, louder.

Lillian neared the table. "I had a premonition."

Art made a loud 'hmph' sound and faced the wall.

"I saw a cauldron," Lillian said, "and seven colourful rocks. A witch was trying to perform a spell, to release their power, but the spell wouldn't work because of the protests of one of the rocks. But she's going to keep trying, and she's going to succeed sooner or later. Unless we stop her."

Just as put out by Lillian's presence as Art was, Dante evil-eyed the younger witch every time she spoke. "Why do you care? What difference does it make to you? What's your incentive to help?"

"My premonition is my incentive. Why would I get a vision of this if it didn't somehow concern me? I just know I have an obligation to help these wots get their gems back before the blue one begins to falter. Its strength can't go on forever." Lillian's smile wilted under Dante's angry stare. "I know who you are, Dante Simms. You and your sisters are highly respected here in Wynne. But you are not the witch these wots need right now."

Not at all to Will's surprise, Foyer jumped to Dante's defence. "We need all the help we can get, and Dante's is as valued as anybody's, if not more so."

"Oh, don't you worry. I've brought all the help you need." Lillian held up a wait-a-second finger, backed up to her bag, stepped over it and dragged it back to the table. The wots all watched patiently. When she tried to swing it onto the table, Foyer, albeit warily, took one end of it and helped her. "Why, thank you, kind sir," Lillian said, smiling again, and Will felt Dante physically stiffen at his side. The bag landed on the table with the same noisy clank as it had when she'd first put it down. She unzipped it to reveal its contents: Weapons. Axes, daggers, knives, and various throwing blades were all tossed onto the table with such carelessness the wots shrivelled backwards. Once she'd emptied it of blades, she turned the bag upside down and shook it. Out fell a selection of small, corked glass bottles, each filled with grainy sand in a variety of colours that reminded Will of his mother's collection of bath salts.

Foyer cast an eye over the mess on the table. "What's all this?"

"These here are some repellents." Lillian waved her hand over the bottles. "You throw them at things, to repel them. I don't have any for wickers or warders, I'm afraid. The green ones are for wenns. I'd recommend you all take one of these each." She rolled the bottles of green sand across the table to each wot, one at a time, and gave the last one to Will, who picked it up and put it to his eye. "I don't have enough for you all to have one of the others," she went on, "but the blue ones are for witches, the red and yellow ones for neethers, and the sort of purple ones here are for badgers."

"Badgers?" Will asked, lowering the bottle from his face.

Lillian stared at Will as though she couldn't understand his confusion. "Yes," she said when nobody else spoke. "Badgers are scary, aren't they?" She glanced around at everybody for support. "No? Really?" She scooped up the five purple bottles and stuffed them into the pockets of her dungarees. "I'll just keep these, then."

Blue peered left and right over his shoulders several times. "What's that? What's that buzzing?"

"There's no buzzing," Foyer said.

Dante listened. "I don't hear anything."

"It's your gem getting through to you," Art said, still facing the wall. "It'll call you to it soon enough."

"He can't go," Dante said. "He'll be killed."

"That's where we come in." Lillian spread the weapons across the table. "We'll follow..." She stopped herself. "Sorry, I don't believe I know your name yet," she said to Blue, but Blue had his hands over his ears and wasn't listening.

The others all found something else to focus their attention on, pretending not to have heard. Foyer kept an eye on what she was doing, but even he was oddly reluctant to respond. Will started to feel sorry for her.

"His name's Blue."

"And you are?"

"Will Morgan."

"Well, Will Morgan, here. These are for you." Lillian passed him three of the corked bottles containing red and yellow granules. "If any neethers get near you, I want you to throw this right at them. It'll get them to back off, so you'll have that bit longer to get away to safety. Oh, and here." She handed him another miniature bottle. This one was empty. "This is very different, and you must only use it in the very gravest of circumstances. Don't use it if there's more than one neether about, because it only has enough in it to kill one of them. And trust me, you do not want to kill one in front of another one, or you're just pulling your own death string."

Will took the bottle between finger and thumb and held it up to the light. "There's nothing in it."

"It's actually a gas that's very poisonous to neethers. But it's also very poisonous to wots, so don't open it around them either."

"What?" Dante spat.

Will held the bottle out to Lillian. "I don't want it."

"No, no, keep it," Lillian insisted. "It could save your life."

"Yeah. But no, thanks."

"Don't be silly. Put it in your pocket."

"No, please, I really don't want it." He thrust it back at Lillian, but before she could take it, it slipped from his fingers.

All the wots, except for Blue and Dyelann, leapt from their seats in blind panic and crashed into each other with all the sense of a herd of spooked horses.

Dante's wand was still in her sleeve when she used it to halt the poison in mid-air, a mere inch from hitting the floor. She picked up the bottle and held it angrily in front of Lillian's face. "How could you bring this into a room full of wots? What's wrong with you?"

Lillian snatched the bottle from Dante's fingers. "It's unbreakable glass. You have to remove the cork to release the gas, and you can only do that when you intend to. It's perfectly safe."

Blue removed his hands from his ears and left the settee. As he edged around the table, Popset hung onto his coat like a child.

"And he's off," Art announced.

"Where are you going?" Will asked, preparing to follow.

Art stood up, checking his tie was straight. "He's being called to his gem, just like I told you he would. I'll leave you with the young witch and her amateur premonitions. So long. Good day. I wish all of you the very best of luck." Striding past Blue, whose efforts to leave were being hindered by Popset's clinginess, the seer exited the hut with a glad snigger.

Foyer stood between Blue and the closing door. "Blue, stop. Think about this. You can't just wander into this witch's territory. She'll kill you. Again."

"I have to. My gem needs me to go. It wouldn't call me to it if I didn't have to go."

"This isn't all on you. It's not your responsibility to fix this." Foyer snarled at Karson. "This is your fault, you know."

Karson grunted in reply.

"No." Dyelann perched on the back of the settee and leaned against the wall. "Foyer's right. It's not your responsibility, Blue. According to Karson here, that burden falls on young Will's shoulders."

These words snapped Blue out of his dozy trance. He pushed Popset away. "How can Will have anything to do with this? Don't start picking on him."

Dyelann, as usual, just smirked.

"Tell me what he meant." Blue glared around at everyone. "No one ever tells me anything."

"It's nothing," Foyer assured him. "It seems some people are under the impression that Will's either the descendant of the Maker, or the Maker reborn, or something like that. You remember the story of the Maker, right?"

Blue's face set in a disturbed frown that put Will on edge. "Will's not the Maker," he said after a brief silence. He sounded calm, but his expression hadn't lost its tension. "You're not the Maker, are you, Will?"

"No," Will said at once.

"He's not, is he?" Blue asked Foyer, forcing a smile that only made his frown deepen.

"I don't know, Blue," Foyer said honestly. "But what I do know is you can't go marching off alone."

Lillian clacked two daggers together. "He won't be alone. We'll all be right behind him. With weapons."

"He's not the Maker, is he, Karson?" Blue pleaded. "Is he?"

"Yes," Karson said with no pleasure. "I believe he is."

The expression on Blue's face made Will feel sick inside. "No, I'm not. I'm just me. I'm not anyone who's not me." Why wouldn't Blue believe him? Why wouldn't he look at him and know he was telling the truth? He wished they'd never come to this place. They had been doing fine on their own.

"So Foyer is right," Karson conceded. "I know I impressed on you that this mess was yours to sort out, but that was before I had all the facts. It was too much to expect of you, I understand that now. None of this is your doing. And…" He struggled to form the words, then coughed them out like they tasted bad in his mouth. "I apologise."

Blue just stared at him for a long moment. "He can't be the Maker! He saved my life. He brought me back from the dead. You know what that takes, don't you? There's a transcript, the mystics..." His face fell, and his voice trailed off. "Oh." He backed away from Will, pushing past Foyer. "You really are the Maker." The door bumped him in the back, and he fumbled for the handle.

"Blue, I said don't go," Foyer warned.

Dante tried to stop him from opening the door. "Hey, come on, Blue, what's wrong?"

"I want to get out of here, that's what's wrong." He wrenched his arm free from her tender hold. "Get off me."

Lillian, now with a small axe in one hand and a glinting twelve-inch-long blade in the other, shouted, "Everyone grab a weapon and follow Blue. Let's do this."

Blue flung out an arm and pointed at the witch. "No. Keep away from me. I don't want anyone following me." He turned to Dyelann. "Especially you." His eyes flicked to meet Will's, and he flinched as though the connection had physically hurt him. "And you." Then he stormed out of the hut and slammed the door behind him so hard the walls shook.

"Why's he mad at me?" Will asked pathetically, cut by Blue's coldness. He looked to the remaining wots, searching for one who could explain. "What did I do?"

"We can't let him go alone," Foyer said again, mostly to Karson.

"Come on, then." Lillian tapped the table. "Quickly now, grab something sharp. I brought plenty to go around."

Dyelann slid off the back of the settee and lifted the nearest dagger.

"You be careful with that thing," Foyer warned, just as Popset fell flat on his face by the door.

"What's wrong with him?" Lillian asked, standing over the badly dressed wot.

"The excitement's just a bit much for him," Foyer said dismissively. He rubbed the back of his neck. "Listen, Lillian, it's nice you want to help us and everything. But - uhh… How can I put this nicely? Wots don't do weapons. Okay?"

Still reeling from Blue's icy departure, Will sat back down on the settee.

Karson sat opposite him. "Don't lose heart, boy. There's much that can be done in only a small amount of time. You just wait and see. We will prevail."

"But why did Blue say that to me?" It was hard to concentrate on anything anyone else was doing or saying, when all he could think of was that last look Blue had given him before leaving. It was like Blue thought Will had betrayed him. "Why did you have to tell him I was the Maker person when I'm not? He hates me now."

"Blue doesn't hate you," Foyer said.

"Yes, he does; he said he didn't want me to go with him and he did this:" Will threw an exaggerated glare at Foyer to demonstrate.

"I think someone's imagining things. Come on, Will. Blue thinks you're great. He's never taken to anyone as fast as he's taken to you. He's – Dyelann!" Foyer lurched to snatch the dagger from Dyelann's hand just as he was about to stab it through Henry's hair. "What are you doing? Idiot."

"Hair doesn't hurt."

Foyer gave Dyelann a swift swipe around the back of the head, to which Dyelann snorted a laugh. Foyer waved the dagger at Lillian. "See what I mean? They can't be trusted to even hold one of these things."

"No problem." Lillian dropped her axe and her knife onto the table with the rest of them and delved into her floppy duffel bag. She unzipped an inner compartment and brought out a stubby wand. The jagged end suggested part of it had been snapped off at some time. "I'm sure Dante and I could stick a charm on them." She pointed the broken wand at the pile of weapons. "What do you think, Dante Simms? Shall we do a little rhyme?"

"Rhyming?" Dante sounded surprised. "Isn't that a bit old-fashioned for a thirteen-year-old?"

For the first time since she'd arrived, Lillian's cheeriness gave way to annoyance. "I'm twenty-two. And rhyming spells are a tradition passed down to me from my grandmother. Rhyming on the spot makes your brain work harder, and when your brain is working harder so is your heart and your blood, which increases your concentration, increases your power. Not rhyming is lazy and makes spells sloppy, and I'd be very surprised, Dante Simms, if you, from your great lineage, did not use rhyme as instinctively as breathing."

There was a definite flash of shame in Dante's eyes, and the brightness was quick to return to Lillian's.

"Okay," Lillian said, all sweetness again, focusing on the weapons that her wand still pointed at. "Let all weapons on this table not, bring harm to any harmless wot, only attack those that cause hitches, like evil wenns, neethers, banters and witches." The wand trembled. A rumbling sound broke out from it like distant thunder. Then a spark shot out of the broken tip, bounced on the first of the blades it reached and spread like flakes of fire over each of the others. "Back it up for me, Dante. My brew stick's not so reliable these days."

Dante didn't look happy about it, but she took her twisted wand from her sleeve and pointed it at the table. A loud pop rang out and the blades shone brightly for less than a second. She lowered it just as Lillian gave hers a dissatisfied shake, and the two wands collided with a sharp clack. The two witches stared at each other, Dante furious while Lillian smiled, backed off and held up her wand in apology. She dropped the stubby wand back into her bag.

"There you go, all done. Scarily easy. Why don't we try it out? Dyelann, go ahead and stab someone."

Foyer held an authoritative arm out to Dyelann, who was eagerly reaching for another dagger. "Don't even think about it, Dye."

Dyelann slowly leaned back.

Hesitant, Foyer lifted one of the smallest knives from the table. The witches watched with interest. He glanced at them, then back at the knife, and pointed it at his hand.

"So brave," Dante said.

And Foyer, needing no more encouragement than that, sliced the blade over his palm without a second thought. "Ha," he said in happy surprise. "Look at that." The blade had disappeared into his hand like a hologram. "It goes straight through."

Lillian nodded, pigtails bobbing. "There you go, see? No danger of any harm coming to any of your boys through their own doing now. So let's hurry and go after Blue before he gets too far ahead. We can't let him reach the witch without us."

"That was actually a… a smart idea, Lillian Scrossly," Dante said, and Lillian beamed with delight.

"That means a lot, coming from you."

Dante showed Lillian a gracious albeit fleeting smile.

"Karson, you should stay here with Cesar," Foyer said. "And Popset," he added as he walked around Popset to get to the door. "Listen, Cesar, next time, if you should happen to sense a witch coming, could you do us all a favour and let Karson know before she's about to walk in? Maybe? Yes?"

Cesar shrugged. "If I can get a word in, I'll inform him at once."

"Good. Thank you. The rest of you, let's move. Henry, Maik, look sharp, come on."

Lillian lifted a large, bronze-handled dagger. "Yes, quick-quick. Don't forget your weapons." She took her wand from her bag and stuffed it into the pocket on the front of her dungarees. "Look after my bag," she said to Cesar. "I'll be back for that."

Will watched the group vacate the hut.

Dante, the last to reach the door, stopped to wait for him. When he made no effort to move, she asked, "What's the matter?"

"Blue told me not to follow him." Will's lower lip protruded slightly, of its own accord. "So, I won't."

"Oh, Will," Dante said, striding over Popset's legs to get back to him. "I forget you've not known Blue long, the two of you seem such close friends. Let me tell you a little something about him. Very occasionally, he'll have a moment of obnoxiousness that we call a strop. But the next time you see him, it's forgotten. You just have to ignore him when he gets that way."

Will couldn't help but think there was much more to Blue's attitude than that on this occasion. Not knowing how to express this feeling to Dante, he nodded and allowed her to help him up. She led him around Popset, shepherded him through the exit, and released his hand as they joined the others between the slanted trees.

Dyelann and Maik walked ahead of the rest of the group, Dyelann grinning from ear to ear and slashing his sword about his head, elated either at being free to play with a sharp object that couldn't harm him or knowing how much his presence would upset Blue when they caught up. It was probably a bit of both.

Foyer and Lillian pushed Henry onwards, one at each side of him. The timid wot held a dagger about the size of a banana tightly with both hands and kept twisting his head to see the hut as if preparing to flee back to it.

Following behind, Dante pulled Will in to lean against her. "It'll be okay, you know. If you really are the Maker's descendant, you will find a way to end all this. And if you're not, you're not. There's no need for you to worry yourself sick about this, is there? Just think of it as an adventure. It'll be something to tell your friends about when you get home."

Will stepped away from Dante to walk alongside her. "I'm not going home."

"Whyever not?"

"My mum and dad hate me. Everyone hates me." He was more upset about Blue turning on him than anything else, and worried that when they caught up to the wot, he'd only verify the fact.

"Nobody hates you. I'm sure your parents don't, and Blue's not even capable of hate. You're probably just tired and hungry."

Sometimes, Dante came out with things that made Will feel like he was with his mother.

"You've been up all night, had a hard couple of days. Would you like something to eat? Maybe a bath and some clean clothes?"

"But…"

"But nothing. I don't suppose there's time for a bath, but I do have a little spell up my sleeve." She shook her arm to drop her wand into her hand, and prodded Will's forehead with it.

"Ow."

"All done."

"What's done?" He peered down at himself. A patch of mud had disappeared from his jacket, but he didn't notice anything else, didn't feel any different. Then he touched his head and felt to his dismay that the gel that had been moulding his spikes had gone, leaving his hair flat, soft, and flopping over his forehead. "Dante!" He didn't even have his cap to cover it.

"Oh." She winced. "Well. I think it looks pretty."

"Pretty?" Will hated that word when used in reference to him.

"Here." Out of nowhere she produced a large glass bowl overflowing with food. Sandwiches, crisps, grapes and several steaming hot potatoes were pressed against a big block of rapidly melting chocolate. She handed the bowl to Will. "You'll feel better with some food in you. And if you need to use a bathroom, you just let me know."

"Dante." He hoped nobody had overheard that. Struggling to hold the bowl, he inspected its contents and decided he most likely would need a bathroom if he was mad enough to eat chocolate-covered potatoes and grapes. A piece of sweetcorn stuck to the rim made the decision for him. "I'm not that hungry," he said, handing the bowl back to her.

"No wonder you're so skinny. Are you sure?" She waved the bowl under his nose, and he got a whiff of tuna.

"Blue gave me something earlier that made me feel like I'd eaten a whole elephant."

Dante threw the bowl over her shoulder. It disappeared before it touched the ground, like some giant invisible creature had engulfed it.

"What are we going to do when we catch up to him anyway?" Will asked. "He said he didn't want us to follow him. Won't he be mad?"

"Blue doesn't get mad, not really. You'll see. As soon as he realises we're only there to back him up, he'll forget all about his strop."

"Are you two coming?" Lillian demanded from a distance. They couldn't see where she was, hidden somewhere among the trees ahead. Will was about to speed up, but Dante held him back.

"Don't rush on her account. As soon as we're out of the limited access area, we'll make our own way to Blue. Get away from that horrid witch for a while."

It didn't make any sense to Will that Dante disliked Lillian so much. She seemed nice enough to him, always pleasant, always wanting to help them.

"I don't know what I'd do if anything happened to the wots," Dante went on. "They mean the world to me. Always have. My sisters say it's a soft spot, but sometimes I think it's more than that. My sisters have the same soft spots for others, you know. Molina feels the same way for wenns as I do for wots. She denies it, but we all know she'd befriend a wenn over a witch any day. Elmer's all funny where wares are concerned. She adores that freaky friend of Blue's, believe it or not. And Harrier, well, she likes wyes, of all things." A bemused little laugh crinkled her brow. "I mean, that really is strange. Most witches can't stand wyes. I've always wondered if there isn't something behind it. Some connection that binds us all to one another. Do you know what I mean?"

Will had begun to hear nothing but jabbering for the last part of what she'd said, too worried about Blue to listen properly. "Yes," he replied, hoping that was the right response. Dante smiled at him, so he presumed it was.

"Will." She lowered her volume a tad. "Can I ask you something? My brother. I haven't seen him in eleven years. I need to know. Is he okay?"

"I don't know," he said, reluctant to get back into this conversation. The last thing he wanted was for her to start crying again.

"Please, Will. I have to know if he needs me. Does he need me?"

Will looked at her face to try and gauge her mood. "Yes," he said. "I think he's been trying to get back to you, but that nasty wenn won't let him. And he can't walk properly, so he couldn't even get up when she made him fall over."

And there were the tears, sparkling already.

"He can't walk?"

"And he's sort of lost most his hair," he added, wincing when he'd said it.

She covered her face with both hands. "What on earth happened to him?"

Will knew she wasn't expecting an answer to that one. "Are you going to help him?"

"Of course." Dante wiped her tears away. "As soon as we've got the gems back to the wots. It's not that I put the wots ahead of Gart," she said. "I love my brother. But Gart's managed without me for eleven years now. I know he can wait a day longer. The wots might not."

"He's been missing as long as I've been alive." The very idea of it boggled Will's mind.

"You're eleven? You look younger." Dante's face locked in thought. "Wait. You're eleven years old? You're eleven... What does that mean?" She rubbed the creases out of her forehead and made an aggravated kind of groaning sound, as if in disagreement with whatever was going on in her mind. "You know, Will, my grandma had a great, fat book that I used to read all the time when I was a little girl. It was full of factoids and myths about everything and anything."

"So?"

"So, there were passages about the Maker in it too. Everybody who believes in the Maker believes he'll return some day."

"Why? I mean, why do they think he'll come back?"

"That's the unclear part. But if you really are the Maker, and you just so happened to have been born around the same time Gart went missing, and you're here now when the wots are in dire jeopardy..." She slowed down. "What if Gart is connected to all this?"

"You said there's no way he would have done it. So did Blue. And that weird Art man said it was a woman."

"I didn't mean connected like that. I meant maybe whoever's stealing the gems had something to do with Gart's disappearance."

"You think it's that wenn? Eve?"

Dante stopped in her tracks. "Eve? Eve is a friend of Molina's. You're telling me she knows where Gart is? You're telling me all the times we've seen that little wenn and spoken to her, she's known our brother's alive and not told us?" She stamped a foot and slapped the nearest tree. "How could she? That heinous little fiend!"

"Definitely her, then."

Doing a double take, Dante said, "Ooh," and waved a hand around. "I can make a portal now. Come on, Will. Let's get Blue."

"How do you know where he is?"

"I don't." She readied her wand. "I've got some of the potion left from when I was searching for the two of you earlier." Her free hand pulled a corked test tube from the back pocket of her trousers. There was a small amount of liquid in the bottom of the tube that looked like the bitty remains of dirty dishwater.

"Gross. What's that?"

"It's for the locator spell. I took it from the brew my sisters and I made when Foyer asked us to try and find the gems."

Will gazed at the little glass tube, intrigued. "How does it know who you're looking for?"

"You have to dip a piece of who or what you're looking for into it. Or something that's physically touched them for a long time. You know, a ring, a sock, a fingernail clipping, something like that. When I took this from the cauldron, I dipped a bit of Blue's hair in it so it would lead me right to him."

She shot Will a quick, embarrassed glance while he wondered if it was worth asking how she'd got her hands on a bit of Blue's hair.

"What? He left a scarf at my place." Her cheeks burned pink. "I didn't steal if from him or anything. There was a strand of hair on his scarf, so I took advantage of it. It's not like I carry his hair around with me or something crazy like that. I'm not some kind of stalker," she said in a loud, flustered whisper.

"You and Foyer both." Will tried not to laugh at her. "What did you dip in the potion when you were looking for the gems?"

"Maik's finger," she said, glad to change the subject. "We stole him away from helping Dyelann for a minute. Trouble is, it didn't lead us to Maik's gem. It just kept leading us to Maik. Which is stupid. I mean, Maik was attached to his finger. Why would we need a locator spell to find something we were dipping into the locator spell? I really don't understand why it didn't work. It's never done that before."

A worrying thought occurred to Will. "If you needed something like Blue's hair to find us when we were at the shop," he said, "how did the other witch who looked like you find us? What did she use?"

Dante stared into space, clinking her test tube against the knobbles on her wand. "Maybe she didn't need a locator spell. Maybe she already knew exactly where you were. Maybe she's watching you."

Will's stomach somersaulted.

"Or," she went on, changing her tone, "Blue's gem would have done the trick, of course. Anyway," she said, louder, like she'd just remembered what they were in the middle of doing. "We have to hurry up and find Blue." With all the skilled care of a surgeon using a scalpel, she sliced open her portal. Then she uncorked the test tube, flicked the liquid into it, and veered Will through the static-crackling light.

Will bumped into Blue's back. The wot grunted in alarm and skipped aside.

The trees were not slanted here but upright and tall. They weren't in No-go Ebb anymore.

"What are you doing here?" Blue asked, flustered.

"Still in his strop then?" Dante said as she stepped out of the portal. "How are you doing, Blue? Are you nearly there yet?"

"Go away." He tried to walk around her, but she walked with him. "I said I didn't want anyone following me."

Will spotted a large, dark shape beyond Blue and Dante just slipping out of sight behind a tree. He peered around Dante as she blocked Blue's way, leaning to see past them both.

"What's wrong with you? You're upsetting poor Will, being like this."

"*I'm* upset," Blue retorted, and Dante's face loosened in sympathy for him.

"This isn't like you. Don't lose hope. We'll find the witch. We'll get your gem back. We will."

Blue barged by her and stormed on his way. "That's not what I'm upset about!"

"Blue, come on. Just stop." She scuttled after him.

Will wanted to follow them but couldn't seem to convince his feet. There was something creeping behind that tree. He tried to call for Blue and Dante but couldn't speak. He glanced after them, lost them, and locked his eyes back in place on the tree.

He coughed to reactivate his vocal cords and a hoarse whisper came out. "Who's there?"

A cold breeze ruffled his hair.

Just as he was beginning to relax and think he must have been imagining things, a vacant voice said: "Nobody."

Immediately on the alert again, he asked, "Who said that?"

"Nobody," the voice said again, in the same dull tone.

"Someone did." Will took a step forward, then another, keeping a quiet footing, intending to sneak up on the stranger, catch him off guard. On reaching the tree, he put a hand on the trunk and swung himself around it. He was both achingly relieved and numbingly terrified to find nothing there. "Where are you?" he shouted, glancing up and down, left and right in his hurry to find the owner of the voice.

Something massive appeared in front of him, and he fell flat on his back in sheer panic. Leaning on his elbows, he could do nothing but wait for the stranger to make the next move.

The man's head was small in comparison to his body; his neck was wider than his face. He wore a sleeveless shirt, probably because no sleeves on the planet could have contained those bulging arms without splitting at the seams. How that hulking body had completely hidden behind a tree half its width was a mystery.

"Who are you?" he asked, hoping no one could hear the erratic thudding of his heart.

"Nobody."

Everything inside Will told him he had to get up off the ground before this bizarre monster of a man broke him in half with one false step. But he couldn't move a muscle. "What do you want?"

The stranger shrugged his hefty shoulders. "Nothing."

Will didn't believe that. "Are you a neether?"

Deep, reverberating laughter pounded through Will's ears like a road drill. The man laughed long and hard, mighty chest juddering. "No." The laughter stopped. "Have you lost your glasses or something?"

Will didn't know whether he needed to be afraid of this person or not, which somehow made the situation worse. "Who are you, then?"

"I've told you how many times now? Nobody. I'm Nobody." He wiped something off the knee of his bulky black trousers.

"Oh, that's your name. Sorry. It's really annoying when people do that."

Nobody's upper lip curled into an ugly sneer. "Yes. It is."

"So, you're not a neether?" Will managed to sit up straighter but his legs were still buckled where he'd fallen.

"Please." Nobody held up his meaty hands, sneer fading. "Don't make me laugh again."

"What do you want?"

"Nothing."

"Is that your brother?"

"Don't be clever with me."

"I'm not."

The sneer returned.

Will gulped.

"You're the one who approached me." Nobody scowled as he spoke. "What's your problem anyway? Little paranoid, aren't we? What's wrong with you? You lost your stick as well as your glasses?"

"I don't wear glasses. And I don't have a stick."

"Oh dear." Nobody smiled. "Who did you tick off for that to happen?"

"Are you a witch?" Will made another feeble attempt to stand, but his legs were unwilling to join him.

Two lines formed deep between Nobody's dark eyes. "Is there something wrong with you?" he asked, sounding almost concerned. "Did you hit your head?"

"No."

"Tell me." Nobody crouched at Will's side to get better eye contact with him. "Have you seriously never crossed paths with a warder before, little witch?"

Will's fingers bit into the soil below. "What's a warder?"

Nobody pointed at his undersized face with two stocky fingers. "You're looking at one. There aren't many of us around these days, I suppose."

"What's a warder do?"

"Let's just say I keep an eye on things in this realm." His cryptic air might have been impressive, except all Will could think was that the warder couldn't be much good at his job if he really thought Will was a witch.

"What kind of things?"

"Things like potential troublemakers."

The answer cemented Will's vague supposition into solid fact: Nobody was definitely bad at his job. Keeping an eye on troublemakers did sound like a good guy's job though, didn't it? Maybe, as a good guy, Nobody would be inclined to help the wots if he hadn't been so bad at his job and actually knew what was going on. Maybe someone should clue him in. Maybe that someone should be Will.

"Like witches who take gems from wots and kill them?" he asked, testing the water. "Those kinds of troublemakers?"

Nobody shifted ever so slightly closer. "What are you saying?"

Will hesitated. The water was acidic and infested with sharks, and he needed to back out.

"What are you saying?" the warder asked again, in just the same tone, like he believed Will hadn't heard him the first time.

"Just what I said."

"If something like that was happening," Nobody said, "don't you think I'd know about it?"

"But it *is* happening. And Karson keeps saying I'm this other boy, but I'm not. And now Blue hates me."

Nobody's eyes glinted, and Will worried he'd said too much. "What other boy?"

Pinned under the muscle-bound man's penetrating stare, Will froze where he lay and stared right back.

"What boy?" Nobody repeated the question, enunciating each word with angry precision to emphasise his want of a reply.

"Hey!" Dante hollered, charging at them with fearsome speed. "Get away from him!"

Nobody backed off without argument, although the witch didn't even reach the height of his massive torso. She lashed out her wand, nearly poking him in the eye with it.

She glanced down to Will when Nobody distanced himself further. "Are you okay?"

With Dante there to defend him, Will felt brave enough to stand up at last. "Yes. He didn't hurt me," he added, feeling obliged to be honest before she unnecessarily attacked the warder.

Dante hid Will behind her back. "This is just a little boy who does not belong here. Harm him, and I will kill you before you can so much as sneeze. Do not test me."

Will couldn't believe how aggressive she sounded. She was deadly serious. And the warder was as aware of this as Will. A glimmer of apprehension crossed his face that Will wouldn't have imagined ever seeing in someone so big and scary.

"You wouldn't care so much about just any little boy, Dante Simms," the warder said. "And neither would your sisters. Or your aunt. Or your brother."

The witch's fingers clasped tighter around Will's arm, but she raised her chin to show she would not be thrown by the mention of her brother. "Don't go near Will again," she said, and she walked Will along with her, keeping her wand poised on Nobody. When they could no longer see him, she snatched it back up into her sleeve and released a frustrated breath. "The nerve of him." She combed her fingers through her hair, unintentionally pulling most of it free from its clip. "Are you sure you're okay?" she asked, stopping to pat at Will's jacket like a worried mother. "He didn't hurt you?"

"I'm fine," he said, and she stroked the back of his head.

"I'm so sorry we left you all alone like that. Blue was in a bit of a state."

"What's wrong with him?"

Dante thought before answering. "Nothing for you to worry about."

"He hates me, doesn't he? Because he thinks I'm the Maker, even though I'm not. Why does he hate the Maker so much? I thought the Maker made him. How could he hate the person who made him?"

"Do remind me. What were you saying earlier about going home to your parents? You'd rather drown?"

"But I don't hate them. Why does Blue hate him, Dante?" he nagged.

"He's scared, that's all. Like I said, it's nothing for you to worry about."

"But he thinks it's me."

"And it might just be you, William, so you mustn't persist!" She curled her arm over Will's shoulders and made a shushing noise at him, like it was his fault she'd raised her voice. "You must keep quiet about this. We can't let anyone find out that you might be who you might be. I may have put that warder off coming after you, but the neethers won't be put off, not for anything."

Will stiffened under her arm, cold with terror again.

"They want you dead. So, from now on, let's just keep quiet about who or what you may or may not be, okay? Let everyone think you're a witch. That's likely the only thing that stopped that warder from tearing your heart right out of you."

Staring up at Dante, Will shuddered.

"Here," she said, releasing him. She scrabbled a hand through the twigs and leaves on the grassy ground between the trees, singled out one of the many dry, brittle sticks littered there, and tapped it with her wand. The stick grew longer and wider, twisting around itself like a piece of rope. It stopped at about a foot long, with a sharp crook in its tip. After taking a moment to admire her creation, she handed the stick to Will. "Keep this with you. If anyone you don't know comes along, you get that out."

Will clutched both ends, confidence rushing back. "Does it do magic?"

"No. It's not real. But I put a little hex on it for you. If needs be, you point it at someone and say, 'Back off', and voilà." She clicked her fingers.

"Vwa what?"

"Give it a try."

Deciding against pointing it at Dante in case it should do anything to hurt her, Will aimed the stick at the closest tree and said, in a blank tone as though reading from a script, "Back off and vwa." A heart-stopping clap rapped his eardrums. Birds darted from the trees all around them, squawking and flapping in outrage. He spun around, expecting to see someone standing behind him with a smoking gun in hand.

Dante laughed at him. "That'll be enough to convince people you're a witch if push comes to shove." Her face changed, amusement fading. "I hope that hasn't drawn any attention our way."

Will twiddled the coiled stick, excited at the thought of a cool new toy to entertain his friends with. "Can I keep this?"

"Yes, of course," she said, inspecting his jacket. Seeing none of its pockets were large enough to hold the fake wand, she poked the stick with her own. It shrivelled a little and she snapped part of it off. A greenish puff of air left it as she handed the larger end back to Will. "I can't believe I left you alone with a warder and you're still in one piece." She gripped his cheek between her finger and thumb in an affectionate squeeze. "Luck was most certainly on our side this time." She slipped her wand away and indicated for him to walk with her. "But we can't let it happen again."

"What is a warder?" Will asked, rubbing his cheek. "Do you think they'd help us?" He took off his trainer to shake out a sharp piece of twig that had somehow got in and wiggled its way down to the toe. Hopping, he pulled it back on. "He said they look out for troublemakers."

"Ha. That's rich, coming from him. As far as the warders and a lot of other idiots in Wynne are concerned, wots should never have been brought into being in the first place."

Will ached with pity for his friends. "Why?"

Dante flashed a reassuring smile at him over her shoulder. "They consider wots an anomaly. Immortality is unnatural. Everything's supposed to die eventually. Even neethers die of old age after a mere hundred years."

"A hundred years," Will repeated in wonder.

"And witches only live to around a hundred and seventy."

"A hundred and seventy?"

She grinned again. "You're impressed by that age, even though you've spent all day long in the company of wots, the youngest of which being two hundred. You're a funny little thing, Will." The seriousness came back to her face again and she came to such a dramatically abrupt halt Will panicked that she'd seen something he hadn't lying ahead, something dangerous, something terrifying.

The up and down hiss of whispering voices permeated the sudden silence. He held onto Dante's arm.

The whispering stopped, and she slapped herself on the forehead.

"What's wrong? What was that?"

"Rats! I forgot to pick up my order for Molina. She'll be furious with me. She wanted those items the minute they came in, without fail." She chewed on a thumbnail, eyebrows contorting in anguish while she thought. "I'll have to go get them. I won't be two jiffies."

Will refused to let go of her arm. He hung on to the witch like his life depended on it, because his life probably did depend on it. "Wait. Stop. You're going away? Why? You can't."

"I know, I'm sorry, but I made a promise to my sister. I completely forgot about it, with everything that's been going on. I won't be long. I just need to pop straight in and straight out. I'll be two minutes."

"What about me?"

"I'd take you with me if I could, but the place only admits witches. I'd have them deliver, but last time, they were two days late and sent the wrong order. It's atrocious service, I must say. The people there are idiots."

Will gaped at her, trying to find the words to convey how angry he was with her, but got nothing. Had she not just been bleating on about how lucky he was to be alive after his encounter with the warder? And yet she was going to leave him, for something as trivial as picking up a package for her sister? What package could possibly be that important?

"Wait right here. Right by this tree. Don't move. You'll be safe. I'll be right back, okay?"

"What if someone comes?"

She put a finger over her lips and shushed him. "Stay quiet. Stay here."

Will threw her arm at her rather than letting it go as she melted into a blast of light drawn by her wand. He checked no one was behind him. Alone in the middle of nowhere, friendless, with nothing but a noisy stick to protect him - why didn't she just go ahead and kill him before she left, get it over with?

The fact she'd abandoned him would have been hurtful enough, but what hurt like a knife to the heart was that Blue had turned his back on him too. How could the wot do that to him? Will had saved Blue's life. They were supposed to be friends. It didn't seem normal that anyone would turn so quickly against a friend over a false accusation, and especially not someone as gentle-natured as Blue. All Will could think was that the Maker must be someone truly, irredeemably evil.

Seconds ticked by and turned to minutes - more than the two minutes promised. His mind shifted into overdrive, and he began to wonder if he'd been led into a trap. What if that witch hadn't been Dante at all? What if it had been the fake Dante who had swooped in and 'rescued' him from a good warder and left him here to be easily found by the neethers? He shuffled, restless. If that were the case, he couldn't stay here. He had to move. He had to hide.

A familiar voice startled him from behind: "Now then, young man."

"Mrs Hoo. What are you doing here?"

The old witch waddled closer, massaging her side like she had a stitch, bony elbow stuck out at a peculiar angle. Her flamingo pink cardigan stuck out like a sore thumb in the midst of the subtle greens and browns of nature that surrounded her. The scarlet shawl on her head hid her wild silver hair from view and clashed horribly with the rest of her outfit. "Oh, please, love," she said, out of breath. "I never married."

"But what are you doing here?"

"I needed a quick word with you on your own."

"Why?" The last time they'd met she stated clearly that she wanted nothing to do with Will or his problems. People around here were too quick to change their minds about things. It was hard to keep up.

The not so friendly look on the witch's face made Will wonder if she too thought he was the Maker.

"Can you remind me, please," she said, "where we left our last conversation? I'm getting on a bit now, young one, and your memory betters mine." She waited patiently for Will to think.

He wasn't sure what she wanted to hear. "You said the sun would burn out and everything would end," he said uncertainly, because it was the last thing he remembered her saying aside from rushing him off.

"Beg your pardon?"

"That's what you said."

She let go of her side. "And what was my reason for saying this?"

Will wanted to say, *How the bloody hell am I supposed to know?* But Foosay was an adult, and he couldn't talk to her that way. So, he forced a cold little smile and muttered, "I don't know."

The old lady picked up the bottom of her frilly skirt and bent her knees to sit on the stubbly grass.

Will followed her example and sat opposite her, cross-legged.

"What else did we talk about?" she asked. "Scilla Simms, wasn't it?"

"Not really. You just said she was the one who'd found out about the secrets to living forever and not you. Remember now?"

"What about the other thing? The private matter we talked about. Privately. You know what I'm talking about?"

Will shook his head, hair flopping annoyingly over his forehead. Damn Dante and her gel-hating spells. "Not really," he said. "Sorry."

"The thing we discussed that I asked you not to tell anybody about."

He racked his brains for the right answer but could not remember her ever having said anything of the sort. Maybe Foosay really was senile, like Blue had said earlier. "You didn't tell me not to tell anybody anything."

"Is that so?" Foosay's face and posture changed then, darkened, stiffened, and she stared at him with such intensity he was taken aback by it. "We all know who you are now, *William*."

A whoop of laughter from Will's left made him jump. Dyelann and Maik skipped through the woodland in Will's direction, fighting with their enchanted blades, stabbing and slashing viciously at one another.

When Will looked back to Foosay, she had gone.

Dyelann noticed him and stopped, only to receive a wallop from the handle of Maik's dagger after Maik got carried away with the attacking. Dyelann cuffed him hard around the ear in retaliation and continued to make his way to Will, leaving a sheepish Maik rubbing unhappily at the side of his head and watching him go. "How did you get out here, kidlet?"

Still shaken by Foosay's parting words, Will couldn't bring himself to speak at first. He peered around the wot's legs for any sign of the witch.

"What are you doing down there?" Dyelann helped Will to his feet.

"Nothing," Will said, glad to see a face he could trust. "I'm just waiting for Dante. I mean, I think it was Dante." He swallowed. "I'm scared a bit." The confession embarrassed him, but he desperately needed someone to tell him everything would be okay.

"You're not the only one. We wots are a bit useless without our gems, no matter how many daggers and swords we wield." Dyelann pulled a face at something behind Will, prompting him to check what was wrong. It appeared that Maik had dropped his dagger point-down through his foot and Henry was stooping to pull it out. "Come to think of it, the more daggers and swords we wield the more useless we are."

"You don't think I'm the Maker, do you, Dyelann?"

"I don't believe in the Maker, Will," Dyelann said, and Will immediately felt better. "But," he said, and Will cringed again, "I do think Karson's right about one thing. It can't be a coincidence that you ended up here when you did."

Someone was coming at them, fast, from a distance. It was Foyer. He sprinted, gasping each breath, not from exertion but panic.

"It's Adrian," Foyer panted, in response to the questioning faces. "I found him." He breathed hard like he had to force the next words out. "He's dead."

Chapter Eleven: The Reaper

On hearing the news of Adrian's death, Henry fainted. He dropped so abruptly that the others heard the thud before they realised what had happened. Even when they did realise, none of them went to his aid.

Maik watched Foyer carefully, as if waiting for him to finish his cruel joke. "Dead? You mean… He's actually dead?"

The knowledge of their loss surrounded the wots in a thick cloud of grief that suffocated Will. He dreaded to think how Blue would take the news.

Lillian joined them in a rush, out of breath, smile for once absent from her face. "I'm so sorry," she said, holding her side. "But we're going to have to push on if the rest of you aren't to suffer the same fate."

Foyer and Maik exchanged wary glances.

"You got quite far ahead of us, Will," Dyelann said. "Did you and Dante catch up to Blue?"

"Yes."

"Why didn't you stay with him?"

"He's really mad with me," Will said shakily.

Foyer, who had calmed down some since he'd stopped running, said, "Of course he's not mad with you. Where's Dante?"

"She went off to pick something up for her sister. I'm glad you guys are here. I thought the bad guys were going to get me while I was on my own."

"That's not going to happen." Foyer's demeanour darkened. "Because I'm not going to let anyone else die. We're going to get Blue and we're going to stick together. I want you all where I can keep an eye on you," he told the wots before sitting Henry up.

"How far ahead is Blue?" Lillian asked Will.

"Quite far. He was upset. I don't think he'd be happy to see me. Maybe I shouldn't go with you."

"Don't be soft, kidlet," Dyelann said. "We're not going to leave you behind just because Blue's spitting his dummy out. You think he's going to be happy to see me? Course not. But you don't see me backing off. Because as much as he hates me, and the feeling's mutual, the upshot of it is, Will, is that Blue's my baby brother. And once it gets through his thick head that you're not the Maker, he'll see what an idiot he is and be begging your forgiveness for being such a child. And that's all he is, a child. More so than you, even."

Somewhat comforted if not baffled by Dyelann's words, Will forced a smile.

"And I know you're his friend," Dyelann went on, quieter. "And we both want to see nothing bad happens to him. Don't we?"

Will nodded.

"So, we stick together."

Foyer gaped in astonishment. "I think that's the most decent thing I have ever heard come out of your mouth, Dyelann."

"Piffle." Dyelann grabbed Will roughly by the shoulders. "Come on. Let's go batter some sense into the idiot."

"Dante told me to wait here," Will said to Foyer, while Dyelann tried to push him along.

"We should wait for her, then. I wouldn't want her to worry about you."

"Oh, no," Dyelann said, letting go of Will so he could mock Foyer. "We wouldn't want that."

Henry groaned and came back to life, limp in Foyer's arms. "What happened? Is it all over yet?"

"Afraid not," Foyer said.

"Oh." Henry sat forward. "I feel sick."

"Just sit and catch your breath. We're waiting for Dante. Then we're going on after Blue."

Henry covered his mouth. "Oh, I feel sick."

"Don't be such a pansy, you pansy," Dyelann said, in a manner intended to make him smile rather than to insult him.

"It'll be okay," Foyer said, unconvincingly.

"You think so?" Dyelann snapped. "Really? We're going to have to face the witch who's already proven she can overpower the lot of us without so much as breaking stride, and even if by some fluke we do manage to outwit her long enough to get our gems back, we'll still have to find some way to keep her from just snatching them straight back again. How exactly do you think we're going to do that, Mr Eternal Optimist? Huh? How?"

A momentary surge of heat burned in Will's head. A flash of frustration coursed in his blood, spikes under his skin, prickling and painful, just for a second making him want to rip himself in two. "The witch's power is nothing on mine," he said harshly under his breath.

Where had that come from? He peered over his shoulder. There was nobody there.

"Sorry, Will, what was that?" Foyer asked.

Will concentrated on Lillian, who had begun to chatter on.

"Thinking negatively is a waste of energy," she was telling them, helping Foyer to lift Henry back up. "You'll do the best you can and that's all you can do. We will prevail. You know why? Because there are ten of us, and only one of her."

"Ten, wow," Dyelann said. "And how many neethers? How many wenns on her side? Even the warders would be against us if they had half a mind to intervene."

"But you mustn't think that way," Lillian insisted. "You'll only hinder us with that attitude."

"And what about Adrian? How much positive thinking will bring him back to us?"

The mention of their friend made Foyer, Maik, and Henry clam up in hopeless despair. Even Lillian was at a loss for words. Forlorn silence fell upon the group. It was broken a long minute later by Dante's return.

"Hey, guys," she said, leaving her portal with a bounce in her step. "What's up? I got Molina's order to her." She zipped up the bright gap in the air behind her. "Everything's okay now." She noticed the glumness on everyone's faces. "What's happened?"

Dyelann answered, somewhat bluntly. "Adrian turned up dead. We were just waiting for you because we wouldn't want you to worry about the boy," he said, imitating Foyer.

It took her a few seconds to find her words. "Oh no... I'm so sorry. Poor Blue's going to be devastated."

"Poor Blue, yes, good grief." Dyelann scoffed angrily and patted Maik on the back in some sort of meagre attempt to console him. "Don't pay any thought to Adrian. He's only the one who died."

Foyer put a hand over his face. "It was awful. I had to pull his body out of the beck along Garrott's hedgerow. He must have been in the water since he went missing." The memory turned Foyer white. "I just can't understand why she only killed Blue and Adrian. She could have killed all of us, but she didn't. Just those two. It makes no sense."

Lillian put a hand to her heart, her dagger pointed down. "Blue's dead?" she asked in a small voice. "When did this happen? Did I miss something?" She frowned. "Aren't we following him right now?"

Replying to Lillian but still looking at Foyer, Dante said, "The witch murdered him yesterday morning. Will brought him back to life." She nodded at Foyer. "That's a very good point though, Foyer. Why did she only kill Blue and Adrian?" She gestured to Henry. "You. The witch took your gem first. How did she do it?"

Henry cowed back. "I didn't see anything. It all happened in a beat. I just woke up and it was gone."

"Sounds like the work of a wenn," Foyer said. "A wenn got Popset too, accompanied by a witch that looked like Gart. Then the witch killed Blue, looking like Foosay. Then she killed Adrian."

Dante's fingers pressed together. "Perhaps once she'd got the first two gems, her power grew enough to allow her to no longer require the wenn's help?"

"Maybe so, but then why didn't she kill Maik? Why didn't she kill Dyelann, or me? She could have done, easily."

"You're right," Dante said. "I was with Dyelann when she took his. She could have killed the pair of us if she'd wanted to."

Dyelann let out a laugh. "Speak for yourself."

Lillian stepped in the middle of the group. "This is all very enlightening, but can we not walk and talk? Come on. We must catch up with Blue before he reaches the witch, and we're just standing here like we've got all day. What is it with you lot?"

"Same when she took mine," Foyer said to Dante, as if Lillian had said nothing. "You were there, Will. You know. We were completely at her mercy."

They were looking at Will, expecting him to speak.

"Yeah," he said. "We were just knocked over on the floor. There was no one even there."

"Come on, you people!" Lillian shouted, loud enough to make Henry jump, and she clanked her blades together. "Didn't you hear me? We have to get to Blue. Now."

Foyer indicated for the group to do as Lillian asked, and they began to move. Lillian drove them on from behind like a sheepdog directing its flock.

"The fact this witch didn't kill anyone but Blue and Adrian definitely implies that she killed them for a reason," Dante said.

Lillian groaned at them. "Obviously, she killed them for a reason. It's because their lifelines to their gems are the strongest, that's why. And you're getting the irony that they were both drowned, right?" She groaned even louder when they turned around to demand an explanation with their expressions alone. "The witch needed those two to die because the water gems are the ones most connected to their wots. Physically connected, I mean. It physically hurts them to be parted."

Dyelann swung back. "I beg your pardon?" The way he glared at Lillian then suggested she had deeply offended him.

"I didn't make the rules," she said. "It's just how it is. That's why the blue gem is the only one actually doing anything to stop what's happening to it."

Clearly having a hard time maintaining his cool composure through his aggravation, Dyelann sucked in a long breath. "You're saying Blue's gem is smarter than mine? Blue's gem is not smarter than mine."

"Give me strength," Lillian whispered, glancing to the heavens. "Of course I'm not saying that. Your gems are all different. Water is energy. Water is life. No life can be sustained without it, therefore, strong life energy." She flicked her pigtails.

It made sense to Will then. If Blue had stayed dead, the spell would have taken place by now. The wots would all be dead already.

"So, do you see now?" Lillian went on. "The very fact that Blue is alive keeps the lifeline alive between him and his gem, which keeps the gem fighting against the witch's spell, which keeps the spell from working, which keeps the rest of you alive." She tapped her dagger against her leg. "Blue's the only thing standing between the witch and her eternal life. You realise she won't hesitate to kill him if she gets the chance? Yes? So why are we still standing here? I did not go to all this trouble just to lose now!" Her face hardened and she shoved her way past Dyelann. "Get a move on!"

Henry scuttled after her, horrified.

With his usual expression of smugness, Dyelann said to Will, "There's an aneurysm waiting to happen. Maybe we'll get to see it if we're lucky."

"Yeah," Will said, and laughed to humour him. After Dyelann and Maik strode on ahead, he asked Dante, "What's an amorism?"

"A what?" Not waiting for an answer, she hurried him along. "Lillian's right. We have to get to Blue. I don't know what I was thinking of, letting him go off on his own like that. When I realised you weren't with us, I knew I had to get back to you. And Blue wasn't exactly kind with his phrasing if you know what I mean. I thought it was just his strop speaking, but now that I think about it, what if there was more to it than that? What if he knows about Adrian?" She lowered her voice. "What if he's given up?"

"Given up?" Will repeated. He gazed solemnly up at the witch before stopping dead and grabbing her sleeve. "We can't let him die. I'm sorry I upset him. I didn't mean to."

"I know."

"How can I get him to forgive me?" He interrupted her before she could reassure him. "I don't want to be this Maker person. I don't even like him, not if Blue doesn't. It's not me."

"Will, I know." She stroked his arm.

"I said I was sorry," he said pathetically. Sorry had been the answer to all his problems previous. There was nothing that sorry couldn't fix. A few years ago, he spilt a bottle of blackcurrant juice over his mother's brand-new cream carpet. Expecting to be grounded for life, he'd been terrified to own up, but one heartfelt apology later all was right with the world again. Even when he had played football in the house after being specifically told not to, resulting in the smashing of his father's favourite ship in a bottle, a simple sorry had gained forgiveness and brought peace back to his family. It made no sense to Will that his apologies weren't working now. Why wasn't Blue there to tell him everything was all right?

"You can't be sorry for something you haven't done," Dante said.

"But I am."

Dante glanced over to the others, who were already well ahead of them. "I need to ask you something," she said. "Why did you say what you said to Karson?"

"What did I say?"

"When he said that rhyme to you, you rhymed back to him," she reminded him gently. "Where did that come from?"

"I don't know," he said, feeling strangely defensive. "I told you, it wasn't me. It just came out."

Dante leaned closer. "Karson knew you would say it back. I know you don't want to be the Maker, but I don't think you have much choice in the matter. People are who they are, and we can't be anything else. I'm a witch. Blue's a wot. You're a boy who may just be the boy these wots have been waiting for."

A sudden chill came over Will. "Blue wasn't waiting for him."

"What was it Karson said to you?" She narrowed her eyes, which were locked on his. "Maybe we can find him in you, Will. How did it go again? I am a wot, my son. I come from your heart. Your will be done."

The words were on his lips before he could hold them back. "I am your wishing will," he said, brow buckling in sheer misery at his inability to control himself. "You come from my heart, wish for me still."

Dante leaned even closer; so close that Will could see his own reflection in the shine of her dark iris. "Who said that?"

"I don't know," Will said.

"It was I." Will continued to speak after he thought he had stopped, and his hands flew to his mouth.

"There's someone inside you."

"Get him out!" Will's arms flapped in panic, and Dante pinned them to his sides. The tightness of her grip frightened him.

"Speak to me. Who are you?"

"You know who I am."

Will shouted, "Someone's talking through my mouth!"

"You're the Maker. What are you doing in Will?"

The alarm faded from Will's face as the other being took control. "The boy's a vessel," he said, leaving Will powerless to speak or move. It felt like he was dreaming of being someone else. Someone much stronger and wiser than himself.

"What do you want? Are you here to help the wots?"

The imposter shook Will's head, slowly, once.

"The wots are your creation. You're just going to let them die for the benefit of some selfish witch?" Dante backed away. "If you aren't here to help, why are you here?"

"The wots possess borrowed power. The sources demand it back."

"What are you saying?"

"The energy I summoned all those years ago must be returned. I'm here to right a wrong."

Another surge of panic helped Will find the strength to recover his own voice. "No!" he shouted. "You can't. I'm not going to let you." Doing his best to emulate Dyelann's innate confidence, he squared his shoulders and took a deep, shaky breath. "So there."

"Get out of him," Dante said in the same chillingly severe tone she'd used to threaten the warder.

There was a long silence. They looked to each other anxiously and waited.

"Has he gone?" Dante asked.

The ground disappeared from under Will's feet. His fingers flexed viciously at the air like it was something solid that they could grip on to and drag closer.

"*My will shall be done!*" the Maker shouted, with such extreme fury that Will's entire nervous system jolted.

He fell back down to earth, legs crumpled under him. His spine throbbed as he picked himself back up, and he swayed, momentarily dazed. "I think he's gone now," he said, blinking nervously.

"I don't." Dante pulled her wand from her sleeve.

Will's eyes followed it. Surely Dante wasn't planning on using that thing on him?

She whipped it up, but Will's hand swiped faster and sent the wand flying from her grasp and clattering against a tree.

"You can't beat me, witch."

Will seethed over the unwelcome words escaping his lips. "What about me? You can't do anything to me."

"Will," Dante cautioned. "Don't."

"I won't let you hurt anyone."

"Foolish boy," the Maker said, somehow making Will fear the cadence of his own voice. "You were part of this plan by my wish. You do not have the option of allowing or disallowing anything I wish to do."

Unsure where to look when addressing himself, Will settled on a patch of space to stare at. "Have you been in me since I got here?" he asked. "Was it you who helped me bring Blue back to life? Why would you do that if you're the baddie?"

"One mistake." The Maker snarled. "There'll be no more."

Dante edged closer to her wand.

Intense heat scorched the palms of Will's hands as the Maker conjured an invisible, shimmering mass of red-hot bubbling gas between them. When it started to ripple and spark with flames, he lifted it, held it high over his head and aimed in Dante's direction.

An undeniable glint of fear passed through her eyes that shocked Will. He pulled against the Maker, battling to stop his own traitorous arms from throwing this bizarre creation, this ball of wet, solid heat, full force at her. A tearing sensation blazed through his tendons as the Maker fought back, but Will refused to give in.

The fireball blew into the ground by the witch's feet, leaving a singed black hole smoking in its wake.

Dante stared at Will with her mouth open.

Gasping, Will checked his hands, expecting them to be burned. They were fine. "I said I wouldn't let you," he said bravely.

Baffled by Will's ability to overpower him, the Maker yelled out with frustration, glaring madly at the metre deep hole in the ground that should have been in Dante.

Will rushed to Dante's wand and handed it to her. She snatched it from him, nearly taking his fingers with it.

"What am I supposed to do now, Dante? This is all your fault. You woke him up or something."

Dante held her wand close. "I'm sorry. I didn't know. He must have been waiting for a reason. There must be something he's waiting for, something that has to happen before he makes his move."

"You're not wrong," the Maker said, a sinister satisfaction in the words.

"Shut up." Will pointed at himself. "He thinks he has more power than you, you know," he told Dante in a tell-tale tone.

"He's not wrong either." Dante sounded worried. "Will, you mustn't anger him. He could blow you up from the inside or anything."

"I knew it. I knew he must be evil."

"After what that poor boy went through, it's no wonder he went a bit mad."

The Maker's anger flared right through Will. "Don't pity me."

"Don't worry," Will said, "I don't."

"I do," Dante admitted. Finally, she allowed herself to stop staring so intently. "I feel sorry for him. I always have. Having his entire family murdered right in front of him, not being able to get them back no matter what he did. That boy created those wots with sheer want of a wish. And the only wish he ever had never came true. I think that's really sad."

Determined not to feel any sympathy for the one invading his body, Will reminded himself that the Maker was a baddie and deserved it. But Dante was right. It was hard not to feel sorry for anyone who'd been through something so horrible. The more he thought about it, the sorrier he felt. "Why didn't it come true?" he asked.

"People can't come back from the dead."

"Blue did," he reminded her.

"That's true. That's true, you saved him."

"Maybe I could bring Adrian back too."

Dante blinked, expressionless. "I don't believe it."

Will turned around to see what she couldn't believe. "What? What is it?"

"I just can't believe we didn't think of this earlier. Come on. Let's find Adrian."

Will grinned. "You know what else I thought of?" he asked excitedly, pleased that his idea had been embraced with such enthusiasm. "What if we make a wish to Karson that all the wots had their gems back? Then they could all go back to normal."

"Oh, Will." Her gait slowed. "That's a lovely thought. But I'm afraid it's just not possible." She quickened pace, leaving Will lagging behind and somewhat flummoxed.

"Why not?" He tried to run but tripped over the stray branch of a bramble bush instead. "Ow," he said, muffled on account of his face being in the grass. The first thing he saw when he lifted his head was a pair of shoes, one purple, one blue, both impossibly tiny. He poked one inquisitively and propped himself up on his elbows to have a quick look for their owner.

Dante stopped and swung back, hair spinning around her head. "Get up. What are you doing? We're in a hurry."

The shoes were only the size of Will's fingertips. He lifted them up to show Dante.

"Wenn shoes," she said. "So?"

"Maybe there's one around here somewhere."

"Most probably. They're like rats; you're never too far away from one."

Will peered into the bramble bush. "Hello? Is anybody there?"

His volume put Dante on edge, and she swooped to haul him onto his feet. "Shh. Don't draw attention."

A sleepy voice came from behind them. "Who's shouting?"

They both whipped around in time to see a wenn emerge from a patch of long grass, where she'd obviously been napping. Her silver hair was stuck up and frizzy on one side. Rubbing her eyes with her tiny hands, she stepped clumsily forwards, and then gazed up at them like she was confused.

"This is Eve's friend Orchid," Dante informed Will.

"I'm not Eve's friend Orchid. Not anymore."

"You've changed your name?"

"Eve is no longer welcome to my friendship. I'll have nothing to do with her. Not since I found out what she's been up to. She's poison. We haven't spoken in weeks."

Dante glanced at Will, then back to the wenn, who was even tinier than Eve and Reese. "Why?" she asked cautiously. "What's she done to upset you?"

"She's in league with some witch. Don't get me wrong, I don't have anything against you people. Except your size; I'm against that. But this particular witch. This witch is evil." Orchid was fully awake now and pacing. She patted her head, trying to flatten her wayward locks and tease her fingers through the tangles.

"Maybe that's the one we're looking for," Will said. "Who's the witch, please?"

"Eve wouldn't tell me her name. It was all 'my lady' this and 'my lady' that. Lady my foot. But she let it slip she was going to help this witch steal gems from the wots." Orchid held up her hands and quickly added, "Now, I don't particularly like wots any more than I like any of you big people. And I don't particularly have a problem with stealing. Finders, keepers, is what I was raised to believe. But the wots' gems? No. Absolutely not. Gems belong to the wots and no one else. Taking them would be like some other being taking my wings from me, my songs. Taking them would be like stealing brewers from witches, horns from unicorns, bods from wickers. It's backwards, is what it is, it's backwards and twisted." Her pitch rose higher. "And I told her so! And you know what she said? She said she'd taken a brew stick from a witch before, and it wasn't the end of the world. She didn't see the wrong in taking the gems if it meant she would live forever. And you know what else she said?" Her voice continued to lift higher the more agitated she became. "She said if I said anything to anyone, she *would* take my wings. Tear them right from my back, she said."

"But you're telling *us*," Will pointed out. "Aren't you scared?"

"She wouldn't dare pick a fight with me," she said, her tone normal again. "Empty threat."

"Orchid," Dante said, "do you know which witch she took the brew stick from?"

"You've probably already guessed. It was your brother. She did it for the witch she's been working with. Dante, Eve has been in alliance with this witch for eleven years. Eleven years."

Clenching her jaw, Dante stared at the branches above as if in private prayer. "To think of her lying to our faces. The brass nerve of her."

The wenn sat down on a root. "I'm sorry about your brother. I mean that."

"So am I," the Maker said, and despite his sincerity, Will bristled with irritation at the intruder using his voice without permission.

"I thought you were meant to be a baddie," he said indignantly. "Make your mind up."

Orchid let out an eerie little warble that could have passed for a laugh. "Does the boy speak to himself often?"

"Only in the last few minutes," Dante said. "We've just found out the Maker is inside him."

The wenn gawked at Will, intrigued. "How did he get there? I thought he died twelve years ago."

"What are you talking about? The Maker died over a thousand years ago."

"Not exactly. He was immortal."

"How could he be immortal if he died?" Will asked, feeling quite clever for knowing what immortal meant.

Dante shook her head in protest. "We'd have known if he'd been alive twelve years ago. The Maker was a legend. Legends aren't legends if they're still alive. They're long dead. That's what makes them legends. Isn't that right…?" She struggled to find a suitable word for addressing the Maker. "Maker?" she finished awkwardly. "See? He's so much of a legend I don't even know his name."

"I heard that he disappeared twelve years ago," Orchid said again.

"Explain," Dante ordered, glaring at Will.

Alarmed by her coldness, Will said, "I don't know!"

"No, William, I was talking to the Maker."

The Maker's grin spread easily on Will's lips. "A rumour began twelve years ago that I'd crossed over," he said. "A rumour brought into life by the very witch you seek. She's a smart one. She overlooked nothing. She sparked other rumours too, the moment she began to put her intricate plan into motion. Rumours all intended to cover her back."

"Who is this witch?" Dante asked.

"I have no idea," the Maker replied, still grinning.

"How can you not know that? You know everything else. And what about you, anyway? Where have you come from? What are you doing in Will? When did you die?"

"I never died."

Will squeezed his chest. "Are you alive in there?"

The Maker took back control and relaxed his grip. "How are you doing this?" he growled, no longer smiling.

"Of course you died," Dante said. "You are dead."

"I live on with the lives I created. I shall not die until they demise."

"Oh, I see. Metaphors. You're still dead though. No getting around that."

"Don't you hear what he's saying?" Will shouted. "He wants to kill Blue and Foyer and the others. He wants to kill them!"

Dante beckoned for Will to walk with her, completely neglecting to say her farewells to Orchid. Will kept an eye on the wenn to see if she would follow, but she simply nestled back down in the long grass, unfazed by their departure.

"Let's focus on doing something positive for now," Dante said, curling an arm around Will. She tapped herself on the forehead. "Gah. I'm starting to sound like Lillian. Anyway, let's go and find Adrian. Let's have you bring him back to life, and then we'll have double the gems fighting the witch. Then we'll all find Blue."

Will was mid-nod when Dante lurched off course through a dense network of spindly trees to their left, almost wringing his neck in the process. "How do you know where he is?" he asked, strangled.

"I don't. I'm guessing."

Strange, Will thought, that she would guess such a specific route.

"This is the way the others would have come from No-go Ebb, you see," she explained, pushing some branches aside to pass through. One twanged back and smacked Will in the face. "The beck Foyer found him in runs this way. Do you think you'll really be able to bring him back to life? It's amazing that you did that, you know, amazing. How did you do it? Do you need ingredients?"

Rubbing his branch-assaulted nose, eyes watering, Will mumbled, "I just did what they taught us at school. You punch where their heart is and breathe into their mouth until they wake up."

"Are you telling me you brought Blue back to life using cardiopulmonary resuscitation?" Her cynical tone suggested she had envisaged Will using a much more impressive method to resurrect the dead and was now sorely disillusioned. "So, were you there when it happened?"

"Well, yeah. I'm the one who did it."

"I meant were you there when he drowned?" Dante said, a little offhandedly. "He couldn't have been in the water for very long before you got there, could he? I'm sorry, Will, but I don't think there's anything you can do for poor Adrian after all."

Every drop of the hope and pride that Will had built up at the thought of being able to save the day splashed out of him and left him torn and empty. "But…"

"What you did only works on people who have stopped breathing for a short while, not on people who have been dead for more than a day."

"But… It worked on…" Will gave up.

The Maker took this as an invitation. "Blue was dead. Well and truly. As a dodo."

"I suppose we'll see, won't we, if we can just find Adrian." Dante rummaged through some foliage with one foot while balancing awkwardly on some scattered rocks with the other. "I can't understand this. There's the beck, right there. Foyer said he pulled him out, but I can't see him anywhere. I wish Dyelann was with us. Eyes like a horse, that one."

"I thought it was eyes like a hawk," Will said, trying to be helpful. "Can't you use your magic to find him?"

"Do you see any clay powder around here? A compass? Pigeons? Because that's what we'd need for a locator brew, which is what we'd need for a spell. And even if we made the potion, what do I have that belongs to Adrian? Come on, Will, use your head."

"Right there." Will pointed at a pair of wood pigeons perched together on a branch directly above them, whose gentle cooing ceased abruptly on realising they'd been spotted. "Anyway, why can't you get all that stuff the same way you got that big bowl of food earlier?"

"That food was already prepared and put away for when I was ready for it." She gave him a funny look. "What, did you think I'd produced it from thin air? Witches can't do that. We have to go to a supplier for ingredients, which normally have to be ordered in advance. Spells really should be thought out carefully, not on a whim. In an emergency, you'd have to go to the black market or try using what you've got in the back of the kitchen cupboards. There's nothing in the back of mine but dust bunnies, I'm afraid to say."

Will strained to see further along the water's side. The sun emerged from behind a cloud and beamed a ray of light between the branches above, directly into his eyes. Averting his gaze, he noticed Dante's face. She was staring, stock still, at something Will had not yet seen, and the sense of danger sent his heart leaping over itself in a painful lurch.

"Stay very still," she whispered, and he fought the urge to throw himself closer to her.

"What's there?" he asked, hardly daring to speak.

Then he spotted it: Something under the cover of trees, between the broken branches and the knotted, narrow trunks. It was crouched forward, its haggard form nothing more than a skeleton draped with flaps of torn, rotted grey flesh.

Another dead body. Only, this one was much deader than Blue's dead body had been. This one was the frightening sort of dead.

Maybe it was Adrian. Maybe he'd been torn apart by hungry animals, and this was all that was left of him. Will didn't think he could give the kiss of life to that. How could he blow into a mouth that didn't even have any lips?

Then the skeleton leaned back.

Had he not been paralysed by fear, Will might have screamed and run at this point.

Anticipating such a reaction, Dante took the couple of steps needed to close the distance between them, prepared to catch him.

The skeleton turned its head over its shoulder to face them, revealing festering eyeballs, its sharp, decaying features locked in a permanent grin.

"Oh, it's okay," Dante said. "It's just a blood reaper." From her laid-back laugh and the casual flap of her hand, Will would have thought she'd been talking about candyfloss or rainbows rather than a creature with the word *blood* in its name. It certainly didn't inspire a feeling of security, being so close to the skinless creature – the skinless creature that seemed disturbingly fixated on him right now.

It was watching Will as if intrigued by his presence there.

"Oh, is that what it is, is it?"

"Don't worry, a blood reaper won't hurt you." Dante clicked her fingers in front of Will in attempt to break his eye contact with the skeleton, but he couldn't look away. "They only kill people who should have died already. Most people die when their time is up anyway. Any stragglers, though, and our friend here will track them down and see they get to where they're meant to go." Seeing his consternation, she asked, "Have you never heard of Death?"

"The one with the big black hood and the big stick with a knife on the end?"

"That's a scythe."

"Big stick with a scythe on the end, then. If he's good at tracking people down, do you think he could help us find the bad witch?" He jolted back with a start when the skeleton moved itself around further.

"No. They're not allowed to do that. Come on. We'd best be on our way."

"Can't you ask him if…?"

"There's no point in asking him anything. He can't talk."

"I *can* talk." The skeleton sprung to its spindly legs. A pair of faded grey trousers more raggedy than Blue's hung loosely from its hips.

"Now look what you've done," Dante said to Will through the side of her mouth. She stuck her chin in the air. "Oh, you can talk, can you? Prove it. Say: Peter Piper picked a peck of pickled pepper."

"Hilarious." The skeleton was not amused.

"Fine, you can talk. Just not with half as many words as the rest of us." She explained to Will in whisper: "No lips."

It made perfect sense to Will that this individual wouldn't be able to talk properly with no lips. What didn't make sense was that it could breathe with no lungs, move with no muscles, or be doing anything at all when it was so obviously dead.

"That's not very nice," he whispered back to Dante, in no way wishing for her to antagonise a creature that killed people for a living.

The reaper's drooping eyeballs flitted back to Will, making a squelching sound as they scraped against the sockets. "Thank you," it said. "Do you need any assistance?"

Will didn't know how to react to that. This undead thing, standing before them like an escapee from a nightmare, was actually offering to help him. How was anyone supposed to react to that?

The reaper bent its slip of a neck to the left, lifeless eyes gazing at Will.

Realising it was waiting for him to say something, he fell back on his good manners and asked, "Have you seen a dead wot around here, please?"

"That's not what you were going to ask him before," Dante reminded him.

"Oh, yeah." Will laughed, nerves preventing him from keeping a steady composure. "You find people all the time, right? Would you be able to find a witch for us?"

The skeleton lost its look of interest in Will then, distracted by the request. "Itch itch?"

Will peeked at Dante for a translation.

"Which witch?" she said, pursing and stretching her lips to their fullest extent over the words.

Will tried to convey an apology on Dante's behalf and his own gratitude in the same smile. "We don't know."

"Then I can't locate it, can I?"

"It's the one that killed the wot we're looking for," Will said. "The one that wants to live forever."

"None exist eternal."

"That's supposed to mean nobody lives forever," Dante said. "I told you he can't speak. Go on. Correct me. Can you speak? Can you say 'speak'?"

Despite the reaper's skull having no eyebrows or facial muscles, visible anger seethed across the bony face.

"Come on." Dante taunted the reaper. "Tell me to shut up. Button it. Zip it."

A piece of tight, brittle old skin that was stretched across two of the skeleton's ribs split apart and fluttered with the breeze. The reaper glared with disgust at Dante, clearly holding her responsible for the damage. "You're a rotten itch that desurze to rot in hell."

"Yet the only thing rotting around here is you. Come along, Will. You can't expect someone without a brain to be useful."

"I hath a grain."

"My apologies." Dante clamped her palms together and bowed at the reaper. "I didn't realise that shrivelled piece of meat flopping around inside that skull of yours constituted a brain."

"Yeah, ell it does." The reaper crossed its arms over its sternum. "And I did see your dead ott."

Will shook Dante's sleeve. "You saw Adrian? Where? Where is he?"

"Gone," the skeleton replied simply, raising its lanky arms to the sides, draping dead skin dangling like torn clothing.

"Gone where?" Dante asked.

"Just gone." Seeing its trousers were close to slipping down, it hooked its fingers into the belt loops and wrenched them back up. "Is this ott inortant?"

Will nodded. "Very. We want to bring him back to life."

"Oh, you do, do you?" The reaper rapped its fingertips against its jaw, bone clipping bone like stones knocking together. "Interesting. I'da thought innossinal. Though, considering who I's talking to, it's ossigle nothing's innossinal atter all."

Will went over the words in his head, scratched through them for any chance he might work them out, and then gave up. Smiling politely at the reaper, he asked Dante: "What's innosigal mean?"

"It doesn't mean anything," she said. "Impossible, is what he meant to say."

Clearly having lost patience with Dante and her mockery, the reaper gave all its attention to Will. "I saw a order not so long ago, child," it said. "I o'erheard it saying it had seen a thing o' great irrortance. I can't hell thinking that the thing he talked o' is you." Then he stared at Will again, waiting for him to acknowledge the information, and again Will strove fruitlessly to understand before eventually relying on Dante.

"What's an order?" he asked her in whisper.

"A warder," Dante said darkly, no longer joking. "Who was this warder speaking with when you overheard him?"

"Alley. The eye."

"An eye?" Will repeated.

"Not eye," Dante said. "Wye. Alley. This makes no sense. Why would a warder be discussing something that it thought to be of great importance with Alley, of all people?"

"Alley has the claret eater."

"She does?" Dante put a hand to her mouth. "I didn't know that. That's amazing."

While glad that the witch and the reaper had put their differences aside long enough to speak civilly to one another, Will was at a loss as to what they were talking about. "Huh?"

"He's saying Alley has the claret vita. There used to be three vitas: The claret, the indigo, and the olive. The claret was for warders, the indigo for wickers, and the olive for harvesters. They're a vile lot of wrongdoers, these beings, you see. A witch with good intentions created the vitas so they'd all have to answer to him and not go around causing trouble anymore."

"A good idea it oz too," the reaper said, nodding, neck bones scraping. "Did a good jog."

"Yeah, until he went and died." Dante said it as if the man only died to be difficult. "Then an honestly disturbing amount of people fell off their rockers trying to be the first to pull the vitas from his cold, dead hands. Fortunately, they all ended up with their own races and were destroyed straight away. At least, that's what I thought."

"Not the claret," the reaper said.

"Evidently. But this is good news for us. If Alley has their vita, we don't have to worry about the warders. They can do nothing without her permission, and she would never let them hurt you, Will."

"I hear the senior calling. I should go." The reaper gave a solemn nod. It gave Will a long look, then reverently bowed its head. "Good luck to you, child."

No one had ever bowed to Will before. His cheeks flushed and he grinned, feeling awkward but honoured.

In the same way that Cesar and Dante had done before it, the skeleton reached its fleshless fingers into an invisible hole and brought them back out holding a long, dark cloak that it swung over its shoulders. With one last respectful gaze at Will, it flicked the large hood over its skull, floated a foot above the ground and swept away, a shadow.

Will watched it go, awestruck. "Wow. He can fly. That's so cool."

"That wasn't flying, Will, that was levitating."

"Is he on his way to kill someone now?"

"Looks that way. Let's just be thankful he's going in the opposite direction."

"That black cape thing was cool, wasn't it? He was cool." His chest tightened with giddy excitement at the thought of telling his friends about this encounter. It was a shame they would never believe him. He wished he'd brought a camera.

"As cool as a corpse can be, I suppose."

A frantic voice travelled from afar, calling Dante's name. Unable to tell which direction it was coming from, Will spun a circle a couple of times, searching. He saw nothing. It called again, louder, and Dante cringed.

"Who is that?" Will asked.

Someone else shouted out, this one calling for Will.

"It's Foyer and Dyelann. Stupid wots. They know we're trying to keep a low profile. What do they think they're doing? Idiots." Dante marched forwards, apparently having no trouble figuring out where they were shouting from. "Come on, hurry up, or they'll have every creature in a ten-mile radius knowing where we are."

The shouts came louder the closer they got, and Dante's frustration grew. By the time she and Will spotted the wots through the weedy trees that covered this part of the woods, she looked about ready to physically attack the pair of them.

"Will you two shut up?" Though she controlled the volume of her voice, the rage within it boomed like a drum. "We have cold-blooded killers after us. *Shut. Up.*"

Foyer trotted to the witch with all the light of love in his eyes, arms out ready to wrap around her, but he came to an abrupt stop when he noticed her fury. He stood a short distance away, embarrassed, and slapped his arms down at his sides. "We were worried."

Dante strode to him and hugged him.

Dyelann gave a demonstrative eye-roll as he passed them. "I'm glad to see you're still in one piece anyway, kidlet," he said to Will. "Do me a big favour, though, and stick with me from now on. Okay?"

Will always appreciated Dyelann's company. Even in the few seconds they'd been back together he'd gained a warm sense of security inside, like the wot's very presence guaranteed their safety.

"You'll never guess what happened," a miserable voice said, and it was then that Will realised Dyelann and Foyer hadn't come alone. Orchid the wenn traipsed through the grass and fluttered her wings to help her over a fallen branch. Her feet were still bare. Two more wenns followed her, both with much darker skin, hair of copper, and wearing green striped tights beneath frilly silver dresses.

"What happened?" Will asked, for the others were acting like they had not heard Orchid speak.

"You'll never guess," she said again.

"Then tell us," Dante snapped.

"Somebody has killed a wye." Orchid dipped her head, and Will was unsure whether she was genuinely sombre about the news or being sarcastic.

Dante took a sharp breath. "What?"

"No, a wye."

"Why?" Will asked in a mournful whine. He hoped it wasn't Esko that had been killed.

"That's right." The wenn smiled gratefully at Will. "These two saw the whole thing. They've been keeping an eye out for any sign of what Eve might be up to for me. Isn't that right, girls?"

Her fellow wenns nodded obediently.

"Tell them what you saw," she ordered, but didn't give them chance to even open their mouths. "They told me the wye was standing there minding her own business, eating some pears – from a tree that rightfully belonged to us wenns, might I add. You were most disgruntled, weren't you, girls? Anyway, just standing there, she was, when a fierce blow from an unknown source shook the great, fat wye from its great, fat feet and…"

"Oh, no!" Will patted Dante's arm while Orchid threw him an angry look for interrupting her. "The pear tree. Alley took that. It was Alley."

His words took a while to sink in. Dante gazed blankly into space.

"Was it Alley?" Will asked the wenns, and all three nodded at the same time. "Who killed her?"

"We…" one of the copper-haired wenns began.

"They didn't see," Orchid shouted over her.

Foyer touched a gentle hand to Dante's arm. "But if Alley's dead," he said quietly, "then who has the vita?"

Dyelann's expression darkened. "Someone who now has an army of warders under their thumb."

"It's worse than that," Dante said. "Whoever it is, they move fast. The reaper we were with not ten minutes ago told us he'd not long since seen Alley alive and well."

"Oh, they move fast all right," Dyelann said, prompting the others to follow his gaze.

A crowd of large, muscular people with oddly small heads just like Nobody's were emerging from the distance, trudging soldier-like in their direction.

"They're already here."

Chapter Twelve: Friends in Low Places

The rumble of heavy feet stamping in synchrony across the grassy ground sent the hairs on Will's arms standing to attention. His fingers curled around the bottom of Dyelann's shirt. "Are they coming for us?"

"Probably. Who knows? We don't know what they want because we don't know who's got their vita. Knowing our luck, it'll be the witch who wants Blue dead." Dyelann stopped talking to tug his shirt away from Will. "You're wrinkling me."

The warders were closing in. Now would probably be a good time to start running for their lives, Will thought. Why were they still standing there?

"They're getting closer," Dante sang.

"Yes, we all have eyes too," Dyelann said. "What do you suggest we do?"

"I'll make a portal."

"I was asking Will."

Shocked by the notion of Dyelann, the one person he felt completely safe with in this place, asking him for suggestions, Will retorted: "Dante should make a portal!" Why Dyelann thought that he, Will, a child, could come up with a better idea than Dante, a witch, he did not know.

"Or," the Maker said, setting Will's teeth on edge, "we could stand our ground and ask them what's going on."

"Don't be foolish, Will," Dante said.

"That wasn't me," Will said, snorting at the concept. "I want to go."

"And ask them," the Maker added, and Will could sense the intruder's desire to laugh at him.

"Will," Foyer said. "Warders aren't really the sort you can have a nice conversation with."

"I'll ask them for you if I must," the Maker told Will.

"No, I don't want you to ask them anything, I just want to go." Will tried to step away but the Maker held him back.

"What's he talking about?" Foyer asked Dante.

Dante took hold of her wand. "Do you remember how we were discussing the possibility of Will being the Maker earlier? Well…" She broke her stare from the warders to look significantly at Foyer.

Dyelann let out a short laugh of derision. "What are you trying to say? Will isn't the Maker, Dante, don't be so soft."

"No, Will isn't the Maker," she said, watching the warders again, "but the Maker's living inside his body. Well, not living exactly, seeing as he's dead."

It was too late to run now. The massive men, and a few even bigger women, came to a stop just a stone's throw away. The one leading the group bent one of the skinny trees aside to stand directly opposite Dyelann. Like the rest of the warders, he had a disproportionately small head atop his bulky neck. Breathing like a growling dog, he curled a lip at Dyelann.

"Excuse me," the Maker said politely, tapping the warder on the back with Will's small hand.

Confusion crossed the warder's rugged little face as he moved, grunting, to see who was addressing him.

"What are you doing? Sixteen of you here together. This is most unusual, is it not?"

Still flummoxed, the leader scratched at his stubbly chin.

"Are you deaf?"

Will stifled his urge to whimper. The Maker was trying to stand up to this huge beast of a man, and Will knew he must not interfere.

"Are you out of your mind, child?" the warder said finally. He clapped his hands together, an inch from Will's face.

Locked inside his own body, Will jumped.

But the Maker did not flinch.

"You should avoid getting under my feet. They could crush you."

The Maker slowly looked the warder up and down. "You're not that big."

Dante stood on guard in front of the wots, braced, ready to intervene. The grip she had on her wand was so fierce Will worried she might snap it..

Mettle momentarily lost under a glimmer of caution, the warder changed tack, like a predator rethinking an attack on a smaller animal that might turn out to have the sharper teeth. "And you're not as small as you look. Are you?"

The Maker's crafty smile teetered on Will's lips. "Tell me. What exactly is going on here?"

"We're hunting. We must kill a wot."

"Tell me who has your vita."

Will could tell that the Maker was just as impatient as everyone else to uncover the witch's identity.

The warder shrugged his broad shoulders. "A witch. We don't know who she is. We can't see her face."

"And why doesn't this witch just kill the wot herself? Why does she need you?"

"We don't ask questions. We do what she commands because we must."

The Maker squinted at the muscular man. "Why? Why must you? Because of a spell? An old spell cast by a long-dead witch." He shook Will's head, goading the warder. "If you had a little more about you, you could escape the power of such a spell."

"It is a strong spell," the warder said with regret.

"Be on your way then."

"To kill the wot," the warder said, as if to remind the child of his intention.

"Do as you must."

"No!" Will shouted, angered by the Maker's disregard for Blue's life. "You can't do that."

"Go ahead and leave now," the Maker said in a tone of urgency, commanding control while Will thrashed and fought and screamed inside his own body.

"You can't kill Blue," he managed to yelp. "I won't let you."

The warder caught Will in both hands and yanked him closer. "*Who are you?*"

Will waited for the Maker to stand up for him. No one said a word. Apparently, his invader had chosen to abandon him in his time of need, perhaps to teach him a lesson.

Dante tried to pull him free, and the warder's grip intensified to stop her. Frightened the pair of them would rip him in two, Will reached into his pocket for his fake wand.

"Back off and vwa!" He swept the wand forth, accidentally smacking the warder across the face with it. The deafening pop sounded out, sending birds flapping from their roosts and the rest of the warders leaping into action. They rushed forward en masse, closing in on Will and their leader.

Then, as suddenly as they'd started to charge, they came to a halt, their focus on something they had spotted behind Will and the others.

Will, panting for breath, turned to see what had saved him.

And there stood Blue, scruffy as ever, his bewilderment clear as he surveyed the peculiar scene before him.

Speechless and immobile, with the warder's hands still clenched around his sides, Will stared at Blue. The fake wand dropped from his hand and pattered on the leafy ground, breaking the silence.

Blue lifted his chin. "Let him go."

The warder obliged, and Will toppled into Dante's protective arms.

The bewilderment on Blue's face fast became alarm when the group of warders began to head his way.

"They're after you, Blue," Will shouted. "Run!"

Blue recoiled, cuffing his shoulder against a tree.

The warders picked up their speed.

Will panicked. "Do something!" he shouted, to anyone, to everyone.

And with that the light dulled, the air thickened, and the grubby ground hit Will square in the face.

Something kept prodding at Will's shoulder. It was annoying and persistent. He pushed it away several times before finally opening his misty eyes. He had to blink hard before he could see clearly again.

Blue and Dante's faces hovered over him with matching concern.

"Oh, it's okay," Dante told Foyer and Dyelann, who were standing close by. "He's awake."

Will sat up. How odd, he thought, that he couldn't remember falling asleep. He stared at the towering trees that surrounded him, their thick, wide trunks and sizeable leaves. What had happened to the weedy twigs of trees that had been there only moments before?

"How did we get here?" he blurted.

"We walked." Dante took his hands and helped him to stand. "Well, *we* walked. Blue carried you. You were out for the count."

"Aren't you the lucky one?" Dyelann said. "Blue's calmed himself now, but I could have done without him forcing me to ballroom dance with him half the way here."

Dante shrugged. "I thought the dancing was quite impressive actually, with him carrying Will over his shoulder at the same time."

Will was relieved. If Blue had carried him to safety, surely it meant all was forgiven. "What happened?" he asked.

"The wenns stepped up and helped us," Dante replied.

Dyelann laughed. "They knocked the lot of us out. The warders got the worst of it. They're probably still lying there now. They'll not know which way's up when they come to."

Anxious to know if Blue was his friend again, Will worked up the courage to talk to him. "How did you find us?"

Blue faltered, evidently just as worried about answering the question as Will had been about asking it.

Dante and Foyer stood side by side, arms entwined, while Dyelann leaned heavily against the nearest tree and looked tear-jerkingly bored.

"Actually, I wasn't looking for you," Blue said. "I was still tracking my gem. But when I saw your predicament…" He shrugged. "I'd started going in circles anyway. My gem calls to me. I can feel it and I know exactly where it is. But then it's not there anymore. It's like it's constantly on the move."

"I'm really sorry," Will said.

Blue kept his gaze glued to the ground. "Don't be. I've been thinking. I was so quick to think the worst of you. You didn't deserve that. And there's no way you're the Maker anyway. If you were the Maker, we wouldn't have been friends, would we? You wouldn't have saved my life, would you? So, don't you be sorry. I'm the one who's sorry." He gave Will a quick, trusting smile. "Okay?"

"Quite sure of that, are we?" Dyelann muttered, peering over his knuckles.

Will glared at him. "I'm not the Maker. You know I'm not."

"Sorry for not listening to you before," Blue said. "You've got to understand, I've always been told the Maker would come back, or the descendant anyway, and I've always dreaded it happening. When Karson said what he said, I suppose I just got scared." He glanced at Dyelann. "I mean angry. I'm not scared."

"Why are you scared of him?" Will asked, talking softly so only Blue could hear.

Blue leaned to Will's height. "The Maker doesn't want us anymore. When he comes back, he's going to unmake us."

"I won't let him hurt you," Will said firmly, deciding then and there that he would fight the Maker with all his heart and soul if he ever tried to unmake Blue. He would reach his hands down his own throat and rip the Maker out if he had to.

Another mirthless smile twitched onto Blue's lips. "There's nothing you can do. The Maker's too powerful." He stood upright.

"He could do things just by believing he could. He's the reason wots exist. And his descendant will be the reason we won't. That's just the way it's always been."

"Yeah, well, the Maker's in me now, and I won't let him do anything," Will said, oozing confidence until he saw the colour drain from Blue's face and realised what he'd said. The wot backed away from him like he was carrying a contagious disease.

Dante hid behind her hands and groaned in despair. "Will, for the love of Chika, think before you speak. Will's not the Maker, Blue," she assured the wot. "While you were gone, we found out the Maker has somehow possessed Will, but they're two different people and neither of them are here to kill you. Honestly."

"Really?" Blue asked piteously. Then he glared at Will. "Then why is he here?"

The Maker answered, "I see the imbalance I've created in this world and wish to put right my wrong."

Will held his breath, wishing he could have stopped the Maker from speaking out of turn that time. Blue was looking at him the way someone might look at a cockroach they found in their meal.

"You want to kill us."

"It's not a matter of wanting to kill you, Blue," the Maker said, and a bubble of hope arose in Will, who was certain he could feel the Maker softening.

"Yes, it is. Of course that's what it's about. The neethers and the witch want our power. The warders want us dead. You want us dead. What chance do we have?"

Will stared sadly back at Blue. If only there was something he could say or do to make this better.

"A wenn told me the descendant of the Maker would kill all the wots someday," Blue went on. "She told me he would want to unmake us. He would live to unmake us."

"I am not the descendant of the Maker. I am he."

"You really don't want to kill them?" Will asked, relieved.

"I keep telling you, this isn't a matter of wanting to kill anybody," the Maker said impatiently. "I need to recover the four powers I summoned and return them to their sources. That's all I want."

"But why?" Dante asked. "Why now? You've waited long enough to just suddenly decide this out of the blue."

"This is no whim, Dante Simms. This was decided centuries ago. It is only now that I've been able to acquire form in a vessel. Until now I have been less than a memory, a nothing, a ghost trapped on this living realm, unable to escape it. And if I don't return the four powers, that's all I will go back to, forever. I'll never be free. I'll never be with my family. And they have been waiting too long for me. They have been waiting far too long."

Dante put a hand to her heart. It took her a second to gather herself. "I'm so sorry for you," she said in the motherly tone usually reserved for Will. "I truly am. But we can't let you kill these wots. They're beyond you now. The gems took on lives of their own; lives you have no right to."

"It is my eternal life that sustains them. Had they stayed the witches they were born to be, they would have been dead long ago."

"But they didn't. They changed. They're wots, and they're not supposed to die."

"And I have no wish for them to die. But returning the four powers to their rightful place is the only way that *I* will die. And I wish for nothing more."

Dyelann pushed away from the tree on which he'd been leaning and said, "Will, are you making this stuff up?"

"It's not me," Will said, while an equally insistent Blue spoke over him.

"The wenn told me you'd be the descendant of the Maker and you'd want us dead."

Dyelann huffed. "What makes you think a wenn would know anything about any of this, Blue? *We* don't even know anything about any of this." He paused. "Hang on. Is this wenn the reason you spent so long depressed and scared witless of every little thing? It took us ages to get your head screwed back on. And all because of some little wenn making up stories? Really?"

"Turns out I was right to be worried, wasn't I?" Blue retorted. "Look at what's happening."

"Coincidence!"

"That's enough," Foyer snapped, ending the fight before it had chance to escalate.

Will appreciated Foyer for that. It would have been great to have had Foyer at home refereeing his parent's arguments these past few weeks. He tried not to think about home. The last thing he wanted was for the Maker to pick up on the fact he was starting to yearn for the safety of real life, where nobody was trying to kill anyone. He didn't want the Maker to know how scared he was. Maybe the Maker was telling the truth about not wanting to kill Blue but maybe he wasn't. They had no way of knowing for sure.

"We need to get back to the others," Foyer said.

"Do you think they found anything out yet?" Will asked. "Me and Dante tried to find Adrian so we could bring him back to life, but the skeleton man said his body had disappeared."

Shocked silence preceded Blue's clipped, "What?"

An icy feeling of self-loathing came over Will. Blue hadn't known Adrian was dead. Think before you speak, Dante had just told him. Why could he never keep his big mouth shut?

"I'm so sorry, Blue," Dante whispered.

"Adrian's dead?"

With palpable difficulty, Foyer said, "We found him while we were looking for you. He'd been drowned."

"I bet you're loving this, aren't you?" Blue asked, and Will was shocked to see Blue had been talking to him.

"Blue," he said, hurt that his friend could even think such a terrible thing of him.

"I meant the Maker, Will." Blue moved away from everyone, breathing faster. "This can't be happening."

Dante tried to twist him back around to face her. "Come on. Look at me. It's going to be okay. I promise. I won't let anyone hurt you. If it means I have to summon the four energies myself, I won't let anyone hurt you. Everything's going to be okay."

"It's not okay, Dante! Adrian's dead."

Foyer stepped closer to Dante. "We arranged to meet up with Maik and Henry in Itchen Hush," he told her quietly. "They'll be waiting for us."

The place name threw Will. Why would the wots choose to meet where Scilla Simms lived? His last encounter with Foosay Hoo may have shaken his faith in her, but even if Foosay wasn't to be trusted, it didn't mean they should blindly trust Scilla. And they certainly shouldn't be taking Blue anywhere near her. He hurried to catch up with Dyelann, who had already started to walk away.

"Do you know where you're going?"

"Of course. I've lived in these parts all my life. I know the place inside out."

"Do you think Blue's okay?"

"Of course he's not okay. He's just found out his best friend in the world is dead and he's never going to see him again. Nobody would be okay with that."

"I'm sorry for him."

"I'm sorry too," Dyelann said. "It's a tragedy that this could happen." He ducked to avoid a low branch. "I'm more sorry for Adrian though."

"I wish I knew where he was. I wish I could bring him back to life."

Only when Dyelann strode on ahead to get away from him did Will realise what he'd said.

"Oops." He winced. From now on he would try to remember not to speak unless he'd considered every word beforehand. "Sorry," he called after Dyelann. Watching him go, he hung back and waited for the others.

"I want to run on ahead if you don't mind," Dante was saying to Foyer. "I need to speak to my auntie Scilla, and she's easier to talk to when there are no wots about." She leaned into him for a long moment before pulling back and flicking her wand out of her sleeve. "I'll see you soon." She sliced open her portal. "Take care of them," she added, meaning Will and Blue.

Will thought she had a bit of a cheek saying that to Foyer. It wasn't like she had been taking the best care of them so far. She kept running off and leaving them, for a start.

"We'll have to be discreet now, you two," Foyer said when Dante disappeared. "We don't want to be attracting any attention. Stealth is what we need. Where's Dye?"

Blue grunted. "Gone off on his own. Typical Dyelann."

"What's he thinking of? We should be sticking together at a time like this."

Guilt pinched at Will. It was his fault that Dyelann had left. A muffled slapping sound caught his ear, and he slowed down to listen.

"Yes, we should stick together," Blue said. "We're the only ones that are definitely on our side. Everyone else is against us. Even Will."

"I am not," Will said indignantly.

"Well, not you. Your alter ego."

Will didn't bother to ask what he meant. "Listen," he said sharply. "Can you guys hear that?"

Foyer and Blue fell quiet.

"It keeps stopping and starting." Will listened harder. "It's coming from somewhere over there." He pointed a finger to an area off the track on which they were walking, where the trees grew closer together, their thick branches blocking daylight.

Foyer slipped away to investigate. "You two stay right here," he said, not looking back.

Blue shifted his weight from leg to leg in his impatience. "Should we follow him?"

"He said stay..." The slapping noise started again, piquing Will's curiosity. "But okay, if you want."

They followed the path of flat grass that Foyer had squashed on his way through.

"Come quickly," Foyer bellowed.

"So much for being discreet." Blue broke into a sprint.

Will ran too, struggling to keep his feet out of the ankle-grabbing weeds.

Blue skidded to a halt and gaped in shock at what he saw.

Foyer watched over a lanky figure flouncing and rolling ferociously in dead leaves and mulch. He shared Blue's expression, and the two wots stood side by side, staring down in stunned amazement.

Will pointed at the grappling man. "It's Gart."

"That's not Gart," Blue said.

Will winced as Foyer tried to help Gart up only to receive a mighty kick in the shin for his trouble. "He won't let anyone help him," he told Foyer, who was hopping backwards on one leg, the other clutched in both hands.

"But we have to help him," Blue said. "Or else we'll be standing here forever, waiting for him to get up."

"No, he can do it." Will stood by Gart's head. "Hey, are you okay? How did you get away from Eve?"

Gart writhed all the more, long limbs flapping in every direction. He screamed out at the top of his lungs, causing Blue to back off and cover his ears.

"Did she hurt you? Where is she now?"

"No care," Gart roared. Finally, with an explosion of effort, the witch pushed himself onto his knees and stumbled into a crouched standing position. He held the precarious pose, knees inverted and knocking together, wobbling in exhaustion.

"Gartaspia?" Blue said, recognising his old friend at last. "What happened to you?"

"Spells." Gart's breath wheezed in his throat. "Lots spells. She practise. On Gart. Spells."

"Someone's been practising spells on you?" Foyer asked, still rubbing his shin. "What spells? Who's been doing this to you?"

"She. He. Ever-for to live." Gart swayed and fought to recover his balance. "Make spell to live ever-for. Try on Gart." He stammered, having as much difficulty forming words as staying on his feet. "Silence! Condemn Gart to silence."

Foyer left his shin alone then, more concerned for Gart. "She wouldn't let you speak?"

"Not let Gart speak who she is. Gart knows. Gart knows."

"Can you describe her?" Blue suggested.

Gart answered with a shake of his head, a jerky movement that unbalanced him again.

"Is she someone we know?" Foyer asked. "Is it someone you thought a friend?"

Gart trembled violently. "No, yes, no, no, Gart. Say. Gart say."

Intrigued, Blue moved closer to watch the eyeball that refused to sit still in its socket. "What happened to your eye? That's disgusting."

"Spell thrown. Thrown in eye. Blind."

"What happened to your hair? Look at it."

Will squirmed, embarrassed for Gart.

"Wrong potion," Gart said, the pitch and volume of his voice fluctuating madly with every word. "She too. She hair bad too. Wild. Wild."

"Foosay Hoo has wild hair," Foyer said quietly to Blue.

"Witch!" Gart shouted, for no apparent reason. "Bad. Now. Can't make hair like was. Can't fix."

"Look at the state you're in," Blue said with dismay. "Look at your face. It's all wrong. All the girls used to have a crush on you. And Popset. Now look at you. You're so weird. You're like a monster.

How could someone do this to you? And how long have those things been on your feet?" Blue didn't notice his blunt words were offending Gart, but Gart was rolling his head and moaning in displeasure the longer the wot went on. "You just look hideous."

"It's Scilla Simms," Will said, speaking quickly during Blue's pause for breath, in case he hadn't quite finished his slew of insults. "It's her. Remember her hair, Blue? It was red, and wild, remember? I knew it. I knew it was her. I said so."

Foyer considered the idea and tried to look Gart in the eye, which Will knew wasn't an easy thing to do. "Was it Scilla, Gartaspia?"

"Yes. No. No. Yes. Round. Round. Try. Try. Wait. Go." Gart bowed his head and gave up. "Gart," he added sourly.

The smirk on Blue's face then bore an uncanny resemblance to the one Will was so used to seeing on Dyelann's. "Can't you just say yes or no?"

"Obviously, he can't, Blue," Foyer said. "Dante's gone to Scilla's. If Scilla did this to Gartaspia, Dante could be in serious danger right now. Come on. Come on, we've got to go. We've got to go now." He dashed clumsily back in the direction from which they'd come, with no sign of the stealth or discretion of which he had only recently requested of them.

Blue tried to take Gart's arm, but Gart shoved him away and screamed piercingly in his face. Blue leapt back, horrified by the sound, and clamped his hands over his ears. "So loud," he said, bending forwards. He groaned. "It's so loud."

"Just don't touch him," Will said. "He doesn't like it."

"It's on and on." Blue squeezed his eyes shut. "So loud. Ringing." He wandered dazedly away, heading the opposite direction to Foyer.

Will rushed to stop him. "Blue. Blue?" He yanked Blue's arms down to uncover his ears. "You're going the wrong way."

"My gem's calling me again. I have to find it. It's getting weaker."

"You can't go. You can't leave me on my own."

"You're not on your own."

"But Gart can't look after me."

"I wasn't talking about Gart," Blue snapped. Regret appeared on his face as soon as he registered the hurt on Will's.

Gart waved his arms and yelped.

It was easy to forgive Blue when his eyes held such sadness. "I can't go back to that house without you." Will upturned the ragged piece of Blue's coat from his hand to expose his bruised, oozing wound. "What if I get bitten again?"

That snapped Blue back to his senses. With an apologetic nod, he returned to Gart and made a grab for his arm again, apparently having forgotten the reaction he had received only a minute earlier. He seemed just as surprised this time when Gart hollered and kicked him smartly on the knee.

"Just don't touch him," Will said, following loyally after Blue as he limped away. He wished Dyelann would come back. Blue clearly wasn't thinking straight, and Gart wasn't walking straight. Neither man felt like safe company.

Gart staggered along behind them, still walking like there were invisible hurdles in front of him every step of the way.

"When I catch up to whoever's done this to you…" Blue balled his hand into a fist and waggled it at Gart.

"What?" Will asked, waiting for him to finish his threat.

"I'll tell her off."

"She needs telling off, doesn't she, Blue?"

"Too right she does. First she pretends to be Foosay, then she starts a fight, then she kills me, then she steals my gem, then she does this to Gart, then she sets a banter on you…" Blue trailed off, scowling. "She needs telling off by someone a lot scarier than me, is what she needs."

"You got that a bit out of order though."

"I'm not out of order, she deserves it. I can't believe it's Scilla. I just can't. She loved Gart like her own son. How could a mother do this to their child?"

"I know," Will agreed. "My mum would never hurt me on purpose." A rough piece of ground tripped him, but Blue caught him mid-fall and hoisted him back up. "Thanks. What about *your* mum?"

"What about her?"

"What was she like?"

"Don't know. I don't remember."

"You don't remember your mum? What about your dad?"

"I don't think I ever had a mum or dad."

That had to be the saddest thing Will had ever heard, and he felt bad for bringing up a subject that must have been painful for Blue to even think about.

Blue laughed.

Maybe not so painful after all.

"What's funny?"

"I was thinking of a joke someone told me once. It was something like, why are parents like ballerinas with no feet… and I've forgotten the punchline, but I remember laughing. Something about them being pointless or something."

Supposing he must have missed the funny part while he'd been concentrating on putting his feet down safely, Will laughed along with Blue, and then cast him a confused squint behind his back.

"Okay, Will." Blue took a deep breath. "Remember, there's going to be a…" A ripping flash of light cut him off, and he raised his hands defensively. "I warned you that time. You can't blame me for that."

Gart whooped in glee, trying heartily to clap his hands but finding it impossible to coordinate them well enough to meet. "Passed it," he sang. "Passed it, passed it, passed it."

Being so close to Scilla's house made Will dizzy. He hid his wounded hand in his sleeve. "What if she's still got that banter?"

"We won't open the door this time." Blue stared at the winding pathway that led into Itchen Hush, deliberating. "It can't be Scilla. It just can't be."

Dyelann called out to get their attention and ran to catch them up.

"How did you get behind us?" Will asked.

"Did you get lost?" Blue gibed.

"Shut it, Eulb."

Blue laughed.

Will was sick of being left out of the jokes. "What's funny now?"

"I'm not a witch, Dyelann. You can call me that as much as you like. I don't care."

"Yeah, all right," Dyelann said grudgingly. "So, have we found Henry and Maik yet?"

"No," Will said. "But we're going to Scilla's house now to rescue Dante, because… Look at what she did to Gart!" He pointed his finger at the wonky man, and Dyelann spun on the spot.

"All right?" He gave Gart a casual nod. Then he said to Blue, "Well. Popset's got an odd opinion of what's hot, handsome, gorgeous, super-duper and a fine figure of a man, doesn't he?"

Gart wailed out loud.

"He never used to look like that," Blue said. "The witch who stole our gems did this to him."

Dyelann jerked his head to the side, an indication for Blue to look that way, and said, "Lillian," with a note of arrogance, as if they never would have seen her had he not arrived in time to point her out.

There was a determined drive in Lillian's step as she approached. Maik and Henry were at her heels, Henry more terrified and drawn than ever. His big fluffy sweater was now red instead of navy, but he still clutched his knife between both hands like a lifeline.

Maik greeted his friend by stabbing him with the harmless blade of his dagger. Humouring him, Dyelann collapsed to his knees and feigned an agonising death while Maik laughed childishly.

"Now then, children," Lillian said, bright and chipper as ever.

"What's an eulb?" Will asked her.

"Why, I've no idea, dear." She smiled. "Where's Foyer?"

Dyelann handed the dagger back to Maik and answered Will's question. "Eulb is Blue backwards."

Lillian reared back like she had a bad smell up her nose.

"It's a big insult to a witch to call them by their backwards name," Blue said. "It's just stupid to everyone else."

Lillian looked ready to slap Blue then. "It's downright impertinent, is what it is. Terrifically abusive."

"What's yours?" Will dug his teeth into his lower lip, thinking. "Na..."

Blue grabbed the back of Will's jacket and yanked him hard enough to knock the word out of his mouth before it got there. "Don't. Don't ever do that. Trust me."

"Where *is* Foyer?" Dyelann asked, concerned at first, but he'd already deduced the answer by his next tired exhalation. "Gone off to rescue Dante."

Blue confirmed the assumption with a nod. "We have to hurry. He won't be able to do anything on his own."

"For once we're agreeing on something."

"I hate you."

Dyelann cackled, unperturbed. "I know you do."

"Rescue Dante from what, exactly?" Lillian asked.

"We got some new information," Blue said. "We think Scilla Simms may be the witch we're after, and Dante's with her right now."

"Right." Lillian didn't sound convinced. "What information led you in that direction?"

"Her hair's mad," Will said, to which Lillian gave a big I-was-right-to-doubt-you nod.

"Many witches have mad hair. It's a witch's prerogative. I don't think that's much to go on, to be honest."

Dyelann clicked his tongue. "Now, now. This is the first time we've had a clue. Let's not blow out the candle before the flame's even hit the wick."

"It is Scilla," Will said. "I bet she's got a Foosay mask. I bet it was her when Mrs Hoo came to me and started asking me stupid questions. She was wearing a scarf around her head. I bet that was to keep her hair covered up so I wouldn't know it was her. And that other Dante at the shop, she had that big hat on, remember?" He pointed dramatically at his head. "So, she must have a Dante mask too."

A distant cry for help rang out through the trees, sending Will's heartbeat into overdrive.

"That's Foyer." Dyelann was already sprinting off before Will had quite processed what he'd said. Maik and Henry raced after him, closely followed by Lillian.

"What are we going to do?" Will asked Blue.

"We're going to save Foyer and Dante," the wot replied.

And they ran.

Chapter Thirteen: Identity

The group arrived at Scilla's house to find the feisty old witch pinning Foyer down on her porch, one knobbly knee planted deep in his backbone. The four wots ran to his aid and pounced on Scilla, knocking her over and landing on top of her like a team of rugby players, all bawling raucously as they did so.

Scilla shrieked and struggled to pull her wand out of the fluffy pocket of her dressing gown. As soon as she had it in her grip, the wots were flung away from her in four opposite directions. Indignant, she hopped back onto her feet, nudged the green towel that was wrapped around her head, straightened her dressing gown, and blew down her nose at her assailants like a flustered horse.

"What do you think you're doing, the lot of you?" Her face reddened the same way Karson's did when he was angry.

"Where's Dante?" Foyer staggered to the porch rails. "What have you done with her?"

"I'm right here." Dante rushed out of Scilla's open door, her plimsolls clapping against the wooden planks. "What on earth is going on out here?"

Dyelann held a protective arm over his ribs. "Give us back our gems, Mrs Simms," he growled. "Come on. We all know it's you."

"Oh, Foyer." Dante put a hand to her forehead and took a deep, disappointed breath.

"Take that towel off your head," Blue ordered.

Scilla's face set like stone. "I beg your pardon?"

"Please?"

If Will had been on a seat, he would have been on the edge of it. He had been right all along about Scilla being the baddie, and she was about to prove it, he just knew it. Or she would, if only she'd do as Blue asked. At first it seemed like she would be uncooperative, for she made no effort to move at all, merely continued to stare the wot down. Then she sighed loudly, thrust her wand back into her pocket and untwisted the large towel from her head.

And out fell very wet, very straight, very blonde hair.

"But…" Blue stammered. "It was all red and big before."

"I washed it! I'd only just got out of the shower when Dante arrived, for heaven's sake. I know it looked terrible, but is having a bad hair day such a crime I deserve an ambush? I put a charm on my shampoo that went wrong. How does that mean I have your gems?"

"It was his idea." Blue pointed at Will.

"You explain it to me, then, young man," Scilla challenged, turning her irritation his way.

A brief silence followed where Will looked at each of the people surrounding him in turn, hoping that one of them might step in at this point and defend him. On seeing that none of them had anything to say, he hastened to explain himself. "Yeah, okay, right, Gart told us the one who had been doing bad spells on him had done something to her hair she couldn't fix, and I remembered what yours was like before, and I thought you wouldn't have been walking around with hair like that if you could have fixed it, so I thought it was you, probably, maybe. But you've fixed it now, haven't you? It can't be you, can it? So, I'm sorry I said that now; because I was wrong." His frightened eyes begged for forgiveness. "Sorry."

Her face twitched. "Did you just say…?"

"Gart?" Dante finished her aunt's question. She dashed down the porch steps to get to Will. "You've seen Gart since I left you? Honey, where is he?"

The intensity of her stare unnerved him. "He was right behind us."

"Yeah." Blue peered over his shoulder. "He's not looking so good though."

"Dante." Scilla plodded down the stairs after her niece. "Dante, are they speaking of our Gartaspia?"

"He's right there," Dyelann said, in the same condescending tone he had used when he'd spotted Lillian. They followed his gaze to see Gart making his awkward way to join them.

Dante sped to meet her brother, and her body hit his so hard Will was surprised the wonky man didn't fall down. She squeezed him like she was trying to crush his bones. He didn't retaliate. He sank into her loving embrace, closed his eyes and held her. For the first time since Will had met him, he looked almost normal.

Scilla, sobbing, waddled in her slippers to her nephew and niece and wrapped her arms around them both.

"Scilla's not the one." Blue sounded discouraged. "I didn't think she was."

"You were right, then," Will said. They were back to knowing nothing at all. But for that particular moment, seeing the three witches so happily reunited, that worry faded into the background.

Scilla rocked her niece and nephew, weeping, while Dante asked, "Where have you been all this time? Who did this to you?"

"Spell, spell, can't tell."

"What happened to you?" Dante pushed him away to arm's length so she could see his face.

Scilla's withered hands were trembling. "My poor darling boy. If a spell has taken your power to tell us who's done this, another will give you that power back. And by hook or by crook I shall find that spell. Whoever did this to you will pay, I promise you that." She stormed back to her house, knocking Henry aside as she passed him.

Henry stood beside Maik, his unblinking green eyes watching her go.

"Well," Dyelann said. "While she's working on that, why don't the rest of us go ahead and run for our lives?"

The warders had found them. They had gathered a few more of their kind along the way too. Each one of them was a huge beast of a man, the three women among them even more so. Massive, muscled shoulders and chests heaved under their clothing, sheer abhorrence in their small faces.

Dante stood protectively in front of Gart and shoved him in the direction of the door.

Blue dragged Will up Scilla's steps by the collar of his jacket. The others were quick to follow, and they all piled into the witch's hallway. While the wots pressed up against the door to keep the warders from coming in after them, Will was left to the rear, gaping at the huge black door at the end of the passage. He didn't know what was scarier, the group of brawny warders behind one door or the skinny banter lurking behind the other.

Scilla joined them in the hall, completely dry and fully dressed in a sky blue trouser suit. A bulky, leather-bound book hung open over both her arms. "Here we are," she said. "See here, a spell."

"Auntie," Dante gasped. "There are warders all over the place out there. They want to kill Blue."

"Yes, I saw them through the window," Scilla said, with not a trace of concern. She balanced the heavy book on one arm so she could point to a passage on the page. "Look here. This is a spell to break a spell. It should do the trick nicely. But we'll have to purchase some ingredients."

The door jolted inward with the force of the warders beating it from the other side.

"Auntie Scilla! They're getting through!"

"Oh, for heaven's sake, Dan, will you focus for a minute? This is important."

The door swung open violently and the wots slammed it back into place, panic escalating.

Lillian, like Scilla, remained unfazed by the invasion and made no effort to help with the barricade. Instead, she wandered casually up the hall, inspecting the walls and the floor with great interest, as if she'd wandered into an art gallery and was admiring its exhibitions.

Finally accepting that her niece needed her help, Scilla passed the book to Henry, elbowed him aside and caught Gart from falling all at once, and then forced her way through the small group of bodies to get to the front door. The warders halted just in the nick of time to stop themselves from toppling in when she pulled it open and asked, "What do you think you're doing?"

The same warder that the Maker had spoken with earlier still led the group, and Will spotted Nobody among the others. None of them looked happy to be there. The leader rubbed at his stubbly chin with the side of a hand, staring down at the little old lady. Then his eyes shifted. They found Blue and stayed there. "We're here to kill that one."

Blue huffed, offended.

"And we must kill anyone who gets in our way."

Scilla hummed reprovingly through her shrivelled lips. "Fair enough. Just wait one minute please." She slowly pushed the door closed and joined the people gathered in her hall. "Quiet as you can," she said, "head for that door. Quickly now." And to Henry, "Bring the book."

She ushered them on, Will protesting every step of the way. When she reached for the black door's handle, he could bear it no more.

"No, stop. I can't go in there. The banter." He thrust his hand to her face, the piece of Blue's coat now stained through and flapping loose. "I'm still bleeding."

"Banter? What banter?" Scilla shoved the door open, sending the bright light from which the creature had emerged flooding upon them. "Don't be so silly. This is just a portal I put in my cupboard, that's all."

Dante took a firm grip of Will's wrist and walked him through the door with her. The others followed one by one, Scilla bringing up the rear. At the other side, the huge, heavy black door was a barely noticeable bronze handle screwed into the base of the last upright tree before they began to grow slanted.

Will took in the half-fallen trees, confused. "This is No-go Ebb."

"That's right," Scilla said.

"But there was a banter."

"This is where banters originated. That's why it became known as No-go Ebb in the first place. People were afraid to come here when the banter population was at its highest. They used to flourish, but now they're dying out. Just like the warders, as a matter of fact. That must have been every last one of them out there. And if I find my house wrecked when I get back, I will personally track down whoever has their vita, take it from their cold, dead hands, and order the vile beasts to track down the nearest volcano and jump on in."

Dante made a sound like a cough mixed with a snort. "You knew about their vita too? Am I the only one who didn't know it still existed?" She glanced around at everyone like one of them might answer. When she saw Gart, she hugged him.

"What were you doing opening my door anyway?" Scilla asked.

Will blinked innocently. "We knocked first."

Scilla took her book from Henry and thanked him. "Now then." She flicked through the pages to reach the one with the bookmark. "Says here we need a feather, preferably from a magpie or a rook. Some citric fruit juice. Oh, and a nut."

"What sort of nut?" Foyer asked.

"Shh! Shut your awful trap, you." Scilla clicked her fingers in front of her face several times as if it would help her to think.

"What sort of nut, Auntie?" Dante asked over Gart's shoulder. "And don't talk to Foyer that way, please."

"Any kind of nut will do the job. And since when do you care how I speak to Foyer?"

"Don't go to Molina's suppliers. Those people are idiots. And since quite recently, for your information."

"My supplier will have what we need, don't you worry." Scilla caught Foyer and Dante smiling at one another. "And what happened quite recently?"

Dyelann laughed. "She found out her uber-denial's had her crushing on an adolescent."

Taking her arms from her brother, Dante gave Dyelann a shove. "You always have to stick your oar in, don't you, you pig? Why don't you just pull it back into your end of the boat and let us row for a change?"

"Greed," Gart said. "Greed ents. Greed ents."

Scilla gave his back a loving pat. "Yes, don't you worry yourself, my darling. We'll get your ingredients very soon."

"Egg. Crow egg. Bulb. Rare root. Sue… Sue…"

"What are you trying to say, my darling?"

"Sue… Wit. Wit. Bean. Sal… Manda. Yo… Yo… Yolk. Rob… Robin."

Lillian rolled her eyes. "Now he's making no sense whatsoever."

A light dawned in Dante. Will could see it in her face, a glimmer of realisation mixed with oncoming dread. "Oh, no," she said. "Oh no. He is making sense. He's making perfect sense. He's listing ingredients. Ingredients Molina had me pick up from the suppliers for her. It's her. It's Molina."

Scilla made a disapproving noise with her lips. "Don't be so ridiculous, girl. Your sister would never do such a thing. What a notion."

Dante sank with relief. "No, you're right." She put a hand to her chest. "Of course it's not Molina."

"No, wait," Will said, remembering their meeting by Karson's Christmas tree. "She had that scarf on her head. We need to see her hair."

"It can't be Mo," Dante murmured, on edge again. She became momentarily transfixed with the swinging motion of Gart's damaged eye, but she shook it off quickly, serious, concentrating. "Gart. Did our big sister do this to you?"

Gart's face turned pink, and his square jaw wobbled. "No, yes, yes, no, no, yes, Gart, Gart, Gart." His shoulders slumped.

"Poor thing." Scilla rubbed his back. "If it really is her, she's in big trouble."

"Big trouble?" Dante repeated, stunned. "Auntie, if it's her… The woman's killing people. She's done this to my brother. She'll stop at nothing for her own selfish means. She has seven of eight gems containing a level of primal power beyond our comprehension. She's out of control. There will be no sending her to her bedroom and giving her a good talking-to. You do realise that?"

"What are you suggesting, Dan?" Scilla asked harshly. "That I kill your sister?"

"No," Dante said immediately. "Of course not."

"More like yes," Dyelann corrected her. "It's her or us."

"Nobody is killing my niece. And that's final."

Will spotted a large, black feather in the grass at the foot of the first slanted tree and made a beeline for it.

"She's been lying to you for eleven years," Dyelann told Scilla.

"She's been working with wenns behind your back," Blue added softly.

"She's betrayed us all," Foyer said.

"Foyer." Scilla held up her hand to him. "Trap. Shut."

Will wandered back to them, the feather held out in front of him like a candle, while Blue sniggered at the reaction Foyer had received from Scilla.

"You know she hates you talking, Foyer," he said with a cheeky grin. "Ever since you said that word to her."

"I wasn't even talking about her." Foyer rubbed his eyes like he was getting a headache. "It's another witch's actual name. I swear."

"What word?" Will asked.

"Backwards name," Blue replied. "If you want to fall out with a witch, that'd be the way to do it."

"Oh." Will offered the feather to Scilla. "Would this one be okay?"

Grumbling incoherently, she dumped her book over Henry's unprepared arms, not minding the dagger he held point up. She took a pair of glasses out of her jacket pocket, shook them open and popped them on. After studying the feather through the thick lenses, she said, "I believe this to be from a pigeon."

"It's from a crow, auntie."

"Oh, a big expert on birds now, are we, Dan?" Scilla handed the feather to her niece.

"Where can we find a nut?" Will asked, eager to help.

"There's one." Dyelann pointed at Scilla, who gave him a fierce glare in return. A subtle grin played on his lips as he retreated a few paces.

"I'll go and get one," Dante said quickly to break the tension. "And fruit juice. Citric fruit."

"Is pineapple one of those?" Will knew where to find that.

With all her usual sweetness, Lillian flashed him a smile and said, "No, dear."

"I'll get some." Dante stroked the feather through her fingers. "I'll see if they have any magpie feathers. Best get it right."

"If I had my gem," Dyelann said, "I'd be able to change that crow feather into a magpie feather in the beat of a heart. In fact, if I had my gem, I'd be able to turn Gart back into his old self just..." He clicked his fingers.

"Karson's still got his," Will reminded them. "Can't he do something?"

"Not very much, I'm afraid." Foyer moved away from Scilla, who looked very much like she wanted to knock him out with the book she was snatching back from Henry. "Whatever the witch is doing to the gems has made them lock down. Our gems are bonded. They're the same entity, see, Will, just in portions."

"Like a pizza," Dyelann said, and Will looked at him in confusion. "Imagine seven of our eight hot, delicious slices have been nabbed from our box, and our leftover slice is cold and rank and upside down now. Probably has sweetcorn on it too."

"What does this have to do with pizza?"

"Nothing. Forget pizza," Foyer said rattily. "That's a terrible analogy, Dye. Anyway, the witch's interference is sending the gems haywire." He watched Will for a sign he'd understood. When none came, he tried again. "Wots have the permission of the four powers to be their keepers. Nobody else does."

"Listen to me, Will," Dante said, unimpressed by Foyer's efforts. "Basically, Karson's gem won't work properly until the rest are back with their wots."

"Why not?"

Dyelann emitted a tired groan and scratched the back of his head. "Because life would be too easy if it did. Don't you listen?"

That wasn't good enough for Will. "But you said Blue's gem waited ages for him. Your gems all worked okay without him, didn't they? What about when you get them back?" He lowered his voice. "Will they not work anymore because you don't have Adrian?"

Foyer barely let him get the name out. "*If* we get them back, the purple gem will be safe in our care until it calls a new wot. Karson kept Blue's for over a thousand years. We began to think it would be forever dormant. Then one day, out of nowhere, there was a baby."

Will mulled over the strangeness of the idea. Babies didn't just drop out of the sky. "Did it steal him?"

"There was no one to steal him from," Scilla said matter-of-factly. "All the wots were once orphaned witches."

So the gems had not stolen babies but saved them.

"But how do you know they were witches?"

Dante smiled at the question. "Because they're too tall to be wenns, too short to be wyes, and too blooming normal to be wares."

"Maybe they weren't any of those things. Maybe they were just regular people."

With an apologetic look at an unforgiving Scilla, Foyer said, "No, we know we were witches. Wares can sense witches. Every time a wot was called, a ware said the same thing, that an orphaned witch baby had inexplicably vanished from the radar. It's not uncommon for witches to die before their time, sadly."

"Most witches do," Dante agreed. "It's a dangerous business being a witch."

This comment appalled and intrigued Will in equal measures. "How come?"

"We have lots of enemies."

"We do," Scilla said, finally relaxing her death stare. "I must say, though, it's mostly the bad witches that drop dead all over the place." To her niece and nephew, she added, "Your mother and father were an exception to that rule, of course. But more often than not they're bad witches who've been stirring trouble and brought it on themselves." She glared at the wots. "I'm sure all your parents did," she told them, with uncalled-for spitefulness in her tone.

"Thanks," Dyelann said. "But I wasn't an orphan. I knew my mother."

"Did you now?" Scilla mocked.

"Yes."

"Okay, before this gets out of hand…" Foyer pushed Dyelann away from Scilla while she demanded yet again that Foyer shut his trap.

"Where's Dante going?" Will asked, noticing the witch slipping away into a line of light.

"Suppliers," Lillian said.

Scilla seemed aware of Lillian's presence for the first time and inspected her suspiciously through her glasses. "And who are you?"

Blue answered for her. "She's Lillian Scrossly. She's Tamzin Rickrack's granddaughter."

Scilla grimaced deliberately. "Pity. I could never stand the Rickrack line. Horrible attitudes when things don't go their way. Her husband always had an odd aura about him too. I hope you take from the other side of your family, girl."

"I take from my own side." The darkness Lillian's face acquired startled Will. It was a shock to see such hatred where he normally only saw kindness. But it was understandable, he decided. Scilla shouldn't make such rude comments about people's families. He'd be angry with her if she put down the Morgans.

"That's just as well. Best to make your own mark in the world when you come from a family like that. You know, I remember you now." She moved her glasses up her nose. "Yes. Joined at the hip with that ware boy when you were a babe, weren't you? Managed to give that tenacious little scrap the slip at last, I see."

Lillian stared glassily at her.

"Good. Good for you, girl."

Henry started to speak but recoiled when everyone, barring the two witches, looked at him. It took him a few seconds to regain his nerve. "What are we waiting for?" he asked. "Why aren't we doing something?"

"We are," Foyer assured him. "We are. As soon as Dante fetches the ingredients, Gart will be able to tell us if Molina has our gems."

"What if she does? What then?"

"What if she doesn't?" Dyelann shrugged. "Doesn't really matter either way, does it?"

"Of course it matters," Scilla snapped. "Every time you open your mouth, futile drivel just pours right out of it. You're aware of this condition, yes?"

A brown paper bag was thrust from a silver-yellow streak of light, followed by a windswept Dante. "Got it."

"That was fast. Good girl." Scilla took the bag and peered into it. She lifted out a dark feather and twisted it to see it shine blue in the light. "Beautiful," she hummed, delving back into the bag for a jar of unlabelled cloudy liquid. "Lemon juice. Lovely." She then tipped the bag upside down and emptied it into her palm. Out dropped one gleaming brown hazelnut. "Hold this," she said, passing the feather to Gart. "This is going to help you, my darling."

As soon as the words left her lips, Gart exploded into a roar of a scream and threw the feather with all his might. It helicoptered gently down to the grass below.

"Gart," Scilla said, annoyed, and leaned over to pick the feather back up before the breeze could take it. "What are you doing?" She pushed the feather back at him. "I want to help you."

The feather twirled back to the ground by his feet while he bawled. The screams continued, loud and without pause for breath. Again, Blue clamped his hands over his ears to block out the sound.

"Stop it," Scilla shouted over Gart's noise, stooping to retrieve the feather. "What's the matter with you?"

"He won't have help," Will shouted. "That's what Eve said. She said he won't have help."

"Confound it. Clever witch has put a spell on him so he can't even have anyone help him. The poor mite. If this is the work of Molina, I'm going to be ever so disappointed in her. And a smidge proud. Anyway, the spell can still work. The feather only needs to be touching him. You!" She pointed it at Dyelann. "Make yourself useful. You too, Blue," she said, slapping one of his hands away from the ear it covered. "Come on, I need you. Hold him down."

Dyelann and Blue glanced at each other uncertainly.

Scilla rushed them. "Come, come."

Gart's screams rang in Will's ears as Blue and Dyelann each grabbed an arm and toppled him to the ground. Blue grew paler the louder the noise became, until he could hold onto Gart no longer. His grip weakened, allowing Gart's arm to shoot free and smack Dyelann on the chin.

Stunned, Dyelann too lost his hold, and Henry and Maik jumped in to help. They each knelt on an arm while Dyelann fought to pin down the thrashing legs.

Scilla placed the feather on her writhing nephew's chest. With the nut in one hand and the now open jar of lemon juice in the other, she stood over him and said in a low voice, "This nut represents new life, this blood of fruit the old, this plume a vein for transference to unfold. Undo the done, on spells adverse. Undo the done and end this curse."

She dropped the nut into the juice. Bubbles rushed up the sides of the glass and engulfed the nut, dissolving it, and the churning liquid blackened and thickened. She tipped the jar over Gart. The liquid trickled slowly, defying gravity, and spiralled to the feather where it was soaked up into the quill on contact. The feather bounced on Gart's chest, flicking up at the sides and turning over. Another feather grew out of it. Then another. Then more. Feathers swirled around each other so fast it was impossible to distinguish anything but a dark blur of movement. A beaked face popped out of the mass. The swirling stopped. Two wings flapped.

The newly formed magpie rearranged its wings so that they folded comfortably on its back, ruffled its feathers and shook its long tail. Settling on Gart's collarbone, it pecked him sharply between the eyes.

"Ow!" Gart shouted, his mad squalling coming to a blissful end. "What was *that* for? Stupid bird."

The magpie opened its wings and took to the skies.

"Yeah, get out of here." Gart jumped to his feet and watched it disappear over the trees. Realising something was different, he paused.

Will grinned. Gart's eye had stopped rolling. His posture was normal, jawline no longer so square. His hair was thick and dark, with the same red gleam his sisters had in theirs. The spell had worked.

"Gartaspia." Dante leapt on him and hugged tight. "You're okay."

Gart raised his hand to examine it over Dante's shoulder. "I really am, aren't I?" He looked past his hand to his auntie Scilla, whose face had lost all trace of its usual severity. "Thank you. You saved me." He left Dante's embrace. "And thank *you*," he said, smiling a warm, grateful smile at Will, a kind and happy twinkle in his deep brown eyes.

"What for?" Will asked. "I didn't do anything."

"Yes. You did."

Dyelann, rubbing the heel of his palm in circles over his injured chin, gestured impatiently at Gart. "Come on then. Was it your sister who did this to you or not?"

"Was it my sister who did *what* to me or not?"

"What do you think?" Dyelann snapped.

"Was it Molina?" Dante asked, reluctant, openly dreading the answer.

Gart frowned at her. "Was *what* Molina?" He glanced around at everybody like he'd only just noticed them. "What are we all doing here? What's going on?"

"Oh no," Scilla grumbled. She hauled the book back into her arms and peered down at the page. "Oh dear. I missed that part. The spell undoes spells okay but has an unfortunate side effect of erasing all memory of said spells. It's the only way it can work, to purge the mind and body of the spell altogether."

A chorus of disappointed groans resonated from the wots.

"Hello," Gart said to Will. "Are you with one of these wots? Have you wished for anything good?"

Dyelann tutted. "I preferred him before."

"I don't believe we've met," Gart said to Dyelann, holding out a hand to him. "I'm a friend of Blue's."

"That's too bad," Dyelann said, and didn't shake his hand.

"Ah." Gart lowered his arm. "You must be Dyelann."

Dyelann tilted his head, questioning how the witch had come to this accurate conclusion.

"Blue told me you were… just a delight." Gart lifted the top of his tattered outfit with two fingertips. "What the heck am I wearing?"

Foyer pressed his forehead into his hands.

"What are we going to do now?" Henry asked over Dyelann muttering about how he *was* a delight.

Branches creaked and leaves rustled from somewhere behind Will. It sounded as if someone was jumping from tree to tree, like a monkey, or Tarzan. Startled, he turned to see what it was. There was nothing. When he looked back, Blue was grasping at his chest and gasping for breath just like he'd been after Will had first brought him back to life.

"It's too late," he panted. "Something's wrong." He staggered. "I can't breathe."

And he collapsed dead at Will's feet.

Chapter Fourteen: A Cat among Mice

Dante and Foyer crouched at Blue's sides, both rocking him roughly, trying to stir him.

Will felt useless. "Is he okay?"

"No," Foyer said. "He's dead."

Will's throat swelled. Everything became painfully real, and he no longer liked this place. He yearned for the peaceful simplicity of home, arguing parents or none. His heart felt too heavy, like it had been replaced with a bag of sand.

Dyelann peered down at Blue. "Don't be stupid, he's fine."

"He's dead!"

Branches shook again, causing Scilla and Gart to spin around to see behind them.

"Neethers," Scilla announced.

Henry shifted about like he had no idea which way to turn.

"Away," Lillian said. "Time to go."

"Neethers," Scilla shouted again, louder, to be heard over the hysteria. "Everyone, be aware, there are neethers here." She pushed Gart ahead of her. "Do not believe your eyes. Think twice before you act!" She and Gart disappeared into the upright trees heading out of No-go Ebb, closely shadowed by Lillian. Henry rushed after the witches, and Maik was quick to follow his lead.

Foyer embraced Dante, who gaped down in shock at Blue's body. He held her tightly. "We have to go," he said. "We have to go."

"We can't just leave him here."

"We have to," Foyer said again, and gripped her hand in his. "Will. Dyelann. Come."

The bag of sand in Will's chest skittered and shook, lightening its load. "No, wait," he said. "I can bring him back to life. I can bring him back to life." He tried to get to Blue, but Foyer stopped him.

"Neethers are coming," he said, using his spare hand to drag Will along with him and Dante.

"No. No, let me go!"

Dyelann trudged along behind them, staring back, clearly having just as difficult a time leaving Blue behind as the others, despite his claims of hating him.

"Let me go! Let me go!" Will fought frantically against Foyer's grip, but the wot was too strong.

"Snap out of it," Foyer shouted, refusing to release him. "The neethers are coming to kill you, Will. We've got to get you away from here."

Something ploughed into Will, snatching him from Foyer's hold. Will tumbled head over heels, the creature falling along with him, and it landed on top of him, an unbearable weight on his bones. It screeched piercingly in his face.

He tried to gasp but his ribs were squashed, and his lungs couldn't fill. He stared up at the creature. It was the shape and size of a man but had no face on its head. No eyes, no nose, no ears, just two jutting cheekbones and a wide, drooling mouth filled with two rows of needle sharp, milk white teeth.

His mind spun. His vision became patchy. Black spots. White spots. He needed to breathe. He needed to get this thing off him. This monster. This neether. It had come to kill him, Foyer had said. It was going to kill him right now. He'd never take another breath.

Two bulges appeared under the creature's grey skin, where its eyes should have been. A pair of sickly yellow eyeballs burst from under the surface to inspect Will. They shrank back and the skin bound itself while the creature squealed again, leaning closer, its hot breath showering him with spittle.

The faceless head started changing. Its grey skin filtered vein blue. Enormous flittering black eyes forced themselves open. The creature morphed into a banter, right there on top of him. He wanted to scream, but he had no scream in him. All he could do was push his injured hand under his back. Blue's piece of coat fell off.

"Foyer," he tried to shout, but the word was little more than a tickle in his throat. "Foyer, help me." He wriggled, pointlessly. "Back off and vwa. Back off and vwa!" He had forgotten that he'd lost his pretend wand and was devastated nothing was happening.

The banter's ugly mouth contorted as it considered where to bite.

A spatter of warm goo slapped Will across the face. Only after he was covered in the stinking viscous fluid did he realise the banter had exploded and he was now wearing its remains. He sat up, gulping air into his burning lungs, and tried to wipe the gore from his clothes as he scrambled to his feet.

Dante, wand in hand, blew hair out of her flushed face. "Serves him right."

Will tried not to let her see that he was trembling. "Blue said banters were too slow to get me," he said weakly.

"That wasn't a banter," Foyer said. "That was a neether. It's like we told you before, they're our opposites. They're the bringers of nightmares. They bring to life what you wish not to happen. It's okay now. They're gone. Everything's fine."

"Yeah, don't worry," Blue said. "We scared them off."

"Blue!" Will couldn't believe what he was seeing. There was Blue: Alive again, like nothing had happened. Will threw himself at the wot and wrapped his arms around his waist. One of the frock coat's buttons jabbed into his cheek, but he just squeezed tighter. "You're alive."

Blue laughed, embarrassed. "Course I am."

"But you died."

"Yes," Blue said. "I thought we'd established that already." He tried to step back from Will, who continued to cling onto him as if he had no intention of ever letting go. "What's the matter with you?" He pushed Will away, quite roughly.

"No, you died again, just now." Will's relief was making him more emotional than he would normally allow himself to be. He hoped nobody noticed.

Dyelann rolled his eyes. "Stop trying to cheer me up, Will."

Foyer stood alert. "It must have been the neethers messing with your head. They're still close by. We have to keep going. Listen, Will, you can't believe everything you see when neethers are about."

Will walked along with them, fingers clamped around Blue's coat. He didn't understand what had just happened. Everyone's reactions to Blue's death had been so genuine. Their shock, their grief, it had all felt so real. How could it not have been real? If you couldn't believe everything you saw when neethers were about, and if neethers were still close by, how could he know what was real now? How could he know what wasn't?

He dropped Blue's coat and fled, as fast as his legs would allow, his every breath a stab of real pain.

Those people might not be who they appeared to be. They could be anyone. Nothing was what it seemed in this place. Blue might still be where they'd left him, for all he knew, dead and gone.

He had to find someone he could trust. The only one he could think of, bizarrely, was Cesar, so he hurtled back into the depths of No-go Ebb to search for the round, tilted hut among the slanted trees. The increasing terror that a banter would accost him any second now sent him running so fast his own legs could hardly keep up with him, and they nearly tripped him three times before an unexpected movement to his immediate left sent him darting off track and skidding to a clumsy stop.

Foosay Hoo waved at him, her rainbow poncho flapping. "Hold your horses, boy," she said. "Where do you think you're rushing off to, all alone?"

His racing heart squelched, and he tried to take off again, but Foosay caught the back of his jacket with an impressively fast arm before the message to run reached his legs.

"Calm down," she said, kind and steady. "Whatever's the matter?"

Panicking that he had been captured, that she would never let him go, Will leaned away. "You're not Foosay. I'm not stupid. Get off me!" In a last-ditch effort to escape he wrenched himself free from his jacket, leaving it dangling in her hand.

She offered it back to him. He just stared at it, afraid that if he accepted it, she would grab him again.

"Who do you think I am? What on earth has happened?" She pushed the jacket closer to him, urging him to take it. When he did, she turned around and fumbled with something at the other side of the closest tree.

Will considered making a run for it while she was distracted, but she plonked a small wooden chair down in front of him and motioned for him to take a seat. Then she brought out a second chair from the same spot behind the tree, ran her hands down the back of her skirt to tuck it neatly under her bottom, and sat.

"Come on. Sit down. Talk to me. Maybe I can help."

Will stared at her, determined not to fall into a trap. "You're just trying to trick me again." Comforted by the sight of her wild, silver candyfloss hair wobbling in all its splendour with the breeze, he grudgingly shuffled around the chair and sat down.

"I came," Foosay said, "because I was a little concerned."

Certain that the kindness she was showing was a façade, Will decided to play along with her and see where it led. "What about?"

"About Blue, actually. Listen, laddie, I know I wasn't in the best of moods when we first met. But after you'd gone, I couldn't stop thinking about what you said about bringing Blue back to the land of the living. It was spinning around and around in my head. Long ago, mystics wrote that a dead wot might be brought back to life, should someone wish for it enough. And I'm not talking wishing in words, I'm talking wishing in the blood. Wishing so hard for something that sheer human will would generate the power to return the wot's lifeforce to its body. After you left me, it occurred to me that the only person ever known to have that kind of power… was the Maker." She raised her thin eyebrows. "Do you know of the Maker?"

"Yes," Will replied, cautious.

"What worries me, my dear, is the mystics also wrote of the Maker having a descendant who will have the power to unmake the wots and end their line altogether."

Will remained steady, aloof, so as not to give the witch an opportunity to fool him.

"You do understand what I'm saying?" Foosay patted her skirt straight on her lap. "I'm not accusing you. I'm just concerned. Where is Blue? Why aren't you still with him?"

His carefully maintained composure was lost in an instant, as Will felt the real need to pour his heart out to the witch. "I didn't know if it was really him or not," he said. "Neethers came and confused me. They made Blue die, but then he was alive again, and one was a banter, and Dante killed it, but I didn't know if it was even really her either. I didn't know what was real."

"But… You haven't killed Blue?" Foosay asked warily.

"*Me*?" Will couldn't believe his ears. Had she seriously just asked him if he'd killed someone? "No!"

"You're not the descendant?"

"No."

The witch sank back in her chair. "That's certainly a relief to hear. Blue gets on my nerves something evil these days, but that doesn't mean I don't care about him. I'd been planning to mix my colours for a chat with my dearly departed aunt, but after you left me filled with uncertainty, I thought my time would be better served finding out more about the descendant. I discovered that he is, in fact, alive and in Wynne as we speak."

"It's not the disnendant," Will said.

"Descendant," Foosay corrected him.

"That's what I said. But it's not him. It's the real one. The real Maker."

"You're saying it's the original Maker?"

"The real one."

Foosay stiffened. "But that can't be. The Maker is dead. Only his legacy lives on. What makes you think it is the true Maker?"

Will shrugged. "The Maker told me."

"You've seen him?"

"No, I haven't seen him. I can just hear him."

"Oh." Foosay paused. "Can anybody else hear him?"

Will slipped his jacket back on, inadvertently exposing his wound to the witch, who rose from her chair with a sympathetic gasp.

"What happened to your hand? Poor child. That looks sore."

Will hid it in his pocket.

"Hmm." She waited for him to relent and let her see, watching him while he watched her watch him, and he made up his mind that no shawl on this planet could have flattened and concealed that vast amount of frizz as effectively as the shawl he'd seen her wearing earlier. Not even a magic shawl. It would be like strapping a poodle under a napkin.

"I think Molina was pretending to be you," he said, thinking aloud.

"And whyever would she do that?"

"She's the one who stole the gems. She keeps pretending to be other people and telling the warders to kill Blue."

Foosay sat back down, too shocked to worry about her skirt creasing this time. "Molina Simms is responsible for all this insanity? And she has the warders' vita? What about the wickers? Where do they stand on all this?"

"I don't know."

"Good. They should stay out of this. We don't need them complicating things."

"It already is complicating."

Foosay smiled at him with such warmth she reminded Will of his grandmother. "And where were you running off to so fast?"

"I wanted to find Cesar." Pointedly, he added, "Blue trusts Cesar."

"Would you like some company?" she offered.

His quick, "No," surprised her.

"What if you should happen upon trouble? I could help. It isn't safe out here for people who look like you."

"Why?" Will was offended. "What do I look like?"

"Like a witch. But you're not a witch, so you can't even defend yourself. It'd be like sending a puppy out with a pack of warring wolves."

"I'm not a puppy," Will said, indignant.

"Well, you're certainly not a wolf." Foosay stared at the bottom of Will's chair and leaned forward in hers. "Did you see that? I saw a mouse."

Will didn't understand her wonderment. "So?"

"Mice have been disappearing from Wynne over the last few weeks. It's a mystery as to where they've been going. But it can't be as bad as everyone's been saying if I just saw one, can it?"

Will remembered the barn owl that had fallen into Cesar's home complaining to the ware about not being able to find any mice.

"Small animals can be sensitive to bad magical vibes," Foosay went on. "They can sense when danger is afoot."

"You think they're disappearing because something bad's going to happen?"

Foosay took a breath as though she would reply, but then changed her mind and gave him another reassuring smile.

"I have to find Cesar now," Will said, an apology in his tone. He stood up.

"I bottled some of the potion I made earlier." Foosay reached into a handbag under her poncho. She showed him a plastic bottle that had once contained an orange flavoured soft drink, according to the label, and shook it at Will as if to prove she was telling the truth.

"Is that like a portal?"

She laughed at him. "Youth today. No, dear. This potion has the power to move an entire house. A portal can't do that. And we don't even have to take the lid off. Where is it you want to go?"

"To Cesar."

"Yes," Foosay said patiently. "And where might we find Cesar?"

"In a little, round, slanty house in No-go Ebb."

"I know of that place. Not even so very far from here. Very good." She shook the bottle at Will again. "Watch this." She cleared her throat. "Now then. Take this young man and me to the old hut in the limited access area of No-go Ebb," she said to the bottle, and then told Will, "Portals won't get you into that place."

"No. Dante told me… Whoa." A tingle shivered up and down his spine, and his stomach rolled over. The spell of nausea passed quickly.

"Here we are."

"Like magic," Will whispered, amazed.

"Not *like* magic," Foosay said. "It *is* magic. Anyway, you're here and you're safe, so I'll be able to sleep tonight at least. You want me to come in with you?"

"No. Sorry. But Cesar will know you're coming, and they might run away."

"Fair enough. Run along. I'll wait here in case you need me."

Will gazed at the witch, grateful to her, and she acknowledged the unspoken thank you with a nod and a smile. He sprinted to the hut, tumbled in through the door, not having expected it to open so easily, and tripped over Popset who was lying right in front of it.

Popset grumbled something.

"Is Cesar here?" Will asked, picking himself off the floor.

"Little weasel scarpered as soon as he heard the door go," Karson said, still seated at the table where they'd left him. "He told us Foosay Hoo was in the vicinity. Did you pass her at all?"

"She brought me here."

Karson's moody indifference quickly became moody concern. "Why aren't you with Foyer? Did you find Blue?"

"Yes."

"And?"

Will shrugged.

"What is-" Karson copied Will's shrug. "-supposed to mean? You don't know? How can you not know? Were you not there? Tell me what happened."

"Neethers," Will said, flustered.

"Are you all right?"

"Yes, but I got confused, so I came back here."

Popset blew loudly through his lips. "You'd have to be confused to come here," he said cattily from where he lay by the door.

"I don't know what's going to happen now," Will went on, hoping Karson would tell him what to do. "We think Molina is the baddie."

"Molina Simms?" he said, in the same way everybody did when they first heard the suggestion, like they couldn't quite wrap their minds around the idea. "And what brought you to this conclusion?"

Cesar flickered back into view by Karson's side, peering at Will with great interest.

"We found Gart and worked it out from what he said to us."

"So not necessarily Molina Simms then," Karson muttered to Cesar.

A quiet knock at the door alarmed the four of them, and they all stared at it.

"Who is it?" Karson asked Will. When he received no reply he yelled, "Who is it?"

Cesar quivered, as if in two minds whether to remain visible.

The door slid open, and the immaculately presented Art poked his well-groomed head around it.

"Hello," he said with a grin that made his moustache bounce upwards. "Ah, perfect timing. I have information for you." Striding carefully over Popset, he let the door close itself behind him.

"Is that so?" Karson said. "Do share."

"The young lady witch that came along claiming she'd had a premonition."

"Lillian," Will said.

"Lillian, Raphael, whatever." Art checked his watch. "I had a little vision of my own. Thought I ought to pop by and mention: You may want to get back to your friends. Quick as you like." There was a smug satisfaction to his tone that irked Will. He stepped back over Popset and let himself out. "Cheerio!" he shouted just before the door clicked shut.

"What do you suppose he meant by that?" Karson said.

Will didn't stay to discuss it further. He scurried around Popset and raced away from the hut, back to where he had left Foosay, and was glad to see her still waiting.

"All okay?" she enquired. "Was he there, the ware you wanted?"

Will nodded. "You've got to take me back to Blue. I think he's in trouble with Lillian."

"Oh, no. What's he done to upset her? Don't tell me he's been throwing horse manure again. I warned him that wouldn't win him any friends."

"No, I mean they're both in trouble." Will shook his hands in frustration. "Art just told us he had a vision about Lillian. He was all happy, and he hates Lillian."

"Art? Artrenamagancer, you mean? The seer?"

"R-tree-no what? Why does everyone around here have such stupid names?"

"Don't be rude. What has the seer got against Lillian?"

"I think he's jealous of her. She told the wots she'd had a prennamission and wanted to help."

"Premonition."

"That's what I said. Prennamission."

Foosay made a thoughtful 'hmmm' sound and held her fingers to her withered face, thumb under her chin. "According to a seer I recently spoke with, our dear Lillian is claiming to be the descendant of the Maker's adoptive mother."

"You mean the witch that took him in?" Will asked, surprised by this new information.

"Yes, apparently so. If this is the truth, there's little wonder she had a vision of what's going on with the wots. It's in her genes to take an interest in their fate. Her mother's grandmother's great grandmother's great, great, grandmother, or however many grandmothers it is, was very much involved in their creation."

"That's a lie!" the Maker shouted, startling Will, who was unprepared for the intrusion. His insides lurched like he'd been walking down a staircase and missed a step.

"Beg your pardon? You know something I don't?"

"I don't know," Will said cautiously.

"She never had any children of her own," the Maker said, his anger prickling under Will's skin.

"Oh, she never, did she not?" Foosay asked. "And how did you happen upon this piece of information? Reliable source?"

"I don't know," Will said again.

"Very reliable," the Maker reminded him. "From someone who knew her better than anyone, in fact."

"Oh." Will nodded. "The Maker told me."

"What's going on here?" Foosay asked. "Are you feeling well?"

"Could you take me to Blue, please?"

The witch showed him the empty bottle. "I used the last of it to get you here." She scowled, and Will wasn't sure if she was frustrated with him or with herself. "I can't even make a portal out of this wretched place. We'll have to walk."

"You will," the Maker said.

"Sorry," Will said, ashamed of himself for speaking that way to an old lady. Of course, he hadn't said it at all, but Foosay didn't know that, and he didn't want her to think badly of him. "It's not me."

"Yes, it is me. And I don't need your help."

"It's not me," Will insisted.

"And I'm not a pup among wolves," the Maker said, taking a backwards step away from Foosay. "I'm a cat among mice." He bowed to her. "Good day."

With that, Will's vision blurred and a frosty whoosh breezed by his ears like he'd stuck his head out of the window of a speeding car. When he next could see, Foosay Hoo had gone, and the trees around them were no longer the slanted ones of No-go Ebb but the solid, upright variety found deeper in the forest.

Blue's worried voice drifted Will's way from somewhere close by.

"How did you do that?" Will whispered, afraid the neethers were playing tricks again.

"I'm the Maker. I can do lots of things."

"But you don't want me to help Blue and Lillian. Why did you bring me here?"

"I want to know why this Lillian Scrossly is claiming to be my mother's progeny. My mother had no children of her own. There was only me."

"Maybe Lillian never said that at all," Will said. "Maybe whoever Foosay talked to got it wrong."

"I need to make certain. Now, stop talking to yourself and find those wots."

"Please don't hurt them," Will begged.

The Maker did not reply.

Accepting the conversation was over, Will followed the sound of Blue's voice and caught up to his friends. Lillian, Henry and Maik were with them now, but there was no sign of Scilla or Gart. Dyelann walked well ahead of everyone else, while Blue trailed behind with Dante and Foyer, jabbering sadly to them. Dante had an arm laid consolingly across his back, but she was deep in quiet conversation with Foyer and wasn't listening to a word Blue said.

"I'm back now," Will called, and the three of them stopped walking to greet him.

"Oh, Will, thank Chika." Dante removed her arm from Blue, who straightened up and stopped sulking. "You had us worried sick."

Foyer called the others back. "Will's here!" he shouted, scattering a few birds, and Dante clipped him sharply around the side of his head.

"What is wrong with you? Do you have a two-second memory or something?"

"Sorry."

Dante seemed sorry too. "I know you are," she said, gentler. She smiled at Will. "At least you're back with us now."

"Where did you go?" Blue demanded, but Dyelann talked over him.

"Kidlet. Do you remember when I told you to stick with me in future? This time, do it. Right?"

Will nodded compliantly. "I got confused."

"That's what neethers do to you."

"I wasn't sure you were all really you, so I went to see Cesar and Karson, because I knew they were definitely still them."

A mischievous look crossed Lillian's face. "What makes you so sure we're really us now?"

"Don't." Blue glared at her. "You'll scare him off again. We're definitely us. I promise."

"Lillian, I think you're in danger," Will said, and she tittered behind her fingers. "No, really," he said, hurt that she'd not taken his warning seriously. "Art said so."

She stopped laughing at the mention of the seer. "What's he been saying?"

The Maker didn't give Will chance to reply. "First answer this: Why have you been telling people you're the descendant of the Maker's adoptive mother?"

Will stayed quiet.

"How did you know that?" Lillian asked.

Will and the Maker continued to wait for her answer.

"I am her descendant," she said. "Or so I've been led to believe." All trace of her previous charm and sweetness vanished. Her face became hard and callous.

"She never had children of her own," the Maker said stiffly, and Lillian clenched her fists by her sides. "Why are you lying?" He set Will's eyes on the witch. "What are you hiding?"

Lillian breathed out sharply through her nose. Then her hands loosened, and she flicked a pigtail. "Okay, so I lied. It's too late now anyway."

Dante squinted. "Too late for what?"

A cruel grin grew on the younger witch's lips. "Exactly. Too late for wot."

"You're not the descendant of the Maker's witch mother," the Maker said, working out the truth as he spoke it. "You're the descendant of the Maker." His sadness weighed Will down. "Mine," he whispered to himself, audible only to Will.

"How do you know?" Lillian screamed, shrill, insane, eyes flashing in fury. "How do you know?" She stormed closer to Will, and he shrank back from her.

Dante shoved her hands into Lillian's back, pushing her viciously away from Will, and Lillian stumbled, staggered, and caught her footing only at the last moment before she would have lost balance and fallen.

She wheezed a laugh as she righted herself. "It doesn't matter. You've only brought my plans forward. That's all." Glowering at Will, she flicked a pigtail in Dante's face, and then raised both hands above her head, fingers curled like claws. When she lashed them back down, the daggers that Maik, Henry, and Dyelann carried sprang from their belts, from Henry's hands, and thrust blade-first into their stomachs, toppling all three of them. They yelped and grunted in shock, in pain, crumpled where they'd landed, taking the handles of the weapons they'd thought safe and dragging them from their abdomens.

Dante's hand dashed for her wand, but Lillian drew hers first and pointed it at Foyer, blasting a gust of fire from its tip that caught his sleeve ablaze. Dante leapt onto Foyer to floor him, desperate to kill the flames before they spread. While they were occupied, Lillian turned on Blue.

"I didn't want to kill you again just yet. It wasn't the plan. But your little friend ruined all that." Her fingers ran up and down her snapped wand. "I don't want the witch to get your power either, you know." She aimed the wand at Blue, twirling it in small circles. "It's rightfully mine, after all. But no matter. I'll just have to take them from her instead of from you."

Dyelann lurched to grab her ankle, unbalancing her and giving Blue chance to dive for cover.

The second Foyer was free from the flames, Dante stood and pointed her wand at Lillian's head.

Lillian laughed provokingly.

"I'll kill you," Dante said.

"No, you won't. You can do nothing against me now, Dante Simms."

The two witches reminded Will of the gunfight scenes in his grandmother's cowboy movies, staring at one another, perfectly still, each waiting for the other to make a move.

Dante lifted her arms in a sudden, vigorous movement that flexed her entire body, heightening her by inches, her wand floating horizontally before her. "Goddess Chika of the South, I summon you. I summon you to take this witch! Take this witch!" She gabbled faster when Lillian aimed the broken wand. "Goddess Chika, I implore you!" Blackness spread over her eyes. Dark red tears spilled down the sides of her nose. "Quick, before she kills me!"

A great wind spiralled through the trees, shaking the branches, blowing up debris that scattered like shrapnel all around, and blustered headlong into Lillian with such speed and strength she barely kept hold of her wand. The wind enveloped her in a cocoon of stampeding air, circling her like a mini tornado. With an ear-splitting snap it disappeared, Lillian along with it.

"Where did she go?" Will asked. He hoped they had seen the last of Lillian.

"Not far enough." Dante patted Foyer's singed arm softly, asking, "Are you okay?" Her hand went to her open mouth when she saw the three bleeding wots on the ground.

Blue knelt beside Dyelann. "Are you going to be okay?" he asked, voice low and, Will could tell, scared.

"Oh, I'm sure, Blue," Dyelann said, eyeing the long bronze blade that lay next to him, red droplets glinting. "We'll be just fine and dandy." He reached a trembling hand behind his back and pulled it back to reveal blood-soaked fingers. "Went straight through, all right." His voice was strained. "What happened to you, Dante? Why did she say you couldn't hurt her?"

"Oh," she gurgled, dabbing blood and tears from her cheeks with a sleeve. "She must have done something back in No-go Ebb when I backed up her spell on the blades. Something to make her immune to my magic when she touched my stick with hers. I should have known. I should have known. I'm so sorry."

"We all should have known," Foyer said, clutching his left arm, which had suffered the worst of the blaze.

Maik and Henry were even quieter than normal, slumped where they'd fallen.

"What shall we do?" Blue asked Foyer.

"I don't know," Foyer stuttered. He turned to Dante. "I don't know," he said again, this time horrified.

Will watched, drowning in guilt. He had caused this. Why hadn't he kept quiet? Why hadn't he handled the situation with more care? And why hadn't he realised that Art had been trying to warn him his friends were in danger *from* Lillian? Will had been worried for her. He had wanted to warn her, to help her. How could she have betrayed them like this? She'd acted like their friend. They'd trusted her. How could anybody be so cruel? His head swam. "I'm sorry," he croaked, but nobody heard.

The Maker forced him to walk aside, out of hearing distance of the others. "This wasn't your fault," he said.

"It was. It's all my fault."

"I misread the information we had too, not just you."

"Who cares what you think? You want them all to die anyway. Get out of me! I don't want you here anymore!"

"I can't do that," the Maker said, softly, not quite a whisper. "I'm sorry. Even if I wanted to, I don't know how."

"Please, can't you help them?" Will begged, clinging on to the thread of hope that the Maker wasn't the irredeemable baddie he'd first thought. "Please? *Please*?"

"I can't. I'm sorry." He faltered. "And if you knew... if you had any idea what I'd been through, you wouldn't ask it of me."

"I don't care." Will wiped his brow with his knuckles. "I don't care what you've been through. You're a bad person."

The Maker had nothing more to say, so Will stamped back to his friends.

"There's a healer at the back of No-go Ebb," Dante was saying. "I can get there and bring him back here. It shouldn't take too long if I run." She lifted her trouser bottoms to show them her navy plimsolls. "See? Sensible footwear and everything."

Foyer wrapped his arms around her, face pressed against her shoulder. "I don't know what we'd do without you."

She returned the embrace and lulled him. Then she shoved him away. "We don't have time for that. I'll be as fast as I can." She shouted to the injured wots, "You three just stay alive. Just stay alive until I get back, okay? That's all you have to do."

"Easier said than done," Maik said with a small smile, and wheezed a shallow breath.

Dante smiled back at him and ran away.

"Why didn't she do a portal?" Will asked.

"You can't make portals into that part of the Ebb," Foyer said. "Plus, summoning beings from other realms to fight for you takes a lot of energy. She'll need time to rejuvenate." He clasped his head in both hands and paced nervously. "All we need now is for the warders or neethers to show up while we're defenceless."

"The wenn was right about the descendant coming to kill us after all," Blue said, in a daze. "Lillian Scrossly though? I knew her grandparents." His eyes regained their focus and he pointed them coldly in Will's direction. "It must have been her mother who was from that line, not the Scrosslys. There was always something off about that family. Something nasty and deep set. Some sort of dormant bad allele was bound to pop open at some point and produce the scourge of all things sordid."

"You're just trying to get a reaction from me, aren't you?" the Maker said, turning his head to stare back at the wot with deliberately intimidating intensity.

Blue clenched his jaw.

Will regained control of his body and forced the Maker's stare away from Blue. "You shouldn't have pulled them out, you know," he said to the fallen wots. "My mum told me, when you get stabbed, you're meant to leave it in."

"Get stabbed a lot, do you?" Dyelann asked.

"No, but my mum's an A and E nurse and she told me," he said adamantly. "You should have left them in."

Dyelann lifted the dagger. "Maybe I should stick it back in, then."

"No!" Foyer and Will shouted in unison, startling Dyelann into dropping the weapon from his weak grip.

"Maik!" Foyer shouted. "Don't you dare close your eyes. You've got to stay awake until Dante gets back."

Will's mind whirled, trying to think of something, anything, to help. "The neethers want to kill me because they think I'm the Maker's disnendant, right?" he asked.

Foyer nodded and corrected him, hesitantly. "Descendant."

"That's what I said. So why don't we just tell them it's Lillian that's the disnendant, not me, and then they'll leave us alone, right? And Lillian will leave us alone because she'll be running away from them when they go after her. Right?"

"Will, you can't 'just tell' neethers anything. They're not going to just stand there patiently waiting for you to explain yourself. And you may not be the descendant, but the real Maker is currently occupying your body, let's not forget. So, if anything, you really are the bigger threat as far as they're concerned."

"Oh," Will said, disappointed. "Oh. Ohhh. *Ow.*" A searing pain burned through his wounded hand. If his eyes and ears hadn't told him otherwise, he would have sworn his thumb was being stabbed into a sizzling frying pan with a fork.

"What's wrong?" Foyer asked, alarmed. "Is that where the banter bit you?"

Will nodded.

"Uh oh."

Will really did not like the sound of that uh-oh. The pain tightened and he gripped his hand harder.

Foyer stood to attention. "A banter must be close by. That's why it's hurting. Until the wound heals, it'll sting whenever a banter comes near."

Will begrudged the inadequacy of the word sting.

"I really thought they were extinct," Blue said blankly, lost again.

Foyer walked another slow circle in search of the banter. "They'll be drawn to the scent of these three bleeding all over the place."

"Oh, do pardon us," Dyelann panted, determined to voice his offence despite being hardly able to breathe.

"How could I not have noticed they weren't extinct before now?" Blue murmured.

"Because you're a clot," Dyelann struggled to say. Blood had spread in a huge wet stain around the slash in his shirt, and he moved his hands to see the damage, choking on his own breath. "Think this shirt's a goner," he joked.

"Foyer?" Henry said faintly, and Foyer rushed to his side. "I feel sick again."

"I'm not surprised," Blue said. "I feel sick too and I'm not covered in my own blood." He left Dyelann's side and began to wander away again.

Will caught his coat before he could go too far and towed him back to the others.

"Sorry. It's my gem. It pulls. It needs me to go."

"You can't," Foyer said. "Not yet. Not alone. Dante will be back soon with the healer. Just, everyone, hang in there."

"My gem's losing strength. I can feel it dying." Blue touched his stomach. "It hurts here. Deep."

Dyelann coughed and winced. "Oh yeah?" He nodded to the blood dribbling between his fingers. "What's that like?"

Blue smiled guiltily.

Unrelenting pain gnawed at Will's hand to the point he felt faint, but he couldn't complain in front of the wots while they were bleeding to death. "You need to go to the hospital." They would have painkillers there, for a start. "They'll stitch you up properly and make you all better."

"Wots can't go to hospitals," Blue said.

"Why not? You're no different from normal people."

"Of course we're different. We're immortal. We're…" He bowed his head. "We're... dying."

"Err…" Dyelann said weakly. "I don't want to worry anyone. But… there's a banter over there." He slumped back. "And it looks hungry."

Chapter Fifteen: Dust to Dust

Will hadn't realised before, because the banter he first encountered had stood upright, but it appeared to be the creature's natural state to walk on all fours. He watched it stretch its neck to sniff the air, toothy mouth opening like it could already taste what was coming. It quivered in anticipation, shoulder blades protruding from its curved back with each slow step.

"Uhh." Blue glanced at Foyer for guidance. "What do we do?"

"I don't know. Dyelann?"

Foyer, Blue and Will all looked down in surprise when there was no snotty reply. Dyelann had lost consciousness.

The banter rose onto its hind legs, the clawed, three-toed feet flexing as they took the weight.

"Stop." Foyer hopped in front of it. "Listen. They're poisoned. You eat them, you die."

A meagre swipe of its arm flung Foyer aside, and Will jolted out of the way. Pulsing pain surged through his hand with every thump of his rapidly increasing heartbeat.

Nose twitching, eyes flittering, the banter moved in on Henry. It reached out three veiny fingers and placed them longingly on the wot's chest one by one. Its back arched further as it lowered itself to Henry's bleeding stomach.

Blue pulled off his left boot and threw it swift and hard, catching the banter directly between its glinting black eyes. It glared like it would retaliate, but changed its mind, Henry's blood too great a lure. Blue yanked off his other boot and lobbed it even harder than the first, again hitting the banter square in the face, and again the banter turned to him, angered by the disturbance. It wasn't distracted for long.

Desperate, Blue lifted a thick, snapped branch. This too was flung at the banter, striking the creature's bony sternum, the old wood cracking apart on impact.

And when this failed to stop it from attempting to drink from Henry's wound, Blue snatched the dagger from the now unconscious Maik, slid the flat of the blade under his coat sleeve, then gave it a ninety-degree twist and pulled it back out, slashing its edge down the inside of his arm from elbow to wrist, shredding both fabric and flesh. He sucked in a deep breath, turning to Will open-mouthed, as though he hadn't expected slicing his skin apart to hurt.

A string of brown drool spilled from the corner of the banter's mouth. Its attention was all Blue's now.

"Blue!" Foyer shouted. "You stupid, brain-dead *idiot.* What were you thinking?"

The banter dropped to all fours and slunk towards Blue.

"Uhh…" He stumbled back, holding his arm out like he didn't know what to do with it. The dagger fell to the grass. "It's coming. What shall I do?"

Foyer crept up behind the banter while it followed steadily after Blue. He whipped the dagger up from where Blue had dropped it and aimed it at the banter's knobbly back.

Will held his breath.

With a quick, sharp thrust Foyer plunged the blade deep into the banter's gaunt haunches. Will flinched at the wet squelch that followed it out. Dark blue-green blood dribbled down the creature's heaving side. It dived at Blue, black tongue licking air, ravenous for the fresh blood that dripped from the tips of his extended fingers.

Foyer stabbed it again, this time in its opposite side.

It whined and coughed. Then it gave up. It limped forlornly away, taking its time in doing so.

Foyer opened Blue's ripped sleeve, shaking his head at him and saying something unintelligible under his breath.

"My arm hurts."

“I wonder why.” Foyer cringed at the sight of the gaping flesh.

“And my coat’s ruined.” Blue flicked the torn fabric to prove it.

“It was about time you got a new one anyway.” Foyer started to wrap the sleeve around Blue’s arm, but Blue skipped three paces back with his jaw open aghast. Foyer sighed at him. “You need to put pressure on it, Blue. Put pressure on it.” He noticed Will watching. “Are you doing okay there, Will? You don’t look well.”

“I’m fine,” Will mumbled, glad that they had no conception of the effect a banter’s presence had on him, the vice-like grip of mortal terror that overcame him every time he even thought of one. The gradually lessening pain in his hand was a relief in more ways than one.

“You sure?” Foyer waited for Will to nod, and then leaned over Dyelann. “Hey,” he shouted, giving him a rough shake. “Wake up.” The body flopped back down when Foyer let go.

Henry and Maik too were silent and still, unresponsive to Blue and Foyer’s scared calls of their names.

“What are we going to do,” Blue asked numbly, “if Dante doesn’t get back in time?”

Foyer said nothing.

They waited in silence.

For what felt a long, long time.

Will heard Dante declaring that she was back a second or two before he saw her. She had a disgruntled and sleepy looking man with her, whose oversized cuffs made his hands appear unusually small. He had obviously dressed in a hurry; his buttons hadn’t been lined up properly when he’d fastened them, so his shirt was askew.

“Come now, Acacia. No time for dilly-dallying. These wots need healing. Get to it.”

Will took his first proper breath since Lillian’s attack and rested against a tree. Dante had done it. She had found the healer in time. Things were finally beginning to go right.

Just as he let himself think so, the fallen wots disintegrated into ash, leaving nothing behind but three large heaps of flaky grey dust.

Dante cried out like she'd been mortally wounded. "What did you do?" She hit the healer around the head with both hands while he held up his arms to protect himself. "What did you do?"

"I did nothing. I did nothing!"

"What did you do, you monster! You were supposed to help them."

Will stared at the dust. The breeze whipped the tops of the piles away, shrinking them before his eyes. Was that really Dyelann blowing away into nothing? Dyelann was the strong one, the one Will depended on. Was he really gone now? He couldn't be gone.

Tricks of your eyes.

"It's not real," he said, out loud so he could be heard over Dante and the healer. "The neethers are making lies again." He squeezed his eyes shut and clamped his hands over his ears, confident that when he next looked the three wots would be alive and well. He could still hear Acacia protesting his innocence, though muffled now.

"I didn't have anything to do with this, I promise you."

"Bring them back," Blue begged. "Please. Heal them."

"There's nothing to heal. I can't heal dust."

Will pressed his hands down harder and hummed to block out their voices. This couldn't be real. Any minute now Dyelann would be standing there with that cocky smirk on his face, telling Will to stop being stupid and to stick with him. He risked a peek with one eye just in time to see Dante tottering away and Foyer chasing after her. The other eye opened automatically as he took his hands away from his ears. Where was Dante going?

"Don't go." Foyer caught her arm and swung her around to face him. "We need you."

"What is happening?" Blue asked, and his distraught confusion brought a lump to Will's throat.

"*Lillian.*" Dante rubbed her face with two rough swipes of her palms. "She must have made a spell so anyone stabbed by one of her blades would turn to dust."

Though still determined this was only his imagination, Will said, "But Blue's not dust."

"Blue? He wasn't stabbed." She noticed the blood dribbling from his fingers. "What happened?" She marched to the dismayed healer and forced him closer to Blue. "Fix him," she demanded. "And if he turns to dust, I will kill you. I will kill you so dead you'll be deader than any dead person ever to have died."

"Okay, okay, calm down!" Acacia yanked himself free. He took Blue's bleeding arm in his small hands and held it for a few seconds. Then he dug his thumbs deep into the wound and squeezed.

Blue hollered and shoved the healer away so hard the nervous man nearly went his length. He held his arm close, not watching the skin begin to scab over, only firing hateful glares at Acacia.

Will searched their surroundings. He wasn't sure what he was looking for, he only knew how badly he needed to see it. A sign. A sign that he was right, that this was wrong. This was all so wrong. His hope began to dwindle. "It's not real," he said again. This time it came out more like a question. "It's just the neethers."

Acacia stalked away, only turning back once to check that Dante wasn't about to set chase. As soon as he saw she wasn't paying him any attention, he ran.

Will watched him go, thinking he should have asked the healer to take care of his hand. Maybe it was for the best he hadn't. At least the bite would let him know if any more banters came along. While thinking this he felt guilty for not thinking about poor Dyelann and Maik and Henry, who were gone.

Foyer and Dante's hands found one another and held on tight.

"We need to tell Karson what's happened," Foyer said. "We need to warn him about Lillian."

"I wouldn't bother if I were you," came a melodious little voice that Will recognised at once.

Eve.

The wenn came to a graceful land on a low-lying branch near to Blue, with an obnoxious twist to her angelic face.

Dante lashed out at her, but Eve evaded the flying fist with a jump and a flutter of wings. Her second landing was not so graceful.

"Hear me out, or I'll sing so loud I'll put the lot of you in a coma for a month." She puffed out her chest to make herself that millimetre taller.

Dante stuck out her chin to suggest she would listen, if reluctantly.

"I know you know I knew about your brother," the wenn said. "And I'm sorry I lied to you." Her nose wrinkled. "Not really sorry. More like disappointed you found out."

"You disgust me," Dante said thickly.

"Oh, would you look at that." Eve pointed a finger at her dinky face. "I don't care."

"You should care. Because usually when things as small as you disgust me, I stamp on them, mop them up in a tissue and flush them down the toilet."

Blue moved closer to the wenn and yelled, "Tell us who you're working for!" Even through his grief he winked an exaggerated wink at Will, which Will decided meant he was only shouting at the wenn in a terrible attempt to intimidate her because of their earlier conversation, which seemed to have taken place a long time ago.

Eve laughed rudely at Blue. "As if I've come all this way to betray the one who will grant me eternal life, when she is closer to unlocking the secret than she has ever been." She sneered. "As if."

"Is it Molina?" Dante asked.

Eve pursed her butterfly lips. "Gart wasn't the only one my lady put a spell on. She's not stupid."

"You lied to me about my brother. Don't lie to me about my sister."

"I cannot tell you either way. Now, if you'll allow me to say what I came to say without interrupting me every two seconds, I am here with a message from my lady. She wants you to stop looking for her. Stop looking or you're going to get hurt. She has already won. All eight of the gems are in my lady's possession now. The power is hers."

"No!" Blue knocked the wenn off her branch with one angry swipe that sent her crashing out of control to the ground.

She coughed, winded, and tried to sit up, delicate wings crumpled over her back.

Dante towered over her. "Give me one good reason not to squash you like a bug right now."

The wenn took an almighty breath, but before her song could escape her lips, the witch slammed a foot on the tiny person and silenced her forever.

Will flinched and had to look away, sickened by the pop and crunch of splintering bones.

"That wasn't going to be a very good reason," Dante mumbled. She wiped her plimsoll clean on the grass.

Blue groaned with revulsion.

"We have to get to Karson," Foyer said, already running.

Dante took charge and directed the group to a pathway of lilac woodchips, which she declared would lead them into No-go Ebb.

Will watched the pale purple spray kicking up from everyone's dragging feet and tried to stop himself replaying the wenn's death on repeat in his head. Will wasn't the sort of person who could even kill a spider deliberately, never mind someone he'd had a conversation with. Eve was evil, no doubt. Will hated the way she'd treated Gart. But had the wenn really deserved to be crushed to death? How could Dante have murdered her like that? Now the witch was leading the way and speaking with Foyer like it had been a normal thing to do. Was murder so common around here that it meant nothing? Neither

Blue nor Foyer had protested. Did they not care either? Should Will not care?

Maybe he had been too lost in his thoughts to notice time passing, or maybe the path hadn't been a long one, but they were off the purple woodchips and back among the slanted trees of No-go Ebb before Will knew it.

He and Blue struggled to keep up with Dante and Foyer. Both were flagging, Blue weakening along with his gem, and Will mentally exhausted from witnessing so many horrible things in such a short space of time.

Blue shivered and wrapped his tattered coat tightly around himself. "What if Karson's dead?" he asked. "If Karson's dead, that's it for us. There's no chance for wots at all."

"Don't say that. I don't want you to die, Blue."

"I know, but if the worst does happen…" He paused, momentarily tongue-tied. "I want you to know I'm grateful for all you've done. And I'm sorry you never got the wishes I promised you."

How could Blue think that Will cared about wishes now? All he wished was for his friends to be okay, for Blue to be happy again, for Dyelann to be alive.

"You're not to stick around and get yourself hurt, okay? You just forget about Wynne and go home, where you're safe."

"Stop it, Blue," Will said gruffly. "I don't want the worst to happen."

Blue smiled. "I bet you… I bet you *wish* you'd never found me in that river."

"No, I don't. If I hadn't found you, you'd still be dead. And so would the others."

Blue's expression grew sombre. "We're all dead anyway," he said, in a voice so low it was barely there.

Will rubbed the sting from his eyes before any tears had chance to surface.

The wots' tilted hut came into sight. Foyer barged through the door so violently he might have knocked it from its hinges had it not been so solid. They could hear him shouting Karson's name. He flounced back outside. "They're not here," he said.

Blue stared at the door. "This is it, isn't it, Foyer? It's over."

"Nothing's over," Dante snapped. "You're not giving up. Not now. You've got to keep fighting."

"I don't think I can anymore," Blue said.

Dante gazed sadly at him. Then she focused on Foyer. "It's up to you, Foyer." She touched his arm. "You have to be strong now." She indicated to Blue with a subtle nod of her head. "Look at him. You're all he has now. He needs you. If you can't find the strength for yourself, find it for him."

A small, tired smile rose on his lips, and he spoke softly so Blue would not overhear. "I've always taken care of him."

"I know," Dante said. "And you're not going to stop now."

"No. You're right. I have to stop that witch."

Dante slid her hands down his arms and slipped her fingers between his. "We'll stop her together."

"Dante's right, Blue," he said, nodding at the witch. "Your gem has never stopped fighting for you. For us. Now we have to fight for it."

Will's eyes wandered to Dante's plimsoll. He told himself off. *Stop thinking about it.* "Who are you supposed to fight?" he asked, looking back to Dante and Foyer's faces. "What are you going to do?"

"I'll summon my sister," Dante said. "She's still a witch, however much stolen power she has. She can still be summoned."

"We can't do that," Blue said. "We don't have her book."

"I'm her blood. I can summon her, book or no."

Foyer let go of her hand. "Do it."

A disconcerting vibration quivered underfoot. At first, Will thought it was Dante's doing, that it was part of summoning Molina, but next came the thunderous rumble of many heavy, stomping feet.

Dante took a step forward, stiff and alert. "Warders."

A black-cloaked figure soared overhead. Will caught sight of it from the corner of his eye, but by the time he lifted his head it had gone.

"Did you see that?" he whispered, but nobody answered.

"Warders don't come here." Foyer stood tall, on guard. "I thought we'd be safe from them here."

"They'll go anywhere the one with their vita tells them to go," Dante said under her breath, letting her wand fall into her hand.

Warders started to appear in the spaces between the leaning trees.

Dante rushed to beckon Will, Foyer and Blue into the slanted hut. She slammed the door behind them and pointed her wand at it. Black smoke wisped from its tip and swirled around the lock for a few seconds before dissipating.

Foyer kicked up the rug by the corner of the settee to reveal a trapdoor in the floorboards. He tugged at the looped iron handle and lifted the hefty panel. A cloud of dust followed it up. Will clambered down the wooden steps after Blue and Dante. The cold, musty air reminded him of his dad's mouldy old shed at home. Foyer shut the door behind them, giving it a quick rattle to flatten the rug back down over the top, and it fell pitch black.

Will struggled to find the floor when he reached the bottom step. "I can't see a thing," he grumbled.

"Why not?" Foyer asked. "Are you okay?"

"We can't see in the dark like you wots can," Dante said. Her wand glowed, illuminating the room enough for Will to see how similar it was to the one above. There was no table in this room though, and instead of a scruffy green settee there were three scruffy green armchairs.

Dante shone her light at the wall opposite the stairway. It flashed over a narrow pine door. "Where does that lead?" she asked.

"It's a tunnel that takes you out of No-go Ebb," Blue said. "I used to sneak out that way sometimes when Karson got mad at me upstairs."

Foyer opened the door for Dante.

"We'll summon Molina as soon as we're somewhere safe," she said as she passed him.

"Nowhere is safe," a deep, echoing voice retorted from inside the tunnel.

Dante retreated, pushing Foyer behind her. Three warders followed her through the open door and into the dreary room.

The tallest of them pointed a bulky finger at Blue. "That's the one."

Will, Dante and the two wots shrank back to the steps behind, the warders matching their pace, evidently enjoying the hunt.

Dante shook the light out of her wand, bringing the room back to blackness.

Blue's hand wrapped around Will's arm and hoisted him up the stairs into the well-lit room above.

Foyer slammed the trapdoor down on the warders, and Dante set the same burst of smoke on it she had used on the front door. Again, it lingered before fading away.

The rest of the warders had not yet managed to force their way into the hut, no doubt due to Dante's charm protecting the door, but the surrounding walls juddered with every collision as their bodies rammed against it.

"I have to think," Dante said. "I have to think."

"Summon her now," Will suggested. "She's the only one who can stop them."

"You're right. You're right. I have to get the vita from her." She clapped her hands together in front of her face and closed her eyes, trying to concentrate over the relentless banging of warders throwing themselves at both doors. "Molina Simms, my sister, I call you forth," she chanted, arms in front of her like she was preparing to catch something that was about to fall from the ceiling. "Molina

Simms, blessed charge of Goddess Nanita of the North, I call you here to me now, my sister."

The door exploded from its hinges and crashed into splintered pieces against the wall. Warders piled in through the entrance like excited ants from a crack in the pavement.

Dante pointed her wand at the warders. "Back! Get back or I will kill each and every one of you."

Her threat had no effect. One of the warders grabbed Blue by his neck and hauled him closer. Blue made a strangled sound of pain, staring at the warder that was suffocating him.

Two of the others caught Dante's arms before she had chance to put up a fight. The wand clattered on the floor. She struggled to escape their grip, and they threw her down with such immense strength it was a wonder she didn't end up back in the basement.

Foyer tried to pick up her wand, but he too was thrown across the room like he weighed nothing.

Will alone did not move from where he stood, though not for lack of trying. He tried to jump into action and help his friends, but the Maker fought even harder to keep him still. For once, the being inside overpowered him, point blank refusing to let him budge.

"Hear me, Molina!" Dante shouted. "I call you here to me *now! Anilom!*"

A flash of light emanated from the wand on the floor, like someone had taken a photograph.

One after the other the warders dropped to their knees, as well-timed as falling dominoes. The one strangling Blue took the wot down with him, not releasing his grip.

"Dante?" Molina said, confused, having dropped from thin air directly in front of her sister. She laughed nervously at the warders surrounding her. "What's going on?"

"We..." one warder said.

"Don't answer!" she interrupted him, startled. Her eyelids fluttered. "Did you really just say what I think you just said, Dante Simms?"

"I had to get you here fast," Dante explained, retrieving her wand. "Tell him to let go of Blue."

Molina glanced at the warder and the struggling wot. "What makes you think he'd listen to me?"

"Just do it. Drop the innocent act, Mo, we all know you've got their vita."

"Don't be ridiculous." She stared at the ceiling.

"They're all bowing down to you!"

"The person with their vita must have told them to do that so you'd think I had it."

"Then you won't mind if I do this." Dante pointed her wand at the warder strangling Blue. Globules of black fluid leaked from the pointed end of the twisted stick. The same tarry liquid then began to spill from the warder's mouth until, with one last gurgle, he keeled over.

Blue stumbled away from the body, holding his neck and gagging as he tried to breathe again.

Molina shrugged her shoulders. "Well done."

Dante snatched the scarf from Molina's head. Her shocked gasp silenced the room.

What was left of Molina's hair was in red, matted tufts that protruded from random parts of her head just like Gart's had been. She tugged the scarf back from Dante and retied it.

"I can't... I can't believe it," Dante stammered. "It really is you. Mo. How could you?"

Molina straightened her scarf and rolled her eyes. "It's not like I wasn't going to share it with you."

"How could you do this to Gart?"

"I was going to share it with him too."

"*How could you!*" Dante slapped her sister smartly across the face.

Molina's expression switched from vaguely interested to savage in a blink, pupils spreading so wide and fast they smothered her irises.

Dante stood fast, her fury closely matching her sister's.

The warders rose and loomed over the witches, breathing like a pack of angry dogs.

Will waited, so afraid of what might happen next that he no longer wanted the Maker to let him move. Everybody stayed frozen in their places for just four or five seconds, but they were the longest four or five seconds of Will's life.

"Kill them," Molina said. "Kill them all."

Before anyone could so much as draw their next breath, Dante lashed out her hand to yank a hidden chain from Molina's neck. She held it up to the warders. A small, ruby red jewel dangled on the end of it from a silver clasp.

The huge men dropped back to their knees.

"What do you ask of us, master?" one asked.

Dante scowled at him. "Drop dead."

The warder's small head slammed onto the dusty floor.

"Oops." Dante grimaced.

Molina made a feeble attempt to catch the swinging pendant, but Dante held it out of her reach.

"I can't believe this of you, Mo. I really can't."

"Oh, give it a rest, Dan. Like you're so perfect."

"I didn't torture my brother for eleven years while crying crocodile tears to the rest of my family. That's sick and twisted and unforgivable and… Oh, how could you?"

Molina pulled a face.

"People are dead."

"You don't say," Molina said, pointing out the two warders Dante had killed. She crossed her hands behind her back. "Anyway, it was nice catching up, but I must dash. Important potion to mix. You understand. I'm sure I'll see you all again soon enough. Goodbye then. Oh, Blue, I nearly forgot. I have something for you, pumpkin."

She patted at her bottom. Then she took something from the back pocket of her trousers. The blade spun through the air, a silver blur, and jabbed straight as an arrow into Blue's shoulder. The force of it knocked him back down. She nodded with satisfaction at him, clicked her fingers and vanished faster than Cesar after a scare.

"Blue." Will finally found his legs and crouched next to the wot. "Are you okay?" The silver skulls sticking out of Blue's shoulder didn't look cool anymore. Just evil.

"Yeah, I think so." He nodded stiffly. "So, you say I'm not to pull this out?"

"Leave it in, wrap a bandage around it, call an ambulance," Will recited, remembering his mother's lesson well.

"Oh, Will." Blue groaned, wrenched the knife out, and dropped it like it was on fire. Blood spilled.

"You're supposed to leave it in," Will said, annoyed that Blue had ignored his clever advice.

"Okay, warders." Dante clapped her hands. "Listen up. I want you to go away and not bother us anymore. Go about your business and don't cause any more trouble for these wots. You hear? I mean it."

Grudgingly, the warders that were still alive left the hut.

Dante tucked Molina's necklace into a pocket and helped Foyer to his feet.

Foyer pulled the top of Blue's coat and shirt off his shoulder to examine the wound. "We should have held on to that healer a bit longer. Can you move?"

"I'm fine." Blue heaved himself up and Foyer guided him outside into the dusky evening. Rainclouds filled the skies.

A shadow swooped over Will, and he glanced up to see what had cast it. As before, it had gone before he could focus.

"I saw it too," the Maker said under Will's breath.

"What was it?" Will murmured, afraid the others would hear.

"I'm not certain."

"It was big."

"What's big?" Foyer asked.

Will's brain scrabbled for an answer that wouldn't get a bad reaction. "Those warders."

Dante pulled the spherical pendant from her pocket. "They shan't be bothering us anymore. Not as long as we keep hold of this."

"It's funny," Foyer said. "I didn't think vitas looked like that. They're meant to be pentagons. And flat. That's what I heard."

Dante rolled the red jewel between finger and thumb. "They responded to it," she said. "This must be it. You must have heard wrong."

"I suppose."

"I'll have to get that healer back."

Blue groaned. "No! We can't just keep healing me and waiting for the next thing to happen. You have to get Molina back here and you have to tell her to give us our gems back right now."

Foyer rubbed his temples and let out a small, stressed laugh. "She's not going to just give them back to us."

"Fine, then take her somewhere and keep her distracted while I go and get them back."

"Great idea," Dante said. "Or, you know, it would be if we knew where your gems were. That's half the problem, remember?"

"That's the thing, I think I would know where they were if Molina wasn't with them. I think they'd stay in one place."

Foyer let go of his head. "Did they stay in one place when she was here just now?"

"How am I supposed to know? I was a bit busy being throttled."

"Okay." Dante swiped her hair away from her face. "You really think you could find them?"

"If you keep her away long enough, yes."

She stared at Blue. Then Foyer.

"It's worth a try," he said.

She paused to consider her options before saying, "Fine. I'll go now."

"But wait." Will didn't like this plan. "How will you get her away from them? And how will you keep her away? What if she hurts you? Or what if she gets back too soon and hurts *us?*"

"Don't worry, Will. I won't let her lay a finger on any one of you." She patted Blue on the back, failing to notice him cringe with pain and pull away from her. "We'll get through this. We'll beat my sister. We have to." She pressed the claret vita into Foyer's palm and closed his fingers around it.

"What are you doing?" he asked.

"You'll have to hold on to this. I can't risk Mo taking it back from me." She squeezed his hand. Then she ran away, hopping on one leg for a few paces to secure one of her plimsolls over her heel.

Foyer's face hardened as soon as she was out of sight. "I don't like her going off alone."

"She's not any safer with us," Blue said.

The black blur rushed by overhead and caught Will's eye for a third time. "Did you see it that time?" he whispered.

"I see what you see," the Maker replied.

"What is it?"

"It looked like a harvester."

"Are you saying something, Will?" Blue asked loudly.

"I... I..." Will worried that Blue would assume he and the Maker were plotting against him. He couldn't let the wot think such a thing. "I was just saying I hope this works."

"It has to work," Foyer said.

Will looked up. A bird stared back.

"What's the matter?" Foyer asked.

"In the tree up there. One of Cesar's kites."

This kite was full grown, much larger than Dreyfus, the youngster Will had followed to Cesar's treehouse.

"I wonder where Cesar is," Blue said. "You don't think he's dead, do you?"

"He won't be dead," Will said. "He would have known she was coming, right? He'd have gone invisible before she got to them."

"No, no, no. He would have fought at Karson's side. He would never abandon someone he was looking after."

Will wanted to support Blue, but he couldn't imagine Cesar stepping up to fight a mouse, much less an evil killer witch.

The Maker chuckled and Will hurried to suppress him, clapping a hand over his mouth. Thankfully, the wots appeared not to have noticed.

"Sorry," the Maker whispered. "It just made me laugh."

"Wares are loyal," Blue said. "Once they befriend you, they'd die for you."

Will still doubted Blue's words, but he managed a nod that could have been construed as agreement.

The kite swept gracefully from its perch and circled its way down, displaying an impressive wingspan for a couple of slow, steady swipes before settling on a lower branch and cocking its head to watch them.

Someone shuffled by their sides, causing the three of them to turn their heads in unison.

A man stood there with them, gazing at the kite with interest. A man who appeared perfectly ordinary, except for the fact he had a small goblin-like creature on each of his shoulders. The goblins were almost identical to one another, the bristly hair sprouting from their heads and down their spines the only thing setting them apart, one being plain black and the other flecked with copper. Both had greenish-brown skin and eyes so large they filled most of their faces, leaving space only for a pair of nostrils and a tiny mouth. Resting comfortably and securely on this man's shoulders, they too gazed up at the bird.

"That's a red kite, that is," the man said. "Very nice. Are you birdwatching in particular or is this just a happy happenstance?"

From the fascination in his face, Will believed him to be genuinely interested.

"What's a wicker doing in these parts?" Foyer demanded. "What are you after?"

"Just out for a stroll."

Will glanced over the man's casual jacket and jeans, wondering how someone so normal had come to be hanging out in the middle of a forest with a pair of tiny monsters on his shoulders. Their eyes met, and Will immediately felt embarrassed for staring. "Dante says wickers are a vile lot of wrongdoers," he said, blunter than he'd meant to.

"Charming," the stranger said.

The goblin on his left shoulder giggled, a giddy, high-pitched noise, so exuberantly he had to save himself from rolling over the wicker's back.

"I won't lie," the stranger said, not at all put off by the creature's behaviour. "There are some rotten apples in our batch. But that's true of every batch."

"That witch made a vita thing for you because you were bad," Will said, silently ordering himself to shut up and stop provoking the wicker.

"That witch was a very stupid man to do something like that. Very stupid indeed. Imagine what could have happened if those vitas had fallen into the wrong hands. Doesn't bear thinking about. That's why we wickers destroyed that indigo vita the second that stupid witch dropped dead. I personally didn't mind so much when he had it. All he wanted was for us to keep to ourselves. That was fine. But if someone else had got their hands on it." He exaggerated a shudder, and the two goblins did the same. "I don't think I could have handled being someone's puppet."

"No," Foyer said sullenly. "I suppose not." He opened his hand and showed the wicker the claret vita. "But I have to hold on to this one for now."

The man stared down at it, and so did the goblins, who each leaned forward and slung an arm around his neck to keep from falling. "What's that supposed to be?"

Foyer froze in position.

"It's the claret vita," Blue answered, tightening his grip on his bleeding shoulder.

"That's not a vita," the wicker said, and the left-shoulder goblin sniggered hysterically for a second time.

Foyer's eye twitched.

"What? It's not a vita," the wicker said again. "It's nothing. A red blob of nothing."

"But the warders..." Foyer squeezed his fingers into a fist around the pendant. "Molina tricked us. I should never have let Dan go."

"It's okay," Blue insisted. "As soon as she gets Molina out of the way, I'll be able to find my gem, I know it. It's begging me to find it. Molina won't get chance to hurt Dante, Foyer. She won't."

"Excuse me." The wicker held up a hand, and the goblins held up theirs too. "Sorry to interrupt, but I think I can help."

Again, Will, Foyer and Blue peered at him as one.

"I just so happen to know where the Simms witch is keeping her ingredients for her so-called immortality spell. Including the wot gems. I could take you there if you want."

The left goblin settled and quietened as the wicker's face became serious.

"What do you think? Need some help?"

Chapter Sixteen: Three of Them

"You'll really help us?" Will asked, beaming with gratitude that was conspicuously absent from the two wots, who had responded to the wicker's offer to take them exactly where they needed to be as though it had been an offer to rub their faces in dog poop. "Really?"

"Of course."

Foyer tossed Molina's broken necklace into the midst of the slanted trees behind him, like he needed an excuse to ignore them.

"Did you hear that?" Will said to Foyer's back. "He'll take you to your gems." No one answered him, so he added a weak, "Hurray," to help them figure out that they should be pleased.

"Why would you do that?" Foyer challenged the stranger. "Wickers do nothing for nothing. What do you get out of helping us?"

The wicker's grin twisted into a mocking smirk. "Right, because we're all heartless monsters. Sorry, I forgot. Anyway, my name's Christian," he said to Will. "My bods, Badmé and Gudmé." The shoulder-goblins waved their fat, four-fingered hands. "They're pleased to meet you."

"Bods?" Will asked.

"All wickers have bods," Foyer informed him. "Can't manage by themselves. Can't even make a decision without a bod."

"That's not true," Christian said. "I make all my own decisions. Unless I'm not bothered either way, in which case Gudmé tends to have the last word." He gestured to the creature on his right shoulder. "Less hassle that way."

"I'm Will," Will said, thrilled something good had finally happened. This man showing up was the break they'd been waiting for, he was certain. "And they're Foyer and Blue."

"Pleasure to make your acquaintance." Christian bowed in jest. The bods both repeated the movement, balancing skilfully on the wicker's shoulders.

Their cheeriness delighted Will.

"So, you want me to take you to the witch's place or not?" the wicker asked the wots.

"This doesn't seem normal to me," Blue said.

"Nor me," Foyer agreed. "A wicker conveniently shows up with the exact information we need, and we're expected to believe that's a complete coincidence? Another 'happy happenstance'? Did Molina send you here? Tell the truth."

Christian's eyes did a quick swirl around their sockets. "Molina Simms doesn't even know I exist. I came across her hideaway by chance. I've been hearing rumours for a while now that some crazy witch has been seeking the key to immortality. I put two and two together when I saw what she was doing out there. You two are wots, right? But what about you?" He and the bods studied Will. "There's great power in you. It's hidden deep, but I definitely sense something. Are you a witch?"

Dante had told Will to let people think he was a witch, and he was about to do just that and lie to Christian - but on second thought, everybody had practically spelled it out for him that being a witch was akin to wearing a 'kill me' sign in this place. So he decided against answering the question at all and smiled stupidly instead.

"No," Blue said resolutely. "Thanks, but no thanks. I'll know my own way to my gem as soon as Dante gets her sister out of the way."

Christian shrugged his shoulders, and his bods shrugged theirs. "I'll leave you to it, then."

Will tapped Blue's arm to let him know he wasn't happy with this outcome. "No, don't go. Don't listen to Blue. He's just crabby."

"And with every reason to be," Foyer reminded him.

"Oh, yes?" Christian pried. "And what reason might that be?" He watched Foyer and Blue exchange glances. "Because a psychotic witch somehow cut you off from your own power and stole your gems from under your noses, maybe?" He laughed at their angry faces. "What? Like it's some big secret? Everyone's talking about it."

Will didn't like the tension. "You don't want the wots to die, do you?" he asked timidly. "Everybody else does," he added, realising just how disappointed he would be if they'd come across yet another enemy posing as a friend.

"It's not on my wish list." The wicker chortled and forced an apologetic smile at the wots. "Forgive the pun."

Badmé busied himself by delving a finger into his flat little nose and having a good rummage.

"Who is this everybody else, anyway?"

"Everybody."

"Clearly not everybody. I don't want them to die. You don't. Miss Simms' sister doesn't."

"I suppose that's true."

"My bods don't," Christian went on, in a manner that suggested he'd missed the part where Will had already agreed with him. Badmé took his finger from his nose and raised it. Christian smiled sheepishly. "Badmé might a little, but that's just his way."

Will decided he did not like that left-shoulder-dwelling goblin.

"Ouch," Christian said, noticing the bloodstained fingers pressed over Blue's stab wound. "That looks nasty. What happened there?"

"People keep trying to kill him," Will said pointedly.

"Oh, right. Are you sure you don't want our help?" Christian asked Blue. "We've no prior arrangements. No commitments, no engagements. No one to see, nowhere to be." He scratched at the back of his head. The bods scratched theirs. "To tell you the honest truth, I'm bored out of my mind here."

"Aren't you the lucky one."

"I know a healer, if you want one," Christian offered, ignoring Blue's uncharacteristic unfriendliness. "His name's Acacia. Nice fella."

Foyer said, "I'm afraid we already frightened that one away."

"I said he was nice, not a fearless warrior. You know they're all pathetic nerve-bags, that sort."

"What sort?" Blue asked.

"You know. Healers, seers, mystics, wares. Artsy-fartsy folk. Namby-pambies. Scaredy-cats." The wicker grinned at himself, and Badmé sniggered his high-pitched snigger.

"I know what you're doing," Blue said sharply. "You're trying to lull us into a false sense of security. Isn't that what he's doing, Foyer?"

Foyer just stared on with distrusting, unblinking eyes.

Will couldn't understand why they were being so uptight. "Come on, guys, he wants to help."

"We thought Lillian wanted to help too, remember?" Foyer said, keeping his voice down while Christian blatantly strained to hear.

Blue doubled over and moaned. "It's happening. Dante must have taken Molina away. My gem's pulling stronger, I can feel it. I can take us to it now, Will. We don't need anyone else."

There was something about Christian, probably the confidence he exuded, that reminded Will of Dyelann, and he didn't want the wicker to go. "Can you follow us?" he asked. "Just in case he goes the wrong way?"

Blue lifted his head tetchily. "You must think I'm really stupid or something."

"You're not stupid, but you said last time you just went in circles, remember?"

"I won't do that this time because… because…" His words drifted off and his face became blank as the pull of his gem took hold. He wandered away.

Foyer followed. "Come on, Will."

Will hung back with the wicker, conflicted. "What about Christian?"

"He can tag along if he must."

"I'm honoured," Christian said dryly, but didn't hesitate to join them.

Will huddled in his jacket, feeling a chill. "It's getting dark," he muttered, unnerved by the prospect of spending another night out in the wilderness. Two nights away from home. His mum and dad must have missed him by now. They'd probably be furious with him when he got back. He told Christian so.

"You live with your parents?"

The two bods acted as surprised as Christian to hear this.

"I'm only eleven."

"Huh. If my brother and I hadn't moved away from our mother by the time we were your age, she'd have killed us." Christian sniffed slightly, and the bods both emulated him at once. Badmé sniffed a little too hard and had to pick his nose again. "The wot's heading in the right direction, anyway."

"Good. About going the right way, I mean, not your mum killing you."

Christian nodded. The bods nodded. "I'd have tried to walk us around the neethers myself, mind. But your wot friend obviously doesn't mind bumping into them."

"We're going near neethers this way?"

"Yip. Lots of them."

"Blue," Will shouted, "there's neethers that way!" When he got no response from Blue, he shouted Foyer's name instead.

Foyer looked back, revealing his concern. "I heard you, Will."

A black blur rushed over them again, and Will stopped to stare up, straining to see against the dull sky.

"What is that thing?" he asked, not minding his volume anymore.

"Perhaps it is a harvester," the Maker said. "Perhaps it's after us. Well. After you."

The kite that Will thought they'd left behind landed on a bough of the closest tree, where it steadied itself and twisted its head from side to side like it was searching for something.

Christian stopped to wait for Will. "Who are you talking to?"

"Myself."

"That's a sign of insomnia."

Gudmé appeared to whisper something in his ear.

"I mean insanity."

"I think there's a harvester following us," Will informed Christian as they picked up their pace. The kite swept along with them, matching their speed. "I don't even know what a harvester is."

"Blargh. Harvesters are the worst. I don't like any of them sort. You know. Harvesters, banters, reapers: Bony killers."

Will could no longer tell where Blue and Foyer had gone or how far ahead they'd got. He hoped Christian knew.

"Being a wicker, I fall into what I think of as the useful sort of folk. Which I'd say includes bods, obviously. Witches, maybe, some of them. Possibly wots if you like. Use*less* sort of folk would include wenns, neethers, wyes. I mean, seriously, what is the point in any of them? Just useless. Oh, and don't forget the oafish thug sort, which would be warders and efferbies." He stopped talking. Something Will hadn't yet seen had his attention now. "Look, there's a witch over there. Hello, witch." He waved a greeting, and the bods joined in with extra enthusiasm as soon as they noticed what he was doing.

Will saw, to his horror, that they were waving at Lillian Scrossly. He grasped Christian's arm, and Badmé leaned over to slap his hand away. "Ow!" He frowned angrily up at the bod. "Please, you've got to help me. She's one of the ones who want to kill Blue."

Christian's cheery smile drooped. "That's not good. What do you want me to do?"

Lillian rounded her shoulders and marched towards them.

"Look after us," Will begged.

"You…" Lillian stormed closer, faster, faster. "You!"

At the last second, Christian stepped sidewards to block Will, who the witch was reaching out to grab with both hands. He stared down at her. His bods matched his hostile expression.

Lillian's cheeks flushed with rage.

"What seems to be the problem?"

"That boy. That boy is the problem. I put on a façade for hours. Hours of playing nice, waiting for the right time to make my move, and that boy ruined everything. I have a job to do, a job he's made twelve times harder, the interfering little maggot."

"What job?" Christian asked, suddenly less worried about protecting Will and more interested in getting some juicy gossip from the new girl.

"To kill the wots," Lillian said, calming down.

"Oh, yeah? Why would you want to do that?"

"A vision came to me. It showed me their power is meant to be mine. I am destined to end the wots, claim their power and become the most formidable being this world has ever known. It led me to the truth, that vision. It was my ancestor who created their race in the first place. It's my birthright to destroy it."

Christian stared at her. "Are you seriously insinuating that you're the descendant of the Maker?" he asked. "You?"

"Indeed I am."

The bods mouthed to each other behind Christian's neck.

"But…" Christian leaned back to take a good look at her. "You're a girl. The descendant's supposed to be a boy. Like this one." He gestured to where Will hid behind his back.

"Well, the descendant is not a boy. She's a woman."

Christian laughed at her. "You're a girl."

"I'm a woman."

"Yeah, the pigtails really emphasise that."

"This has nothing to do with you. Why should you care what happens to the boy?"

Christian considered Will, as if he needed to see him to think of a reason. "He's only eleven. Leave him alone."

"I will." The witch flicked her plaits behind her shoulders as she walked away. "I'll go after bigger game."

"You're so selfish," Will called after her.

"Ah, let her go," Christian said, quite calm. "She's going the wrong way anyway. Don't worry. I'll see you get somewhere safe from the likes of mad witches."

"She's a murderer, Christian. Foyer and Blue are the only ones left."

"Hey, I don't want to see the wots disappear any more than you do," the wicker assured him, and Gudmé nodded his agreement. "I like wots. They live forever. At least, they're supposed to. And that's great. They're dependable." He yawned, either tired or bored, and walked on, signalling for Will to follow while the bods tried to force themselves to yawn too.

Despite knowing Foyer and Blue's reservations, Will couldn't find a reason not to trust this man. He followed without question.

"What are wickers, Christian?" he asked, trying to ignore Badmé, who kept pulling unfriendly faces at him. "What do wickers do?"

"What sort of question is that, when we're chasing your friends into a pack of neethers that want to kill them? Hang on. Do the neethers want to kill them?"

"They want to kill me."

Christian stopped so abruptly, Badmé nearly overbalanced. "Then it's not very clever to take you right to them, is it?"

"Yeah, but…"

"Yeah-but nothing." Christian rolled his eyes. Badmé quickly copied the action. Gudmé, however, had not noticed, having been slouched against the wicker's neck with his eyes closed. "We'll go a safer way to the witch's place. We'll meet your wots there."

"If they get there alive," Will muttered.

"They'll be fine. Come on." Christian ushered Will to the right of where they'd been heading. "We'll take the scenic route. Which just so happens to be a shortcut."

A rancid whiff of off fruit blew their way, and Will curled his lip. He didn't have time to vocalise his disgust. Heavy footsteps accompanied the rustle of leaves and the snapping of branches.

"Don't let them get me," Will begged.

"What now?" Christian casually waited for whoever approached to reveal themselves.

A huge, bearded man lurched into sight. Will recognised Esko and was relieved to see an established friend. But the wye didn't look like he was about to reciprocate any feelings of camaraderie. Fury burned in his eyes, just visible beneath the jagged, fuzzy brow. The fearsome scowl etched on his face brought back the same instinctive fear that had bristled in Will when he'd seen the giant for the first time.

"Hello," Christian said. Badmé gave a half-hearted wave.

Esko's tree trunk of a leg brushed against the wicker as he passed. "Get out of my way," the wye said in a rumbling voice.

"Charming," Christian said, and Badmé's wave turned into a rude gesture.

"Wait," Will shouted to the wye. "Have you seen Blue?"

"I have not." Esko did not stop. "And I care not. My Alley is dead because of this feud between wots and witches. She is dead. All I care about now is finding her killers. I will not rest until they are buried." He said no more. The sound of his footsteps soon dimmed into the distance.

Will turned to Christian for reassurance. Badmé tried to slap him away again.

"You know him, do you?"

"He's Blue's friend."

"Nice bloke."

"He was before."

"Is that so?" Christian nodded. Badmé nodded. "Wyes aren't trustworthy, you know. Like I said, useless. Prone to hissy fits. Hissy fits, bad breath, and parasites."

"You mean they like hot beaches?" Will asked, confused.

"Ha. You're an odd one, you are. Come on, get it shifting. We want to get there before your friends or it's not much of a shortcut, is it?"

Badmé stared at Will as they walked. Will stared back, determined not to be intimidated by something so small.

"So, what's a wicker, Christian?" he asked again, hoping he might get an answer this time.

"It's short for Quicklewicker. We originally came from Quicklewick. How did you become involved with the wots' plight anyway? Were you just minding your own business when their bus went by and jumped on board, spur of the moment?"

"There wasn't a bus."

"It's a metaphorical bus."

"There wasn't any kind of bus."

Christian smiled like he was amused, although Will had no idea what was so funny. "So, what did happen?"

"I found Blue in the river," Will explained, thinking hard, wondering where and when everything had gone wrong. "I helped him out and we decided to find his gem."

"You've found it now. Mission accomplished."

"I hope so. I really don't want Blue and Foyer to die."

"That would be a pity."

"It's not fair."

"Not much is," Christian said. "No need to whinge about it."

Gudmé awoke with a start, like he'd been about to fall.

Badmé sniggered and pointed at his twin. Then he stared thoughtfully down at Will as though trying to decide something and stuck out his tongue.

"Your bod's sticking its tongue out at me."

"Don't take it personally. Now then, what's-your-name. Will. Listen to Christian. We are going to a place in the farthest reaches of Wynne. It's called Arrrflangenblahhh. Or something."

"Huh?"

"I can't pronounce it," Christian admitted. "But it's a dark place."

"It's getting dark anyway." Will glanced at the cloudy sky. "It's going to rain."

"Dark in the other sense of the word. Like, evil. Nobody really goes there, which is probably why Miss Simms chose it as a hiding place. Oh, and that poor witch she kept there. I saw him through the window a couple of times. Barbaric, what she did to him."

"You're nosier than my mum. You just went snooping around a window for no reason?"

"Who said it was for no reason? I heard someone screaming and went to see what was wrong. Like you've never snooped by a window? Everybody does it."

"What were you even doing there? You said nobody goes there because it's all dark and evil, so why would you be there?"

The wicker scoffed. "What are you getting at? You think I must be evil, just because I was in a place where nobody goes because it's evil? Don't be so paranoid. I'm not evil. I just like it in Arrrtaflaffanaaagh. You want to know why? Because when I'm there, people leave me alone. There's nobody bugging me, or telling me off, or trying to kill me, or throwing fits, because nobody there is interested in me. Even the harvester there leaves me alone since I bought a few bits and bobs off him."

Will frowned at him.

Christian walked faster. "Come on, get a move on or I won't bother helping you anymore. I could do without the earache, to tell you the truth."

There's no need to be nasty, Will thought to himself, but didn't dare to speak the words out loud. Unfortunately, the Maker wasn't so restrained.

"Then don't."

Christian stopped and turned. "Beg your pardon?"

Will laughed in a weak attempt to mask his embarrassment. "That wasn't me. If I say anything rude, it's not me. Just ignore him."

"Ignore who?"

"The other me. He's not actually me, but he just talks whenever he wants to, as if he is me. But he's not. It's really annoying."

"Kind of like your version of a bod?"

Will screwed up his face, uncertain of how to respond. "Okay," he said: The magic word to bring confusing conversations to an end.

"Oh, okay." Christian continued to walk. "So, this bod of yours can just take the reins and control what you do and say, whenever he feels like it? That's got to be rough."

"He's just annoying. I don't have to listen to him."

"Watch it," the Maker warned.

Christian laughed. "That's brilliant."

Badmé sniggered along with him, despite most likely having no idea what he was laughing at. Will didn't know what was so funny either.

"There's two of you in one body."

"Only because he snuck into me while I wasn't looking. There wasn't two of me in me until I came here."

The Maker's discomfort twinged through Will. "That is not quite true, as it happens."

"What? What do you mean?"

"I've been living with you for a few months now."

Will put his hands on his head, flustered. "No, you haven't. I'd have known if you were in there that long."

"In fact, you wouldn't, because clearly you didn't."

"You're such a liar."

"I never lie."

"Liar!"

Christian's eyes lit up.

"Shush your mouth and hush yourself," the Maker hissed. "Don't you remember where you are, what's after you? Do you want to die? Do you?"

"It's your fault they want to kill me. They think I'm your stupid disnendant because of you."

Christian's face dropped, grimly serious. "Hang on. Hang on just one second there. Who exactly is this bod of yours, Will?"

The Maker ignored Christian and went on speaking to Will. "That is not true. They came to that conclusion because of what you did to Blue, and I had no part in that."

"Yes, you did. You did it!" Will stamped a foot.

"No, I didn't."

"Yes, you did."

"No, I didn't, you impossible, impertinent child, you are wrong."

Will punched himself in the ribs and recoiled from the pain.

"You can't reach me in here," the Maker said after Will had finished coughing. His smugness grated on Will's nerves. "You'll only hurt yourself if you try."

"Hey!" Christian yelled. "Who is this bod of yours, I asked."

The Maker threw a chilling glare the wicker's way. "Keep out of it and take us to where we need to be."

Badmé returned the glower, but Gudmé and Christian weren't so sure.

"I don't think I will," Christian said. "Goodbye, Will."

"No, please, please don't leave me on my own." Will skipped around to the front of Christian. "You can't leave me with just him. He doesn't want to help me. He wants Blue and Foyer to die so he can get the power back from their gems."

Christian hesitated. "Same as Miss Simms? And that little girl witch?"

"Yeah. But he doesn't want to live forever like they do. He just wants to die." Will hoped Christian might stay and help if he understood the full direness of their situation.

"If he just wants to die, why doesn't he just kill himself? Why does he need power from the gems?"

"He just does. He's in mortal."

"You mean he's immortal?"

Will's blood surged hotter for a long second and he gritted his teeth. "That's what I said." Intense pain coursed through his hand.

It caught him off guard and he clutched it, wincing, forcing himself not to cry out.

"What's wrong now?"

"My hand..." He pressed his fingers over the scabbing wound. Then he remembered what Foyer had told him. "Oh, no, oh, no... There must be a banter somewhere here." His airways tightened.

"Hey, hey, relax. Banters aren't scary."

"Yes, they are," Will retorted, offended by the suggestion it was wrong to fear such obviously terrifying creatures.

"They're nothing to worry about. They don't even attack you unless you're bleeding." Christian noticed Will's hand then and pointed at it with a hint of embarrassment. "Oh. I see the problem. A banter bit you once already, I take it. I trust you found an antidote to their poison?"

"Duh," Will said, and Badmé stared down his tiny nose at him. "It hurts. It hurts so bad." He rocked back and forth, hoping for a little consolation.

"Seriously, do you ever stop whining?" Christian's response lacked the compassion Will had been fishing for. "Be grateful you've got a good warning." Sticking up an index finger to shush Will, he cocked his head. "Do you hear that?"

Will heard nothing, but the thought of a banter on its way knocked him sick.

"Someone screamed. I definitely heard a scream. Come on. Let's go see who it was." Christian dashed away, calling for Will to follow, any thought of leaving the child behind apparently forgotten in his curiosity over who was in trouble now. Will had never known anyone so nosy.

They reached a barricade of ferns and nettles between a group of trees and Christian peered around the side of it. When he said nothing, Will looked too. His heart pounded faster.

Three banters. Three banters were crouched over a wriggling, white clad person. It was Cesar. Will recognised the bright white outfit. The banters had the ware tight in their grip, each one busy drinking deeply from where it had sunk its teeth. Cesar was covered in bruises and scratches from falling out of his tree, Will recalled. The poor ware would have drawn those banters to him like moths to a flame.

Three of them. Three banters. There were three of them. Will couldn't think. He couldn't move.

"Okay," Christian whispered. "Maybe they're a bit scary."

"Pathetic," the Maker grumbled.

Cesar's struggling was becoming weaker. He was dying. Blue's loyal friend was dying, and Will was just standing there watching it happen. He had to do something. He tried to find the courage to intervene. But what could he do against them? What could he possibly do?

He took a sharp, strained breath and leapt out into the open.

The banters turned to him, their huge black eyes shimmering with satisfaction.

Christian joined Will and stood at his side. "What are you doing?" he asked through clenched teeth and a vexed smile.

The banters inched back from their meal. One of them wiped at its grotesquely malformed mouth with the back of its vein blue, three-fingered hand. It seemed they'd finished with Cesar now and were content to wait for their dessert to manifest. Their nostrils flared greedily, necks stretching for a better look at their next potential snack.

Christian sidestepped into Will, trying to nudge him back behind the ferns. "That's right, keep waving that hand under their noses. Why not pass them some knives and forks while you're at it?" He shoved again, harder this time, and the bods crawled down his jacket to join in. "Come on. Time to go."

"We can't," Will said, unable to tear his eyes away from the closest banter's hideous, knobbly sternum. He couldn't move his feet. They felt heavy, too heavy to lift. The banters were closing in, and he did nothing. "What about Cesar?"

"Forget Cesar. Those things will kill you."

Will wanted to tell Christian he would have to find a way to stop them from killing him; he'd just have to. But no sound left his lips. He wasn't breathing. His heart pumped away but it was running out of oxygen to keep going. He told himself to breathe, commanded it, but his throat locked tighter.

Taking the breath for him in the form of a contemptuous sigh, the Maker assumed control and took one bold step to the oncoming bloodsuckers. Before he could do anything more, a flurry of movement darkened the sky, casting a huge, mutating shadow. No fewer than thirty of Cesar's kites rushed to his aid in a din of piercing cries, flying at the banters like launched missiles, slashing the thin-skinned creatures with beaks and talons, their forked tails and streamlined bodies flitting in all directions.

The banters swiped their claws in retaliation, but their defence went unnoticed. Their strikes, which would have knocked any of the wots clean off their feet without trying, were useless against these birds. They passed through the feathered bodies just like Lillian's weapons had passed through the wots before she had undone her spell.

Eventually, damaged and bleeding, the banters stopped fighting back. They stalked away in their unhurried fashion while the birds continued their frenzied dives and swoops.

Shaking, Will regained control of his body and hobbled to Cesar, terrified the ware was already dead. He had to swallow a few times before he could talk. "Cesar?" He prodded the ware, avoiding the wet patches of red that saturated the glaring white shirt. "Are you alive?"

Cesar's beady eyes opened.

"Why didn't you go invisible?"

"I did. It makes no difference to banters. They hunt by scent."

"Please don't die."

"Oh, I'm sure I'll be fine." An uncertainty crossed Cesar's face that Will knew was not intended.

"I'm sorry."

"It's not your fault," Cesar assured him. "Where's Blue?"

"He's gone to find his gem."

Cesar struggled a raspy breath and lifted himself with a shaky arm, the other cradling his rib cage. "It was Molina Simms. It was her all along."

"We know."

"She has all the gems now. She came. She took Karson's gem. I couldn't protect them."

"Are they dead?" Will asked in a croak of a voice.

"No. When the banters came, I told them to run. They're wounded, you see, and I didn't want what just happened to me to happen to them. It's the last thing they need." Cesar gazed down at a splash of blood on his sleeve. "I get the feeling they didn't hear me telling them to run though," he said. "They were gone so fast."

Will smiled at him. "Blue knew you'd stick up for them."

Cesar stopped staring at his arm and noticed Christian. "What's the wicker doing with you?"

"Helping, I think."

"I'm glad Blue has faith in me," Cesar said, distant and unfocused. "Tell him I have the same faith in him. Tell him I know he'll live through this. They all will."

Will didn't have the heart to tell him that Dyelann, Maik, and Henry were already dead.

"You can leave me here," Cesar said. "It's okay, honest. Go ahead and help Blue. I'll be fine. My kites will take care of me. They always do." On Will's confused expression he added, "You think I've never been bitten by banters before? My kites know the location of every healer in Wynne."

As Will began to stand, Cesar's hand darted out and dragged him back down. "Don't trust the wicker!" he said hoarsely, and Will stared straight at him until he released his grip. "You be careful, boy."

"I will."

"Good lad."

Will waited to ensure Cesar had nothing more to say. Then he headed warily back to Christian.

"He's okay, is he? Good." Christian beamed. "See? Things work out sometimes, don't they?"

"Sometimes," Will agreed.

"Yes," the Maker said stiffly under Will's breath. "Sometimes."

Chapter Seventeen: Darker Places

"Here we are," Christian announced, as though presenting something he was truly proud of.

Rainclouds blanketed the twilight sky, but Will had seen enough during their trip through the darkness to believe what Christian had told him about nobody wanting to be anywhere near this place. It was an appropriately creepy spot for the likes of wicked witches and headless horsemen, but he doubted any sane person would have stuck around for the joy of it. Even the trees looked evil here, with their sharp, twisted, armlike branches and hunched backs, straight from the setting of a gothic fairy tale.

The building Christian had led them to was little more than a shack covered in patches of filth and black mould. The roof tiles were cracked, displaced, and littered with dead leaves, rotten branches, and shrivelled conkers from the haggard horse chestnut that towered behind it.

"This is where she kept Gart?"

"Yip."

Will walked timidly up the broken steps to peer through a grimy window. An inch of dirt layered on both the inside and outside of the glass blocked his view, but he could vaguely make out the small flame of a candle flickering eerily in the grimness. "Poor Gart."

"Yip."

Will pushed at the rotted door. It bent over slightly at the top as it scraped across the floorboards. A strange, tangy smell hit him when he crossed the threshold, like someone had slopped old vinegar all over the place. There was a small fireplace in one corner of the room. Dark purple flames licked the base of a black cauldron. Above the cauldron was a shelf, on top of which sat the eight wot gems, each of them dull, speckled with a dusting of sooty residue.

Excitement and fear bounced around in his heart. Then doubt. Last time he had been this close to the gems, they hadn't been gems at all.

One of them quivered. Its smooth edges drummed against the shelf, clearing itself of the black powder, which dispersed in the air around it like cigarette smoke, revealing the blueness beneath. Will moved closer, wondering. Was it encouraging him to take it? Was it asking him to keep it safe for Blue?

A hammer and chisel were laid neatly in front of a fat, black wax candle that slouched, dripping on the mantel. They too were finely sprinkled with the sooty black dust.

"What should I do?" Will asked the Maker, barely daring to speak in this place for fear of alerting Molina to their presence. "Should I…?"

The Maker said nothing.

Will's throat felt dry and tight, like he'd swallowed a cup of flour. "Here goes nothing," he mouthed. He stretched the bottom of his jacket out to create a pouch, and with one swift swipe of his arm he scooped the eight gems from the shelf. He wrapped the material around them and clutched the bundle.

Then:

The force.

The energy.

It engulfed him.

His blood bubbled, gushed through his veins. He felt every breath of air absorb into his lungs and circulate through his body as his heart bulged and contracted, pounding, squelching, whooshing. Vibrations hit the marrow in his bones. He felt every nerve, every cell, every fibre of his being...

Every...

...fibre of his being...

His skin tingled, danced, prickled like static. He was lighter than air, and yet solid as a bull.

He was...

...invincible...

"Will! No!"

The urgent scream breezed his way from the door behind him, so distant it verged on frivolous. Someone was shouting? What did it matter?

Then a moment of wonderment: Who dared to shout at him?

He saw Foyer by the door as plain as day, the darkness meaningless to him now.

"Will." Foyer edged closer, his growing dread palpable. "You have to give me the gems. Please."

Will heard his friend's plea, wanted to help him, but found himself arguing - arguing in his mind - with himself.

"Will, please. The Maker cannot have our gems."

The Maker doesn't have them, Will thought. I do. I have them.

Foyer braved another hesitant step. "Will?"

Blue peered around the door.

Blue.

His friend.

Blue wanted his gem. And the gem, trembling beneath the fabric of Will's jacket, wanted Blue even more.

"He cannot have our gems," Foyer repeated, voice tight with impending fear. "He'll kill us, Will. He'll kill us."

"What's happening?" Blue asked with a quiver of uncertainty.

Thunder rumbled. The rain that had been threatening for hours finally began to fall, rapping loudly on the tiles above their heads and spitting in through the cracks.

"I'm not sure," Foyer replied.

"He's flipped." Christian pushed Blue aside to see inside the shack. "Look at those eyes. They're not even human anymore. Look at him, he's flipped. I told him talking to himself was the first sign. I told him so."

"Talking to himself?" Blue repeated. "Wait. Will's got our gems, and the Maker's in Will. The Maker's got our gems!" He yelled at Foyer, "What do we do? What do we do?"

Will knew he would never allow the Maker to take the gems. Even as he thought it, the fact occurred to him that the Maker had made no move to seize the gems, or, for that matter, to do anything else at all.

"What do we do?" he asked, repeating Blue's question to let them know he was still on their side. The words felt separated from his mouth. He was split three ways right now, body, soul, consciousness, held together only by a thread of life as fine and as fragile as a spider's web.

A glimmer of hope crossed Foyer's face and he took another step closer. "You don't have to do anything. It's okay. Just let them go."

The blue gem erupted from Will's grasp, scattering the rest across the room, and he yelped as they ripped across his wounded hand. One of them landed directly in the cauldron and hit the bubbling liquid with a solid plop.

The taste of power Will had received tore from him so violently he felt like it had turned him inside out. Nothing worked. His legs crumpled like paper. He was blind, deaf, and unable to feel anything other than the pain in his hand and overwhelming emptiness in the unhinged vessel that was his body.

Then the many candles in the shack gushed to life, their flames roaring up like Bunsen burners, bringing Will's senses back in time for Molina's dramatic entrance. The witch stood in the doorway, dripping wet, a look more dangerous than the storm raging above set on her face. She lashed out her arms. The gems, including the one that had sunk into the cauldron's boiling brew, flew to her like paperclips to a magnet, and she caught them, holding them before her without physically touching them. All the gems except for Blue's hovered there at her mercy, huddled together in the space between her open arms.

Blue held his gem, which showed no sign of trying to join the others, stare locked on Molina, who stared right back at him.

"I already had you killed once," she said, her red lips twisted with hatred. "I swear, there'll be no coming back a second time. Give it to me."

Blue pressed his gem to his chest, squeezing it tighter and tighter. A flash of panic lit in his eyes, as if someone had looped an invisible rope around his neck.

"Give me the gem. Now."

Blue smirked at the witch, finding his nerve.

Dante forced her way past her sister, shouting, "Sorry! I'm sorry. She sussed it out, but I'm here now. I'm here." She spotted the gems in Molina's hold and gasped in astonishment. "You really have them. You really… are a complete–"

"Kill that wot!" Molina shouted. "Kill him, kill him, kill him!" Beside herself with fury, she kicked a hole in the wall.

Warders closed in around the shack. They pressed up against the windows, surrounding them.

Blue, Foyer, Dante and Christian were all forced further into the building, while one by one the warders filed in through the door.

Will was afraid to watch, so sure he was that this was the end, but he couldn't look away.

A swipe of Dante's wand sent the warders falling on their backs, until two charged her from behind and pinned her against the wall while a third tried to prise the wand from her impressive grip. At least three others trampled over Foyer in their determined efforts to reach Blue.

Molina loomed over the scene, a queen bee commanding her hive.

And Will, helpless, powerless, terrified, did nothing.

"There," the Maker said. "Right there. I saw it, so you must have seen it too."

Will couldn't understand what he was saying.

"The vita," the Maker snapped impatiently. "Get the vita."

Still shaking in a frenzy of shock and pain, slouched awkwardly on the witch's floor and only narrowly being missed by many pairs of stomping great boots that could have crushed him to death at any moment, Will searched for the vita. Even if he could spot it, he doubted his own ability to stand, never mind steal an object of such value from the immensely powerful witch currently watching every movement of every being in the room.

"We can get it."

A shimmer of red caught Will's eye. The pentagon-shaped disc glinted in the candlelight. It peeked from the breast pocket of Molina's petite jacket.

"You have to let me." The Maker raised Will's hand, barely able to keep the arm still in its weakened state.

As quick as the bolt of lightning that streaked at that very moment, the vita dived from the witch's pocket and into Will's open palm.

"Stop!"

The warders did stop. They faced Will, an army of automatons, awaiting his command. Only, he didn't know what to command them.

"Stop," he said again, trying to catch his breath, trying to see if Foyer was okay where he lay strewn on the floor, trying to see if Blue was still alive, and trying to sit up all at once. "Stop."

"You!" Molina's anger surged Will's way. "You sneaky little brat, how did you do that?"

"Remember," the Maker said in a shallow voice that only Will could hear. Will was not sure he had opened his mouth at all. "We are cats among mice, you and I."

"Good, Will, good," Dante praised him, yanking her wand back from one of the warders. "Tell them to seize her."

"Don't you dare," Molina said. "I'll kill every last one of them, and then you."

Will stood up. "Leave us alone. Just go away."

The warders began to exit the tiny building.

"Don't go far," Molina called after them, marching across the room to get to Will. The gems floated along with her, still trapped in her hold. As she precariously removed a hand from its position around the gems to make a grab for the vita, Will threw back his head and popped the disc to the back of his throat, swallowing it down faster than he'd ever swallowed anything in his life. She clawed his arm and swung him up off his feet, dangling him in front of her. "Don't think I won't rip it from your stomach, child."

Dante rushed to rescue Will from her sister. "Don't even suggest such things." She eased him from Molina's grasp and set him down with remarkable steadiness. "What's got into you? Are you insane?"

If Molina had felt anything like what Will had felt when she touched those gems, he knew exactly what had got into her. He secretly wanted them almost as much as he wanted the wots to have them. He wanted that feeling back. That feeling of being the one and only thing that mattered in this world and that nothing - nothing - could touch you.

Molina turned to where Blue was standing, and Will tensed with fear. Fear for his friend, who was in real danger now.

In the time it took Molina to open her mouth to speak, Blue disappeared in a puff of blue smoke, his gem along with him.

Will laughed. He was scared, and nothing was funny, and he knew it was the wrong reaction, but he laughed anyway, because Blue had escaped. The wots had a chance again.

Molina dashed forward to clasp at the remaining blue wisps, as if she thought she might be able to drag Blue back. She pulled off her bandana and threw it to the ground, screaming curses until she was purple in the face, tufts of red hair waving uncontrollably on her otherwise bald scalp.

Christian snuck up behind the enraged witch, entranced by the gems that were bobbing around her like planets around their sun. While she was distracted, he picked one from the cluster and passed it up to Badmé, who balanced it between his stubby four-fingered hands and stuck his tongue out at the mad witch.

Her screams subsided. Slightly crouched, breathing heavily, she stared at the left bod through eyes that grew darker with each passing second.

Badmé examined the orange gem with interest, seemingly oblivious to the rage he was causing. He held it proudly before them all. In the light from the candle flames, the orange gem glowed amber.

It hurt Will to see it, knowing Dyelann would never reclaim it. "He's dead because of you." The words rolled from his tongue before he could think to stop them. "He's dead because of you!"

Molina didn't acknowledge Will but stood up straight and took a sharp breath as though he'd reminded her of something. "He has to die." Saliva that had accumulated during her temper tantrum glistened on her lips and chin. She retrieved her bandana and gave it a quick shake. "You can keep the warders," she said to Will. "I don't need them." Then she turned to the wicker. "The gem or your life."

Christian just smiled at her.

"The gem," she said again, firmer, slower, "or your life."

Everyone stayed quiet while Molina and Christian stood with equally stubborn stances and equally serious stares.

A sopping wet woman crashed through the doorway. Two long seconds ticked by before Will realised who it was.

Lillian Scrossly, panting for breath, glanced around the musty shack. "Is he dead?" she asked Molina. "Blue. Is he dead?"

"The closest thing to." Molina held out her elegant hand to the wicker, obviously expecting him to pass the orange gem over to her.

Lillian quietened when she saw the gems hovering around Molina. "Those belong to me. They're mine."

They're *mine*, a tiny voice nagged in the back of Will's mind. He shook the thought away, scolding himself.

"You forget your place," Lillian said, closing in on Molina. "I am the Maker's descendant, *me*. I am the one who is to end the time of wots and retain their power, *me*. It is my destiny, *mine!* Now, hand them over!"

Dante grinned, though Will couldn't begin to imagine what she had to smile about. She groped for his hand. Her warm touch calmed his trembling arms.

"Foyer," she whispered. "Quickly. Come."

The wot pushed himself up with clear difficulty and stumbled closer to Dante in a lurching stagger of a movement. Molina was too focused on Lillian's outburst and Christian's audacity to notice, and he reached Dante and Will without anyone caring to stop him.

"Let's go." Dante took Foyer's arm. "Come. Out the back."

Will hadn't been aware that there was a back exit, but Dante opened a concealed door beside the fireplace in the back wall and led him and Foyer out to safety. The solid curtain of rain soaked them through to the skin in under a minute.

"We can't leave the gems," Foyer said, struggling to make himself heard over the whipping and rustling of hundreds of branches thrashing in the howling wind. Only then did Will see the full extent of Foyer's injuries. Blood oozed from the corners of his mouth. He was curled over in discomfort, barely able to keep on his feet, both arms wrapped around his ribs. One foot stuck out at a funny angle and scraped across the ground when he took a step.

"Don't worry, it's okay. We'll get them back." Dante held the side of Foyer's face, both of them blinking against the rain. "Are you okay?"

"Dante," he said wistfully, but she shushed him.

"Neethers are coming. We have to go. Lillian's in there spouting about how she's the descendant. The neethers want the descendant dead. If we're lucky, they'll rid us of her. Molina will concentrate on hunting Blue down, so as long as he keeps moving in the opposite direction, he'll buy us time." She waved them away from the shack.

Foyer limped along beside her, grimacing with each step.

The discomfort of the ice-cold rain beating on Will's head and slipping under his collar only added to his misery. "I'm so sorry. This is all my fault."

"How so?" Dante asked.

"I had the gems. I had them. If I'd have just given them to Foyer quicker..."

"It doesn't matter. Whatever you'd done, Molina would have returned before you'd passed them back."

"Not if I'd been quicker."

"Yes, if you'd been quicker," Dante said sharply. "She acted the second she sensed they were back in the wots' hold again."

"Yeah, when Blue's gem got away from me," Will muttered.

"No." Dante clamped her hand around Will's again. "It was the moment you were about to give them up, Will. And that was strong of you. You have no idea how strong."

Will wanted to believe her, but he knew the truth. As much as he had wanted to give them back to the wots, he would most likely have held on to the gems for much longer, had the blue one not fought itself free. The shame was hard to bear.

They made their steady way back to the heart of the forest, where the trees grew thicker and friendlier and sheltered them from the harshness of the heavy rainfall. It was back at the giant Christmas tree under which Will had seen a gem for the first time that they found Karson and Popset, both unhappily holding their bleeding shoulders. And a fresh feeling of hope finally crept back into Will's heart.

"Dear God, what happened to you?" Karson asked with revulsion.

Foyer's eyebrows buckled at these words, dipping below his dripping fringe. "I was trampled by a herd of warders," he said sullenly over the rumble of thunder. "What happened to *you*?"

"Molina happened," Popset answered when Karson brushed it off as nothing. Both Popset and Karson held their hands firmly to their stab wounds, which were identical to Blue's and in the same spot on their shoulders. Will couldn't decide whether Molina was a very bad aim or a very good one.

Dante placed an arm tenderly around Foyer, offering herself as a prop. "I still can't believe my sister is doing this."

"We need to get out of this weather." Karson indicated to the swirling downpour with an unnecessary jolt of his neck and took a stride back so that he was sheltered under the spiny branches of his tree. The others stared at him grimly until he said, "Are you waiting for a written invitation?"

There wasn't much space, so they huddled close together. Will didn't mind. He stood with Dante, leaning on her left side while Foyer leaned on her right, and his eyelids began to feel too heavy to keep open. For the first time in his life, he longed for someone to order him to bed.

"You were saying?" Karson asked Dante. "About your sister. You're appalled? Never would have imagined that anyone with your same blood could be such a soulless, psychotic, murdering…"

"Karson, stop." Foyer's arms were clamped around his body, to shield himself from the cold. Or to hold himself together. "Leave her alone. It's not her fault."

"You always did have rose-tinted glasses when it came to this witch," Karson said. "But never mind that. Where's Blue? Did he find his gem?"

"Yes, he has it."

Karson smiled. "Maybe he's not such a useless beggar after all."

Popset looked nervously from Karson to Foyer and back again. "So, we're good. If Blue's got his gem, there's still hope, right?"

"That's right," Karson said. "Now, quiet down and let the people with brains in their heads try to work something out. What about the others?" he asked Foyer. "Are they still with that Scrossly witch?"

Dante's side knocked into Will, as if Foyer had unbalanced her, and she had some trouble holding him up for a second.

"I'm sorry," Foyer said. "They're dead. They're all dead, Karson. Lillian Scrossly tricked us. She killed them."

Foyer's words hung in the air while the news was processed, somehow amplifying the din of lashing rain whipping around them.

Karson flicked his free hand over his gleaming wet hair. "We should have known better than to trust a witch. Who do we have left?"

"Just the three of us." Foyer moaned in pain or despair, or both. "And Blue."

"You're joking. Popset and Blue. The… the idiot and the useless scruff are all we're left with?" Karson's fingers tightened around his wound. "I… The… It…" He gave up. "Four wots are dead? Four? This is absolutely unacceptable."

"Oh, is it?" Foyer said. "Oh, well then, if you say so. Let's go and let Dyelann and Henry know how stupid they are for getting themselves killed. Let's tell them to snap out of it, shall we? We'll tell their corpses they're bang out of order and give them a good talking to, shall we?"

"All right," Karson interrupted. "Point taken."

Another flash of lightning lit their faces under the branches, and Will automatically nestled closer to Dante.

"You, boy," Karson said to Will, with an uncharacteristic look of respect. "You brought Blue back to life. You could do the same for the others, could you not?"

An ear-splitting crack of thunder shook the air around them.

"Even the Maker can't bring people back from the dead," Dante shouted over the tail end of it. "Why would you expect Will to be able to do such a thing? Why would you put the burden of such an impossible request on his shoulders? That's not fair."

"Don't speak to me of fair, witch," Karson said angrily. "You think it fair that we wots are being extinguished before our time and can do nothing to save ourselves? You think it fair that I have to beg a child for the lives of my kin?"

"He can't do it!" Dante shouted.

The numerous flashes of lightning that followed shadowed Popset's eye sockets as he pleaded with Will for something they all knew he couldn't give. "Can you?"

Will barely heard the next clap of thunder for his stampeding thoughts. "Can I?" he asked himself, in whisper.

"Thank heaven Blue got away with his gem," Foyer said between pained breaths.

"Thank heaven," Dante repeated in humble agreement.

"Actually," the Maker cut in with swift coldness, "you can thank Will."

Will stared at his feet.

Karson asked, "Beg your pardon, boy?"

"It was he who got rid of Blue," the Maker replied impatiently, lifting Will's head to look at the confused wot as he spoke to him.

"I did not."

"I'm sorry, but yes you did. Blue's far too stupid to realise he was only endangering everybody by hanging around. He never would have left willingly. You wanted him to go, so he went. You did it."

"I didn't," Will insisted.

"Stop arguing with me."

"What's going on?" Popset asked.

Dante touched Will's back to get the Maker's attention. "Where is Blue now?"

"How should I know? Will's the one that did it."

"I didn't, I didn't, I didn't!"

"You did, you did, you did!" the Maker said, mocking him.

Will tried to think of exactly what had happened the moment Blue disappeared. All he remembered was the giddy relief when he knew Blue was safe. Of course he'd wanted his friend to run away and save himself, but he'd wanted that many times in the past couple of days and it hadn't happened. He didn't have the ability to make someone vanish into thin air. But – and the thought came to him progressively, causing a shot of anxiety-fuelled adrenaline to rush through him – what if he did? What if the Maker was telling the truth? Where was Blue? Where had he sent his friend?

"I didn't." It was all he could manage to say.

"If you did," Karson said, "you did a good thing."

"Very good," Dante agreed.

"And you're right about Blue being stupid," Karson added.

"Hey." Dante scowled, insulted on her friend's behalf.

"Yeah, come on, Karson, there's no need for that." Foyer sucked in a long breath. "Leave the poor boy alone. You're breaking him. Did you know that? Nothing he does is ever good enough for you. You have to stop putting him down, just stop it."

"Calm down, Foyer. He's not even here."

"I mean it, Karson. You have no idea how much you matter to him, how much your opinion matters to him, and you never have one good word..."

"It's not like he's even here to hear what I say. What are you getting your knickers in a twist about?"

The two wots spoke over each other, neither pausing to let the other finish.

"Can't you see how miserable you make him, when he tries his best for you and it's never good enough?"

"Can't you see how miserable you make me…?"

"You're going to drive him to depression or madness if you keep on…"

"When you go on and on and on and on…"

"You'rc not happy unless you're bossing everyone around, because everything has to be your way, only you know what's best…"

"You all drive me to distraction, and you *should* all follow my lead, yes, too right you should…"

"Like you're the big 'I Am'…"

"I'm the one who'll be going mad, never mind anyone else…"

"And I'm sick of it!" Foyer shouted, bringing the rant to an abrupt end. The shout jarred him, and he had to close his eyes to steady himself and catch his breath.

Karson gazed into space, a contemplative expression on his tired face. Then, as if Foyer had said nothing, he forced a smile at Will. "So then, lad. If you had indeed wanted to send young Blue away," he said carefully, "and good thinking that was too, but, if you had, where do you think you would have wanted him to go?"

Such a simple question. Will had no idea how to answer.

"Somewhere he'd be safe," Dante said, nodding, trying to jog his memory.

His face was as blank as his mind. He didn't know where to look, didn't know what to think.

"Somewhere Molina couldn't find him," Dante suggested.

"Yes, but I don't know."

"Never mind," Karson said. "He'll turn up eventually, I suppose."

Foyer and Dante glowered with icy frustration, but Karson remained oblivious and went on.

"As long as he's safe from the witch, it isn't a problem. We can worry about him later."

"I'm worrying about him now," Dante said.

Will's "Me too" was muted under the growl of angry thunder that followed another flash in the churning sky.

"Our priority right now is getting those gems back from the witch before she finds him," Karson insisted.

Popset, who had recovered from his earlier bout of hysteria and was back to being the level-headed man that had tried to stop Will and Blue from opening the black door in Scilla Simms' house, said, "I agree, and we mustn't let the neethers get them."

"Or the Maker," Foyer said, aiming a look at Will that unsettled him. He was unsure if it had been one of wariness or accusation, but either way it hurt.

That familiar dark flutter rushed past overhead. Will shielded his eyes from the rain with both hands and tried to see between the thick evergreen branches. The harvester - or whatever it was - was still following him. Cold raindrops ran down his face and neck. His jeans stuck to his legs, heavy and sodden, making it uncomfortable to bend his knees. A voice in the back of his mind said, 'hospital'.

"Hospital?" he repeated, thinking the Maker had said the word to him. The curiosity passed as fast as it had come when the sweeping movement above caught his eye yet again. "Did anyone see that?" he asked, straining his voice over the increasingly noisy weather. The thunder's growl became an overwhelming roar and more lightning flashed.

"See what?" Foyer asked, wincing.

The branches that had been sheltering them could no longer hold back the rain and the drips grew heavier.

"Up there." Will pointed a finger to the sky. "A harvester. It keeps flying over me."

"Come now, don't be absurd," Karson said. "Harvesters can't fly. You're imagining things, boy. It's just the clouds moving in the wind."

Being called absurd nettled Will, who had only been repeating what he'd been told. Surely the Maker, of all people, would know if harvesters could fly or not. He waited for the Maker to step in and explain. But the explanation did not come.

"Maybe it was a neether," Dante said, still looking up.

"Can they fly?" Will asked.

"They can do anything."

Will gulped. "Anything?"

"Anything that can be construed a nightmare."

"A flying harvester would frighten you, Will?" Popset asked.

Will didn't even know if a non-flying harvester would scare him. "No."

"Then why would a neether choose that guise?"

Will felt like he didn't know anything at all anymore. Popset's words were starting to sound like gibberish. He saw the shadow pass again and took cover behind Dante and Foyer, burying his head into the dip of the witch's back. "Make it go away."

"It's okay." Dante flicked her wand out of her sopping sleeve. "Come on, boys," she said as she cut open her portal. "Let's get out of this rain."

Eager to get away from whatever hideous creature was following him, Will was the first through the portal, barely a second after Dante had finished opening it. The warmth of indoors wrapped around him like a comforting hug at the other side. A log fire blazed away before a large, grey sofa. Soft lamps lit the room to a cosy dimness.

Two identical heads appeared over the top of the sofa to see who was there. Harrier and Elmer sat up, surprised to see Will, even after Dante and the wots joined him.

"Explanation?" Harrier said.

Dante, still supporting Foyer, stared at her sisters as she said, "I don't need to explain coming into my own home with some guests." She sealed her portal. "Which you two happen to be too, you do remember?"

Harrier slouched back behind the sofa so that they could no longer see her. Elmer, however, continued to stare unabashed.

Dante sat Foyer down on a wooden chair by the table, and then patted the back of a dark blue armchair. "Come, Will, sit."

Will basked in the glorious warmth and comfortableness of the chair as he sank into its corduroy cushions. The clicking, crackling fire and soft, cheerful background music dimmed the ferocious rapping of rain against the windows to dreary insignificance.

"What's wrong, Dan-Dan?" Elmer circled a finger in front of her face. "You look upset."

Will expected that Dante might next gently break the news to her siblings that their eldest sister was not the wonderful woman they'd always believed her to be.

"Turns out Molina is the one who's been stealing the wots' gems so she can make a spell to live forever, and I'll probably have to fight her to the death any time now," Dante said with dashing bluntness. "That'd be why I look upset," she added, circling a finger around her own face to mimic Elmer.

Elmer continued to stare, apparently unfazed. "No, that's not it. Something else."

"Oh." Dante relaxed her defensive stance. "Blue's missing. I'm worried about him."

"That's it." Elmer nodded. "Don't worry so, Dan-Dan. You worry far too much for those wots."

Dante stroked a hand down Foyer's arm as she took the seat next to his. "You'd soon have something to say if someone were trying to kill all the wares. You'd not just sit there and do nothing then. What if little Cesar was the one fighting for his life?"

"Oh, no. No. Yes, I'm sorry."

"Well, he is," Will said, butting in before really asking himself if that was a wise move.

"Who is what?" Dante asked.

"Cesar. He *is* fighting for his life."

Elmer drew herself from her seat in one strange sweeping movement, as though she'd been pulled up by the shoulders rather than using her legs. "What's wrong with Cesar?"

Harrier flounced from the sofa with a yelp of dismay. "What did you just say about Molina?"

Elmer held up a hand to her twin. "Just a tick, Harry. What about Cesar?"

Will sat up awkwardly from the comfort of his armchair. "He got bitten by banters."

"They caught him?" Karson asked, an unmistakable tone of guilt in the question.

Elmer rushed around the sofa. "We should find him. We can't leave the poor little guy out in this weather if he's hurt. When did this happen? Wares only have a few hours before the poison takes effect."

Harrier followed her twin. "Who cares about the blipping ware right now?" she snapped at Elmer, before turning on Dante. "What are you accusing our sister of exactly?"

"Don't you dare speak to me that way, Harry," Dante said. "Molina's the one who deserves that anger, not me. You know I'd never lie about something like this. Molina did things to Gart. It's her fault he's been missing all this time. She kidnapped him. She hurt him. She's not right in the head."

Harrier fell quiet but continued staring angrily.

"We've missed out on some stuff, huh?" Elmer said, stunned.

Foyer looked up weakly to smile at her. "A few small details."

"Four wots are already dead," Dante went on, "and she's after killing the rest. She's cooking up a spell to create immortality from their gems. We have to get them back to the wots before it's too late."

Harrier's enraged expression did not change but she forced herself to aim it away from Dante by facing the nearest window instead.

"It does all seem very anti-Mo-Mo," Elmer said. "But what about Cesar? Shouldn't we go and find him?"

"Be my guest." Harrier flung the living room door wide open. "I'm going to Molina's place."

"She's not there," Dante said. "Don't think she won't turn on you if you get in her way, Harry. You can't trust her."

Harrier lifted a long black cagoule from the mahogany coat-stand by the door and slipped it on, scoffing indignantly at Dante while she fastened the buttons and flicked up the hood. Without saying another word, she barged by Elmer, disappeared into the hallway and headed out into the storm. There was a loud bang as the front door shut behind her, either slammed in temper or caught by the wind.

"Stupid witch!" Dante shouted after her.

Elmer clasped her hands together. "I'm all worried now. Oh, Dan-Dan, why did you have to bring these people here?" She clicked a button on the radio and silenced the happy acoustic music. "We were all settled in for the night, and now Harry's gone and Mo-Mo's some kind of monster. What's Auntie Scilla going to say?"

Will sank back into that oh-so-sweet armchair. His eyelids drooped so low he gained a blurred view of his own eyelashes. He felt himself sag, ready to drift away to dreamland.

An excruciating stabbing sensation in his wounded hand woke him straight back up. He sat bolt upright, clutching his wrist, hoping the pressure might cut off the pain. It didn't.

Dante roared in frustration when she realised what was wrong with him. "Banters! Perfect. Just what we need. They're popping up everywhere now, aren't they?"

"It's us they're after," Karson said gruffly. "Wot blood is their favourite, it being so rare that we bleed. It also tends to be a case of the more superficial the wound, the higher the appeal."

Will squeezed his wrist tighter still. "Please do something," he said, choked.

"Never fear, little one," Elmer said sympathetically. "There's a spell on this house. No one can enter uninvited."

That information was good to know, but it didn't help his hand.

Elmer perched on the back of the sofa. "So, what's the plan? How are you going to get the gems back from Mo-Mo? I assume asking her nicely won't achieve much."

"Good assumption."

"We have no plan as such," Karson said, hanging on to his lapels and puffing out his chest. Even with the blood-soaked slash in his jacket and dripping with rainwater he somehow managed to look pristine. "We are biding our time."

"For what?"

For once, Karson had no words.

"There's only one thing you can do, then," Elmer said.

Popset gave an amused snort. "You have an idea?"

"Yes," Elmer replied, clearly confused as to why he would find that something to snort at. "You need to funnel the four energies into new vessels. If you make new gems, the energies will come right back to you. And Mo-Mo will be left with… very pretty rocks."

"Actually," Foyer said over Popset's derisive noises. He took a sharp breath. "She might be on to something. We could do what everyone wants to do ourselves before they get the chance."

"What are you prattling on about?" Karson flicked some water from his neatly buttoned sleeve.

"We could use Blue's gem to do a spell, like Elmer said. Unite all the powers with his."

"That would be a very dangerous thing to do." Karson's back stiffened. "And I say no. No. Absolutely not."

"We'd separate them again straight away," Foyer said. "When Blue has all the power, he can call back our gems, and we'll put it all back where it belongs before any harm's done. Elmer's right, it's the only way."

"It's not the only way. It's no way at all. It cannot be done."

Elmer nodded understandingly. "Pessimism."

Karson leaned back so that he could look down his nose at Foyer as he said, articulating each word to emphasise how serious he was, "It is not worth the risk."

"If we do nothing, she's going to kill us."

"Not if Blue's gem stays safe."

"So, what do you think we should do, keep Blue hidden away somewhere until Molina dies of old age?"

"Whatever we're doing," Dante said loudly, "we need to find Blue first. Do you remember anything yet, Will?"

Will hadn't expected to be dragged into the conversation and couldn't think of anything to say. His hand hurt too much to think about much else.

"Why ask him?" Elmer asked.

"He's the one who sent him away," Dante explained. "He just can't remember where he sent him."

"That was rather careless."

"I didn't do it on purpose," Will said.

"Oh, cutie-cakes." Elmer smiled reassuringly. "Nobody's careless on purpose."

"Ugh, my hand is killing me." Will tucked his hand under his armpit and leaned over it. His wet clothing clung to a different part of him every time he moved. Just as he opened his mouth to ask Dante if she had a magic-sucky-towel he could borrow, a flash of lightning revealed a face at the window behind her and he gagged instead, unable to speak for panic. A banter had found them. It was pressing its gaping, lipless mouth against the glass.

Dante twisted her neck to see what had spooked him. She sighed angrily and dropped the canvas blind over the window to block the creature from view. "Just ignore it." She rushed to Will's side and crouched by his chair. "You have to think, Will. Please. It's so important."

Easy for her to say, Will thought, but there was no ignoring the agony and the gripping fear that the banter brought with it. Didn't she know he wanted Blue back as much as she did? If he knew where Blue was, he would tell her. He hated her looking at him that way, with those needy eyes pressuring him for answers he didn't have.

"Where would you go for safety?" Foyer asked, with none of the intimidating urgency that Dante had acquired. His calm patience eased Will enough to be able to think logically, for a moment at least.

"I'd probably go to my mum," he admitted.

Dante widened her eyes. "You've never sent Blue to your mother?"

Had he? Had he somehow sent Blue to his house? Will pictured the scene. What would his parents say to a stranger turning up in their kitchen? Their child was missing. They'd probably call the police.

No, surely not. He would have known Blue wouldn't be safe there.

The little voice he had heard earlier came back to him: 'Hospital.' Finally, it dawned on him.

"Hospital. I'll have sent him to the hospital."

"Oh, *William*." Dante stood up. "Why on earth would you do such a thing?"

"He'll be safe at the hospital. They'll look after him there."

"We'll have to go and get him." She pointed her wand at herself and her clothes instantly dried. She did the same for Will and the wots. The heavy denim peeled free from Will's legs, and he cuddled his jacket around himself.

Foyer attempted to heave himself up, but Dante pushed him straight back down.

"Where do you think you're going? You can't go to a hospital looking like that. They'd have your botty hanging out of a gown in two seconds flat. And you can sit yourself down too," she snapped at Popset, who'd made a move forward. "They'd think you escaped from somewhere. And no thanks, Karson," she said when Karson was about to speak. "We don't need you bossing everyone about either."

"Of all the disrespectful..."

"I'll come," Will said over Karson's grumbling, keen to get away from the banter that lurked by the window. Its shadow hit the blinds every time the lightning glared, and the pain in his hand was making him sick.

"Damn right you'll come. I'm not going into a place like that by myself."

"Place like what? It's only a hospital."

"Hold my hand while I make the portal and think as hard as you can about this hospital of yours for me." She held out her hand to him and pulled him out of the comfy chair.

Closing his eyes, he envisioned the hospital where his mother worked. He thought of the big automatic doors at the entrance, leading to the reception area that tried so hard to look welcoming and relaxing but was always full of worried people under ugly lighting. He thought of the corridors, the shiny grey floor that his mother wouldn't let him slide on, and the mint green walls.

A slap on the back shoved him into a blast of light. The pain in his hand reverted to a slight tickle under his skin for the next few seconds, and then faded to nothing. He wiggled his thumb around and enjoyed the relief.

It was too dark to see once the portal had gone, but Will knew they'd reached their destination. The air reeked of disinfectant that always reminded him of his mother. He patted around the wall for a switch and clicked on the light, which buzzed before it flickered to life and revealed a small storage room filled to the brim with neatly stacked boxes.

He pushed the door open an inch and peeped through the gap. "It's okay. There's no one about."

They stepped out into the oddly quiet corridor.

"So, where is he?" Dante asked.

"Let's go look."

They moved swiftly, peering through the glass panel in the door of every room they passed. The soles of Will's trainers squeaked as he tried, and failed, to slide on the shiny floor. It was more fun in socks.

"I can't see him," Dante said impatiently.

"We've hardly looked yet." It was a big building with a great many rooms on each floor – did the witch really expect to find Blue in the first place they looked? They'd probably have to comb the entire hospital.

At the end of the corridor, Will knew he'd been proven wrong. Three doctors, two security guards, and several bemused nurses were gathered outside one of the rooms, which could only mean one thing: They'd found Blue.

One of the nurses in the group spotted Will.

Will froze when he noticed her notice him: Him, Will, the missing child of her colleague and good friend Sandra Morgan.

Chapter Nineteen: Safe Real World

Olivia Banks was one of Will's mother's best friends, the mother of one of his schoolmates, and a responsible adult, and there was no way she was going to let him go once she got her claws into him. She would call his mother and he would be forced to go back home. He wouldn't be able to help Blue.

"Will?" Olivia jig-jogged in her hurry to get to him. "Are you okay, love?"

He tucked his hand under Dante's arm.

"Where have you been? Your mum is worried sick about you." Olivia glanced suspiciously at Dante. "Who are you?"

"Veronica Martingale," Dante announced, affecting a bizarre, over the top posh accent that made her sound like she had a peg on her nose. "It's a pleasure to meet you."

"What are you doing with this boy?" Olivia held out her hand to Will as if she expected he would take it. Will just stared at it and held Dante tighter.

"Oh, he seems to have latched on to me," Dante said in the same exaggerated, overloud voice, and she tugged her arm free from Will's grip, smiling pleasantly at the nurse. "I think he must be lost, the poor mite. There's a nice little boy." She patted him on the head like a dog, and he snarled at her like one. "I'm trying to find my husband. Blue, is his name."

Olivia's face softened. "I see. Could you please go and speak to the doctor over there?" Still reaching out for Will's hand, she called out to one of the men gathered by the door. "Doctor Jenkins? This lady knows our mystery guest."

Dante gave Will a comforting look before joining the people down the corridor.

"Love, I have to call your mum and dad, and let them know you're safe," Olivia said. "I can't tell you how worried everyone's been about you. Your poor mother's been out of her mind. Good lad for coming here. You know you're always safe here."

"You can't tell my mum." Will hid his hands behind his back when she reached out for one again. "Please. Not yet."

"Of course I have to tell her. Everyone's out looking for you. Come on. Come with me."

Will tried to keep one ear on what Dante was saying to the doctor, but Olivia was blocking it out. "It's okay," he said. "I'll wait here."

She made another grab for his arm, but he jerked back out of her reach.

"I'll wait here. Honest. You can tell my mum. I was just scared. Because she'll be cross with me."

"Oh, honey, she's not in any way cross with you, I promise." Olivia laughed with relief. "She just wants you home, safe. I need to go and get my phone. Please, please, promise me you'll wait right here. Right here. Do not move."

Will just smiled.

She checked he was still there four times as she hurried away, and she whispered to another nurse as she went, obviously telling her to keep an eye on him.

"We have to do something," he said to the Maker as soon as Olivia was out of earshot. "We can't let her tell my mum. We have to stop her."

"Would that make you happy?"

"Yes."

"Very well. It is done."

Will looked around. "What's done? We didn't do anything."

"Speak for yourself. I've just erased that woman's recollection of the last ten minutes. And I did it just for you."

"Ten minutes? We didn't even see her for that long."

"You can thank me later."

Will took his body back from the Maker's control and, after a quick scan of the people down the hall to check he didn't know any of them, made his way back to Dante.

"He's not dangerous or anything," she was saying. "Why can't I just take him home?" When she saw Will at her side, she gave up the pretence and dropped her fake accent. "You know what? Enough talking." She waved her hands at them. "Shoo. Go on. Off you go."

The doctors' faces gave away their thoughts, that perhaps the strange, black-coated young man in the room behind them was not the only crazy person to arrive in the building today.

"Why aren't you leaving?" Dante glanced worriedly at Will and said, "Rats." Fast as she could manage, she whipped Will in front of her and pushed him into the room, slammed the door closed, and pressed her back up against it to barricade it should the people in the hall attempt to follow them in. "Blue, hey, it's okay," she said. "We're here."

Blue had been huddled in a corner, coat wrapped tightly around his shoulders with the collar raised to cover the lower half of his face, but he released himself when Dante spoke. Crouching so he couldn't be seen through the window, he rushed closer. "What, in the name of everything with a name, is going on here?" he asked in a harsh whisper. "There I was, standing with Molina, ready to defend my gem to the death, and the next thing I know, I'm in a room full of people all wanting to poke me and telling me to get undressed. What sort of sick psycho-hole is this? How did I even get here? I couldn't get out, you know, I've been trapped here. My gem's not working."

"My stick isn't working either," Dante chuntered, gnashing her teeth.

"But why?"

Will heard Olivia calling his name from the corridor. He ducked under the window, next to Blue. "You didn't change her memory at all," he said crossly to the Maker. "She still knows I'm here, and she'll have told my mum where I am now. My mum'll come and get me, and I won't be able to stay with you guys anymore."

"Will," Dante said for his attention, stunned. "We are trapped in here, with a bunch of people out there who think we're a sausage short of a barbeque, and your biggest concern is that your mother knows you're safe?" She banged the back of her head against the door. "What is *happening?* Why can't we use our magic?"

Olivia's face appeared at the window, giving Will a shocking flashback of the banter at Dante's house. "It's all right, honey," she shouted, rattling the door handle. "There's nothing to be scared of. You're safe here. All of you are. Come on out."

"This place isn't real," the Maker said.

"Yes, it is." Will wondered why the Maker would come out with something so outlandish. "My mum works here."

The Maker shook Will's head, patient but stern. "No. This isn't the real hospital. This is some imaginary version of it, where there are no scary banters, no scary magic. This is the place you crave when things get too much for you. This is your safe real world."

Dante gesticulated rudely to Olivia through the window. "Oh, confound it, William! You've gone and got us stuck in some imaginary world where we can't use magic. How exactly are we going to get back home? We're well and truly stuffed, aren't we?"

"I can't tell you how glad I am to see you two," Blue said. "Or three, even. They were making me think I really was mad for a bit, especially when my gem wasn't responding to me."

"Well, I really am mad, getting madder by the minute. How could you do this to us?"

"It was an accident." Will resented the insinuation that he'd deliberately caused this situation to inconvenience them.

Dante abandoned her post at the door to hold manically on to Blue's arms. "What does this mean?" she asked him. "What does this mean, really? Will can just click his fingers and render us helpless as two blind bunnies with their legs cut off? What does this *mean*?"

Blue drew back from the hysterical witch, eyes filled with concern for her.

"But I didn't do anything," Will insisted.

"You don't ever think you're doing anything," Dante said, glaring madly at him. "But you're doing things all the time. All the time. You're probably doing something right this second, standing there, looking all innocent."

"Hey, come on now." Blue hushed Dante.

"I'm not," Will muttered.

The door began to open, and Dante and Blue slammed it back into its frame. Whoever had tried to open it backed away.

"How are we going to get out of here without your brew stick or my gem?" Blue asked.

"Ask *him*!" Dante shrieked, losing touch with her sanity.

"How did you get us here, Will?" Blue spoke in the same calm and unrushed way that Foyer had back at Dante's house. It took the pressure off.

"I didn't even know I'd done it. I didn't do it on purpose!"

Dante jammed a fist against her breast. "Good grief," she panted, "this must be what a heart attack feels like."

There was a sharp knock at the door and Olivia peered through the window again. "Come on out," she called, waving a large syringe by the glass. A squirt of liquid dribbled from the needle. "We'll make you all better."

Will cringed. "No, I hate needles."

"Isn't this meant to be your safe place?" Blue asked. "Why would there be needles in your safe place if you don't like needles?"

Will was sick of being asked questions he did not know the answers to. Everyone seemed to think this was all part of some plan of his. How could they think he would want them to be stuck here, powerless?

But then he remembered. He remembered longing to be back to normal whenever things had become too scary, just like the Maker had said. Whenever things had become dangerous, he'd yearned for home, for reality, where magic was just pretend, because magic was – well, it was wrong. It was something he could not understand or control, so of course it was wrong and frightening. Somehow, his subconscious must have decided that if magic was so wrong, surely a normal, familiar place where magic did not exist was right and safe. And this hospital was the least magical place he could think of. So, he had brought his friends here, for safety. He had stripped them of their magic.

"But how could I have done that?" he whispered to himself.

"You've got the Maker in you," Blue said. "It's like I told you, he can do anything just by willing it to happen."

"I did not will *this* to happen," the Maker said firmly. "I am powerless here too."

"What does this mean?" Dante asked again, in a hiss of a voice as crazy as her eyes.

Blue sniggered, and Will looked at him in surprise. "It means Will's more powerful than the Maker."

Dante stopped breathing so heavily and stared at Will, momentarily frozen. "So, the Maker possesses a body in which to return the four energies to their sources, and that body turns out to belong to the only being in the history of time with the power to stop him?" Too deep in thought now to fret so much, she slouched against the door. "Don't you think that's a bit too much of a coincidence?"

"No such thing as coincidence," Blue said, mimicking Karson. "Will's come to save us. Save us from being unmade."

"Yeah, that or to get us stuck in some freaky hospital with not a thread of magic between us."

Will wished there was a way to make her see. He wasn't powerful. When he had touched the wots' gems – then he had been powerful. Now he was just Will.

"Why do you think I had to wait all this time?" the Maker said, the unexpected interruption to his thoughts startling Will. "Why do you think I've had to wander in spirit as nothing, as a bodiless, heartless, bloodless ghost of the child I'd once been, for hundreds of years? I didn't think I'd ever be in a position to return the energies I summoned. I didn't think I'd ever get another chance to pass over. I'd given up. But then, there it was, out of nowhere. I felt a pull."

He fell silent.

"What pull?" Dante asked impatiently. "You mean Will called you to him?"

"I didn't," Will said with a stubborn frown.

"You did." The Maker relaxed Will's face. "That was it. It was like you called me to you. Not intentionally, of course."

"Nothing Will does is ever intentional," Dante retorted, prompting Blue to cast the witch another complaining glance.

The Maker went on as though Dante had said nothing. "I felt a compulsion to leave Wynne for the first time since I stumbled across it at ten years old. And I found you, Will. You were one of many children, but you stood out to me. Seeing you was like seeing a splash of colour after centuries in a world of grey. And when your game was over and you started to leave, all I knew was that I couldn't let you go. So, I snuck in."

"That's disgusting!" The thought of a dead spirit stalking him and creeping into his body while he went about his day oblivious was severely disturbing to Will.

"I should have known, when you brought the wot back to life, the strength that lies in you," the Maker went on. "For that is the one thing I could never do."

The door rattled again, and Dante punched it.

"Come on out now," Olivia's chirpy voice trilled. "The police are here, and they're going to force their way in if you don't."

"You don't know your own power yet," the Maker said. "I didn't know mine either, not until I'd lost my family and found my witch mother."

"You have to get us out of here, Will." Dante struggled to keep the door shut.

Will didn't know what she expected him to do.

"This isn't a safe place anymore," Blue told him. "If I could use my gem, I could get us home. I know it's not safe there either, but at least it's real. This place isn't real."

It felt real enough to Will. Even so, a tug of excitement niggled at his heartstrings. Was he, little Will Morgan, really some all-powerful being that could save the day? *Of course not*, a voice of reason interrupted the outrageous notion. If that were true, Dyelann, Maik and Henry would still be alive. His parents wouldn't have been at each other's throats for weeks. He would have been able to control himself when he'd had all eight gems in his possession and would never have let Molina take them away from him.

"There's a fire exit," he said, pointing to a door at the back of the room.

Blue, still crouching, ran on bent knees to investigate. "There's no way this was here before," he said, pushing the door open. "Dante, it's clear. Come on, let's go."

The exit opened onto a stairway. Blue let Will and Dante through first and closed the door behind them. Dante darted up the first couple of steps, but Blue caught her hood and yanked her back down.

"What are you doing?" he asked, perfectly calm. "Why would you go up? What are you planning on doing, flying off the roof?" He proceeded to drag Dante by her hood, until she fought herself free and patted down her clothes, running downstairs alongside him.

Will tottered behind, his legs tiring. "We've got to get back to Karson and Foyer," he shouted.

Blue stopped, and Will, yet again, nearly crashed into his back. "Karson's alive?"

"He and Popset are both at my house," Dante said, pleased to give him the good news. "They're with Foyer and Elmer. They're safe."

A wide smile spread over Blue's face, and he hopped gleefully down the last three steps to the next fire escape.

Will pushed the bar on the door and swung it open with a determined shove.

Generously spaced trees thrashed in all directions with the monstrous gales outside. Rain lashed down from swirling clouds that blocked out the moon and stars and cast a strange blue-grey shadow on the world.

"I didn't know this hospital was in Itchen Hush!" Blue shouted over the din.

"It's not." Will turned around. Goosebumps prickled. There was no sign of a hospital ever having been.

"You must have wanted to come back here more than you knew." Dante pointed her wand at herself. The raindrops began to bounce away an inch from hitting her, like she was shielded by a sheet of Perspex. "My brew stick works!" Her body slumped with relief. "Oh, Will, thank you. Thank you so much." She laughed. "Gosh, I nearly panicked there for a minute."

"Really?" Blue said. "You hid that well."

"I don't live in Itchen Hush of course," she added, "but that's not a problem now." She kissed her wand and gazed adoringly over the glistening wet wood. "I missed you so much," she told it, and then swiped a portal open with it. Rain disappeared into the hole of light, and Will could hear Popset complaining before they'd even walked through.

"Now I'm drenched again," the wot moaned as they emerged in Dante's warm, cosy home. "Thank you very much." He rubbed at the wet patch on his stripy sleeve like it was something revolting.

The stabbing sensation in Will's hand flared. Groaning, he headed back to his armchair and bounced into the snug cushions, sitting on his hand in another useless attempt to curb the pain.

Blue yanked Popset into an exuberant hug, ignoring his protests. "You're alive!"

"You're soaking me." He gave up trying to struggle free and went limp in Blue's arms. "I'm glad you're well too."

"Yes, jolly good," Karson said.

Though Foyer was slouched weakly over Dante's kitchen table, he still managed a menacing glare, daring Karson to say anything unfriendly to Blue.

"Now then, Blue." Karson scraped his chair back to stand up, and Blue let go of Popset to pay attention. "These people want to do something terribly foolish, and they're going to want to use your gem to do it. Now, lad. Do the sensible thing and take your gem far away from them while you still can." Responding to Blue's growing alarm, he clarified, "That was the only reason they went to find you, to get your gem."

"That's not true," Dante said. "That's not true, Blue. We just thought if we drew all the powers into your gem, we could get them away from Molina. That's all." She wandered around her table and stood behind Foyer. "Tell him, Foyer." He didn't respond. He had either passed out or fallen asleep, but he was still breathing, so she leaned over to kiss the back of his head and let him be. "It'll be okay, you know. What do you think?"

The worried knot between Blue's eyes loosened, and he sat on the nearest chair.

Elmer popped up from the sofa and peered over the backrest. "I think it's the only way you'll do it. Mo-Mo was strong enough even before she had your gems. How else do you propose you get them back from her?"

"Don't get roped into it, boy," Karson said.

"We're not roping him into anything." Dante kept her focus on Blue as she spoke, probably to refrain from punching Karson in the mouth. "All we'd do is a little spell to drain the powers from the other gems and shift them all into yours. That's all."

"Isn't that what Molina's been trying to do all along?" Blue asked, dubious. "If she can't do it, how are we supposed to do it?"

"There must be a way she's missing," Dante said. "The Maker's witch mother did it for him."

"You mean she did it *with* him," Popset corrected her. "Blue's right, we won't be able to do it. Not on our own." His face drooped, as though the likelihood of this plan failing miserably had only just occurred to him.

Dante rested on the arm of Blue's chair, and he looked up at her like a child who had just asked his mother if the rumours he'd heard about Santa were true. "Lillian Scrossly believes she's the Maker's descendant."

All too aware of the Maker pricking his ears, Will gritted his teeth against the incessant pain and made an effort to listen too.

"If that's true," Dante went on, "Lillian's family must have inherited his books somewhere down the line." The forced smile she had worn until then changed into a more genuine one. "One of those books must contain the spell we're after."

The Maker exhaled irritably, and Will hoped the others realised it was the Maker and not him being disrespectful. "Lillian Scrossly had no inkling of her connection to me until recently. That much is obvious. My spells were never written in any book. And let's not forget, I never needed a spell to combine the powers, only to split them. You do remember why we needed to split them?"

"Yes, yes," Dante said, aggravated. "We all know the dangers, but it'll only be for a short time, and we'll put them straight back."

Elmer, who had been watching the Maker speak through Will as if fascinated, recovered her apathy and wandered to the window. She pulled back the blind and Will started at the sight of the banter's face flashing in the lightning. Its mouth gaped with longing, puffing a cloud over the rain-spattered glass with each hot breath.

A flitter of blackness rushed behind the banter just before Elmer released the blind and allowed it to swing back into place. Will lowered himself into his cushions, trying not to panic.

"Will," the Maker said urgently. "I saw it. That is no neether. And it's not a harvester either."

"What is it, then?"

"And I don't think it's here for you."

Will crawled out of his seat and headed for the window, wondering if he dared to peek out. A loud crack from the banter's claws on the glass decided that for him, and he backed away.

"It's a reaper." The Maker's excitement bubbled inside, infectious and giddy. "And it's here for *me*."

Chapter Twenty: Repercussions

Popset did a double take at Will, as if unsure he'd seen right - for how could anyone in their right mind possibly find something to smile about at a time like this?

"It's finally going to happen," the Maker whispered in one long breath.

"What's going to happen?" Dante checked Blue's face like he might know. "Did I miss something?"

Blue had been staring at his feet for a while and apparently hadn't been listening.

The Maker approached Blue. "Pass me your gem."

"Like I'd ever trust you with it," Blue said, too distracted by his feet to put any emotion into the words.

Will felt in control of his body again and took that to mean the Maker had given up speaking. "I think he's just trying to be helpful." He had no idea why he should want to stick up for the Maker but did so all the same. His hand throbbed mercilessly. No matter how hard he squeezed, no matter what position he held it in, it hurt no less. He wished the banter would go away. The adults here reckoned he could create an entire building full of people with the great magical power he supposedly possessed. If he could do all that, how could he not make one banter disappear?

"Blue?" Dante said.

Blue still wasn't paying attention. "Yes?" he said, a polite but automatic response to hearing his name.

"What do you think?"

"I think… I think I'm not wearing any shoes." He hitched up his trouser legs and revealed the dazzling white socks to everybody.

"Huh," Popset said. "How could you not have noticed that earlier?"

Karson, Will could tell, was quietly admiring their impressive cleanliness.

More annoyed now than intrigued, Blue asked, "Where are my boots?"

"You threw them at the banter when..." Will wavered, remembering Blue's valiant efforts to save his friends from the fiendish creature, only for them to be taken from him at the last moment. "When..." He didn't know how to say it.

He didn't need to.

"Oh. Right." The sombre glimmer in Blue's eye changed to a perplexed squint. He lifted one foot. "Look. Dirt." He twisted his sock around so they could see the bottom, which was soiled black.

Dante took a quick glance. "That's what happens when you walk around outside with no shoes on."

Karson clicked his tongue loudly, in a way that implied he was disappointed but not surprised that Blue's socks weren't as impeccable as they had first appeared.

"That's not possible. My socks don't get dirty. They've a charm on them that never allows dirt to stick to the fibres."

"In that case," Elmer said, leaning over for a closer look, "perhaps it isn't dirt."

"Of course it's dirt. Look." Blue gestured with an irritated flick of his hands. "Filthy."

With everything else that was going on, it didn't seem right to Will that a pair of dirty socks were getting so much attention. "So what? Put them in the washer."

Elmer, on all fours now, stared at the socks, her face only inches away. "It looks like soot," she said, just as Blue turned self-conscious and tried to hide his toes back under his trouser leg. "Perhaps it's sewitt?"

Thinking that Elmer had repeated the word 'soot' in a funny accent, Will grinned.

"Can't be," Dante said. "Can't be, can it? Where could he have stood in sewitt?"

"What's sewitt?" Will asked as soon as he realised they meant something different, and Dante snapped out of her concentration to answer him.

"It's a dusting of an extremely precious mineral that doesn't even exist in this reality. It has to be purchased from the otherworld."

"Blackbone," Karson said.

"Yes, that's it. It's practically priceless. Immune to…" Her concentration-frown returned. "Immune to all rival magic," she said slowly. "Like charms to keep your socks clean." Glaring around at everyone like she thought one of them might be hiding something from her, she asked, "How on earth did he get sewitt on his feet? Has anyone seen any? Where have we been?" She sucked in a long grating breath. "Please tell me Molina doesn't have sewitt. Did anyone see any at her place?"

"There was black dusty stuff all over," Will said. "On the gems and everything."

"On the gems?" Dante grasped her hair, moving so Elmer could get by. "Was there a funny smell in there?"

Blue stopped staring at his feet. "Now you mention it," he said, "there was something a bit…"

"Vinegary," Will said.

"Yes." Blue pointed an unenthusiastic finger at him.

Dante let go of her hair and growled accusingly. "For the love of Chika. Why didn't you tell me that? I don't have a sense of smell. I didn't know."

"Definitely sewitt, then," Elmer said.

"Where did Molina get sewitt from?" Dante sounded more and more like the crazy lady she had become at the hospital. "It's impossible to get your hands on that stuff. Impossible. And how are we supposed to get the powers back now, if she's using sewitt to keep them?" She grumbled for a minute or two, twitching, kicking at the floor, and then she stopped. She stood still, took a deep breath and held up her hands. "Okay," she said. "Let's not panic."

The rest of them calmly glanced at one another.

"But this is bad," she went on. "She's obviously been using the sewitt for her spell, and that's a bad, bad sign. We won't be able to use witch-magic to draw the power to Blue's gem." She seemed nervous when she asked Will, "Will you help us? Please?"

Will stared back at her. Didn't she know by now that all he wanted was to help? "I'll try."

"Not *you*, William."

"Why do you keep calling me William like that?" Even his mother didn't call him William.

"I shall help you," the Maker said.

Karson dipped his neck in a quick bow.

Dante's eyes bored into Will, and he shifted a little. "Why's he suddenly changed his tune, Will?"

"I think he's trying."

"He's very trying," Blue agreed. "But at least he seems to be making an effort." He reached out from his chair to nudge Will. "Can I trust him with my gem?" he asked quietly, as if that would somehow prevent the Maker from overhearing.

Will wanted to give the Maker the benefit of the doubt but couldn't help fearing the worst - that this was all part of a plan to win their trust only to betray them in the end just like Lillian had.

"Can I?" Blue pressed him.

"I think so. I think you might have to."

A heavy spatter of rain rapped against the window in a fierce gust of wind, startling everyone apart from Blue, who didn't react at all, just continued staring like he'd heard nothing.

Elmer lifted the blind again to yell abuse at the loitering banter.

Blue carefully held out his arm, the gem still encased in the vice that was his hand. He stayed in that position for a while, contemplating. "Okay," he said eventually, and unclenched his fingers to present the blue gem to Will.

"I don't want it." He took a clumsy step backwards, shocked by the offer.

"He's giving it to the Maker, William." Dante took the gem from Blue's open hand, and he didn't take his gaze from it for even a blink while she carried it away a couple of steps, bobbing it up and down as if to get a feel for its weight.

"Rin," the Maker said in a small, almost shy voice.

Karson, Popset, and the witches looked at Will.

"Sorry?" Dante asked.

"Rin. It was… It is my name."

A strange, uncomfortable silence fell upon the room, and Elmer turned her back on everyone to fiddle with the blinds again.

"Rin." Dante smiled graciously. "That's lovely to know, sweetheart."

"Sweetheart?" Popset mouthed.

Blue jumped out of the chair and snatched his gem back from Dante.

"Blue, you only had to ask if you wanted it back, you didn't have to tear my hand off."

"Sorry, I just…"

"Give it to me." The Maker held out Will's bleeding hand.

Blue stared at it, taking a while to gather the courage or the will to pass over his most precious possession to the one who could take it away with a thought. Slowly, cautious, he settled the gem in Will's injured palm.

The moment the stone touched the wound, the skin sealed itself over, leaving no scab or scar in its wake. The pain ceased. Will was grateful - but he was holding Blue's gem.

"There," the Maker said.

Will flinched, feeling the Maker's anguish, the conflict in his mind: Here he was, with a gem in his hand, tasked with uniting the four energies again. Now what would he do? Help the wots and give them back their borrowed power? Or would he return that power to its rightful place like he'd had his mind set on doing for hundreds of years?

"You said you'd help," Will whispered. "You said."

"And I shall," the Maker said, making the decision there and then. "There's a reaper here for me. I saw it. So, yes, I shall help you, and help you fast." A flicker of hope made its way to Will's face in a smile. It was the Maker's and his own too.

The Maker tossed the gem upwards, so hard that Dante ducked as if she thought the roof would cave in. Blue cringed at the sight of his poor gem about to crash into the ceiling. It didn't get a chance to hit anything. In the split second it took to leave the Maker's hand, he stopped it and sent Will floating into the air after it.

Words boomed painfully in Will's head, but not a sound left his lips.

"*Eight come one, I will it be…*"

Blue's gem glimmered, then shone brighter and brighter, until blinding white light swallowed the room. The last thing Will saw before he had to close his eyes was the banter recoiling from the window.

"*…Seven be gone, come back to me.*"

For a minute, the air that beat across Will's face felt like the rush of heat that blasted out on opening an oven door. It cooled. The light dimmed. Will dared to open his eyes.

Something was different. At first, he couldn't quite fathom what had happened. Then Dante screamed out loud in horror and despair, and Will knew.

She shook Foyer, who was still slouched motionless over her table. She shook him harder the longer he didn't respond, until she was all but lifting him from the chair.

Karson and Popset's bodies were both slumped on the floor. Even collapsed and dead, Karson looked neat and tidy.

The gem began to drift gently back down.

Will couldn't remember dropping from where the Maker had been levitating, but his feet were now on solid ground, and the blue gem, complete with the power from all eight, was falling his way. The Maker readied himself to catch it.

"You killed them!" Dante's wand was suddenly in her hand, pointing Will's way, and he was flung through the nearest window.

Falling in a cascade of shattered glass and fierce raindrops, he landed in a pitiful heap on the grass below. Warm liquid dribbled over him along with the cold rain, an odd and sickening sensation. Unable to move for fear of the pain that he was sure would kick in at any moment, he lay still where he'd fallen.

Then Dante was there, sweeping the glass away from him with several swipes of her wand, and she took his hands to help him up. "I'm so sorry, Will. Are you hurt?" She hugged him. "I'm so sorry."

"He said he'd help." The loudness of the storm drowned out his voice.

Dante guided him to the front door. When they walked in, they saw Blue. He stood in the centre of the living room, gem back in his fist, with a peculiar look of serious and profound hatred on his face. Air rushed in around him from the open door and his coat fluttered against his legs like a super-hero's cape.

Elmer backed up to Will and Dante, watching Blue like he was a rabid dog. "We shouldn't have let him take it back," she told them.

"I didn't intend to," the Maker said, accusing eyes on Dante. "She threw me out of the window before I had chance to do anything."

"Threw *me* out of the window," Will chuntered.

"Not good," Elmer said, still backing away from Blue. "Very not good."

Dante took a step closer to him. "Blue? Come on." Another step. "Come on. It's okay." Her gaze kept flitting back to Foyer. Every time she saw him, she quivered as though the crack in her heart was breaking open even further. "We need to get the other gems back, right now."

Blue's eyes were dark, staring, and cold. He didn't look like himself. "What's the point, now they're dead? They're all dead."

"The energies must be separated," the Maker said. "It must be done. The time you waste keeping hold of that gem, the neethers are out there, fast becoming more powerful than they've ever known themselves to be." He marched past Dante, stood before the wot, and held out a commanding hand. "Give it to me and I can right this wrong. I can end it all right now."

These words struck the wrong chord in Blue, and his pupils dilated bigger than they should have been able to as he visibly tensed. "This was your plan all along. To steal our trust and kill us all." He gave his head one slow, solemn shake. "I will not let that happen."

With that, he vanished into a burst of blue smoke.

"We cannot allow him to keep that gem." The Maker snaked around Dante to break her attention from Foyer. "Do you hear me? The neethers exist only to balance the power of the gems, and with such concentrated power in the blue one theirs shall grow to compensate. This cannot be allowed to happen."

An absurd chorus of laughter sounded from outside the house: Laughter that surrounded them, the same laugh coming from twenty or more different mouths.

"I think they heard you," Dante said, a nervous whisper. She ran to the smashed window and stuck her head through the blinds that hung dejectedly from their broken rail. "I can't see them."

The laughter rang on.

"But I can hear them."

The neethers were taunting them. Will's heart skittered and flopped.

"Don't worry," Dante said. "They can't get in here."

The door clattered against the wall, sending a framed picture crashing to the floor along with the coat stand. A slim, faceless figure, dressed in dark and fluttering rags that weren't in the least bit wet despite the torrential rain floated through, pulling itself slowly into the living room by grasping the doorframe with long, spindly fingers.

Another followed, identical to the first. Then another.

Dante darted back across the room to stand protectively in front of Will and Elmer. The creatures had no eyes and no expression, so it was impossible to tell which way they were looking, but Will just knew they were staring right at him. Three more drifted in behind the others.

"Give us the child," one rasped deeply through a thin-lipped mouth that grew above its chin as it spoke. The mouth elongated and stretched. The neether held out a hand to Will, its fingers uncurling and opening out one by one.

"Okay," Dante said. "Maybe they *can* get in here."

Elmer blew a raspberry. "You think?"

Will unwittingly found himself craving his normal, real life again.

A pair of animalistic black and gold eyes blinked open from the smooth skin above the neether's cheekbones. "The child," it said, voices overlapping like several had spoken in unison.

"He's not who you think he is," Dante said. "He isn't the Maker's descendant. Leave him be."

The neether blinked its new eyes. It was hard to tell if the creature was curious, angry, or indifferent.

"Leave him!" Dante poised her wand.

It blinked again. The eyes disappeared back under the skin then reappeared larger and blacker when they next opened. "Hand over the child, witch." There was no emotion. Every word was spoken with a strangely laid-back, rumbling drone. "Or we shall take it from you."

Regardless of everything that was happening, and despite the triviality, it stung Will to be referred to as an 'it'.

"He is not the Maker's descendant," Dante said again, louder and firmer.

"No." The Maker confronted the first neether. "I am no descendant."

The neether breathed out a long, wet breath, like someone with a bad chest cold. "You arc he."

It spun twice where it hovered in mid-air, so fast it blurred, its long arms catching Will and the witches and sending them scattering across the room. Elmer landed just short of the fireplace. Dante smacked into the wall. Will went head over heels and landed painfully on his knees, but the Maker had him straight back on his feet and returning to the neether that had pushed them. The others floated around this one like they were awaiting its instruction.

"You seem to forget," the Maker said, "I am your creator." He rubbed Will's finger against his thumb. "I can snub you out like a candle if I so wish."

The neether's eyes and mouth slid a fraction down its face. "You have no form. Your wishes mean nothing. The wots have outgrown you. And so have we."

A delighted chuckle from the hallway made everybody look. Some of the neethers grew bulging eyes in the backs of their heads to save themselves the trouble of turning.

Glad of the attention, Molina smiled. "Looks like we have a full house already." Her bandana was knotted firmly back in place on her head, and she was soaking wet through, dripping murky water all over.

"Molina, my carpet!" Dante shouted.

To Will's tremendous surprise, Molina actually looked guilty. Then she collected herself, and her face changed again.

"You tell me where Blue is, right now, or else…" She pointed at Will. "I'll kill the boy."

Grinning mouths sprouted on the neethers' empty faces. Some of their grins kept growing until the sides almost met at the back of their heads.

“That’s it,” Dante said, choked, and she barged past the six neethers to reach her sister. As soon as she was close enough she slapped Molina across the face, leaving the vague red outline of a handprint behind.

Molina rubbed her inflamed cheek and rolled her tongue around her mouth, probably to check she still had all her teeth. She stared daggers at the wall. Then she turned that stare onto Dante. “I let you off with the last one,” she said. “But that hurt.”

“Good! I’ve lost friends because of you. I’ve lost…” She couldn’t finish.

Not a trace of sympathy crossed Molina’s face. She had shown more remorse for dirtying the carpet than for hurting her heartbroken little sister. A smile teetered on her lips, an amused sparkle in her eye.

“Why doesn’t she throw her through the window?” Will muttered, and the closest neether moved jerkily to look at him. Its eyes swelled and shrank again before it returned its attention to the witches, apparently interested in the family feud.

Another angry gush of wind blew in through the open door and rushed through the house to the broken window, flapping Will’s jacket as it passed. The contents of his pocket clinked. He slipped a hand in to investigate. His fingers met something cold and hard. Glass? It took him a second to remember the corked bottles that Lillian had given to him. Neether repellents. He’d completely forgotten he had them. What was he supposed to do, just throw them? He only counted three. Would that be enough? He stared at the nearest neether, afraid that it might somehow be reading his mind.

“Oh, you’ve lost friends?” Molina feigned shock. “Well, poor little Dante. Don’t give me that holier-than-thou rubbish. You’re no better than I am. You murdered my best friend in cold blood then wiped her off your shoe and carried on with your life without once stopping to think of me, so excuse me if I'm not cut up for you right now."

Dante twitched with irrepressible anger. "You're *evil,*" she said. "So was Eve. I'll never forgive you. Look what you've done." She stepped back to show Molina the table where Foyer had been slumped. Foyer, however, was no longer there. "Where is he?" She glanced around the room, pushing neethers out of the way to clear her view. They floated aside like hanging clothes being swept across a wardrobe rail. "Where is he?"

"You," the first neether said, moving close behind Will's back.

Will's fingers tightened around one of the repellents.

"The Maker. You must be destroyed."

Will tugged the bottle from his pocket, tearing the fabric in his haste, and hit the neether with it. The glass crunched against its side. Red and yellow grains of sand exploded from the bottle, a dusty cloud in the air.

Then Will could hardly take a breath. Everything went wobbly.

The neether looked curiously down on him, hovering higher and higher. Except, it wasn't hovering higher - Will was stooping lower. His knees slowly gave way beneath him until he was too low to stay upright. He toppled onto his side, paralysed and numb, vision blurred.

It occurred to him then that he had been very unwise to trust something that Lillian Scrossly, the enemy, had given to him.

I am such an idiot

. It was his last thought before all went dark.

Chapter Twenty-One: The Agulga Sphere

Will's eyes needed time to adjust to the newfound dimness, but he didn't need to see to know where he was. The whiff of mould and old vinegar had already given it away.

A flash of lightning, dulled through the filth on the windows, lit the room for barely a second. Long enough for Will to see that he was not alone.

"I can't believe it," Lillian said, with her hands set smugly on her hips. "I can't believe you were actually dumb enough to use the potion I gave you." She smiled, pleased with herself. "I'm glad I gave them to you now."

Will's equilibrium returned in fits and starts. He struggled to drag himself up from the grimy floor.

"I gather the power has been funnelled into the one vessel again," the pretty witch went on, in that bright way of hers that Will used to believe was her natural pleasant nature shining through. How wrong he had been. "The Simms witch certainly left in a hurry. You see, she couldn't quite understand how it had happened, and so quickly. I hear she went to great lengths to retrieve a -" She laughed. "- an extraordinarily rare, mystical matter to protect those gems from anyone else's interfering magic. So, if not magic that took those powers, then what?" She leaned casually against the wall. "I don't really care about that. I'm just glad it got her away from me. The woman's a raving lunatic."

"Whereas you're such a sane, rational little girl?" Christian said. The wicker, who had been lurking in a corner out of Will's sight, emerged from the shadows. His bods were fast asleep on his shoulders. "How are you, anyway?" he asked Will, buttoning his bulging jacket pockets. "Less psycho than when we last saw you?"

Will smiled nervously.

"I'm still very angry with you, young man," Lillian said. "But I'm pleased to tell you it worked out for the best that you ruined my plan. Like I said before, you've certainly sped things along."

"Okay," Will said, uncertain.

"Yes, it is okay." Lillian swaggered across the little room to peer out of the front door.

Feeling a bit woozy, Will planted his hands onto the filthy shelf above the fireplace to steady himself. A small purple flame still flickered in the ashes beneath the cauldron. Sooty black sewitt covered every surface. Will could feel a thick dusting of it under his hands and between his fingers, the soft texture of flour. "What are you going to do?" he asked quietly.

"Well," Lillian answered in her usual cheery tone, "first, I thought I'd track Blue down before that tiresome Simms witch gets to him. Then I thought I'd kill him, properly this time. After I've claimed my rightful powers, of course. Then I thought maybe I'd take a trip. Somewhere nice and warm, with sunshine, none of this rain. And then I thought I'd sit back and enjoy my happy ever after."

Will didn't like the sound of that. Shouldn't the good guys be the ones who lived happily ever after? He shuffled to the door.

"Err…" Lillian blocked his way. "Where do you think you're going?"

"Outside?"

"No." She smiled sweetly. "No, I don't think so."

"But… You said…"

"I said I'm still very angry with you. That's what I said."

Christian stood by Will's side. "Hey. You also said you'd leave him alone. Remember? Something about going after bigger game?" He indicated to the door with a lift of his brow. "Go on. Go get your bigger game, girlie. Go pick on someone your own size."

Lillian rummaged in the pocket of her dungarees and continued speaking to Will. "The repellent I gave you was really a potion meant to bring you to me so I could kill you if the time was right." Her teeth scraped across her lower lip while she made a show of deliberating. "The time is right," she said with a shrug, aiming her stunted wand at Will. It crackled.

"Hey, come on now," Christian said, backing off. His bods slept soundly, undisturbed by the commotion.

Will's hands instinctively shot up to shield his face just as a translucent, sparking blast burst from the wand's tip. The force hit his palms, driving him backwards, bending his arms against its weight. And then it stopped. Resisting sudden nothingness, Will's arms flung the energy back in the direction from which it came. It flashed like a fork of lightning, straight into Lillian's heart.

She fell flat on her back, silent and motionless, eyes and mouth wide open.

Will gasped for breath. It took his brain a few seconds to register that the witch wasn't going to get back up. "It wasn't me," he croaked, stunned. "Was it you?" he asked the Maker.

"No," Christian said, returning to Will's side. "I thought it was you."

"I did nothing," the Maker replied, ignoring Christian.

"Well then." Christian nudged Lillian none too gently with his foot, and Will had to look away. "What happened?"

The Maker flipped Will's hands to show him his black palms. "Your hands. See that? It's sewitt."

"Sewitt?" Christian asked.

Will showed him his hands.

"Oh. Soot."

"No, sewitt. It's magic." The words Dante had used to describe it escaped him. "It does something. It stops other magic."

"I suppose that explains it." Christian shrugged. His bods rose and dropped with his shoulders but did not stir. Badmé was lying on his back with his legs dangling down Christian's front, while Gudmé was face down with his legs dangling over Christian's back. Neither of them looked particularly comfortable but were sound asleep regardless.

"What am I going to do?"

Christian found a stiff blanket on a wooden stool next to the door and draped it unceremoniously over Lillian. "Would you like me to get you back to the wots?"

The offer rankled Will. How did this man have the audacity to act like nothing had happened, after what he'd done? "You tried to steal Dyelann's gem."

Christian snorted a mocking laugh. "We only looked at it. Unlike some fiery-eyed, gem-hogging hypocrites who shall remain nameless. Come on, you whiny little whinge-bag, I can take you back to your friends."

One last burst of rain rattled the windows, and then eased into a gentle drizzle as the storm finally reached its end.

Christian waved a hand in front of Will's face. "Hello? Anyone in there?"

"You can't take me to them," Will said, watching the weather through the open door. "They're all gone." He kept his head angled in a way that kept Lillian out of his peripheral vision, trying not to think about the fact she was lying there dead under a mouldy blanket. Trying not to think about the fact that he had killed her. He looked at Christian, completely at a loss.

"I'm sorry about your friends. Really. Maybe it's time you went home."

"He can't go home," the Maker retorted.

"He can go wherever he wants," the wicker said. "You can go wherever you want, Will."

"I know," Will said.

The Maker made an angry noise in Will's throat. "You know nothing. You have no idea what pains I went through to get you here. All the things I had to do for you to finally get the message. It's a good job I broke you when I did, too; I had no idea that any of this was happening with the Simms witch and my newfound 'relative' over there." He flicked Will's arm in the direction of Lillian's body, and Will stiffened, determinedly keeping his eyes averted. "We could have arrived too late. Then what would have happened? You were such hard work, Will. You just refused to listen to me. Refused to leave your cosy little life. That's why I had to do what I did."

A nip of nervousness tightened inside Will.

"I had to do it. For the greater good."

Christian listened, intrigued. "What did you have to do?" he asked, his chronic nosiness surfacing again.

"Your parents. They never…"

Will waited patiently for the Maker to formulate the words, not sure he wanted to hear what was coming.

"Very well, I confess. I knew you'd never leave if I didn't give you a reason to go, so I stooped as low as a neether and got inside your head." The Maker's shame flickered in Will's thorax like a candleflame. "I had to get you to Wynne somehow," he added, as if he thought that might justify his actions. "I am sorry, Will."

It took a minute for Will to put together exactly what the Maker was telling him. "You mean," he said hopefully, "my mum and dad weren't really yelling at each other all the time? It was all just pretend, to upset me?"

"Yes," the Maker admitted. "And, like I said, I am so s-"

Will whooped for joy and jumped into the air with excitement before the Maker could finish.

Christian grinned at Will's glee.

Will had lost count of the sleepless nights he had spent listening to his parents' harrowing arguments. None of them had been real. Nothing had changed. They loved each other. They still loved him. Everything was going to be okay. If the Maker had been a corporeal being right then, Will might have kissed him.

The rain stopped falling completely, leaving a crisp freshness in the cleansed air that breezed into the hut.

"I'm happy that you're happy," the Maker said. "But you're going to stay and see this through, yes?"

Will nodded, raring to go.

"Good. Then we will begin where we left off. But first, let us take advantage of the witch's filthiness."

Will refused to look anywhere near Lillian.

"No, not *that* witch," the Maker said. "Molina Simms left sewitt all over the place. Use it. Cover yourself with it. It'll protect you." He began to scoop it up from the shelf and pat it onto Will's jacket. Will quickly took over and continued to sprinkle the black substance all over his body. He rubbed it into his hair and tried to use it to remould his spikes. This idea, like his hair, fell flat.

Christian stifled a yawn and peered out of the doorway. "At least it's stopped raining. That's good. Your soot won't wash out."

"Do you think I've put enough on?" Will presented himself to Christian. His battered and torn outfit was covered in black handprints, and he'd smeared it across every inch of visible skin. He felt like a chimney sweep from an old movie.

"Yip. Come on. I want to see what happens." The wicker invited him to exit the hut with an elaborate arm gesture, which Gudmé copied weakly in his sleep.

Will couldn't get out of Molina's shack fast enough. He hoped he wouldn't end up regretting being glad of the company. Cesar had explicitly warned him against trusting Christian.

"Great. So now you're all magically protected with… soot… Where are we going?"

"It's not soot," Will said, pleased to be the one correcting someone's pronunciation for once. "It's sewitt. We're going to Dante's house. You know the way, right?"

"Aren't you forgetting something?" the Maker asked.

"What?" Christian and Will said together.

"Me. I'm helping you now."

"Yes," Will said, wondering what he was getting at. "Thanks."

"Yeah," Christian laughed, "we really appreciate you, Mr Maker, sir."

"No, you pair of..." The Maker let out a puff of vexed air like there wasn't a good enough insult in his vocabulary for them. "I'll take you to the Simms' house."

"Oh, yeah." Will remembered the Maker's teleportation powers. "Like before, when you left poor Foosay in the middle of nowhere after she'd been nice to us." He nodded at Christian. "But I don't want to leave him."

"Really?" The Maker sounded astonished to hear that. "But he's so irritating. Don't you find him irritating?"

"*You're* irritating," Will countered. "But I don't want you to go either."

The Maker took back control but said nothing, and Will felt the odd, fuzzy twinge of an emotion that wasn't his own. He, the Maker, was touched.

Christian wavered. "Umm… Are we going or what? Because I'd appreciate it if we could get there before these two start wakey-wakeying." He waggled a finger at his bods.

"Very well," the Maker said. "I can bring him along, if you wish."

Like it was so easy, Will thought, suddenly indignant. With the ability to blip from place to place with no need for portals or potions of any kind, the Maker could have had Will at the shop and slurping back pineapple juice in no time after he'd been bitten by the banter. Instead, he'd been left to travel on foot for hours, in pain, scared for his life. That didn't seem fair. Wondering if the Maker could sense his emotions the same way he had begun to sense the Maker's, Will concentrated on projecting his bitterness about this.

A loud thump from behind them immediately eliminated the bad feeling. Something scary was about to happen. Anything the Maker had done before was irrelevant if they remained on good terms now.

Another thud. And another. Heavy footsteps. Esko appeared from the dark shadow of creepy gothic trees to their right. He circled the grubby hut twice, and then bent low to peer through one of the windows. Realising he was being watched, he turned.

"You two again," he boomed. "Where's the witch? The witch that killed my Alley, where is she? I know she has been here. A seer told me of this place. Where is she? Tell me." He ducked to challenge them eye to eye, hot breath hitting Will hard in the face. "Are you working with her?" Those unruly brows of his sank unnaturally low while he waited for Will and Christian's response. "Are you?"

"No way!" Will shouted back, offended. When he saw the angry glint in the giant's eye, he hid behind Christian.

"Let's not hang about," the Maker said.

The air felt like ice, so cold it burned. A blur of colour followed, and the next thing Will knew, he and Christian were standing by Dante's broken window.

Will dropped to an unsteady crouch, afraid that the neethers inside would see them.

"What the… Where the… What…?"

"Shh!" Will grabbed Christian's arm and dragged the wicker down to his level. "They'll hear you."

"Who will?" he asked loudly, nudging Badmé back into place on his shoulder.

"Shh!"

"Told you we shouldn't have brought him," the Maker whispered. "He'll probably get you killed. Then what will we do?"

Will chose to ignore the comment rather than tell the Maker to shut up, which is what he would have preferred to do. Slowly, carefully, he rose to the height of the windowsill to peek into Dante's dully lit living room. Glass crunched under his trainers, and he flinched at the sound.

"Be careful you don't cut yourself," Christian said, a sarcastically emphasised whisper.

Will stood up properly and stuck his head into the house. There was no sign of anyone. Not the witches, the neethers nor the dead wots. Other than the blind gently flapping in the breeze, everything was still. "Where do you think everyone went?"

"They've probably run off to find Blue," the Maker said. "We probably ought to be doing the same."

Will looked through Dante's window at the spot where they'd last seen Blue: Filled with hate and mad with grief. Maybe mad with power too. "Maybe we should leave him alone. You saw what he was like." Blue's empty face flashed in his head, and he put his arms around himself, hoping the Maker wouldn't pick up on how scared he felt. "You don't think he'd kill me, do you?"

"Not in a million years," Christian said, his conviction putting Will's fears to rest. "Wots are not killers. They're just not." He stood up and brushed some shards of glass from the bottom of his jacket. "Thanks for pulling me into the pool of broken glass by the way. Lucky for you, wickers are tough."

"Why, what would you have done?" the Maker asked. "Bled on me?"

"Yes, actually. And banters love wicker blood."

Will smiled. "Sorry."

"Forget it." Christian froze in place as Badmé snored and rolled over. The little creature settled again, and Christian let out his breath. "He shouldn't wake up yet, but he can sense when there's trouble afoot. Always on guard, this one."

"Yes, it certainly looks like it," the Maker said. "Anyway, let's think about this logically. The last thing Blue said was that he wouldn't let me get his power. So, where would he have gone from there? Somewhere he thinks I would never think of."

"Where's that, then?" Christian asked.

"I'm the wrong person to ask. It's somewhere I would never think of."

"Can't you just use your magic to bring him to us?" Will asked.

"It's not magic, Will," the Maker said, and it surprised Will to hear what snappy authority his own voice was capable of projecting. "It's much more powerful. It's energy. It's human spirit. It's *will.*"

"Me?"

"The other type of will."

"I know." Will hadn't known.

"Do you even understand what magic is?" the Maker asked. "It's an exchange with the earth, that's all. It's having one thing and swapping it for something else. What I do, what my wots do, what you have proven you can do too, it's so much more than that. It's better."

"How?"

"The earth gifts us. It asks for nothing back."

"Okay," Will said. "Can't you use your stuff that's better than magic to bring Blue here, then?"

"Blue has the entire culmination of the four powers streaming inside him now. He'll be able to fight against my will."

"What about mine?" Will ventured to ask, trying not to sound arrogant.

The Maker didn't reply.

Christian jeered. "Nothing to say to that, has he?"

"We shouldn't have brought him," the Maker said. "So tiresome. Listen. Maybe I cannot summon Blue, and maybe you cannot either. But together? Together we might have the will to guide him to us."

"Wow," Christian said, amazed. "You really think I could help?"

"Not you, idiot," the Maker snapped.

"I don't know how," Will said.

"It's simple. You want Blue to come back to us, right?"

"Yes."

"Want it more."

Will looked to Christian for encouragement of some sort.

"Don't look at me. I'm just the tiresome tagalong."

Want it more. Will closed his eyes. Want it more. Come on, Blue. Come back to us. I really, really want you to come. He squeezed his eyes shut tighter. "I don't think it's working."

"No, he's resisting us. Try harder."

Come on, Blue. Will screwed up his face to concentrate. Come here. Come back to us. And he really did wish for his friend to be there with him. He was worried about the wot out there, all alone and upset.

"Young Will."

A hand tapped him on the shoulder, and he choked on his own alarmed gasp.

Foosay Hoo patted him on the back until he could breathe again. "My goodness, you're filthy," she said, wiping her hand clean on her poncho. "I'm so glad I found you. There was a strange clarity that passed my thoughts not half an hour ago, and I knew I needed to tell you. You see, I told you a lie. Not deliberately, mind. At the time I told you this lie I had no idea it was a lie at all. But now I know the real truth."

"What are you going on about?" Will felt too frazzled to mind his manners, and he could tell the Maker was annoyed with her.

"I was wrong when I told you Scilla Simms discovered the secrets to eternal life. It wasn't Scilla Simms at all. It was Tamzin Rickrack."

"So?"

"So, don't you see? How could I have made that mistake? Why did the memory return to me now, out of the blue? I'll tell you why: Because someone has been using magic to change it."

"Interesting," the Maker said. "Your change of memory rather seems to have coincided with Lillian Scrossly's time of death."

"Will killed her," Christian said.

"I never! I didn't do anything. I didn't kill her."

"Listen to me," Foosay said impatiently. "I'm trying to tell you something important. The truth returned to me in its entirety. I remember everything. And I remember that Lillian Scrossly cannot possibly be Lillian Scrossly. Lillian Scrossly died eleven years ago, when she was an eleven-year-old child. She was murdered."

Something twisted horribly in Will's stomach.

"So, who was the girl claiming to be Lillian?" the Maker asked.

"I believe it was Tamzin," Foosay said. "Tamzin must have changed herself when Lillian died. She must have become Lillian and lived out the child's life for her. Everyone's memories were changed. We were all made to believe Tamzin was the one who died that day, and not her granddaughter."

Christian was positively glowing with delight, listening eagerly to the gossip.

Will was baffled. "Lillian was never really Lillian? It was her gran who wanted to kill the wots? It was her gran who…"

"You just killed," Christian finished.

"That's right," Foosay said before Will could protest his innocence. "Not long before Lillian's murder, Tamzin made a wish to a wot for the ability to cheat death."

"What are you saying?" the Maker asked. "Are you saying Tamzin is still alive? Now?"

Will felt lightheaded. Would Lillian be a zombie now?

Christian hooked his thumbs in his trouser pockets and leaned back against Dante's house. "That witch looked pretty far dead to me."

"The wish she made enabled her to survive death," Foosay explained.

"She wasn't really Lillian?" Will asked again, saddened. Poor Lillian, the real Lillian, had been murdered when she'd been the same age Will was now. It dawned on him just how much he had been counting on his age to be the thing that would save him in the end, to be the reason nobody would really harm him. Now it seemed his age meant nothing. Eleven-year-olds were not exempt, after all.

"Oops." Christian noticed he was squashing his bods on the wall and moved away from it. "Tamzin's been fooling everyone all these years," he said as he checked his bods for damage. "That's sort of impressive. Also sort of demented."

"You're right about that, son," Foosay agreed.

"We're looking for Blue," Will told her.

"Yes," the Maker said. "And thank you so very much for interrupting us with that delightful news bulletin of yours. We were on the brink of bringing that wot right to us, until you showed your face. We almost had him, Will."

"Do you think Lillian's gone after him?" Will asked. "Tamzin, I mean." He'd been so busy trying not to look at Lillian's body after her death, would he have even noticed if she'd stood up and walked away? Surely Christian would have.

"Hey, look," Christian shouted, hopping down from Dante's porch. His fleeting absence had gone unnoticed until his return. He thrust a crumpled piece of notepaper into Will's hand. "I found this."

Will started to ask how he'd been in and out of the house so quickly but was distracted when he opened out the paper and saw his name in the scrawled blue ink. He held it under the porch light. "Will… Go to Cesar's dance…" He frowned at the page.

"Place," the Maker corrected him.

"Oh." Will read on. "Foosay told us Blue had gone there. Molina was not happy to see her, let me tell…" He flipped the note over. "You."

"I found it inside," Christian said, as if he expected a thank you.

"I certainly said no such thing." Foosay snatched the note from Will. "I never saw Molina. I only came here to tell you about Tamzin. I have no idea where Blue is." She hmphed at the handwriting. "I must say, I am getting rather tired of this wretched witch using me as their scapegoat."

"But it was Molina who was pretending to be you," Will grumbled, frustrated by his own confusion. "How could she pretend to be you, in front of herself?"

"There's a question you don't hear every day," Christian said.

"It was Molina, I know it was. It had to be her." All the evidence had pointed to Molina. Whenever she'd worn someone else's face, she had covered her head to hide her incurable baldness. Why would anyone else bother to hidc their hair? But, unless Molina somehow had the ability to split herself in two, there was no way it could have been her after all. Will rubbed his forehead. "It was Molina, wasn't it, Mrs Hoo?"

"Oh, lad, I wish I knew." She huddled under her poncho. "It's chilly out here. I'll be off now, I think."

"Aren't you coming with us?"

"I'm going home," she said, as if surprised that Will had expected anything else. "I only came because I thought my new information would be important to you."

"As if you care," the Maker muttered.

"Of course I care." Her frail voice turned gentle, and she put those kindly grey eyes on Will that reminded him of his grandmother. "I care deeply. But I cannot help you further at this time." Then she strutted away. She did not look back.

"Now what are we going to do?" Christian asked, a bizarre tone of innocence to the words, like a child whose toy had been snatched from him.

Will shivered in a sudden chill. A colourful blur smudged in front of his eyes, and he rubbed them with his sleeve. "Go to Cesar's, I suppose. Like the note said."

"Look around you," the Maker said curtly. "How slow are you people?"

Will almost laughed when he saw they were standing right beside the massive tree trunk that led to Cesar's home. He bent his neck back to see the shabby hut in the branches above. A plank of wood fell from one rusty nail that had been holding it up and broke in two where it landed by Will's feet. "How did we get here?"

"I brought us here while you were wasting time daydreaming," the Maker said. "Let's just all shut up and get up there."

Will heaved himself onto the first step with none of the exuberance he'd had the first time he climbed this tree. "I can't believe you brought him," he said, flailing a foot until it regained traction on the slimy, wet wood. "I thought you didn't like him."

"I absolutely do not," the Maker said. "But you seem to enjoy having him around. So, I thought, why not?"

"That was nice of you."

"I am nice."

Will pulled himself onto the platform of the rickety old treehouse and rolled into Cesar's wonderfully warm, welcoming home. The aroma of freshly baked biscuits took the unpleasant smell of musty weeds from his nostrils. It was like stepping into another world.

They peered around the extravagant room. A single kite stared at Will from where it perched on the back of Cesar's red sofa. Its face was silvery and striped, dangerous hooked beak narrow and long, eyes a mesmerizing pale green, and it looked about as happy to see Will as Cesar had when they'd first met.

"We should be quiet," the Maker whispered, breaking Will's eye contact with the bird. "It could be a trap."

Will nodded.

"Wow!" Christian's voice blasted out, shaking the quiet from the room. "Would you look at this place. Who said wares are simple creatures?"

The Maker smacked Will's hand into Christian's breastbone. The wicker overbalanced, fell backwards and disappeared on his way out of the door. Will winced at the grim thump that followed. He briefly worried about the sleeping bods before he saw the kite reaching a leg out for something, using its long, scaly toe like a finger. Its talon pierced a scrap of paper just like the one Christian had found at Dante's house.

The Maker was quick to snatch the note from the bird, causing Will to panic over his recently healed hand so close to such a sharp set of claws. The fear was soon forgotten when he got to work on the scrawled writing.

Will read aloud, squinting. "Want a... cracker."

"What's wrong with you?" the Maker interrupted. "Can't you read?"

"Yes, I can read." Will scowled, annoyed that he couldn't see the Maker to glare at. He went back to the note. "Wait at… carrot." He scoffed. "I can't read this writing."

The Maker held the note steady. "It says: Wait at Cesar's for our return. Won't be long. Wish us luck." He screwed the paper into a ball and threw it, not caring where it landed. "As if we're going to wait around here. Stupid witch."

"Dante wrote it?"

"I assume so."

"Her writing's worse than mine. And I'm eleven."

"Yes, yes, you are eleven," the Maker said, unimpressed. "Congratulations."

Will sat down on the sofa, his back to the bird. "How old are you?"

"Far too old. I should have died centuries ago. Yet I live on. Live on without actually living."

"How come? How come you didn't die?"

"I was never entirely certain. It was because of what I did with the four powers, I know that much." The Maker smiled weakly. "But that doesn't matter now. I saw the reaper come for me. He will come again."

"I don't want to die." Will was afraid to even speak the words.

"Of course you don't. You're a child."

"But I thought you were too. They keep calling you a boy. Karson said you were just like me."

"I know what he said. It makes me smile. I love the nature of my wots. They're good all the way through, all eight of them."

Will's throat tightened when he remembered the horrific truth. "There's only one now."

"I know." The Maker went back to what he'd been trying to say. "I was a child. I grew. I had a child of my own, with a lovely witch, my beautiful Sanshé Sing." His growing sadness ached in Will's chest. "But when the time came that I should have died, the spirit of the child I had been the day I summoned those powers lived on. That is who I now am."

"So, you really are just a kid?"

"A kid," he repeated coldly. "Yes. A child with the memories of a man who lived a lifetime and should have died."

"You're starting to give me the creeps." Will wiggled his shoulders to stop his spine from tingling. Something brushed against the back of his neck, and he sprung from the sofa, spinning around mid-leap to see the kite that he'd already forgotten about. It sat in its spot on the back of the sofa, watching his every move.

Christian staggered into the room. "What did you push me for? You almost woke them."

The bods still slept soundly on the wicker's shoulders. Will wondered if they'd been fastened in place somehow.

"Lookie, lookie at this place," Christian said, any anger he might have been feeling quashed by the sight of such splendours. He gazed at the lavish paintings on the gleaming walls, marvelling at the intricate detail to the unicorns and dragons they depicted, then wheeled around when he noticed the kite. "Hello," he said to it kindly, reaching out like he wanted to stroke it. The broken torch that Will had left on Cesar's coffee table distracted him midway. "What's this?" he asked, picking it up. He gave it a shake and its light came on.

"Hey," Will said, not sure whether to be impressed or annoyed. "You fixed it."

The beam of light reflected from the corner display cabinet, attracting the wicker's attention.

"Look at those." Discarding Jonah's torch, Christian slunk to the cabinet and peered through the glass at the treasures inside. It contained a peculiar array of trinkets, most of which were fashioned from stone or metal. The centrepiece, a large, glass-like orb, glinted aqua blue where the light touched. It could have been a giant bubble, for how delicate it looked. Not one doomed to twist and contort with the air only to burst into nothing, but one captured in time, a permanent, perfect sphere.

Christian yanked the cabinet door open.

"Don't touch it," Will said, darting over the carpet to stop him. "You might break it." He glanced over his shoulder to check for adults, forgetting for the moment that Christian actually was one.

"Look," Christian said, awestruck. "An Agulga sphere, a real live Agulga sphere." He circled his hand an inch over the top of it. "This is truly incredible. Do you know what this is?"

"An Agulga sphere."

"Exactly."

"Is that good?"

"It's unbelievable."

"What does it do?" The ball's resemblance to a giant marble made Will long to roll it. He never would, of course. He knew better than to touch things that looked expensive and fragile.

"I have no idea what it does," Christian replied, sounding ready to pop with excitement. "But I've always wanted to find out."

Will was confused. "What's so special about it, if you don't even know what it does?"

"Special?" Christian lowered his voice when he remembered his sleeping bods. "Special," he said again, quieter, "is not the word for this thing. I can't believe your ware friend has it just sitting here out in the open, and nobody's taken it." He paused and cocked his head.

"Don't steal it," Will said, knowing exactly what the wicker was considering.

Christian laughed and held up both hands. "Me? Steal? What do you think I am? A giant wenn?" His casual posture backed up his words, but his greedy eyes, glittering and fixed on the orb, told a different story.

In the hope of removing temptation, Will moved to close the cabinet's door.

A furious, whistling bolt of wings and claws launched itself at him, and Will jolted back in shock, protecting his face. His shoulder hit the cabinet, rocking everything inside. The orb tipped from its golden holder. It rolled gratingly across the surface of the glass shelf. Will followed it with his eyes, powerless to catch it in time. He tried anyway. It grazed his fingertips on its way to the floor, where it shattered into a thousand sparkling pieces over the beautiful carpet.

There was no time to fret for Cesar's loss. Pain seared every nerve like he'd been sliced in half from the top of the head down. He staggered blindly across the room until he toppled, crashing into Cesar's coffee table, completely incapable of stopping himself. A most revolting nausea rippled through his insides, and he begged himself not to be sick.

Christian's shocked exclamation ricocheted around the walls. "Oh my G…!"

Will passed out.

Chapter Twenty-Two: Meeting the Maker

"Wakey-wakey," came an annoying voice that Will was certain he'd already ignored once. Maybe even more than once.

He wanted to roll over and go back to sleep, but there was something wrong with the bed. Something kept jabbing into his back.

"Come on, lazy bones."

Christian's face hovered ominously over him. The bods hung from the wicker's shoulders to stare at him too, bright-eyed, bushy-tailed, and very much awake.

A soft, pristine white blanket fell off him as he sat up. It had been nice of Christian to cover him up, Will thought. Of course, it would have been even nicer if he'd moved him off the broken coffee table first. Rolling his eyes at the wicker, he rubbed the sore patch on his back where a piece of wood had been poking him for who knew how long. He felt like he'd been asleep for days. He choked on his yawn when he saw the dazzling glass fragments that had once been Cesar's sphere and remembered what he'd done.

"About time you got up," Christian said. "Something amazing happened." He took Will's wrists and hauled him roughly to his feet. "Something absolutely amazing." He grinned. The bods grinned.

Someone moved behind Christian. It was a child, about Will's age – a skinny child, dressed in tattered clothing, with black hair so short to his head it looked like it had only just started to grow back after having been completely shaved off.

"Who are you?"

"It's me," the strange boy said with a bright white smile.

Will still had no idea. "Who?"

"Me," the boy said impatiently. "Rin."

Will glanced at Christian for a clue, and then back at the boy. *"Who?"*

"The Maker, stupid."

He faltered, pondering what had just been said. Then he waved his arms frantically. "You're not in me anymore!"

The Maker jumped on the spot, just as excited as Will. "Look at me," he cried. "I'm my old self. I'm back in my old body!"

"His very young body, even," Christian said. "It's nothing short of a miracle," he added, with a respectful little bow of his head, which was immediately aped by his bods.

"It had something to do with the Agulga sphere," the Maker explained. "You touched it just before it broke, and next thing, I'm being torn right out of you. I've been restored." He took Will's hand and slapped it to his scrawny chest. "Feel that? That's my heart, Will. My heart. It's beating. Feel it?"

Will felt it all right. A soft, rhythmical drumming. He left his hand there for a moment after the Maker let go, until he suddenly felt awkward and moved away to look around. Despite the place having no windows, the room was lit with natural, sunny daylight now, as opposed to artificial lamps.

"Have I been lying here all night?"

"Yip." Christian and the bods nodded. "Quite a lot of the day too."

What a waste of time. "What about Blue? Is he all right?"

"We've not heard from him," Christian said happily. "We've just been having so much fun celebrating. Isn't that right, Rin?"

The Maker nodded exuberantly. "I must admit, I am verging upon ecstasy. I haven't felt my heart beating in hundreds of years. I haven't felt anything at all. Just feel that blood gushing." He pressed his fingers to the pulse in his neck.

Will couldn't help but consider the possibility that what was happening now was only happening in his imagination. Perhaps the neethers were trying to fool him again. They only brought nightmares to life though, he assured himself, whereas the Maker leaving him and his body alone at last was more of a dream-come-true.

"How?" he asked, posing the question like a challenge. "How did that ball make you jump out of me?"

The Maker composed himself, Will's seriousness obviously getting through. "I know Agulga spheres are used in protection spells," he said. "All I can think is that when you touched it, it tried to protect you. And the only way it could see to do that, with you being in no direct danger, was to get me…" he struggled to explain, "…out of you. That's the only explanation I can think of that makes any kind of sense."

"But that doesn't make any kind of sense."

The Maker beamed. "It's so good to meet you, Will." He grasped Will's hand again and shook it firmly. "Properly, I mean. I have so much to thank you for. Do you know what it means that I'm alive? Do you have any idea at all?" He hopped onto Cesar's sofa and raised his arms to the ceiling. "It gives me a second chance to die. The reaper that's been following us must have known this was going to happen. It must have been fated all along." He took a deep breath to calm himself, stroking his cheeks as though all the grinning had made them ache. "It is truly wonderful."

"But you're still going to help us, right?"

"Absolutely. Absolutely I'm going to help you, after what you've done for me."

A relieved smile spread across Will's face. "Okay." He stretched his back to wake himself up. "What day is it?"

"I lost track of days a good eight or nine centuries ago, my friend."

"And I don't care," Christian said.

The Maker bounced from the sofa cushions, leapt through the air, landed smoothly on his hands and somersaulted across the carpet to the front door, where he rolled straight out.

Will stumbled after him, expecting to find the Maker in a damaged heap at the foot of the tree. But no, he was standing safe and sound on his feet, gesturing for Will to follow. Will clambered down the makeshift steps, taking care not to be caught by any pronging nails.

"What are you doing?" he asked the Maker, jumping the rest of the way as soon as he was close enough to the ground to avoid injury.

"I thought you'd be eager to get going."

"Yeah, but where?"

Christian dropped from the shabby treehouse and landed neatly, barely having to bend his knees to do so. The bods both did a little jump of their own on Christian's shoulders to replicate the movement.

"To find Blue, of course," the Maker said.

"But you said he'd go somewhere you'd never look." Will was certain they'd already had this conversation.

"I believe we'll find Blue exactly where we would expect to find him, because he'll be expecting us to look where we *wouldn't* expect to find him. You see? So!" The Maker twisted into an elegant spin, elated at being in control of his own body again, and clicked his fingers.

Dizziness took a hold of Will, and he held his head, feeling like it would drop off his neck otherwise. An icy gush of air made him shiver. "I don't like it when you do that," he said, rubbing his arms to warm himself up, and he blinked hard to focus the blur in front of his eyes. When the fog lifted, he saw the trees were all sloped at the same bizarre angle, where they'd frozen in time in a long-ago storm. The Maker had taken him to the wots' tilted hut.

"You think Blue's come back here?" he asked. "You forgot Christian," he added, noticing the wicker's absence.

"It's not forgetting if it's intentional. But you're right. I'm sorry." The Maker scratched his head with the tips of his fingers, leaving them there for a few seconds longer than necessary as if to reintroduce his sense of touch to the texture of his hair. "I believe we'll find Blue in the basement. And I believe the witches would not yet have thought to look for him here."

Will put on a deliberately suspicious expression, not trusting this new Maker and wanting him to know it.

The boy sped to the hut, graceful, light as a cat in his battered pull-on shoes, and held the door open for Will.

"What makes you think he's here?" Will asked once they were inside.

The Maker kicked up the rug from the trapdoor that led to the basement. "This place belongs to the wots. Blue would have spent a lot of time here over the years. He told us he used to sneak off to the basement."

"Yeah, to get to the way out, not to lurk in the dark," Will muttered, annoyed that the Maker thought he knew Blue better than Will did, and even more so that he was probably right to think it. Shaking it off, he insisted to himself that he did know Blue better, and there was no way they would find him creeping about in a pitch-black, smelly basement.

His thoughts were interrupted and refuted by Blue's uncharacteristically cold voice sounding from the darkness.

"How did you find us?"

The Maker lit an old-fashioned lantern on the wall and exposed the room to Will in flickering firelight.

Blue stood in the corner by the exit, swaying, unbalanced. He clutched his gem so tightly that a trickle of blood seeped between his first two fingers. Dark rings circled his eyes, making his face appear ghostly white, hair hanging drably over his forehead. His eyes strained upward, following the Maker with burning hatred.

"This was the only place I could think of where you'd feel safe," the Maker said, with no sign of his recent glee. "I never wanted to hurt you, Blue. I still don't. I don't even want to return the powers anymore. They're yours. I promise."

Blue continued to shake and stare, seething. "Your promises," he said, jaw stiff, "mean nothing to us."

"Blue," Will pleaded.

Blue didn't take his eyes from the Maker, merely held up his gem-free hand to Will, indicating for him to keep out of it. "Leave. Leave now or…"

"Or what?" The Maker held out his weedy arms, inviting the grief-stricken wot to do his worst. "You'll destroy me? You'll kill me?" A dry smile passed his lips. "Who are you kidding? You don't have it in you to harm anyone. If you did, your gem never would have chosen you."

"You know nothing about any of us," Blue retorted. "We want you gone. We want you gone."

The Maker dropped his arms. "And if I wanted you gone as much, you could disappear forever," he said. "Only, I don't. I want to help."

"We don't trust you," Blue said, with a dark burst of laughter. "None of us trust you." He pointed his gem at the Maker, still gripping it far too tightly. "You're our maker. You're our destroyer."

"You're wrong."

"You hate us for not bringing your family back to you, but we have no control over life and death. You hate us for being unable to do something you never gave us the ability to do!"

"I don't hate you." The Maker sounded stunned that Blue didn't already know this. "I never hated you. I hated *myself*." Sadness quelled his boldness. The revelation visibly altered his perception, as though it had never encroached the outskirts of his imagination before today: The wots had harboured guilt all this time for being incapable of fulfilling the wishes of their maker - and they resented him for it. "I still do."

"It was already decided the day you made us. You were always meant to end us."

"You're not listening to me," the Maker shouted, patience failing. "I am not going to end you."

"No," a happy voice agreed over the sound of feet clapping sharply against wooden steps. "That's my job." Tamzin, still playing the role of Lillian, swept elegantly across the room to join them, a huge smile emblazoned on her face, pigtails swinging over her shoulders.

The memory of her dead body under a mouldy blanket flashed in Will's mind.

"You, boy." She pointed at Will. "You know how I was angry with you before?" she asked in that sweet manner of hers, nodding. The sweetness turned sour. "I'm so far past angry now, child. Nobody uses my own magic against me and gets away with it. Nobody."

"Nobody," Will said, heart missing a couple of beats. "Nobody. *Nobody!*"

"That's right. Nobody." Tamzin looked at Blue as if he'd patted her on the back and startled her, even though he'd not moved an inch out of his wobble zone. "You. Be a good little wot and hand over the gem. Come, come, boy, we don't have all day."

His quivering head didn't move from its position, but his eyes flicked from the Maker to the witch, and he locked his cold stare on her instead.

"She's not Lillian," Will told Blue, breathless with uncertain fear. "She's Tamzin. Lillian really died when she was eleven, and Tamzin changed herself, so she didn't have to…" He wasn't sure how to phrase it.

"Cope with the loss," the Maker finished for him.

Fire in her glare, Tamzin turned like a shark through water to face Will. "How do you know that?" she bellowed. "How do you always know these things?" She glanced at Blue and the Maker, then back to Will, aiming her broken wand at each of them in turn, again and again. "That power is mine. I want it. I want it. I want it now!"

"I don't want it," the Maker reminded Blue, perfectly calm. "I just don't want the crazy lady to have it. I know that's what you want too."

Blue's cold gaze remained on the witch. "It's ours. We won't let anyone take it from us."

The door behind Blue burst open, and all four of the Simms sisters bludgeoned their way through it. The sight of Dante standing side by side with Molina threw Will. Was Molina a goodie now? Was Dante a baddie? He wanted to demand answers, but Dante was focused on Blue, who still hadn't moved. His stare still had not left Tamzin, and his grip had not loosened for even a moment from his gem.

Molina took Blue roughly by the arm and tried to unlock his fingers. "Give it back to me!"

Dante dragged her sister back and pushed her violently to the floor. "I told you what would happen if you did that."

Scilla and Gart followed the sisters into the room. With a look of shock on his now handsome face, Gart automatically stooped to help Molina up.

"Leave her there." Dante pointed her wand at her brother, who backed off. "You might not remember what she did to you, but I do." She turned her lip back at Tamzin with the same abhorrence as Blue. "I really wish I could describe how much I hate you, Lillian Scrossly."

Tamzin smiled. "If only you knew how little your opinion meant to me."

"It's not Lillian," Will said. "It's Tamzin." He didn't know why this fact was so important to him. It was only a name, after all. A worthless detail, really.

"Tamzin?" Scilla repeated, her old eyes glistening with intrigue.

Tamzin held her hand out to Blue. "The gem. Give it to me."

Dante instantly jumped in to shield him from her.

"Think sense, woman," Scilla said, stepping in front of Dante, as protective of her niece as Dante was of Blue. "There are nine of us, against one of you. How do you think you'll fare in this fight?"

Molina picked herself up, huffing at Scilla. "I hope you aren't including me in that number." She sneered down her nose at Tamzin.

"Get out of here," she said, low and harsh. "You will not get in my way anymore."

Someone put out the light, and Will listened in alarm to the violent scuffle that followed. He had no idea what was happening, could see nothing. A cold hand closed around his and he did not know whose it was. It led him away, rather roughly, and he didn't know whether or not to start resisting. There was a seven in nine chance that the person was someone on his side, so he tried to keep his nerve and presume it was a friend.

The thumping and crunching of bodies colliding with the floor and with each other sounded from all around, indistinct voices shouted, and the jubilation of the Maker's echoing laughter boomed. But there was no sound from the person holding Will's hand. He would just have to wait until he could see again. They passed through the door into the cool air of the tunnel beyond. Their feet tapped against the concrete, and the sound of the fighting dulled.

"Where are we going?" he asked.

"We're getting you away from here." Blue's voice put Will's mind to rest. "We can't stay around those people anymore, but we can't let them hurt you while we get away."

"Why do you keep saying we?"

Blue didn't answer, just continued to drag Will along. Soft light eventually emerged, and Will could see at last. The tunnel narrowed until he could have just about touched both sides at the same time.

"Maybe you're safer without us," Blue said.

Will dug his heels in and anchored the wot to a stop.

Blue stared blankly ahead, shifting his weight restlessly.

"Blue," Will said, and Blue shot him a fleeting glance. "Are you all right?"

"No. We're not all right. We're dead."

Will freed his hand from Blue's grip and reached for the one holding the gem. Blue took a sharp breath and yanked it away. Will gave him a stern look intended to point out how absurd he was being.

He reached for it again and this time Blue let him uncurl his stiff fingers from the gleaming gem. The sight of the bruised and bleeding palm made Will wince, and he sucked a breath through his teeth.

"Blue," he said, aching with misery. "What are we going to do?"

Blue hesitated. "I just want my family back. I'd give up my gem forever to get them back."

Will stared at a smeared fingerprint of blood on the edge of the gem. "They're following us, aren't they?" he asked. The Maker and the witches were no doubt hot on their heels by now.

"They will be. They all want my gem. All of them."

"The Maker's got a reaper following him about and he's really happy. He thinks he's going to die. That's why he wants to help now. Maybe you should just let him help."

Blue disagreed, even before Will had finished speaking. "No. We don't trust him."

"Karson trusted him," Will said, and noticed the comment rattle Blue. "You said Karson was always right," he pressed. "You said he was your leader and you had to listen to him and do what he said. Right?"

Trembling, Blue closed his fingers around the gem and blinked, finally able to look Will's way. "He did trust the Maker, didn't he?" he said, and Will nodded earnestly. "It was just me who didn't trust him. Not all of us. And I'm speaking for them. I don't have the right, do I?"

Will stayed quiet.

"Do you think…?" Blue held out the gem, arm shaking uncontrollably. "Do you think I should give it to him?"

"No. No, don't give it to him, just let him help you split it back up again like he was supposed to do. The only reason he didn't was because Dante chucked me out of the window."

"Yes. Because they all… they all…" He couldn't say it out loud. "You're right though. You're right."

Will peered into the darkness of the tunnel behind. "What do we do? Do we wait for them?"

"No." Blue snapped his gem back up again and staggered on along the dim corridor, shaking his head and muttering angrily under his breath.

Will followed, unnerved by Blue's unpredictable new mood swings. "What? What's wrong?"

"No! No waiting."

"Why not?"

"Because. Because! Don't you see? Can't you see what's going on? They're trying to trick us."

"Who?"

Blue stopped, turning so quickly his coat fluttered. "What do you think is going to happen when the energies are split eight ways?"

Will stared back at him, unblinking, not knowing how to answer.

"They'll get new ones." Blue faced the wall beside him and rested his head against the bricks.

"New whats?"

"Exactly," Blue said, heartbroken.

And then Will understood. The gems would choose new wots, and the only family Blue had ever known would be replaced by strangers.

Blue sniffed and stood back from the wall, struggling to stand steadily without the support. "I'm not the one who's supposed to decide important things like this."

"Don't worry, dear boy." That sickly sweet voice of Tamzin's echoed down the hall. "You don't have to make any decisions whatsoever." She tip-tapped closer, pointing her snapped wand. With the barest amount of effort, she flicked her wrist and Blue spiralled into the opposite wall.

He laughed mirthlessly, rubbing his free hand down his nose, seemingly to check it hadn't been flattened. "Are you forgetting something, Tamzin? I have the gem."

"That's one thing I most certainly have not forgotten." Her tone could have frozen water.

"I told you." Blue's expression changed. Instead of anger, there was hurt. He looked at Tamzin like the long-lost friend she was, rather than the enemy she had become. "When you were a child, I confided in you. I told you all about my nightmares of the Maker's descendant. I told you he would eventually find us and kill us all. And you told me it was just a dream. It could never happen. You said there was nothing and nobody in the world evil enough to do such a thing."

Tamzin laughed cruelly at Blue's memory. "I was a foolish child. And you still are."

Disappointment fell over his face. "I never, ever would have believed it would be you."

"I don't think I would have either," she agreed. "It's funny how this *disgusting* world can change a person. But that's enough chitchat. I am going to ask you nicely just one more time." She took a long, satisfied breath, and held out one hand, the other still aiming her wand fervently in Blue's direction. "Hand over the gem. Now."

"Or?"

"Or die. You choose."

"No."

"I know you're endowed with your borrowed power," Tamzin said, "but you would be a fool to underestimate me."

"Like you say," Blue said, his head still appearing to find his neck an unstable sitting point. "I am a foolish child."

Deep, growling breaths rumbled from the lighter end of the tunnel, causing Tamzin to turn. Blue barely acknowledged the newcomer, or the fact that Tamzin was no longer facing him, just continued to stare at her, awaiting her comeback to his last comment.

"You called, Master?"

"You're slow," Will said, only wondering after it was already too late to stop the words if this was a rude thing to say. "I called for you ages ago."

Nobody closed in on them, shoulders hunched to keep his little head low. "I was nowhere near when you called for me." The warder dropped, grudgingly, to his knees. "What do you request of me?" he asked, bowing his chunky neck forward.

Tamzin broke into a shrill burst of hysterical laughter. "What on earth did you think this brute's presence would accomplish?"

"I don't know," Will mumbled, suddenly embarrassed.

Riled by Tamzin's mockery, Nobody drew himself to his full height and swore when his head clonked the ceiling, which only made Tamzin laugh harder. "I can do you a great deal of damage, witch," he said, seething with contempt. When she didn't stop laughing, he slapped his hands together in a mighty clap that frightened Will out of his skin, and a surge of flames roared to life in an arched fountain of fire as he drew them apart.

Tamzin's laughter ended in a regretful moan. Nobody flicked a finger through the flames, sending a shimmering ribbon of fire to the witch's snapped wand. Fire engulfed the crooked piece of wood instantaneously, catching Tamzin's fingers, and she shouted out in pain, lashing tapering red-gold spirals and zigzags of rippling light and smoke through the corridor's shade. Quickly realising her mad flapping was useless, she tossed it to the concrete and stamped the fire out.

The warder imitated Tamzin's earlier laughter while she picked it back up. "That's the thing about witches." He pressed his hands together to extinguish the flames he had conjured, bringing the tunnel back to darkness. "You're nothing without your little sticks."

"That's where you're so wrong." She pointed her blackened wand at him. "But I do like what my little stick can do. Want to see?"

A gushing torrent of wind swept the warder off his feet. He cracked his head on the ceiling for a second time and bumped from wall to wall all the way down the tunnel like he was nothing more than a ping pong ball.

Will checked Blue's face for a sign it was time to panic. The wot appeared strangely calm, which didn't comfort Will in the slightest. It only made him worry that Blue had finally lost his mind and had no idea of what was going on around him at all. If Blue had looked in the least bit concerned about their predicament, at least Will would have had someone to be afraid with.

Tamzin laughed at the warder being carried away and waved him bye-bye. While she was distracted, Will took the opportunity to nudge Blue.

An odd little smile grew on the wot's face. It took a while for Will to spot what had caused it, but when he did, he could have smiled too. Dante was storming up the corridor, wand poised at the ready.

Tamzin's laugh stuck in her throat. "Dante Simms," she shouted, as if blaming her for something. There was a momentary stillness while the two witches eyed each other. The silence was broken by Tamzin's disgruntled sigh. She put a finger firmly down on Dante's wand, dipping its aim to her feet. "Foolish, foolish girl. Your brewer is useless against me, remember? You made sure of that yourself."

Dante scowled. "You tricked me."

"Yes," Tamzin agreed proudly, "I did. Even the boy has more power against me than you do now." She nodded at Will. "He killed me once already, and I don't mind admitting I still have no idea how he did it."

Will hid behind Dante and peered around her at Tamzin. "I didn't kill you," he said, but the comment went ignored.

"You should probably be cowering behind him," Tamzin said. "Not the other way around."

"You're probably right," Dante said, worry creeping into her tone.

Tamzin lifted her wand.

Dante, too quick for anyone to protest, lifted Will and held him in front of her to take the force of the blow. Hanging from her arms, wondering how she could be such a coward, he prepared to scream his lungs out as soon as the imminent pain hit him.

No pain came. As before, the sewitt that covered him bore the brunt of Tamzin's attack and blasted the fiery force straight back at her. Her pigtails caught alight, and her scream rang out like a siren. The repulsive stench of burning hair filled the corridor.

Dante put Will down, grunting under his weight. "Come on," she shouted over Tamzin's noise. She touched Blue's arm. "Let's get out of here."

"Okay."

The next step Will took was not on the hard concrete of the corridor but sinking into a colourful woodchip pathway out in the open air. He glanced around, startled. He had felt nothing; no change of temperature, no nausea, no blurred vision, no dizziness, and he was certain that Dante hadn't had time to make any portals.

"Wow, Blue, how did you do that?" Dante asked.

"I've got the gems," he said sadly.

"Oh, Blue." She pulled him into her arms and rested her head against his lapel. "I'm so glad you're okay. I've been so worried."

Maybe she had been worried, but not so worried that she hadn't taken the time to plait her hair, change her clothes and paint her nails yet again in their absence, Will noted. He had never known anyone change their nail colour so often. This time they were black to match her combat shirt.

"Blue?" Will said. "If you could do that, why didn't you get us out of there ages ago?"

"It didn't cross my mind until Dante suggested it," he admitted, flashing his endearing lopsided smile. His eyes still gave away his exhaustion and grief, but his neck had regained its composure for now, keeping his head from wobbling so much.

Cesar appeared beside them, bedraggled and bloodstained. "Something terrible has happened," he said, close to tears.

"What?" Dante and Will asked in unison.

"My Agulga sphere has been destroyed. This could only be the work of malevolent evil. My kites are no longer protected. Two were killed in their efforts to get me to safety. Two. Two."

Guilt stabbed at Will like a knife. He gaped at the ware, speechless.

Dante gave him a consoling pat on the back. "There-there."

"Two," he said again, with a loud sniff.

Blue glared at Will. "What did you do that for?"

Will backed away, shocked. How did Blue know? "What? What do you…? What?"

"What," he said again, slower, "did you do that for?"

"I didn't. I didn't, honest. It was an accident. We were looking for you," he gabbled to Blue, "and there was a note from her." He pointed at Dante. "Then Christian was messing about in that glass cupboard, even though I told him to leave it alone. Then *his* kite attacked me and pushed me into the cupboard, and the ball fell out and I tried to catch it, but I couldn't, and it smashed. Then everything really hurt, and I got knocked out, and when I woke up, the Maker wasn't in me anymore, and he said it was because the gulgy sphere did something and I'm so sorry, I'm so, so sorry." He panted, terrified that they'd hate him.

"That's…" Blue said blankly. Then he frowned, confused. "I was just asking why you kicked me." He looked over his shoulder. A young chimpanzee was sitting right behind him with a bicycle bell in its left hand. It peered up at the wot, dinged the bell, then leaned backwards and kicked him sharply on the back of the leg. Blue stepped away from it.

Cesar stared at Will with that same aggravated, accusing expression he'd worn when they'd first met. "It was you? *You* broke my sphere?"

"It was an accident. I never touched it. Your kite attacked me."

"He would have been trying to protect it. He must have thought you were going to take it. You shouldn't be nosing through other people's property, Will, it's just not right."

"I wasn't. It was an accident." He caught sight of a flicker of black above.

"It's okay, Will," Dante said. "I'm sure Cesar doesn't blame you."

Will watched the sky, waiting. Sure enough, his black-cloaked follower flew overhead yet again and disappeared.

The reaper.

"Of course I blame him," Cesar said angrily. "Why wouldn't I blame him? It was his fault. What? What's the matter with you?" He looked up. "What are you looking at?"

Dread stole Will's ability to speak straight away. "The blood reaper," he said after a couple of false starts. "It's still following. It's not here for the Maker like he thought. It's after me."

Chapter Twenty-Three: Unravelling

After a brief scan of the sky to see if they could catch sight of Will's mysterious follower, Cesar and Dante returned their attention to Blue, whose head had begun to wobble again.

"Are you okay?" Dante asked.

It was hard to tell if he'd shaken his head or nodded in response to the question.

"I just can't understand why everyone died except for me," he said. "Karson warned me not to let the Maker join the gems with mine. I should have listened to him. Why didn't I listen?"

"No. Blue, no. I don't want you thinking you've wronged Karson. He knew exactly what would happen when we joined those powers, but he thought he would be the one left standing. That's why he allowed you to do it in the first place. Do you really think he would have let you hand over your gem to his precious Maker if he'd thought for one second he would drop dead?"

Cesar nodded his agreement. "That's right. Back in No-go Ebb, Karson warned us that if the witch joined the gems together, your life forces would be severed, and you would all die."

"Exactly," Dante said. "You. That's what he said. *You*. Not *we*. And he wouldn't have been beating himself up about it either, Blue, so why should you cut your heart out for him?"

"Because they're my family, Dante. And they're all dead because of me."

"It's not your fault."

His expression darkened again, grief and confusion superseding his ability to control his emotional responses. "If you knew it would kill us, why did you let me do it?"

"I didn't know it would kill anyone."

"You said Karson told you it would."

"He did, but he said lots of things in No-go Ebb, Blue, and most of it was nonsense. I didn't believe him." She moved to touch him, but he stepped away. "Do you honestly think I'd have asked you to do it if I'd known? If I'd thought for a moment…" She broke off, stopping to dig her black nails into the back of her head. "I hate my sister. I hate her. This is all her fault. It's not your fault, or Karson's, or anybody else's. It's all down to her."

All outward trace of Blue's resentment faded away. "I can feel the powers growing the longer they're together," he said. "Karson would have been able to deal with it. But not me."

"You have to part them."

"It's not just me getting stronger," Blue continued, panic rising. "The neethers too. I can feel them. They're searching for Will as we speak." His pupils contracted and dilated madly. "They want you dead, Will. They want you dead, and the stronger they get the easier they'll find you."

Will took another worried look at the sky. Was that why the blood reaper was following him? To ensure the neethers killed him? "Please, Blue," he begged. "Just part them. You have to."

"I have to get the gems back from Molina first."

Christian's laughter reached their ears before they saw him approach, at speed. "Hey, how about that? Right on cue." His two bods were enjoying acrobatics on his shoulders. They slung themselves into a sitting position as soon as the wicker came to a stop beside Will. "Couldn't have timed that better if I'd got a seer involved."

Cesar sprang into the air, swiped Badmé from Christian's shoulder, and tackled the unprepared wicker to the ground, who let out a startled yelp as the ware's small hands tightened around his neck.

Dante clamped her arms around Cesar's waist and dragged him off Christian. "What are you doing, you idiot, are you crazy?"

"He killed my kites," Cesar shouted. "It's his fault they're dead."

"It was an accident," Will said again, saddened and guilt-ridden at the thought of the birds being hurt.

"What are you talking about?" Christian lifted Badmé back onto his shoulder. "I didn't kill any kites. I would never harm a bird. I love birds." He rubbed his neck. "Crazy ware."

Badmé and Gudmé also rubbed their necks, subdued from the unprovoked attack.

"It was the gulgy sphere," Will explained as Christian stood back up. "When we broke it."

"Ah. Right." Christian shuffled his feet. "Forget that for now," he said, the fleeting moment of shame apparently over. "I have what you want." He shook out the contents of his jacket pockets. Seven gems scattered across the bark chippings underfoot.

Blue gathered them together. "How did you get these?"

"Quite easily actually. I took them from Molina's hideout in Arrrrtenflaffannaaargh. She wasn't so possessive of them once their power had gone, for some reason." He turned to Will. "Where's Rin? Thanks for ditching us, by the way."

The admiration Will had initially felt for Christian flared back up again. "That was the Maker. How did you find us?"

"That was the hard part. I followed *him*." He pointed up.

Will expected to see the blood reaper, but the only thing moving above them now was a small kite, perched unsteadily on a spindly branch at the top of a tall, thin tree.

Cesar's face lit up. "Dreyfus! Thank heaven he's alive. That young one will wander off. He scares the life out of me." He offered an arm to the bird. "Come, Dreyfus. Come on."

The kite hopped from its branch as though it would fly down to Cesar, but instead it turned tail and flew clumsily on its way.

"Just as the saying goes," Cesar said. "You can lead a kite to water, but you can't make him drink."

That didn't sound right to Will. "Maybe he didn't know you had a drink for him."

Blue had lined the gems in a neat row while the others had been watching Dreyfus. He placed his left hand on the white gem, which was first in the row, and his right hand on the black at the other end. "I don't know if I can do this," he said quietly. "I don't know what I'm doing."

"Wow," Christian said. "He's as much of a whinge-bag as you are, Will. No wonder you two get on so well."

The bods leaned over the wicker's shoulders to watch what Blue was doing.

"It'll be all right," Dante reassured him gently. "The powers' natural state is to be four separate entities. They'll help you. You'll see."

Blue closed his eyes. The ripped sleeve of his coat had fallen open, revealing his bare arm, and after a short, charged silence, veins bulged under his skin, swollen and dark. Will tried not to look, thinking Blue would be embarrassed if he knew. But Blue hadn't noticed his veins, or the fact that his face appeared greyer and deader than it had when Will had dragged his corpse from the river. He was too deep in concentration to even react when Dante shook his shoulders and begged him to stop.

"Why are you telling him to stop?" Christian gibed. "You're the one who told him to do it in the first place."

She lifted a hand as if considering slapping Blue out of his trance but resisted the urge.

Nothing happened for a minute or two, other than Dante getting more and more worked up, but eventually Blue's gem, the second in the row, glowed like a neon light. The white gem lit up next, not as bright and for only a moment, the way the weapons had done when 'Lillian' had cast her spell on the blades. The yellow gem flashed, then the red. Blue's gem dulled. The droplets of blood that remained on its surface glistened.

Blue's face, though still too pale, regained its life in a matter of seconds. His veins relaxed to their normal state, hidden away under his skin. "I did it," he croaked, slumping. "They're four."

"Well done." Dante hugged him while he was too tired to protest. "I knew you could do it. It's all going to be fine now. You'll see."

"No." Blue shook his head, which was no longer a wobbling wreck on his neck. "It won't be. I can hear the neethers. They're so angry. They know what I just did. They're coming. They don't care about Will anymore. It's me they're coming for. They want to bury my gem far, far away, somewhere it will never be found. And me." His eyes were glassy and haunted. "They're going to bury me, Dante. Bury me where I can't get out and I'll never be found."

"We won't let them do that," she said in a voice that, while firm, was not as confident as it might have been. Will wasn't the only one who noticed. Christian and the bods exchanged doubtful glances. Cesar vanished for two seconds then forced himself to be visible again and apologised.

"We won't," she said, more determined this time. "We won't let them take you or your gem anywhere. In fact, the sooner you split the powers back into eight the better, because you'll weaken them all the more. Then they won't be able to take you and bury you anywhere, never mind somewhere you'll never be found."

Blue nodded, eyebrows wonky and low, like a child lost and frightened in the dark.

"Out of the way, kiddies," Scilla shouted. She trotted their way from the same direction Christian had come, wheezing and holding her side.

Gart loped effortlessly behind her. "There's a crazy wye after us," he yelled in disbelief. "The Itchen Hush barrier's been broken. Wye came right through. Don't ask me how. The world's gone mad!" He overtook his aunt, then slowed to let her catch up. "Come on, seriously, it's like a scene from a dinosaur movie back there."

"Don't hurt it," Scilla warned Dante as she passed. "Harrier would never let us hear the end of it. Just get out of its way. Come on, move yourselves. No time for messing around."

"We're not messing around," Dante called after them, indignant.

"First time for everything," Scilla shouted back.

Dante huffed a few times as she watched them go.

The stomping rumble of heavy feet came into hearing distance.

Christian stood taller and stretched his neck to improve his view of the giant's imminent arrival.

"Must be poor Esko," Will said.

"How on earth did he break through the Itchen Hush barrier?" Dante asked. "That spell's been unbroken for centuries."

Remembering the Maker's words regarding another *old spell cast by a long-dead witch*, Will said, "He must have had a little more about him."

"We'd better get out of here," Cesar said. "Dante, we need to get Blue to my tree. He can separate the powers undisturbed there."

The witch didn't have time to take out her wand before Esko bulldozed through the trees, snapping several branches in his haste. Will covered his nose, but the scent of bad fruit wasn't nearly as strong as it once had been in the wye's vicinity.

"Are you after Molina?" Dante asked him.

Esko was unrecognisable from the laid-back creature he'd been when Will had first encountered him. Anger and grief had turned him into a monster. He didn't stop moving but slowed to converse with Dante as he passed by, visibly forcing himself to calm down enough to speak. "Yes," he said, lips twitching. "And the other one. They are in league with one another, I know that now, and they shall both suffer for what they did to my Alley. The murderous beasts deserve everything that's coming to them."

"What other one?" Dante asked. "Why are you chasing my brother and my auntie?"

"The old one says she will never betray her niece. But she knows what the witch has done, and she knows where she is. She knows and she will tell me."

"What other witch are you talking about?" Dante shouted, desperate for answers. "Who is Molina in league with?"

"The blonde one." Esko sneered. "Rickrack."

Dante's jaw dropped. "You think my sister is in league with Tamzin Rickrack? That's impossible."

Esko stopped edging away. "Rickrack could only change her features to look like the Scrossly girl because she was the child's grandmother." He pointed his sausage of a finger at Dante. "You witches can only change your appearance to that of a member of your own flesh and blood family. I shouldn't need to tell you this. If Rickrack is not working with your sister, how could it be that this wot saw Foosay Hoo take his gem and drown him? Tell me that."

"What are you talking about?" Dante asked, flustered. "Tamzin Rickrack isn't related to Foosay Hoo."

"You know nothing." Esko stood back to his full height. "I will find those witches, and I will make them pay." He shoved the nearest tree, inadvertently shaking its wet leaves and causing a mini rainstorm to spatter dramatically down on them all. "They shall rue the day they thought they could treat a wye like nothing in this day and age," he yelled as he stomped away.

Christian slapped Blue on the back, open mouth stretched in a delighted smile. "I love being around you lot. No one ever tells me anything like that." His bods reached behind his neck to slap each other on the back. "That little girl really is an old woman with pigtails, and she's related to the crazy old witch with the poodle-head. That's brilliant. Tell me that's not brilliant."

"It's *not* brilliant," Will said sullenly.

Dante stared at Cesar in wonderment. "I can't believe I forgot. The wye's right: The spell to change your appearance into that of another person can only be applied to blood relatives. How could I have forgotten that? I knew it, and yet it didn't register at all. It's like the knowledge was stolen from my mind." Her wonder quickly declined into frustration. "But Tamzin and Foosay can't be related."

"Actually," Cesar said, "Tamzin Rickrack's father was Emmett Hoo. She is Foosay's half-sister. She took her mother's name. I couldn't recall this before, just the same as you, Dante. I knew it, but I couldn't access the information until now."

Dante lowered her voice. "Someone made a spell to tamper with our memories."

Christian elbowed Will. "Just like how Foosay only remembered the truth after you killed Tamzin."

"I didn't kill her," Will grumbled.

"Wait a minute," Dante said, looking like a cartoon lightbulb should have been floating above her head. "After Will disappeared from my house, Foosay came to tell us we'd find Blue at Cesar's treehouse. But that wasn't Foosay, was it? That must have been Tamzin."

"Mrs Hoo was there when we read your note," Will said. "We didn't know how Molina could have pretended to be someone else in front of herself."

Cesar, who was glancing worriedly about him like he felt exposed to danger, said, "Molina's been plotting all this for at least eleven years, since she kidnapped Gartaspia. But Tamzin has been living a most quiet and normal life as Lillian Scrossly throughout that time."

"Bit of a coincidence though," Dante said darkly. "What if they've been plotting together the entire time?"

"Before Lillian died," Cesar said, "Tamzin made a wish for the power to keep from crossing to the land of the dead, which would give her the ability to resurrect herself in the event of her death. She devised a complicated spell to reverse her own age, in the hope of living a long, youthful life until she was ready to pass on. But Lillian's murder drove her mad with guilt, for not making the same wish for the child she loved. She went to the wots to beg them to let her remake her wish. But of course, it was too late. Wots can't bring people back from the dead."

"If they can't bring them back to life, how can they stop them from dying?" Will asked. "Isn't it the same thing?"

"No. Once someone has passed over to the land of the dead they can never come back. It's a one-way door. Tamzin's wish was for the ability to keep her soul locked in her body while she recovered herself. If she had asked for this to happen indefinitely, it would have been beyond the wots' power, but she was smart and asked for it to happen only a certain number of times. All the memories changed after that. After that, it was Tamzin who was murdered, not Lillian, while Lillian lived on peacefully with her grandfather."

Dante flinched. "So creepy. Tamzin must have changed everyone's memories to keep Lillian alive in some twisted way."

"It doesn't seem so high on her list of priorities now. She seems to be more interested in keeping herself alive. And forever this time."

"But why would she suddenly change her entire outlook and betray her granddaughter's memory like this? It doesn't make sense."

"Maybe it was because of her vision," Will said. "When I met Jonas in the-"

"Jonah," Blue corrected.

Will bit back a grumpy retort. "Yeah. Him. When I met him, he told me he was worried about Lillian because she'd gone off with something on her mind and hadn't gone home. Maybe it was the vision that was on her mind."

"Makes sense," Dante agreed. "If the vision showed her she was the Maker's descendant, it must have changed everything for her. But it still doesn't explain how she got mixed up with Molina. How could she possibly have known what Molina was up to?"

"Molina must have been in the vision too," Cesar said. "Her actions may well have triggered it in the first place. Tamzin probably tracked her down and made a deal to steal the gems together."

Dante ruffled her hair with both hands, groaning. "I sort of wish I hadn't squashed Eve now. She could probably have answered a lot of these questions for us."

The reaper flashed by overhead and Will tried desperately to ignore it. If he ignored it for long enough, maybe it would get bored and go away. He wished Dante hadn't mentioned Eve. The crunch of her tiny bones replayed cruelly in his head. He forced himself to pay attention to Cesar, who was talking again.

"We wares are supposed to have finely tuned senses when it comes to things like this. How could I not have noticed my memories were wrong?"

"Never mind you," Dante said. "What about Art? How could a seer have missed something like this?"

"Art didn't like Lillian at all," Will said. "Maybe he knew she was bad all along."

"I wasn't particularly fond of her myself," Dante reminded him snootily. "The only reason Art hated Lillian so much – Tamzin – so much was because he was put out that she's only a witch and she had a vision. Seers can't stand anyone else seeing anything." Dante rubbed her forehead. "Is it just me who's getting a headache from all this now?"

Will shrugged.

"But Molina and Tamzin were so hostile to one another," she said into her hands. "Why would they act that way if they were working together?"

It seemed like Dante was hanging on to any last straw she could find to believe her sister wouldn't ally herself with Tamzin. Will didn't see what difference it made. A baddie working with Tamzin or without Tamzin was still a baddie either way.

"It was all an act so we wouldn't know," Christian said, bursting with joy, which Will felt was inappropriate.

"Why would they care if we knew?" Dante asked.

"Because it diminishes the element of surprise. How they kept this secret all these years is incredible. I can't keep secrets for ten minutes."

"Pah," Cesar said. "That's because you're the biggest gossiping nosy parker this world's ever been subjected to."

Christian shook his head firmly at Badmé, as if reacting to something the bod had said. "Maybe so." He faced Cesar with a smug chin lift. "But at least I'm not a namby-pamby, arty-farty, little fancy-pants ware."

Dante interrupted before Cesar could retaliate. "In the basement in No-go Ebb, Molina told Tamzin not to get in her way anymore. Maybe they fell out."

"No," Christian said, like the thought upset him. "It was all an act."

"I think I know my own sister."

"Oh!" Christian said in a high tone. "I'm *sorry*. I was mistaking you for someone who *didn't* know their sister had been torturing their own brother in Artenflaffanargh for eleven years."

It was the last thing Will heard from them before realising he was alone. At first, he thought Blue, Cesar, Dante, and Christian had all disappeared, but on second glance noticed the trees around him had changed. He was the one who had disappeared.

"Hello?"

The Maker stepped into view, startling him.

"It's you. You scared me."

The Maker didn't react. His face was set solemn and cold. "I'm a fool," he said.

Will fidgeted and checked over his shoulder. "No, you're not," he said. "Did you bring me here? I was with Blue and Dante. Do you know where they've gone?"

Again, the Maker did not change his expression.

"What's wrong?"

The Maker stroked his fuzzy head. "It's over."

Prompted to say something by the long pause that followed, Will asked, "What is?"

"Any hope of any chance I ever had of being with my family again." The boy's voice cracked. "It's gone."

"Why?"

"Because there's no reaper, Will, you know that. You know that."

"It doesn't matter. It'll be okay."

"No, it won't. Not if there's no reaper."

"You'll just have to die later. Everyone does."

"Not me."

Will fell silent. The Maker's defeated posture was beginning to frighten him.

"I'll just go back to floating around in the cold, able to see and hear but never sleep. Never feel, or taste, or communicate, or do anything other than exist. Forever and ever, just existing, as nothing. A sentient ghost." He wrapped his arms around himself. "I can't do that again. Not now I recall the feeling of my heart's beat. Not now I have known warmth, and touched the ground, and breathed the air, I just can't. I need you to understand that. Do you, Will? Do you understand?"

Will understood.

"I am truly sorry," the Maker said.

"What for?"

"You do understand. I know you do. If I have to live forever – if I *have* to – then I have to stay in my body. I have to." He squeezed himself tighter, like he was afraid of slipping out of it there and then.

"I don't get what you're saying." Will's chest tightened. He did get what the Maker was saying.

"I am sorry. But I have no choice. I have no choice."

Panicking that the Maker was about to attack him, Will clamped his eyes shut in vain attempt to concentrate through the fear. All he had to do was want it…

I want to go back to Blue. I want to go back to Blue. I want to go back to Blue. He checked his progress. The Maker was still with him, still staring. He tried again, repeating the words in his head so fast that even his inner voice got muddled. *I want to go back to Blue, back to Blue, black to Blue, black to Boo, back to Blue! Please. Please!*

"Will?" Blue smacked his back to make him look. "What just happened?"

Will sank with relief at the sight of his friends. "The Maker wanted me."

"What for?" Dante asked. "Was he worried about you?"

"No," Will said, thinking how nice that would have been. "He just wanted to tell me he's not on our side anymore."

"What? Why not?"

"Because he wants to live forever, same as your sister and Lillian. I mean Tamzin."

Christian, who had been easing gradually closer into the huddle so he could hear the conversation better, withdrew quickly. "But I thought he wanted to die."

"Yeah, he did when he thought the reaper was there to take him back to his mum and dad, but now he knows it's not. Now he just wants to stay alive so he doesn't go back to how he was before."

"He could always jump back into you again."

"No!" Will said, appalled at the suggestion.

"No, that's not the answer," Dante agreed. "Of course he wants to keep his own body now. Poor thing. It must be tough for him."

Will could scarcely believe what he was hearing. "Poor Maker?"

"Yes. I feel so sorry for him."

"He wants to kill Blue."

"I know, Will, but…"

"He wants to kill Blue," Will said again.

"Put yourself in his place. What would you do? None of this was his fault, you know."

Blue had reverted to the shaking, hunched wreck that Will had hoped they'd lost when the powers had been separated. "We can't win this. We can't fight our maker. He's our destroyer. I knew it would come to this. I knew it. I knew we couldn't trust him."

"No, we can win this," Dante told him firmly. "You have to think positive."

"How can you say that? There are only four of us. Four of us against the Maker, the descendant, and your sister."

"Who are just three."

Christian counted the group, including himself and his bods, on his fingers several times and said, "Hey."

"You have your gems now," Dante said. "That puts you well above the league of Tamzin Rickrack. We already know Will's got enough wishing will lurking in that little body of his to overpower the Maker when push comes to shove, and I've always had more magic in my little finger than Molina's ever dreamed of. And then there's Cesar." She glanced doubtfully at the ware. "Who gees-up the numbers," she said with a shrug. "And let's not forget the warders are on our side if needs be. And this wicker might help us out. So, when you think about it…"

"The neethers are stronger than I am," Blue interrupted. "There are too many. It's hopeless. Foyer agrees with me."

Dante took an angry step back and glared around the wot as if hunting for someone to blame for his remark. "What are you talking about? No, he doesn't."

"He does. He says it's pointless to go on."

"Foyer would never say that to you."

"He keeps telling me I might as well just leave my gem for the neethers and be done with it."

Dante scoped as far as she could see between the haggard trees surrounding them. "No wonder he's acting so strange," she murmured to Will and Cesar without moving her lips, her back to Blue. "Someone's messing with his head."

"Nobody's messing with my head," Blue retorted.

Will watched Blue's eyes turn darker and lighter as the pupils continued to enlarge and shrink over and over.

"Blue, I don't think Foyer's really Foyer," Dante said worriedly. "It's a neether or something. You don't listen to them."

"He said you wouldn't believe it was him. That's why I didn't tell you he's been with us."

Will didn't mean to, but he found himself holding Dante's hand.

Cesar turned invisible for a second or two. "There's nobody here," he said when he came back. "Certainly nobody who's dead. I think he's just imagining things."

Blue glared at the ware. "I'm not crazy."

"That's debatable."

"He's standing right beside you. He came back to help me because he knows how much I need him. It's because Dante told him he was all I had. She made him feel guilty when he died, so he came to look after me."

"No," Dante insisted. "Cesar's right this time."

"He's been with us since we left No-go Ebb."

A soft pressure touched Will's calf, and he dropped Dante's hand to dart away from it. "Something just touched me! On the leg, I felt it."

"That was Foyer," Blue said. "He's trying to show you he's here."

Christian was quick to point out, "You said he was standing next to the ware."

"He was. He moved."

"Death gives you super-speed, does it?"

Dante shook her wand from her sleeve. "We need Foosay Hoo. She can mix up her mineral colour potion thing for us and try to make contact with Foyer and the others. Then you'll see."

"You mean you'll see," Blue shot back, but he seemed heartened by the idea.

"What is the colour thing?" Will asked. "Why does Mrs Hoo have to do it? Can't you do it yourself?"

"I'm afraid not," Dante said. "It's a rare gift attributed to very few witches. Foosay is the only one I know of."

"What is it though? Mrs Hoo was going on about it before. She said she was talking to her auntie. But her auntie's dead."

"You'll see, Will." Dante lifted her wand.

"Forget the portal," Blue said.

A brief whir of light passed Will's sight, then Foosay's cottage was right in front of him. Another large lump of cheese had been left on the breadboard at the front of the house, which was back in the clearing where he and Blue had first come across it with Esko.

Foosay opened the door just as Dante aimed her fist in a knocking position. "What are you doing here?" The old witch stretched her neck out to see past Dante. "Come in. Quickly, now." She grasped Blue's coat in one hand and Will's jacket in the other and lugged the pair of them into her hallway, allowing Cesar, Dante, and Christian to follow in behind before the door slammed shut of its own accord.

"What's the whispering about?" Dante asked, mocking Foosay.

"There was someone out there." Foosay rushed to her window and tweaked back the curtain to see outside, in her hen-like way, reminding Will of the first time she had dragged him into her house. Then, he had been worried she would eat him. How silly that seemed now he knew better.

He joined Foosay by the window and tried to see what she was looking at, but she pushed him back with an arm, gasping dramatically.

"Keep away from the windows." She tugged the curtain shut. "I said there's someone out there."

"Who?" Cesar asked.

"I'm not sure. I think there was more than one. I looked out and there was nothing. A second later, poof, there was something."

Dante hummed. "And then we came to the door?"

Foosay nodded.

"Did you stop to think it was us you saw?" Dante mimicked Foosay's hushed voice, and Foosay did not look amused.

She buttoned her lime green cardigan and looked carefully at each of her visitors in turn. "What are you all doing here?"

Dante answered for everyone. "We need you to mix your colour potions and get in contact with Foyer and Karson for us, if you would."

Foosay's thin lips parted. "Foyer and Karson are dead? Oh, Blue, my love. I'm so sorry."

"So, you'll contact them for us?" Dante pressed.

"I would if I could, but I'm afraid I can only contact spirits that are in the land of the dead."

"That is where they'll be," Christian said. "Seeing as they're dead and all."

"No. Wots cannot pass over to the land of the dead like other living beings do. They're not supposed to die, you see. They are bound to their powers that still exist here in the living plane."

"That's not what you said before," Will argued. "You said I brought Blue back from the land of the dead."

"No, I said you'd brought him back to the land of the living. And that you did, my dear."

"Back from where, then?"

"My dear, I really don't know. All I know is that as long as the four powers remain here, the wots cannot pass over."

"They're all around," Blue said. "It's not just Foyer now. They're all here."

In response to Foosay's startled expression, Dante said, "Don't listen to him. He's not thinking straight."

"Foosay's lying. She's in league with them. She doesn't want to help us."

Foosay leaned closer to Dante and quietly asked, "Who am I supposed to be in league with, dear?"

"She knows full well." Blue approached Foosay with dangerous focus. "We're on to you, Foosay Hoo. We know."

"That's nice, dear," Foosay said. "But keep your distance." She didn't need to touch him to shove him back.

Blue seethed at being treated in such a way. "See?" he said to Dante. "She's got something to hide."

"What's going on in that head of yours?" Dante patted Blue's arm gently, like he was a distressed pet in need of comfort. "Hush now. Trust me." She turned her head abruptly to confront Foosay. "Tell me the truth, Foosay Hoo. You're aware of your connection to Tamzin Rickrack, yes?"

Foosay settled herself on a chair and neatened her crumpled skirt. "You refer to the fact we share a father? Yes. I'm aware. The question is, how could you possibly know about that?"

Dante indicated to Cesar with her eyes.

"Of course." Foosay bared her teeth. "I remember all of a sudden why wares are so horribly unattractive to my eye."

"Because they're short?" Will guessed, and Cesar scowled at him.

"Answer us this, Foosay," Dante went on, serious. "Did you help your sister to get her hands on the gems?"

Foosay got up from her chair and stormed across the room to stare into her empty cauldron. "Get out of my house. I want no more to do with any of you." She waved her arms, ushering everyone to the exit. "Go on. Out. All of you, out."

Dante stood her ground and held up her hands to apologise. "We didn't come here to accuse you. We need your help."

"And because I'm unable to do what you ask, you decide to turn me into the enemy," Foosay said, still trying to shoo away her unwanted guests.

"Not at all. I was only asking for Blue's sake."

Hoping to calm the situation, Will crept between Foosay and Dante and gave Foosay his best innocent face. He had wrapped many teachers around his little finger using that face. "I know you're not the baddie, Mrs Hoo." He smiled at her.

She gave up flailing her arms. "I am so sorry about what's happened. But, Blue, you cannot truly believe I would ever do anything to hurt you. Come on, you're a wot. Can you not sense what it is I wish for?"

Blue shot her a wary couple of glances, his overwhelming confusion evident in his conflicted expression. "Foyer wouldn't lie to me."

"No, he wouldn't," Dante agreed.

"Listen to me, dear." Foosay shifted closer to Blue, speaking softly to soothe him. "Young Will here has already proven wots can be brought back to the land of the living. Wots belong here. Because they're never meant to die, they don't go on to the land of the dead. And because they don't go on to the land of the dead, they don't cross over the void that it's impossible to retreat onto. Think about it, all of you. Just maybe we can get them all back."

Will checked everyone else's reactions to see if he could get excited yet. No one reacted much at all.

Blue wobbled. "Foyer says they're gone and can never come back," he said in a strained voice. He looked hopefully at Foosay. "I want you to be telling the truth."

"Foyer would never do or say anything to hurt you," Dante said. "If this person is upsetting you, you have to know it isn't him."

Blue closed his eyes and whispered, "But he's standing right there."

"Tell him to go away. Tell him, if he's really your friend, he'll leave you alone."

"He says I can't be left alone. He doesn't trust me to keep the gems on my own. He's right. I have all the power anyone could ever wish for, right here in my hands… and I'm just losing it."

"You listen to me." Dante grasped him by the arms and shook him until he looked at her. "It's not Foyer. Ignore him. Ignore them all."

Still holding him steady, she asked Foosay, "What do you suggest we do now?"

Foosay opened a cupboard door that was disguised in the wall. "I'll do my colours, as you asked." Three shelves inside the cupboard were lined with tidy rows of jars filled with fine powder in various shades of blue, purple, green, red, and brown. Glass clinked noisily as she picked out the darkest of the green and two of the red jars. "I prepared these earlier to contact my dear aunt. She is also Tamzin's aunt." She slammed the door shut. "Which of course you already know," she added, giving Cesar a nasty look while she unscrewed the caps from the three jars. She dumped the contents carelessly into the cauldron. Three loud pops shot out like gunfire.

A twinge of fear prickled the back of Will's neck. "What's going to happen?" he asked.

"Nothing you need to be afraid of," Dante replied.

"What is that stuff?"

He'd aimed the question at Dante, but Foosay was quick to answer.

"The red is magically ground jasper from the otherworld. It brings forth the soul you wish to find - or the soul that wishes to find you. The green is dust of beryl. The emerald stops any evil spirits from passing through the void that must be opened to communicate with the dead."

"I thought you said they couldn't get through the void," Will said nervously.

"Life cannot pass back. Death can. If given the chance." Fire whooshed to life under the cauldron. "She's coming." The light from the flames cast shadows that danced across the walls.

The cauldron popped again. Its contents emitted a puff of green smoke, from which a ghostly face formed that blinked like it was waking up from a long sleep.

"Auntie." Foosay pulled a chair up to her hearth and sat. "How are you, my dearest?"

"My child." An ethereal whisper joined the shadows in their dance around the room and chilled Will to the core. "Why do you beckon me here, in this unusual way, at this unusual time?"

"My guests have questions that I hope you might answer."

"I do have knowledge you seek," the airy voice said from all around them. The face in the green mist grew more defined, more feminine. "Alice Montgomery is in danger."

"Who is that?" Dante asked. "What does she have to do with anything?"

"Alice is an old friend to the wots," the spirit said. "She has been protecting this one for over a century."

"This one?" Dante pointed at Blue. "*This* one?"

"Yes. One hundred and fifty years ago, Foyer Naxlar saved the life of Alice Montgomery. The two grew close."

Dante's fingers curled, making fists of her hands.

"So close, in fact, that Alice devoted her life to Foyer's request."

"What request?" Foosay asked.

"To protect the young wot. Alice Montgomery spent her entire life making sure no harm ever came to him, for this is what the one she owed her life had asked of her." The green face flickered. "Foyer asked the witch to keep an eye on the young wot once while he was temporarily absent, taking care of a problem elsewhere. Alice took the request much further than he ever intended. She kept an eye on the child for the rest of her life."

Dante relaxed her hands. "She didn't stop him from being killed the other day," she reminded everybody.

"She could not," the spirit said. "Molina Simms was aware of Alice. Before she and my niece Tamzin began their attack on the wots, they saw to it that Alice was no longer a threat."

"Alice is the witch who saved me from the banter," Blue said. "Isn't she?"

"That's right. She never let one near you again."

"That's why I thought they were extinct." After a quick glance at everyone to convey his surprise, Blue refocused on the face above the cauldron. "What did they do to her?"

"My niece Tamzin transformed her into a mouse," the ghostly voice said, "so that she would be powerless against them. Molina Simms was not satisfied with this act and tasked a group of wenns with killing every last mouse in Wynne in an effort to eliminate Alice."

Again, Will remembered the owl in Cesar's treehouse complaining about disappearing mice.

"Find her," the spirit said, evanescing with the smoke from which she had appeared. "Find Alice Montgomery, and you will have a valuable ally back in play."

Chapter Twenty-Four: Buried

The never-ending mass of solid, grey-brown tree trunks all around them was enough to drive a person mad. Will was beginning to feel blinded by them.

"This is a waste of time," Dante said. "We're on a wild goose chase."

"Wild mouse chase," Will agreed.

"One teensy-weensy little mouse in a forest this size," Dante grumbled on. "It's like looking for a needle in a haystack with an extra twelve haystacks piled on top of it."

Cesar trudged along at her side. "It does feel futile. We're wasting precious time here."

Dante changed her tune then. "Maybe if you stopped moaning and started doing something useful for once, we'd get along quicker. Come on. You're the one who can talk to the animals for us. Ask around." She clapped her hands sharply in front of his face. "Come on, shake a leg. Some time this century."

Cesar's beady eyes shrunk in his face and his ears turned red.

"No need for that," Foosay cut in before the shouting match started. "Will and I saw a mouse in No-go ebb. We should head there."

"You think the mouse you saw was…" Will struggled to remember the witch's name. "Anna?"

"Alice," Blue corrected. "I've heard Foyer mention her before. He said her name in front of Scilla Simms once, and Scilla hated him after that. She thought he was calling her by her backwards name. Took great offence." His tone softened. "I never knew who he was talking about. It's weird to think she's spent her life looking out for me and I barely even knew she existed."

"She sounds nice. I hope we can find her before she gets eaten up."

"The boy's right," Cesar said. "There are many hungry birds of prey out there. If one of them spotted her, she'd have no chance at all."

Dante's wand dropped into her hand.

"Please, my dear," Foosay said with a condescending chortle. "Put that away. Here now." She reached into the woolly pocket of her cardigan for a small plastic bottle. "This potion will get us much closer than any portal could." She shook the bottle, sloshing its grotty contents into a foamy mix of tiny bubbles, and said, "Take us all to the area of No-go Ebb that lies a few yards short of the lilac path. The spot where Will and I met while he was searching for the wots' hut in the limited-access area around the corner from…"

"Foosay," Dante interrupted, loud and aggravated. "You can stop describing it. We've moved already. And my portal would have quite easily got us here, I'll have you know."

Foosay lifted her bottle and peered through the glass to see how much potion remained. There was little more than a drop in the bottom when she tilted it. She tucked it back into her pocket. "This is where we were, isn't it, dear?" she asked Will. She ducked behind one of the slanted trees. "Yes, look. My chairs are still here." She wiggled one of them out into view.

"You're a strange lady, Miss Hoo," Cesar said.

"This is where we saw the mouse." Foosay pointed at a patch of grass. "Let's hope it's the one we want."

Will hadn't seen any mice but didn't want to contradict her.

Blue squashed a clump of nettles aside with his foot. There was no time for Will to wonder when or how Blue had retrieved his boots. The dead mouse he'd exposed in the middle of the patch of nettles pushed all other thoughts out.

"Or let's hope it's not the one we want," Dante said.

"Yes, let's indeed hope this isn't our Miss Montgomery," Foosay agreed sadly.

Knowledge as clear and indubitable as sunrise being a morning event came to life in Will's mind and gave him the confidence to inform the group: "It isn't her."

"But how can we know for sure?" Dante asked.

"I just know." It unnerved Will, not knowing where this information had come from, but it was as though someone had explained to him exactly where to find the witch they sought without anyone having spoken a word. "And I know where she is too."

Cesar folded his bloodstained arms. "Oh, you do, do you?"

"Yes. She's hiding where Foyer keeps his gem. She doesn't know he's dead. She's waiting for him to come home."

"How stupid of her," Cesar said. "Wouldn't it be more sensible to try finding a ware, seeing as how Foyer would see only a mouse and have no idea it was her?"

"Well, you're not exactly being a lot of use right now, are you?" Dante said. "How come you can't sense where she is anyway?"

"Maybe because she's a mouse," he retorted, offended.

"How do you know where she is, Will?" Blue asked, cringing away from something or someone that the others could not see.

"I don't know how I know. I just know."

"Could you not have told us that before I wasted all my potion getting us here?" Foosay waggled her empty bottle at him.

Dante gave Foosay a smug smile as she took out her wand.

"What if the Maker did something when he took you away before?" Blue said to Will, while Dante made her portal. "What if you're leading us into a trap?"

"It's not a trap. Trust me."

"I'm trying to."

"Come on." Dante guided Blue into her portal.

Will tripped on the other side, but Christian caught him with remarkable swiftness. "Thanks." He brushed himself down and noticed the wicker appeared uncomfortable. "What's wrong?" he asked, realising Christian hadn't spoken in a long time. It was unusual for Christian to have nothing to say.

Blue pushed past the pair of them, muttering, "I don't know why you keep wasting potions and making portals." He rushed to the tree under which Will had first met Foyer and began scrabbling around in the grass with both hands.

Cesar jogged after him. "That's no way to find a mouse. I'll just ask her to come out if she's there."

"She's hiding in the next tree," Will said, pointing to the one he meant, feeling positive. "There's a space between the roots where she's dug a hole."

"How do you know?" Blue asked again, heading for the tree. Cesar bopped him out of the way with his hip.

"Miss Montgomery? Are you in there, please?"

Just as Will had expected, a mouse emerged from between two thick roots that bulged from the ground. It squeaked and chittered wildly.

"It's really her," Cesar said, laughing.

Dante laughed with Cesar, whereas Blue threw Will a suspicious glance.

"Miss Montgomery, how can we turn you back into a witch?" Cesar listened while the little brown mouse stood up on its hind legs, its nose twitching and tail flicking, and then he translated for his companions. "She says there's nothing we can do. Only Tamzin can reverse the spell."

"That can't be true," Dante said. "Spells can always be reversed. Just look at what Auntie Scilla did for Gart."

The mouse bared yellow teeth at Dante.

"Calm down, Miss Montgomery, that's the name of her auntie. She wasn't insulting you."

"Oh, for the love of Chika. Listen up, Little-Miss-Mousey, we've got work to do. We're all in serious danger here. Foyer asked you to protect Blue, did he not? Well, you're not doing a very good job of it, are you?"

"Dante," Cesar scolded. "That's not fair. She's been doing an exemplary job of keeping her promise for a hundred and fifty years already."

"Yes, until he actually needed help. Poor thing's terrified of what the neethers are going to do to him."

"They're going to bury me alive!"

"Shh." She patted his arm consolingly. "See?" she said to Cesar.

The mouse stayed perfectly still, its shiny black eyes on Dante.

"Foyer won't be coming back, I'm afraid," Cesar said, in response to a question that nobody else had heard. "He's dead."

The mouse lowered its front feet, forgetting to be angry with Dante.

"Yes, we know he's immortal," Cesar said, losing the politeness in his tone. "He was murdered." He listened a while, then glanced at the others as if she'd said something interesting.

"What is it?" Foosay asked.

"She says wots don't die. They stay in the land of the living."

Foosay flapped an arm to dismiss the remark. "I already told you that much."

"No, you told us you don't know where they go. Alice says they just stay here, bodiless. Like…"

"Like the Maker," Will guessed.

"Exactly. She also claims she can feel power emitting from you, Will. She says the wots would be able to feel that power too, and they'd be drawn to it."

Dante said, "Hang on. Are you saying they'd do what the Maker did? They'd go inside Will's body?"

"All of them?" Will's train of thought trundled to a wonky stop. It had been hard enough sharing a body with one other person; he couldn't imagine having seven of them trying to chime in and take control.

"Only one way to find out," Cesar said.

"We have to talk to them," Dante guessed.

"That's right. They can't surface unless someone addresses them directly. According to our witch-mouse here, anyway."

"That'll be why the Maker never said a word until I asked him who he was." Dante smiled hopefully and spun to face Will. "Foyer, are you in there?" she pleaded, grabbing Will's shoulders.

"Ow, Dante!" Will ducked out of her grasp. "Let go of me."

"I'm sorry." She stroked her hair flat. "Come on, Dan, calm down," she chuntered under her breath.

Blue stared at Will. "Who are you?"

And immediately that familiar feeling overcame Will, of being taken over from the inside, unable to control the words that left his lips.

"I'm the wicked wenn that gave you your nightmares, Blue," Will's voice said in an eerie drawl. "I've come back from the dead to give you this message: Ha-ha, I was right. You big idiot."

Blue reacted like someone had flicked him between the eyes. Then a smile sparked alight. "Dyelann?"

"No fooling you, is there?" Dyelann smiled through Will's face and patted Blue sharply on the arm. "And that isn't really Foyer talking to you, dumbo. It's just some vision Molina sent to mess your head up."

"Oh."

"How are you doing?" Dyelann asked, serious then. "You okay?"

"I am now," he said earnestly. "Is everybody in there with you?"

"No. It's just me. Only one of us could fit in, otherwise Will's eyes might have fallen out."

"Eurgh, gross," Will said. "Why does everyone keep jumping into me?"

"Shh, never mind that," Dyelann said, forcing Will out of the driver's seat. "All you've got to do is get me out of you the same way you did the Maker, and then everyone'll hop in you one at a time so you can do the same for them, and we'll all be alive again." He grinned excitedly. "Genius, no?"

"No!"

Blue twisted his hands together. "Yes, come on, please, let's do that, please."

"You can't," Cesar said. "My Agulga sphere was shattered."

"Maybe it could still work," Blue said. "We could try, couldn't we? Maybe we could fix the sphere. Or find a new one."

"There are only three in the entire universe," Cesar said shortly. "And mine is completely shattered. Entrusted with my family since the dawn of time, practically, and I'm the one whose possession it is in when it's destroyed. The thought makes me ill."

"Can't we fix it?"

"It is shattered," Cesar said again, slower.

"And it really hurt last time," Will muttered, remembering the intense suffering he'd endured when the Maker had finally left his body, like he'd been guillotined from the head down.

"That's a bit selfish, Will," Dyelann said.

"Is Foyer okay?" Dante asked.

Dyelann rolled Will's eyes at the question. "Aside from the whole being dead thing, yes. Just fine and dandy." He changed his tone to say, "Oh, leave it out, Foyer. No. No, I'm not being messenger-boy for you. If you wanted to say something to your girlfriend, you should have stepped up and possessed Will, shouldn't you?" He shook Will's head. "I did not. I did not. Just shut up. Go float into a volcano."

"What's he saying, Dyelann?" Dante demanded. "Come on. Stop being such a pig."

"But it's such a good plan," Blue said in exasperation. "We have to find another sphere. We just have to."

Cesar drummed his fingers on his chin. "There's got to be another way. What do you suggest, Miss Montgomery?"

Alice leapt back into the roots, out of sight.

"Hey!" Dante pointed accusingly at the hole. "Where does she think she's going?"

"She says the Rickrack witch is close by." Cesar turned his back on the mouse. "And she's right. Maybe we should disappear too."

"Not without the mouse."

Dyelann flicked Will's arm casually. "Piffle. You don't have to run away from Tamzin, Blue. You've got to stop thinking you're not good enough or old enough to handle the power you have now. You are handling it. And… You're doing a good job. Better than any of the rest of us could have done."

Blue aimed that familiar look of suspicion Will's way again and said, "You're not Dyelann."

The thought frightened Will. If it wasn't Dyelann, then who?

"What are you trying to say?" The attitude Dyelann projected quelled Will's fears in an instant. "You think I'm incapable of being supportive? I mean, yes, Foyer did tell me to say all that stuff, but just because he told me to say it, doesn't mean I don't agree with him. I mean, I sort of don't. I sort of think a donkey in a tar pit could do a better job of… Okay, okay." He gestured to an invisible person to be quiet. "No. I believe in you as much as Foyer does. Of course I do." He smirked. "Of course."

"You're a pig, Dyelann," Dante said. "Guys, we have to leave. Before Tamzin gets here."

"Nonsense," Dyelann shouted. "Stand your ground. All of you against one of her, easy."

There was a movement behind Blue. Will seized control of his body, cutting Dyelann off before he'd finished speaking. He recognised the graceful, floating bodies, weightless tattered cloaks flowing and fluttering, their long bony fingers groping at trees as they passed to gently pull themselves along through the air.

Five neethers came into sight, and Will feared more would soon join them. He pointed, frantic, too afraid to speak.

In Dante's haste to pull out her wand it snagged the fabric of her sleeve, and she gave it a few tugs to free it. A roaring flame erupted from her elbow, and she shrieked in shock, flapping her arm in desperation to kill the fire.

"It is a rather dangerous place to keep your brew stick, my dear," Foosay said to her, reaching for her own.

Will lurched to take cover at Blue's side.

The neethers swarmed around them, predators closing in on their prey.

Dante and Foosay put out the fire but were immediately attacked by two of the neethers. Christian and Cesar were nowhere to be seen. Three neethers circled Will and Blue, watching them with eyes that grew and bulged and retracted on their heads along with gaping mouths and flaring nostrils. They circled closer and closer until the tails of their rags met the front of the one behind, joining them into one snake-like beast ready to constrict them.

One of them broke out of the circle and morphed into the form of a banter. It dropped to all fours and flew at Will like a wild animal. His bones juddered when he hit the ground. The back of his skull cracked against the hard base of a tree. Everything began to spin out of control. The world swam around him in a blur, like he was clinging on to an unstoppable roundabout.

The neether-banter's head dived, and a sickening pain spread through him as its teeth punctured the flesh on the top of his left arm, deep into the muscle. Its glinting eyes flickered with delight over the warm blood that flowed into its black mouth. And Will could do nothing. He could not even call out for the help he knew wouldn't come. His head throbbed, his arm felt as though it was hanging on by a thread, and he could see just enough of what was happening around him to know that Blue had gone. They had taken Blue.

"No," he coughed, furious. The neether bit even deeper into a lower part of his arm and sent a jolt of excruciating pain screaming through his body, but he was still angrier that they had taken Blue.

His thoughts came crystal clear: 'I want it off me. Get off me, get off me, get off, off, *off!*' He drew a long, harsh breath. "Get off!" His right arm lashed out. The neether soared through the air like a launched missile and crashed against a tree. It rolled down the trunk, disintegrating into a wisp of spiralling pink dust.

Will stared at where it had been, shocked by what he'd done, gasping for breath and trying to focus his eyes so everything would stay still. He reached a shaky hand to feel the back of his head and brought it back to check for blood. There was none. It took him a second to find the courage to check his arm, which he was certain would be shredded beyond repair. But no. There was a scuffed patch of fabric on his shoulder and nothing more. He grabbed it and squeezed. It was still attached.

"Where's Blue?" Dante was turning on the spot, staring in all directions. "They've taken him."

Will searched the trees for a glimpse of his friend, knowing it was hopeless. They'd be long gone by now.

"I promised him I wouldn't let anything happen to him," Dante said. "Now look what I've done. I've let him down. I let them take him. How could I let this happen?"

"This was not your fault," Foosay soothed. "This wasn't anybody's fault."

"Yes, it was," Dyelann said, forcing Will to stand still. "Blue didn't lift a finger to stop this. He's the only one of us with the power to do something about this, and he won't put his brain into gear and realise he's not just a useless waste of space."

Dante turned furiously on Will and jabbed her finger hard into his sternum. "That's because of you, Dyelann! You and Karson, drumming it into him all his life that he isn't any good, that he is a useless waste of space. So, if this is anyone's fault, it's *yours!*"

Dyelann was dumbstruck.

"You make me so mad!" She spun a dramatic circle, roared in anger, and marched away.

"Where are you going?" Will shouted after her.

"To find Blue!" she screamed back.

Will watched her go, wanting to follow but knowing she didn't want him to. "At least I've still got you guys," he said nervously to Foosay. "Where's Cesar and Christian?"

Foosay hummed. "I'm not sure."

"What are we going to do, Mrs Hoo? How are we going to get Blue back from those horrible people?"

Foosay stood beside him, silent while she contemplated the question.

Will pressed on. "Can't you split the gems up for him? Then they won't be able to hurt him. That's what Dante said."

"No, my dear. Even if we could somehow manage to part the power into all eight gems, the neethers would make him join them back. Wots are strong enough to hold their own in most conflicts, but not one against all the neethers. Not one so young and suffering with grief like poor Blue. Wots aren't made for fighting."

"He'll be okay." Will spoke the words with confidence but his heart doubted it.

"I'm thinking about the mouse," Foosay said. "My aunt called her a valuable ally. There's not much value in her if all she can do for us is sniff out cheese, is there?"

Discombobulated by the subject-change, Will felt himself go blank.

"I'm having an idea, my boy. Come." Foosay bustled to the tree that was hiding Alice. She looked back at Will, waving him over. "Get the mouse. Quickly now. Get your hand in that hole."

Unwilling to risk being bitten, Will stayed put and ignored the request. "What idea?"

Foosay picked up her wand, and he expected that she might use magic to extract the mouse. Instead, she poked the wand into the hole and rattled it roughly around Alice's hiding place like she was stirring cake mix. "Get out here, Alice."

"What idea?" he asked again, wondering if the witch was having trouble hearing him. She was pretty old, after all.

"To turn Alice back into a witch, of course. That's what we need to focus on right now." She kept her eyes on Will while she spoke to him, still poking her wand around in the hole. "When I mentioned cheese just now, it made me think of home," she explained. "And that made me think of my Ours. Witches keep a book of our own from a young age, which disintegrates when we die. But we also have a family book called an Ours, which is handed down from generation to generation." With a disapproving scowl, she added, "That's what I caught you and Blue thumbing through."

"Sorry."

"My Ours belonged to my father's family. I'm wondering if perhaps the remedy to my half-sister's spell can be found within its pages. She is my father's daughter after all."

"Like when Scilla was looking in that big book for a way to get Gart back to normal? Was that their Ours?"

"No, it was their Theirs," Foosay replied patiently, though she seemed a touch aggravated by the question. "Only they would call their Theirs their Ours."

"Hey, Mrs Hoo?"

"Yes, dear?"

Will smiled, embarrassed to ask. "Why do you have cheese outside your house?"

"It's very bad luck to keep cheese *inside* your house."

"Really?" That was probably the cause of Will's bad luck, then. His parents always had cheese in their fridge at home.

"It also gives you nightmares," she said, giving the hole another aggressive jab.

Will winced. "You'll hurt her."

"We need to get going. Are you coming with us?"

"You can't go now. You've got to stay and help me find Blue and everything."

"Don't worry. We'll be back." She lifted her wand. The mouse clung onto the end with all four of its dinky feet, delicate bald tail coiled around it like a tiny snake. "We won't be long." Foosay got the last drop of potion out of her pocket. Then she was gone, and Will was alone.

The depth of the forest seemed endless from where Will stood, and it all looked the same no matter which way he turned. Where had everyone gone? Where was he supposed to go? How could a place that was teeming with life look so vacant and dead?

"I'm still here, Will," Dyelann reminded him chirpily, settling his heart, which had begun to thump too hard again.

"Dante's really mad at you. Couldn't you have just said you're sorry? Then she wouldn't have left."

"Oh, she would, Will. They're temperamental, these witches."

An uncomfortable silence fell as Will waited for Dyelann to tell him what to do. He was just about to ask, when the wot began to speak.

"I don't mean to get at Blue so much, you know," he said quietly, and Will understood that Dyelann was saying this in confidence. "I suppose it was just because he was the youngest. When I was growing up, the blue gem was practically mythical. We lived in awe of it, every single one of us. Everyone anticipated the coming of the final wot as something miraculous. The coming was supposed to change everything. It was supposed to complete us." He sighed deeply.

Will listened politely but couldn't help but wonder what the reason was for Dyelann's sudden sentimentality.

"But he just didn't show up for so long. And when he finally did, nothing happened. His arrival changed nothing. Not for the better anyway. He was just a normal little boy. People were rather disappointed in him. Especially Karson. Karson's attitude changed towards all of us after that. He'd taken care of that blue gem all his life. He would never let anyone else touch it. But he gave it to Foyer, and it was Foyer who named Blue and took care of him. Karson didn't want to know. It's like he gave up. Foyer was happy Blue's arrival didn't change anything, you see. He was happy with how things were. Still is, as a matter of fact. So, you see..." Dyelann sighed again, like his own story was depressing him. "We expected an all-powerful saviour to bring a miracle, and instead we got a stupid child who did nothing but play practical jokes. Just a child who knew nothing of anything."

Will paused to check that Dyelann had finished speaking. Then he said dubiously, "But everyone starts off like that. Even all-powerful savers. You guys were the stupid ones, not Blue."

Cesar materialised by his side with no warning. "He said saviour, not saver," he said without missing a beat. "What's going on? Why have the witches gone so far away?"

"Dante ran away in a huff," Will explained. "Foosay went home to turn Anna back into a witch."

"Alice. Where's Blue?"

"Neethers took him. Where have you been?"

"Pah, I went after Christian. The wicker's only gone and stolen the gems. The powerless ones, that is. I saw him taking them and chased after him. He outran me, of course."

Will lifted his arms anxiously, using them to ask Cesar for some sort of explanation. When none came, he slapped his hands firmly over his head, aghast. "But why would he steal them?"

"I told you not to trust him, didn't I?"

"But Christian was the one who gave them back to Blue in the first place! Why would he steal them again? I don't get it."

Dyelann removed Will's hands from his head. "Wickers never do anything without a reason. Why did he show up and start hanging around in the first place? That's what I want to know. There was no reason for him to do that, that I could see."

"First things first," Cesar said. "We have to find Blue. If anything happens to him, that's it. The wots' connection to the gem will be snubbed out and who knows what will happen?"

"If we were alive, we'd be able to follow his trail and find him," Dyelann said. "But it's like existing without existing. We can do nothing to help anything. We feel nothing except the power emitting from you, pulling at us, flaring out a signal like two great beacons."

"Two?" Cesar asked, stretching the word out longer than necessary.

"Yes. The Maker has as much of a pull on us as Will."

Will laughed out loud, hands raised high with jubilation, and he stared at the cloudy sky, smiling in sheer delight over the fresh and wonderful feeling of hope.

Cesar watched him like he was fascinated by his behaviour. "Care to share? Explain your excitement, please."

"The Maker's just like me, isn't he?" Will said, lowering his arms. "One of the other wots can go in him like Dyelann's in me, can't they? The Maker's on the same side as Dante and Mrs Hoo's evil sisters now. You guys can find things out and stuff. Like a spy on the wall."

"Or even a fly on the wall." Cesar nodded. "Good thinking, lad."

Dyelann held up a hand. "Hang on, hold that horse. You expect one of my living-dead chums to hop into their creator and start pulling some strings?" he asked, apparently astounded at the suggestion. "That's unbelievable. Why didn't I think of that? I think Maik should do it." He pointed Will's finger at what looked like thin air, jumping up and down giddily.

"Stop it." Will settled firmly on his feet. "I don't like you doing that to me."

The ground beneath him gave, and he wobbled, trying to keep his balance. "What…? Whoa!" The root-covered soil crumbled under him, and he fell a good five or six metres until he reached solid land and collapsed in an undignified heap. "Ouch."

He coughed in disgust at the foul earthy taste of the dusty air. It smelt of old unwashed potatoes. A stream of light shimmered in through the small hole above but only highlighted the fog.

"What happened?"

"We fell into a weird underground sort of chamber," Dyelann said, as if Will hadn't worked that one out for himself.

"That's because of you and all your jumping around like an idiot. You must be making me heavy, being in me."

"Oh, leave it out. You sound like a moaning old witch."

"I can't see anything."

"Me neither. It's awful. Do you think you've gone blind?"

Will strained to see something, anything, through the dust. "But wots can see in the dark, can't you?"

"Not when I'm in you, I can't."

The same strange sensation of something brushing up against him that he'd felt earlier touched him again, and he jumped with a start, bouncing back onto his feet. "What was that? Something touched me."

"I felt it too. It was probably just some roots. Relax."

"Are you all right?" Cesar shouted from above ground.

"No!" Dyelann yelled at the top of Will's voice.

"Yes, we're fine! Don't be such a baby, Dyelann."

"Me, the baby? You're the one jumping out of your skin because of a stupid root on your – Agh!" He sprang forward when it touched him again. "What was that?"

"I thought you said it was a root," Will whispered, instinctively crouching. "Cesar! I think something's down here."

A shadow appeared over the blur of light above as the ware leaned over the hole to shout, "That's very likely, boy!"

"I beg your pardon?" Dyelann demanded.

"You're in an efferby burial chamber. There's usually a lot of creatures hanging around those things, grave-robbing and eating the dead and such."

"Gross!"

Something hard and thick wound itself around Will's ankles. Before he could look down to even try to see what it was, it wrenched back, sending him falling with a rib-rattling thump on the dusty ground. An indistinct, guttural sound escaped him. The grip on his legs tightened to a painful pressure, and he scrambled on all fours, kicking out, fighting against it with everything he had.

"Let me go!"

Immediately his leg was released. He tumbled forwards. "Who's there?" He stretched his eyes as open as they would go. It was too fast. By the time he'd seen it move, it was already coiled around his waist, dragging with brute force. He felt like he was on the world's worst theme park ride as he soared through the air and was thrust headfirst into the mouth of a tunnel. He slid straight down, trying to catch himself, but his fingers couldn't dig far enough into the sloppy mud to anchor him. The tunnel led to another chamber, where he landed splat on the puddle-ridden ground below.

There was no dust here. The air was cold and zesty. A wide beam of light from another tunnel lit the area an eerie blue, light enough for Will to see the rocky walls and the glittering surface of the filthy water in which he sat.

"What's going on?" Will asked, catching his breath.

"We've got to get out of here." Dyelann hauled Will up and waded through the puddle to get to dry ground.

"Will?" a frightened voice echoed.

"Christian? What are you doing?"

The wicker crept into view, ashen, jumpy, not his usual confident, cocky self.

"Why did you bring me down here?"

"It's not me. It's Gudmé. He's gone crazy."

There was only one bod on Christian's shoulder. Badmé was hugging the wicker's neck with his face hidden and his little tail in the air.

"What? What do you mean?" Will babbled, nervous. "What are you talking about? What happened?"

"Shh. Not so loud." Christian pulled Will by his jacket to a muddy wall. "I don't know what happened. After Foosay Hoo summoned her dead aunt from the spirit realm, something happened to Gudmé. I don't understand it. At first, he was just saying things Badmé usually says. It confused me. Badmé only says things like that to be clever, but Gudmé meant them, he really meant them. Once the neethers attacked he made me take the gems and run. Then he threw us down here and left us. He took the gems with him too. I don't understand why he even wants them. They're useless anyway."

"How could Gudmé do all that? He's only this big." Will poised his finger and thumb an inch apart and glared at Christian.

"Will, what's wrong with you? He's a bod. *Bod*, as in, short for *bodyshifter*. He can be as big, or as small, or as strong as he wants. You didn't know that?"

"No," Will said, still sceptical. "Why do they stay so small if they can be as big as they like?"

Christian pointed to Badmé's hairy back. "So they can sit on my shoulders, obviously."

Will stared at Christian. "Foyer said all wickers have bods. I thought they were, like, attached to you or something."

"They are. They never leave their wickers, never. This is what makes no sense. It's not normal, Will. It's not normal!" He grabbed Will and shook him dramatically.

"You're not normal," Will said when he stopped. "What's he brought us down here for?"

"Not just us." Christian stepped back and looked down a slippery bank.

Will peered down at a mound of filthy sludge. "What is it? What's down there?"

Christian crossed his arms tightly over his stomach. “The neethers buried him there. Way, way down. Buried him alive. Your wot. It’s Blue. That’s his grave.”

Chapter Twenty-Five: The Takeover

Will slid clumsily down the bank, scraping sidewards on his knees half the way, and dropped into the claggy mud below. White hot burning seared his skin when he stuck his hands into the mound of slop that Christian had said was Blue's grave, like he'd reached into acid. He yelped and backed off, pressing his hands under his armpits.

Christian looked down at him. "Yeah, we already tried that."

"We've got to get him out!"

"He'll have suffocated by now, Will. There's too much mud."

"No," Dyelann said, checking Will's palms for damage while he had control of the body. "He's not dead. He'd have joined us, otherwise. And the neethers would be dead too."

Christian sat on his haunches and bent over the edge of the bank like a gargoyle. "What tosh. That's like saying if all the witches dropped down dead right now, so would all the warders."

"You don't know what you're talking about," Dyelann told him. "I didn't believe it at first either, but it's true. The neethers do want to merge the four energies. But they know if Blue dies, the energies will return to where they were summoned from and the neethers will cease to exist. They need Blue alive. I know he's alive. He's not buried here. He's not buried anywhere. Why would they bury him before the energies were merged anyway? That makes no sense."

"All I'm hearing when you speak is blah, blah, blah, bliddy blah," Christian said childishly.

"Quite a lot about this makes no sense, come to think of it," Dyelann went on, undeterred. "Why would your bod turn against you and take gems that have no power in them? Why would he then leave you down here with Will, right where the neethers have supposedly buried Blue? Why?" Dyelann stared as if trying to find the answer in Christian's face. "It all seems a little convenient."

"Convenient?" Christian shouted, and Will thought this was the first time he'd seen the wicker lose his temper. "Convenient for *who?*"

"You've been plotting something way before you just happened to bump into Will and Blue."

"Hey, I resent that. I only ever tried to help. I took Will to the witch's place, just like he wanted."

"Rather convenient that you just happened to know where that was."

"I've stuck up for him and looked out for him and been there for him. I've done everything I could." Christian stood up and held out his arms. "What else do you want from me?"

"The truth. What are you really sticking around for? Where's your bod really gone? Who really threw us down here? Why?"

"I'm telling you the truth. I only wanted to help."

"There's no way Blue's down there," Dyelann muttered, glancing at the mound. "You're full of it. And we are out of here. Come on, Will."

Will planted his feet to keep Dyelann from walking away. "No, we can't leave Blue here."

"Are you not hearing me, kidlet? Blue isn't here. It's a trick."

"But he told us the neethers were going to bury him. He told us this would happen."

"Yes, and who just so happened to be there when he told us, listening, taking everything in?" Dyelann argued. "Him, that's who." He snarled up at Christian.

"But what if he is?" Will stared at the heap, an uncomfortable judder in his stomach. "I believe Christian."

Christian let out a bumptious, "Ha!"

"We can't just go without him," Will said again, less sure this time. Carefully, he wiggled a stone the size of half a brick out of the mud. "We'll use this." Lowering himself to his knees, he scraped aside some sludge with the stone, keeping his fingers well clear, scared of being burned again.

Dyelann's anger simmered inside him.

"Please," he said under his breath, digging faster. "Please just help me."

"I don't believe him," Dyelann whispered. "I don't trust him. There's not an ounce of truth to what he says. His bod did *not* go evil because of some colour-mixing séance Foosay did. The bod did *not* throw us in here. The little oik's probably hiding in his pocket."

"Stop it, Dyelann," Will begged, working harder to push the sludge aside.

"I'm telling you, Will. I don't know why, but that wicker is lying. He is lying to get you to do exactly what you're doing."

"Don't you want to get Blue back?"

"He isn't here, damn it!"

Will threw the stone across the chamber.

"Will?" Dyelann said quietly.

"What?"

"I can't move your legs."

Will tried to stand. His bottom left his heels but that was it. He had sunk into the thick mud and couldn't free his knees. "I'm stuck." He tried to wiggle himself out but only sank further. "I can't… Christian, help!" He glanced up the bank to where the wicker had been. "Erm. Dyelann?"

"Yes?"

"Christian's gone."

Dyelann didn't respond immediately. "Yes," he said. "I noticed that."

Will sank another couple of inches and gasped in horror.

"I suppose we're sinking because I'm making you so heavy?" Dyelann asked sarcastically.

"No," Will whined. "You're right. Christian's done this on purpose." He hid his facc in his hands. "People keep changing. I thought he was my friend, and he's just left us here."

"Oh, for... You're not going to cry, are you?"

"No." Will folded his arms, hating Dyelann for suggesting such a thing.

"Oh, so you'll sulk instead? Yeah. That's a great help. Great help, Will."

"Well, what do *you* want to do?" He sank deeper all at once to his waist and cried out, terrified.

"Something other than scream, you mean?" Dyelann made a grab for the dry ground behind them, but Will snatched his arm back and wrapped it around the other as if that would keep Dyelann from taking it again.

"Don't get my hand stuck too."

"You have to drag us out, you idiot."

"Now you sound just like Karson."

That shut Dyelann up.

"I'll just…" Will stammered. "I'll just want us out. Come on. Come on, brain." He squeezed his eyes shut. "I'm not stuck in the mud, I'm not stuck in the mud, I'm not stuck in the mud, I'm not…"

"I don't think this is working, kidlet," Dyelann interrupted, opening Will's eyes.

"Shut up, Dyelann, you're spoiling it!" Down he went again, until the mud was tight around his chest, swallowing him. "Uh!" He raised his arms above his head. "We're sinking!"

"Well spotted, genius."

The mud crept up to his shoulders. "What do we do? What do we do?"

"Summon Dante. She'll get us out of here."

"I don't know how." Will could hardly breathe for the weight of the sludge collapsing in around his neck.

"We need her book."

Fear was all that kept Will from laughing in Dyelann's face. That, and the fact the wot currently had no face to laugh in. "Oh, you know what, Dyelann? We don't have her book!"

"It's all right. Foyer's here. He knows the incantation well. We're lucky he's such a shameless stalker. Yeah, okay, Foyer, whatever you say, just hurry up and tell us before Will drowns in this disgusting filth. Okay. Okay. Right. We summon you here to us, Sister Simms of the South. Come here to us now. Bring yourself forth to us, blessed charge of Goddess Chika of the South. We… *What?* No, there's no way I'm saying that." He shook Will's head stubbornly, even as the mud slopped over his chin and choked him.

"Just say it!" Will squawked.

"Stuff that rubbish. Dante! Dante! Dante Simms, sister of an evil goat from hell, I summon you! Get your backside here, right now, Dante Simms!"

A cold rush of wind blew over Will's head, and a black cloud formed at the other side of the muddy mound. It swirled, circled, and spat out the hazy shape of a woman who landed heavily on the wet ground with a splash. When the black mist dispersed, Dante stood before them with an expression of bewilderment etched on her windswept face.

"I haven't been summoned in years. I'd forgotten how intrusive and downright rude it is."

"Help me." Will waggled his arms at her. "Please!"

She pointed her wand at him. When nothing happened, she darted closer and grasped his hands in hers. His shoulders felt like they were disconnecting from his body as she threw all her weight back to haul him out. He gradually slid upwards. With one last determined tug she dragged him free, and they both collapsed on top of one another on the firmer ground behind them.

"What happened?" she asked. "What on earth are you doing in a place like this?"

Will wrapped his aching arms around the witch and hugged her. "You saved me. You saved me."

"I wish we could say the same about Blue. I can't find him, Will." She looked up, exasperated. "It's like he's disappeared into nothing. I've searched everywhere. I'm worried he's no longer in our reality."

Will let go of her, trying and mostly failing to keep his lip from wobbling. "So, he's not down there?"

Dante glanced to where he pointed. "No."

"Christian said he was. Then he left."

"Which one's Christian again?"

"The wicker that was hanging around like a bad smell," Dyelann said.

"Oh, Will. Didn't anyone ever tell you wickers are a vile bunch of wrongdoers?"

"Yes," Will said, humbly. "You did."

"I'm very wise." A faraway look crossed Dante's face, promptly followed by one of queasiness. "Okay, this is the weirdest thing ever. I'm being summoned again." Her eyes blackened, and she grabbed Will by the shoulder. "You can come with me," she gasped, just as a vacuum sucked them upwards into a white void.

Solid ground slammed into Will's soles like he'd been dropped from a great height, and he nearly fell over.

"Oh, Dante, good," Foosay said. "Sorry about the summoning. We saw Will do it, and we thought it was a good idea. Now listen, I have good news."

"You've found Blue?" Dante said, a hopeful guess.

Will relaxed when he saw they were in Foosay's living room. The neat line of gem replicas sat untouched in their place on the dressing table. He stared at them wistfully.

"No, I haven't found Blue. Not yet. But we're well on our way." Foosay smiled and held out her arms to the doorway. "Alice, my dear, do come in and introduce yourself."

A frightfully frail old lady pottered shakily in from the hallway. Her thin hair was wispy and white on her head, and she wore a pleated grey skirt, a drab cardigan and blouse, and a ruby pendant the size of a tangerine that hung from her spindly neck.

"This is Alice Montgomery. She'll find him."

Will was pretty certain he could guess what Dante was thinking. This old lady barely looked like she could remember her own name, never mind how to find someone who seemed to have fallen off the face of the earth.

"So," Dante droned. "You're not a mouse. Good for you."

"No, I'm not a mouse." Her voice was small enough to have belonged to a mouse though. "Thanks to Foosay, here. She's a most talented witch."

"Yeah-yeah. So, you're going to find us our wot, are you?" Dante clicked her tongue. "Where to start, I wonder?"

"Oh, don't worry about that, young lady. I already know where he is."

"Sorry, what's that now?"

"Yes, I know."

"Any chance you'd mind divulging that minor piece of information?"

"Of course. Here." The old witch took something resembling a wrinkled black prune from her breast pocket and tossed it in Dante's direction with a flick of her bony wrist. Dante failed to catch it, and it fell to Will, who automatically snapped it up in both hands. He'd intended to pass it straight to Dante, but the moment it touched his skin he was overcome with a flash of bright light in his head - then a startling image of Christian's broken dead body lying blood-soaked on the sodden muddy ground.

Petrified, he threw the prune down like it was poison and grasped Dante's arm to steady himself. He held his breath, trying to block what he'd just seen from his mind, but the memory kept flashing back, like photos in a flip book, getting bloodier and bloodier.

"What's the matter, Will? What's wrong?" Dante scooped up the strange black ball. "Oh, it's a seer's eye." She smiled at it, but her gladness quickly faded. "Oh. Blue. There you are. How could I have missed him?"

"Where?" Will asked, still grimacing. "Where is he?"

"Didn't you see him?" Dante passed the seer's eye back to Alice. "He's right where you said he was. He's right where we've just come from."

Will stepped away from the witches, needing some space to deal with his rising resentment. He wished he could move away from Dyelann too.

Blue really had been buried in that chamber. And they had left him there.

"I told you!" Will shouted at Dyelann, pointing at himself. "Christian told you! He was telling the truth and now he's dead."

Foosay touched Will's shoulder and made him jump. "Christian's dead? That's what the eye showed you? Oh, that poor lad. That poor lad. He didn't deserve that. One of the few wickers with any decency and something like this happens. No wonder the others don't bother."

"Killed by his own bod," Alice said, slipping the seer's eye back into her pocket. "Tragic. So very tragic."

Dante pinched the bridge of her nose. "What is going on around here lately? Everything's so backwards. Why is all this happening?"

"We've got to go back." Will tugged at Dante's arm to snap her back into action. Why was she just standing there? "Come on. Come on, take us back. We've got to get him out. I told you he was there. I knew we shouldn't have left. I told you Christian was telling the truth."

Dyelann managed to stop Will long enough to speak out. "I know, Will, I'm sorry. Okay? I'm sorry!"

Foosay passed a small bottle to Dante. "I made more travel potion. Where are we going?"

The next time Will blinked, he and the three witches were in the dank chamber of the efferby tomb. He didn't stop to think. Ignoring the shivers from the trip, he skidded back down the slope to where Blue was buried, disappointed to see he'd hardly made a dent in the mound where he'd been digging.

"Careful," Dante called out, clambering after him. "You'll sink again. There must be another way to get him out." Taking care not to step into the sloppy mud, she crouched down to hold her palm an inch above the supposed grave. She hummed. "There's a curse on it."

"It burned my hands."

"It will have done." Dante tried to see up the slope. "Where are Foosay and Alice?"

Will followed her eyes to the ground above, where the two old witches should have been.

"Foosay?" Dante stood upright, worry creasing her forehead.

There was a movement. Will was relieved, expecting Foosay and Alice to appear. But it was Christian that stepped forward.

Christian stood in the very spot he had occupied before and lowered to a gargoyle-crouch just like before, except this time dark blood oozed from the gaping slash wounds on his face, neck and chest, soaking through his clothes. His broken neck forced his head to an ugly angle. His eyes were glazed, dead, but staring right at Will, who stared back, frozen in fear.

"Will." Dyelann clenched Will's jaw. "I'm not sure what you're seeing but I can tell you it's not real. It's just a neether. It's in your head. It's showing you what will scare you the most. That's all it is."

That was no consolation. The words changed nothing. Christian was still dead, mangled, shuffling closer to the edge of the slope, closer to Will.

He retreated a few clumsy paces.

"Will, you're - uhh!" Dante's warning was cut off by something large and heavy that swung from the rocks above and ploughed into her.

Will tried to take another step back but his feet wouldn't budge. He was stuck, sinking again.

Dead Christian descended the slope.

Will struggled so hard to free himself he felt his leg bones flex. The more he fought against the gluey mud, the faster it devoured him. It was up to his knees in a matter of seconds. The broken wicker drifted ever closer, pointing a bloody finger his way, and Will strained with all his might, only to be sucked down in one big gulp, to his stomach.

"Someone, help," he screamed. "Please help!" He couldn't breathe. The earth swallowed him in faster still as he thrashed and writhed for his life. "Dante! Help! Help!"

Then grim reality hit, as he saw Dante fighting off a constantly morphing neether: Help was not coming. He was going to go under, he was going to suffocate, and he was going to die.

The back of his head and his ears were submerged. He fought to keep his mouth and nose in the open. Sound became a mere rumble. All he could see was Christian's expressionless dead face staring down at him. He took one last deep breath.

Then he was under – completely under. Only his arms remained in the outside world, but they were useless and immobile, stuck above his head. He was trapped. Cold mud clamped around him, in his ears, his nostrils, squeezing too hard, and he needed to breathe, he needed to breathe. Down, down, he kept sinking.

A peculiar sensation occurred. His legs felt like they were dangling in space. Strong hands took hold of them and pulled, drawing him through the gummy mud and back into murky air. He crash-landed and hit stony ground bottom-first, gulping deep, noisy breaths.

He curled into a tight ball, head between his knees. "I thought I was dead," he whispered. "I thought I was dead."

"So did I."

Will lifted his head and saw Blue's dark shadow towering over him. Nothing was clear through the dimness, but he saw enough to be able to throw his arms around the wot and cling on to him. "Are you okay?" he asked, letting go. He knew Blue wasn't the cuddliest of people.

"Not really. The neethers used magic to make this place impenetrable. They obviously didn't count on you being covered in sewitt."

Will looked around. The walls and ground appeared to consist of solid rock. "Is this a cave? How do we get out?"

"That's the problem, isn't it?" Blue sounded distant.

Will couldn't see his face properly in the shadows, but the wot's tone worried him. It was the same tone he'd had when Will and the Maker had found him in the basement of the tilted hut in No-go Ebb. He sounded wrong.

"That's the problem, the how. How to get out. How to not be stuck anymore. How to unstick and the how of how to do it."

Will stayed still, watching the wot's dark frame nervously.

"You shouldn't have come here. Now you're in it too. That's not fair. I should never have dragged you into this mess. When we first met, I should have sent you home and been on my way. Now you're stuck here with me forever and ever and ever and ever."

"Always fretting," Dyelann said, with a brutal edge to his tone. "Always complaining. Come on, kidlet, pull yourself together."

"Dyelann," Blue said. "Stuck with Dyelann forever and ever. Will… How could you do this to me?" It almost sounded like Blue was joking.

"You can get us out of here, Blue," Will said bravely.

Blue gazed up at the solid stone above, through which Will had somehow slipped in. "Maybe I could pop you back out the way you came."

"No." Will scowled, annoyed at the suggestion that he would leave Blue behind. "I meant all of us. We all have to get out of here." The memory of what waited for him out there - neethers and Zombie-Christian - sent a shudder rolling up and down his back. "But we can't go that way. Christian's out there."

"He's not so bad. I thought he was at first, but he started to grow on me. I thought you were friends with him."

"I was, but..." Will stopped to consider his words. Maybe telling Blue that yet another friend was dead wasn't a good idea. "His bod went crazy and killed him."

To Will's surprise, Blue laughed.

"What's funny?" he asked, offended on Christian's behalf.

"You were serious?"

"Blue!"

"All right." Again, Blue peered up at the area Will had fallen through. Then he shifted his eyes to the walls, to his feet, and finally back to Will. "I really don't know what you're expecting me to do."

"Fine. Lift me back up there, and I'll go get more sewitt and bring it back for you."

Blue nodded. "Okay." He clamped his hands together, ready to boost Will. "Step up."

Will stood on Blue's palms and was startled by the swiftness with which the wot threw him up, plunging him back into the gooey substance above. His head burst out into the open and he gasped for air.

The scene was almost exactly the way he'd left it. Christian still stood by the sloping wall of mud. Dante continued to fight off the neether, with ebbing vigour.

One thing was different: The Maker stood at the highest point of the chamber, staring down on them like a lord over his realm.

"Maker," Will shouted. "Help me. Please help." He was already sinking again. Blue's push had only raised him so far and now he was stuck again, completely helpless for a third time.

Dead Christian transformed into the shape of a neether, with only one huge eye on its blank face that fixed inquisitively on the Maker and bloated like a bullfrog's throat. The neether that fought with Dante also backed away in one sweeping, floating motion.

The Maker skated gracefully down the slope to get to Will and reached for his hands. Though grateful for the help, as soon as he was out of the sludge Will backed into the wall behind to get as far away from the Maker as he could, suspicious of his intent.

The Maker turned to the neethers. He raised his arms. The neethers both straightened out and lifted their faceless heads, as if the Maker had them on invisible strings. With a mighty swing of his weedy arms, the neethers were flung together with such force the collision burst the pair of them into a cloud of pink smoke.

No one spoke for a tense moment.

"What's going on?"

The Maker twisted himself around dramatically to face Will. "I'll tell you what's going on," he said. "We're all in here."

Will's heart fell over itself. "What?"

"I said," the Maker said, slower, "we're all in here. All of us. Me, Karson, Maik, Adrian, Popset, Henry. All of us."

"Foyer?" Will asked, uncertain whether he was excited or scared. "Really?"

"Yes, really. We did what you said, we all jumped in. It was the only way we could overpower him, all together."

Dante hugged the Maker's scrawny body. "Foyer, is that really you?"

The Maker hugged her back.

Then he pushed her harshly away, knocking her two paces back. "Not just him, witch. Get your grubby mitts off us."

Dante snarled.

Will laughed. "This is amazing. This is brilliant. This is…"

"Who called you out?" Dyelann demanded.

One of the Maker's eyes twitched.

"Who called you out?" Dyelann asked again, impatient. "You have to be called out before you can take control of the body, right? So, who called you out?"

"Cesar did."

This answer didn't satisfy Dyelann. "You were down here with us when we were sinking the first time," he pressed. "You helped us summon Dante."

"I know," Foyer said. "I was there. I do remember. It wasn't all that long ago."

"My point exactly. How did this happen so fast?"

"When you and Dante disappeared, Maik called me, and we went for it right away. Once Cesar told us his idea, he told us he would approach the Maker and call us out as soon as he arrived. There was no time to hang about."

"How did you get back here so fast then? And why did you come here? How did you know we'd be here?"

"Dye, relax, come on. Trust me, it's me. It's all of us." He waved the Maker's arms. "Hello."

Will interrupted Dyelann's attempt to sneer with an enormous smile. "Oh, this is so brilliant. Everything's going to be okay now, isn't it?"

"Sure it is, Will," Dyelann said. "If we can just forge up our own bodies to live in and get our gems back, it'll all be just peachy."

"Dyelann," Foyer said in a sigh of a voice. "That's enough, all right? Will's got the right attitude. Positivity, that's what we need.

"We need to get Blue out of that hole." Will pointed down to where he'd been stuck. "*That's* what we need."

Foyer stared down at the mound, shaking the Maker's head. "We can't. We can break the curse so we can get to him, but we can't get him out. It's all psychological with neethers. He's only trapped because they made him believe he is."

"Tell him, then," Will said.

"He won't believe the Maker."

"Fine, I'll tell him."

"It's not that simple. Remember when they made you think Blue died? We were talking to you, trying to get you to see sense, but we couldn't get through. The belief's too strong."

Will stared at the mud. "You've unblocked it now?"

Foyer nodded.

"So, he can hear me?"

"I should think so. If you shout loud enough."

Drama was Will's weakest subject at school. But he was determined to make this performance believable. Blue wouldn't let a silly thing like being trapped stop him trying to help someone, Will was certain.

He thought of Christian's bloody corpse closing in on him. Eve's little body splitting and crunching under Dante's foot. The banter's teeth stabbing into his flesh. Conjuring his deepest terrors and forcing them to the front of his mind, he bent over the mud and screamed, "Blue, help! *Help!*"

The wot appeared from thin air in a frantic rush to Will's rescue.

Will's scream briefly turned into a cheer when he saw his idea had worked but ended as a startled yelp when Blue bashed him aside and flew at the Maker. "No, stop," he shouted, hurting his throat. He grabbed Blue's coat to hold him back. "It's Foyer, it's Foyer!"

Blue glared at him, then back at the Maker.

Foyer nodded brightly. "It's okay, it's me. And the others. We've possessed him good and proper. There's nothing he can do about it. Nothing. And this is the Maker we're talking about." He laughed. "Isn't that funny? In a way?"

Blue didn't laugh.

"Yes, well. Don't worry your head. We're sorted now."

"Sorted?" Blue repeated. "*Sorted?* You're all dead. I've only got four gems. There are still two witches out there intent on taking our power. And let's not forget - you're all dead!"

"Don't be too cheerful, Blue." Foyer's gaze kept veering to Dante, and she smiled sweetly at him every time. "Listen," he said, giving Blue his full attention. "It's going to be okay. We'll work out a way to get the Maker to render Molina and Tamzin powerless and bring us all back to life. Piece of cake."

"The Maker can't bring people back to life," Blue reminded them. "He never could." He looked away. "I've been thinking," he said reluctantly. "I know what has to be done now. And it's my decision to make."

Will expected Dyelann to interrupt with a sarcastic comment at this point and was surprised when the wot said nothing. There was a respectful silence that Blue also seemed to have picked up on, as his nervousness all but vanished.

"What decision is that, Blue?" Dante asked quietly.

Blue lifted the witch's hand with his fingertips, staring down at her black nails. It was like he'd grown up all of a sudden. No longer a lost, frightened child, but a man who knew exactly where he was headed. "You'll know soon enough," he whispered. He gave the back of her hand a quick peck before dropping it like a hot potato and reaching into his pockets. "But first things first." He brought out the white gem. Then the red and the yellow. Last came his own. The blue hue of the cave accentuated its already inimitable beauty.

It shuddered, and Blue's pupils spread wide and black over the whites of his eyes. Veins bulged under his greying skin.

Will gripped Dante's hand.

"Blue, what are you doing?" Foyer shouted. "We don't want the powers joining, we want them separating. You're just doing what the neethers want."

Blue dropped all the gems but his own carelessly to the ground. "Don't worry. They'll be separated before any harm is done."

Foyer looked wistfully at the three powerless gems laid at Blue's feet. "Then, won't you be needing those?"

Blue's fingers caressed the blue gem while he gave it one last sorrowful look. Then he let it go. It landed with a sharp crack on top of the others. "I don't think so, no."

Will wanted to ask why, but he dared not ask the question out loud. Dyelann seemed to hear it regardless.

"Because he's crazy," he said. "Are you sentencing us to death now?"

"You're already dead," Blue whispered, refusing to meet his eye.

"We could live again. Everything's on our side now." He gestured to their surroundings with Will's arms, glaring at Blue. "Everything except for you, that is."

"I don't know how you can say that to me."

"If your decision is to keep the power for yourself and let us float around in our fun little afterlives until the end of time, then it is *not* your decision to make. How dare you?"

"All the decisions from now on are mine. Seeing as I'm the only one still breathing."

Dante's hand tightened around Will's. "Blue, this isn't you speaking."

"It is. I know I sound cruel, but I'm not. The Maker's descendant was always going to unmake the wots. The time has come. It's now. This is just what was always meant to happen. It's inevitable."

"So you're just going to roll over and give in?"

Blue's face crumpled in anguish. "It's not about giving in. I won't let anyone take the powers. I promise."

A surge of fear sent a flutter to Will's chest. Blue wouldn't keep the powers for himself. If he wasn't going to let anyone take them, there was only one option left. "You're going to kill yourself, aren't you?" he said in a small voice. All eyes turned to him. "Please don't."

"Come on, I'm not going to kill myself." Blue ran an unsteady hand over his head. "I'm just going to give the powers back to the earth, that's all. Put them back where they belong."

"Which will *kill* you." Dyelann made an angry growl of a sound under Will's breath, cursing Blue.

"Just like the Maker wants," Foyer murmured, cold disappointment in his words.

"Yes. And now I understand why." Blue's sad voice pleaded for their understanding. "If they go back to where they belong, we're free. We'll stay together. The Maker will go back to his family. The neethers will be gone. It'll take away the possibility of immortal evil, forever. Maybe it will even absolve Molina somehow, I don't know."

Will put a hand to his stomach, sickened. "What about what you said before, about a world without wishes and how horrible it would be?"

Blue smiled dryly. "There will always be wishes," he said. "Maybe they'd be more special if the ones that came true were worked for." He appealed to the wots in the Maker. "Don't you see? It's the only way."

"We could try though," Foyer said, little over a whisper. "We could try and find a way to come back to life, and things could go back to the way they've always been. Don't you want that?"

"Of course I do," Blue said longingly. "But you know it's not possible. You know. And I don't want to be alone. I don't want to be fighting off neethers and bad witches and whoever else tries to steal the power. It would happen eventually. You know it would. Then what? We all stay here forever, like the Maker had to do, going mad, watching while our power goes to evil? No. I'm sorry, but no."

An unrelenting ache grew inside Will that he knew did not belong to him. It belonged to Dyelann. On the outside Dyelann came across as unflappable, tough, sometimes even uncaring - but Will knew the truth now. Pain was spreading from Dyelann like ink from a leaking pen, blotting through his heart and into Will's.

"Great," Dyelann said, and Will was impressed by how he retained his composure despite the devastation he endured inside. "If you've got your mind all made up about this already, why did you bother joining the powers? Huh? Why not return them right now?"

"You know I can't do it myself." Blue wrapped his ice-cold, trembling fingers around Will's wrist. "I have to make sure Will and Dante will be safe first. Then it will be time."

"Time to snub out our race forever," Dyelann said.

Blue closed his eyes. "I'm sorry."

Daylight streamed all around them, blindingly bright after their time underground. They were out in the open, by the hole that Will and Dyelann had fallen into the efferby tomb through. Trees flittered noisily in the thrashing wind. And Blue was gone.

Chapter Twenty-Six: Last Wishes

The ever-persistent shadow flitted by overhead but, as always, vanished in the second it took Will to register its presence. He'd nearly forgotten about the blood reaper until then and was all at once dragged back to his frightening realisation he was not too young to be killed in this place and almost certainly would be. Of course, Blue intended to end it all before Will had the chance to be hurt – but that wasn't what Will wanted. Will wanted the wots to live, for them all to be saved, for the bad guys to pack up and leave them alone. There was no chance of that ever happening though. The baddies would never give up. Blue knew that too. That was why Blue had chosen the only way out.

Will scanned the sky for the reaper he knew he wouldn't find. It seemed to know exactly when he was looking and when he wasn't, only ever allowing him to catch a glimpse from the corner of his eye.

Dante scrunched her hair in both hands and muttered to herself, while the Maker stared into the distance.

"Where's Blue gone now?" Will asked her. "What's he going to do?"

"Oh, Will, I don't know what's going on in his head. I don't know what he's going to do. I just don't know. I can't believe this is happening."

Dyelann grunted. "Believe it, sister."

Dante bared her teeth, livid. "My *sister*." She spat like a feral cat and pulled her hands away from her head, leaving her hair sticking out mad-professor-style. "This is all her doing. She's my big sister. I've loved and trusted her my entire life. How could she betray me like this? How could she betray Gart, and Auntie Scilla, and everybody? I just can't believe it."

"Believe it already!" Dyelann snapped. "Because it's happening and there's nothing any one of us can do about it."

"Except talk some sense into Blue." Dante glanced guiltily at Dyelann. "Unless he already is seeing sense. I mean, I understand, in a way, why he's doing what he's doing. And I know how brave he is to have made that decision alone. But… But…"

Foyer put a consoling arm around her and said, "I know."

One of the other wots took control of the body and pushed her away with unnecessary force.

"Stop doing that," she said through gritted teeth, finding her balance. She held Will by his elbow. "Will. You. You're the answer. Remember how you took us to your hospital, how we had no powers? You created a whole new reality out of nothing, a building full of people who never existed. If you have the ability to do that, then you have to be able to put a stop to all this. You have to."

The Maker's small frame juddered in a violent spasm. His eyes, dull and sunken, turned red, the sheer effort of taking control of his body long enough to speak bursting his blood vessels. "The boy can do nothing," he wheezed.

Dante curled her lip. "What woke *you* up?"

"He can do nothing," the Maker said again, sinking as his strength waned. He staggered and took a laboured breath. "Not anymore."

Will's already glum heart deflated with disappointment.

"It was my power, never his," the Maker explained. "Don't misconstrue," he added, steadily lowering himself to sit on his knees. "He has incredible will. He must, to have been able to suppress me while I shared his body. But it is not wishing will. It is something very different."

"Do you really expect us to believe that?" Dante chided. "You couldn't have possessed him if he were an ordinary child. You would have possessed someone centuries ago if you could."

The Maker heaved another deep, grating breath and slumped sidewards. "Quite right. There is nothing ordinary about him. His essence drew me to him and allowed my spirit to pass into his body, but that was nothing to do with wishing will. It was nothing to do with magic either. It was something else. Something unique. I didn't understand before, how he could take another's power and manipulate it, strengthen it, use it without even thinking about it. But I see it now."

Dante stooped to the Maker's level. "Go on, then. What?"

"He is an elite."

Dante stood up and turned away, snorting. "You're crazy. You're just trying to delay us so Blue will go ahead and do exactly what you wanted doing in the first place."

Dyelann's annoyance scrunched Will's face. "Come on. We've got to stop him before he gets to those witches."

"You're already too late," the Maker shouted, swaying with the effort of holding back the wots inside him. "And I'm telling you the truth. The boy was stronger than I was while I possessed him, but it was my power he honed. You saw what happened when he touched the gems. That was Will's reaction to their power, not mine. He overpowered me because he is an elite. That is the only reason. That is the only reason I could possess him in the first place. And that is the only reason he could bring Blue back to life."

Dante took Will firmly by the hand. "Just ignore him," she said kindly, as though she thought the Maker's words had hurt him. "Foyer, please, just shut him up, can't you?"

"What's an elite?" Will whispered to Dyelann.

"A dead person, Will," Dyelann muttered back, allowing Dante to drag him along behind her. "That's why you can believe he's a liar."

A nervous knot tied itself up in Will's stomach, and he automatically searched the skies for the reaper. "He thinks I'm dead? Why? Why would he think that?"

"He's just trying to spook you. Don't worry about that. Worry about Blue. Worry about us."

The Maker staggered slowly after them. "Why do you think there's been a reaper over his head this whole time? It can't understand what it's seeing, that's why. It's never seen a living elite before. It's probably expecting the child to drop down dead any second. Or wondering if its brethren missed a job eleven years ago."

"We're not listening," Dante sang.

"Where are we going?" Will asked.

"To find my sister before Blue does," she snapped, taking out her frustration in every word.

The Maker coughed, fighting for air. "I told you, it's too late. Blue's been gone longer than you think. He conjured up a stun potion for us before he left. A strong one."

Dante dropped Will's hand, caught her wand from her sleeve and swept it up to open her portal in one fluid motion. After a quick fumble in a pocket on her trouser leg, she lifted out a small test tube, bit and spat out its cork, and flicked the watery contents into the light. "Come," she said, snatching up Will's hand again and glaring at the Maker. "Foyer, please shut him up and get in here."

Will stumbled through the portal and bumped into Foosay's woolly back. She and Alice were hiding behind a tree, peering around the trunk for an obscured view of Scilla's house and whispering urgently to one another.

"Oh, hi," Will said, pleased to see friends.

"Shh!" Without so much as glancing his way, Foosay grappled for his arm and yanked him to her side.

Dante and the Maker arrived, and they too were instantly hushed and hidden by the elderly witches.

"What's going on?" Dante asked. "My portal wasn't supposed to bring us here. It was supposed to take me to my sister."

"Your sister is in there." Foosay indicated to the house. "She's with Tamzin."

"And they have Blue," Alice said gravely in her tiny mouse voice. "I have failed him."

Foyer took her withered hand in the Maker's. "You've always been a guardian angel to Blue, Alice. You could never fail him."

"But I have, my dear friend, for he is locked away with the enemy." She narrowed her colourless eyes. "You've changed somewhat, Foyer, my dear-heart."

Foyer smiled.

Dante eyed the two of them with jealous disgust, and then craned her neck to get a better view of her aunt's cottage, detest in her glare. "I need to get Blue out of there. Will, do your thing. Try and will him out. I know you can do it. I know you can."

"No, don't you move, boy," Foosay said. "Dante, your sister is not to be underestimated. Alice's eye revealed to us that Molina acquired some extra power of her own. She stole it from Goddess Nanita of the North, after summoning her under false pretences."

"She did *what?"* Dante raised a fist and struggled to restrain herself from thumping the tree they stood by, swelling with suppressed fury.

Foosay shifted back and forth like she wanted nothing more than to burst into the house herself. "Blue didn't know what he was walking into, the poor lad."

Alice fiddled with her shrivelled prune. "I fear he knew exactly what he was walking into. If anything happens to that young wot, I shall never forgive myself. Not ever. We must do something."

Cesar flickered into view between the elderly witches, startling Will. "If you have any suggestions, I'm all ears," he said. No one else was remotely fazed by his sudden appearance. "The witches are growing in strength, but Blue is a living conduit now and will only be losing hold over his. The longer this goes on, the more powerful the neethers become."

"I've got an idea," Will said with a determined nod. "Send in some badgers."

The group broke their stares on the cottage to look at him.

"Tamzin's scared of badgers," he clarified. "They'll scare her off."

"Or," Foosay said, "how about this?" She brought two dainty glass bottles out from under her rainbow poncho, each containing a fine floury powder, one red, one green. "I could ask my auntie to talk some sense into her. Tamzin may listen to her." She knocked the bottles together and hummed in thought. "We just need to lure her out here first."

"Which will leave the rest of us with just one foe," Foyer said.

"And I'll deal with that one," Dante said darkly. "Stealing the power of her honourable protector and guide from the otherworld, the nerve of her, to betray her family heritage like this. I will never forgive her. When she comes crawling back to me on her hands and knees, begging me for understanding and forgiveness, I'm going to look down on her and say…" She tossed her hair. "*No.*"

Will tried to see the cottage. "Do you think he's okay in there?" He stepped away from the tree, but Foosay caught him and yanked him back, one-handed, faster and stronger than Will would have ever expected from such an old lady. "I just want to look through the window."

"Let him go," the Maker rasped, and Dante turned her vicious glare his way. "He's an elite. Fortune will favour him."

"An elite?" Foosay repeated in a faraway murmur.

While she was distracted, Will made a dash for the house, ignoring the angry cries that followed. Crouched low to avoid being spotted, he tiptoed up the porch steps. Adrenaline coursed through him like a scream bubbling his blood, readying him in case he needed to run. His leg muscles ached in anticipation. He hid under the window, bracing himself. Quietly, slowly, he reached up and touched the sill. His breath caught as he lifted himself to the pane. If they saw him – would they kill him?

A blast of pain scattered his senses as the window burst open and slammed into his face. The blow would have floored him had someone not seized his arm and hauled him inside. His friends called out to him, but he was already flat on Scilla's carpet, head spinning from the bash. All the adrenaline that had been building, now he had no use for it, turned into crippling nausea.

Holding his throbbing nose, he blinked his blotchy sight into focus. Tamzin's face swirled together, a picture of glee.

"Oh, look," she chirped. "My two favourite halfwits in the one room." She twizzled one of her pigtails around a finger. "Why, oh why do you keep coming right on back to me, child? You're like a boomerang, always coming back just to be thrown about some more."

Slumped in the corner of the room, blood oozing from his nose and his ears, Blue looked more dead now than he had when he'd actually been dead, and Will's sickness and fear were forced into submission by an overpowering surge of loyalty. He had to protect his friend. Look at what was happening to him. Blue was a good person, with a good heart, and he didn't deserve to be suffering like this. Will let go of his nose, forced his leaking eyes to meet Tamzin's, and wobbled onto his feet.

"Why don't you take a seat?" Tamzin grinned. "Enjoy the show. You see, Molina Simms and I are trying to get the four powers out of this wot. We need them for a spell to give us our eternal life. Well," she whispered, "*my* eternal life." She put a finger to her lips. "Shh."

"But you have that anyway." Will wondered if there was any chance of appealing to Tamzin's better nature. Maybe she wasn't such a monster. She was just an old lady who missed her granddaughter, after all.

"No." Tamzin twirled her stubby, charred wand between two fingers and slipped it neatly back into her pocket like a gun in a holster. "I may have my wily ways of cheating death, yes, a few tricks up my sleeve. I can reverse my age and appear young again. But I'm not immortal. I can't keep this up forever. I can't…" She stopped. "Wait. Why am I justifying myself to you? I can't stand you, you little worm. You killed me. You wasted one of my lives."

"Why do you want to live forever, anyway?" Will tried again. "What about Lillian?"

Hatred flashed in Tamzin's eyes.

"Don't you love her anymore?"

Just as Tamzin's rage was about to burst to the surface, Molina stalked into the room.

"What's this?" She stared at Will. "What's he doing here?"

Tamzin flounced past Molina and kicked Blue viciously in the ribs. Will recoiled as if he'd felt the pain himself, deciding then that Tamzin really was a monster. There would be no appealing to her better nature. She had no better nature.

"Stop." Molina held up a hand. "If he's here, my sister won't be far behind."

"Who cares about your sister? If we don't get those powers out of him soon, I swear, I'll kill him."

"That's what he wants you to do, you brainless hag."

"How can you be so nasty?" Will demanded. "You're supposed to be his friends. He's never done anything to you."

"He's the reason my granddaughter's dead!" Tamzin screamed in Will's face and knocked him backwards into the wall.

Will hurried to push himself back up. "If you're too selfish to think of anyone else but yourself when you're making wishes not to die, that's your fault, not his."

Tamzin's mouth fell open in disbelief at Will's words. "How do you…? How do you…?"

Molina caught Tamzin's upper arm. Her fingers curled like talons, long nails digging in. "If that wot dies before we have those powers, they disappear forever. If that happens, so help me… I have been working too long and too hard to ever let that happen. I've sacrificed too much to ever let that happen. Do you understand me?"

Tamzin glared at Molina and said nothing.

"You hear me?" Molina shouted, making Will jump with fright.

"Who do you think you are?" Tamzin said, intimidatingly fierce.

"You have to stop this," Will begged.

Tamzin wrenched her arm free of Molina's intense grip and raised a hand as if to strike Will. He flinched and cowed back, but her arm stopped mid-swing. The ferocity in her face changed drastically into an expression of mortal dread.

Molina turned to see what had happened. So did Will. And he smiled at the sight of a real live badger snuffling around the doorway.

Tamzin backed into the open window, hyperventilating as if the Devil himself had walked in. She grasped at the sill, preparing to leap through it, but froze in position when Foosay appeared at the other side.

Foosay smiled, waved, then flicked a handful of her green and red powder into the room. It hit the air like a puff of talc and gradually settled on the ghostly surface of a small, invisible person. At first Will thought Foosay must have accidentally thrown her potion over Cesar, but the dust sparkled and began to melt away. The vague human shape grew more defined, until there was a child of Will's age left standing there; a girl whose blonde hair was tied in pigtails just like Tamzin's. The profound sadness with which she gazed up at Tamzin made Will's heart ache for her.

"Grandma?"

Tamzin's face crumpled in grief. "Lillian? Baby?" Tears spilled down her cheeks. Right there before their eyes she withered, fast motion, into the worn old woman she'd been hiding from the world for the last eleven years. Her dungarees loosened around her flesh that aged and shrank away. The shine dulled from her hair, blonde faded to grey, and it thinned until the bands that tied her pigtails slipped free.

Lillian took one of Tamzin's thin, freckled hands between her own, still gazing at her as though she hadn't changed at all. "I have to tell you this. You need to know who murdered me. It was Molina Simms, Grandma."

Tamzin took a fleeting glance at Molina, who stood guard at Blue's side, but looked straight back to Lillian, at a loss for words, shaking her head.

"Please don't do this," the little girl went on. "Don't help her. She murdered me to make you sad. She knew who you were. She knew before you did. She knew everything. She wanted you hurting so that when she was ready for you, you would be there to help her with only blackness in your heart."

"Baby, I…" Tamzin shook her head again, weeping freely, clearly struggling to think straight. "I just love you so much. I'm so sorry, Lil. I'm so sorry."

"I know that, Grandma." Lillian smiled. "I've always known that."

"Ohhh," Molina groaned. "Give me a break. Please. I'm about to lose my breakfast." She snarled and aimed her wand at Lillian's ethereal form, which swirled away into the air like smoke from a blown-out match.

Tamzin collapsed in a folded heap on the carpet. "How could you? How could you kill an innocent little girl in cold blood for your own selfish gain?"

Molina grabbed her viciously by her wispy, grey hair, and leaned over to spit the answer directly into her ear. "The same way you were ready to kill an innocent little boy for yours."

A shocked cry of pain from Tamzin was cut short when Molina shoved the old lady's head towards the floor and let go of her. Only then did Will see the torn-out chunk of hair and scalp dangling from Molina's fingers, which she was quick to push into the narrow neck of a glass bottle she'd plucked out of her jacket pocket. She replaced the screw cap, shook the murky brown liquid twice, and slid the bottle out of sight.

Tamzin stared at the badger, shaking where she stooped. "My God. What have you turned me into?"

Molina suddenly had Will by the throat, and she gave him a violent shake. He was a rag doll to her, nothing more. He yelped and gagged and tried to apologise to her, tried to beg her to stop, but couldn't make a sound.

"I've worked too long for this moment for you or anyone else to screw it all up at the final hurdle, Rickrack. This is my moment. This is my time. I've earned it."

An enormous, thick-skinned hand crashed through the window and wrapped around Molina's neck, causing her to release her hold on Will's at last.

Esko peered through the window at the witch dangling from his grip.

"Let go of me," she said, articulating each word. "I am warning you."

"You killed my Alley!" Esko roared, matching the witch's madness. "Now I'm going to kill you."

She rolled her eyes at him. "Gudmé," she said. "Get him off me."

A harmlessly small spider that Will hadn't even noticed in one corner of the ceiling grew bigger and bigger as it skittered down the wall with freakish speed. The dog-sized spider, still growing, took a leap through the window and transformed into a huge, ugly, stripeless tiger in mid-air, large enough and solid enough to knock the wye clean off his feet.

Molina brushed herself off. "I warned him," she said, as if she'd been the reasonable one.

Will ran to Blue and desperately shook his arm. "Come on, Blue, wake up. You've got to wake up." He lost his hold. Spectral hands took him by every limb, swept the floor from under him and threw him back across the room, where he smacked into the wall with a painful crunch.

Molina wagged a finger at him. "Hands off the wot."

The door burst from its hinges, and finally some reinforcement arrived. Dante, Foosay, Alice and Cesar all rushed to Will's aid. Unfortunately, before they were able to reinforce anything, Molina introduced all four of them to the same wall she'd just thrown Will into. They landed on top of him, squashing him against the carpet.

Yelping in a suffocated panic, he struggled to free himself from the mass of arms and legs.

A loud thumping sound drew his attention: Neethers darkened every window, flinging themselves aggressively at the building like crazed animals. They were all around, all wanting in.

"Stay back!" Molina showed the creatures her palms, and apparently the neethers could approach no further. Floating bodies were even colliding against the open window like it was solid.

Molina's anger was so intense her eyeballs seemed to bulge from their sockets. She took the bottle back out of her pocket. The liquid inside was now inky black. She gave it one last shake, kissed it, and threw it at Blue like she intended to kill him with it. The neck of the bottle broke against his chest and its contents evaporated into a blast of steam as if it had struck scorching heat. Ballistic, wild-eyed, Molina pointed her wand at him.

Blue's limp body lifted. A quivering wave left him, crystalline sparks bursting from the pulse of energy, and it shimmered its way towards Molina. As soon as it was all gone from Blue, he toppled back to the floor.

She laughed with excitement at the wave rippling up her body, on and on until it was a manic scream of jubilation.

The neethers that surrounded the house howled out in unison, a haunting chorus, like a pack of wild dogs.

Will, along with Dante and Cesar, looked on in stunned disbelief. Molina couldn't really have the power. She couldn't really have won. Could she?

On hands and knees Will shuffled to Blue and patted his arm. "Blue? Please wake up."

A neether shifted its position behind one of the windows and allowed Will a glimpse of the battling giants through the gap. The tiger-monster had clawed Esko's huge torso open like a slab of meat and was hanging over him, yellow fangs bared in his face, as though merely holding the wye in place until he received further orders. The neether slammed itself back into its place against the glass, the impact creating a crack that splintered and spread out across the window like a spider's web.

Molina drew a deep breath and released it steadily, eyes closed. "I did it," she whispered, hoarse from shouting. "I possess more power than any single being ever has in this world before me. I shall live forever, a Goddess in my world. My world." Her pupils were gigantic and black and took over the whites of her eyes, as Blue's had done before her. She floated just like a neether, those massive, inhuman eyes staring intensely at Will. "And the first thing I am going to do for my world… is rid it of you."

The Maker banged on the door for attention. "You cannot kill him," he announced, propped up against the doorframe. "The child is an elite."

Molina floated closer to the Maker. "Nonsense. You'll see when his insides are splattered all over this room just how 'elite' he is."

"It's true." Foosay's silver candyfloss hair wobbled as she lifted herself stiffly up from the floor. "He's telling the truth. A touch of the lips, A wish in the blood, Alive an undead, A soul born of good. That's the transcription of a centuries-old premonition, Miss Simms. It's what is needed to bring a dead wot back to life. You can't kill him."

"You think I fear a higher power now?" Molina's eyes flared in mad ecstasy. "I *am* a higher power. I don't care if he's an angel from heaven or a demon from the deepest circle of hell. If he is indeed an elite, he should have been dead a long time ago." A spiteful smile crept onto her face. She slowly turned to Will, pulling an enormous blade from somewhere behind her back. "So, let me help you with that."

Blue lurched onto his feet and threw himself in front of Will, just in time to receive the dagger that spiralled his way. The tip of its point protruded from his chest, right in front of Will's face.

Will stared at it in shock. Blood accumulated and dribbled. Holding Blue's arms, willing the wot to stay on his feet, he tore his eyes from the dark, wet tip of the blade to look at Blue's face. "Please don't die," he squeaked, tears stinging.

"It's okay," Blue whispered. He took a shallow breath. "I worked it out. It's going to be okay."

The life left him in moments. His light dimmed and down he fell. Will stood fast, convulsing with agonising sobs, hands still poised where Blue should have been.

Tamzin stood in the centre of the room, no longer a quivering, broken old woman but a fierce and angry witch with a look of devilment about her that rivalled Molina's. Clutching her stumpy wand in both hands with such force it snapped into two jagged pieces, she shouted, "Return you now Fire, Air, Water and Earth. Return here now powers inherent from birth!"

An immense shudder of energy sprung from the remains of her black wand and enveloped the entire room.

Molina's skin turned paper white as the wave of energy she stole from Blue retreated from her. It wobbled around her, distorting reality. An almighty snap caused a united cry of pain from everyone in the room. They were all sent catapulting backwards as the power exploded, sweeping over everything in its path and shaking the walls around them.

The neethers emitted ear-splitting howls of despair. When the shockwave hit them, it reduced each one of them to a cloud of pink dust.

Molina lay in a disfigured heap on the floor, some of her bald head visible under her twisted bandana.

"I loved that baby girl more than anything in this world," Tamzin said. "And you stole her from me."

Molina, trying to sit up, let out a strange laugh of disdain. "If you love the dead child so much…" She lifted her wand in a trembling hand. "Join her!"

Tamzin snatched the wand away from the weakened witch and aimed it down, right over Molina's heart. "This," she hissed, "is for my granddaughter." She pressed the point of the wand into Molina's chest and bore down on it. Molina's horrific wail continued to echo around the house after it had stopped.

Tamzin stood. She rubbed the top of her head. She walked out of the house. Her feet rapped against the hollow porch as she went. Then, barring Will's gentle whimpering, there was silence.

Dante stepped around her sister's body to get to Blue. She dropped beside him and lifted his head and shoulders into her embrace. "Oh, Blue. What have you done?"

Foosay rushed to Will and hugged him in her grandmotherly way, rocking him back and forth. "You're okay, dear. You're okay."

Will's heart was broken. He was not okay.

Alice poked Molina's back with the tip of her boot. "She's dead."

"Good," Dante croaked, but Will knew she didn't mean what she'd said. She looked at him hopefully through red, weeping eyes. "Dye, is Blue with you now?" she asked in whisper. "Is he here?"

"Dyelann's gone," he tried to say, but his throat was locked so tight the words could not escape. She must have read his lips, for she immediately looked to the doorway for the Maker. There was no sign of him.

"He disappeared," Esko said gruffly from behind the broken window. "The bod. He disappeared."

"He's not the only one," Foosay said softly, lulling Will. She gazed at Dante, who still held Blue in her arms. "I'm sure he and the others are fine now. They will have passed on."

A sob caught in Dante's throat. Tears dripped from her chin. "But I don't want them to pass on. They're wots, they're not meant to pass on. They belong here with us. With me." She stroked her fingers through Blue's hair, like that might somehow revive him. "This can't be real."

Will backed away from Foosay and headed woozily for the door. "I want to go home," he said. "Please, someone, take me home. I just want to go home."

Dante laid Blue back down and gave him a gentle kiss on the forehead. Then she stroked his hair back one last time. "I'll take you home," she said, standing. "Come on." She rested an arm around Will and the two of them guided each other out of the house.

The porch creaked as they descended the steps. Birds sang and twittered happily in the brightness of the day outside. And Dante and Will, quiet in their shared grief, wandered out amidst the trees.

All Will could see was a murky blur through his tears. The image of Blue's pouring blood hammered relentlessly through his mind. It was too much. He wasn't aware of falling, but he was suddenly on his knees in the grass, unable to breathe for the rock-hard lump in his throat. He felt like he would choke on it. Dante knelt beside him and held him, hushing him, but he was inconsolable then, crying like he'd never cried before. This time he didn't care who was watching.

"Listen to me, Will," Dante said. "You did everything you could. You gave them a bigger chance than they would ever have had alone. I know they're so grateful to you."

"Doesn't matter," Will warbled, pressing his soggy face to his sleeve. "Blue's such an idiot. He shouldn't have let her kill him." He sniffled. "He shouldn't have let her kill him."

After a few minutes, Dante stroked Will's back and took a sharp breath. "Do you know what an elite is, Will?" she asked.

He didn't answer. He didn't care.

"Well," Dante went on. "When a special type of soul is brought into this world, a soul that is very pure and very good, they are taken by the angels to be protected and nurtured. And these chosen souls are called the elite. They become very special beings, like angels, that guide and protect the living from their home in the otherworld. They're usually taken before they're born, or within their first two years of life, before this world can damage them."

Will didn't move. "I can't be one, then," he muttered. He couldn't understand why she was even telling him this now. It didn't matter. Nothing mattered. Nothing would ever matter again. He gave another big sniff.

"You're an amazing anomaly." Dante leaned back to get a better look at him. "It was foreseen a long time ago who could bring a wot back to the land of the living. What Foosay said back in the house, about the lips and the blood, all of that; it's you, Will. You brought Blue back to life. It was meant to be. It was for a reason."

"What reason? So he could just die again?"

"If you hadn't saved Blue when you did, my sister and Tamzin would have taken the four powers for themselves. Between them and the neethers, they'd have torn this world apart." She took another deep, pensive breath, and then anger blazed in her eyes. "I can't believe how much I hate my sister. I'm glad she's dead." More tears spilled.

"No, you're not."

"If Tamzin hadn't killed her, I would have."

"No, you wouldn't."

Dante closed her eyes. "No," she whispered. "I wouldn't."

"I just wish we could do something. Everyone says you're one of the greatest witches, right? Can't you do something? Anything?"

"I can't bring people back to life, Will," she said carefully. "I can't turn back time. What else do you want me to do?"

Will didn't know. He didn't know anything anymore.

Something moved around in his jacket pocket, and he swatted it unthinkingly. It squeaked. Normally, a pained squeak coming from his pocket might have given him cause for concern, but he could barely summon an interest right now. He watched a rat-sized lump wiggle its way to the surface until the top of a hairy head emerged. A gremlin-like creature climbed free and jumped to the ground.

The instant Dante recognised the bod, she sucked in a breath to shout out and bounced to her feet – but then did nothing. She watched in wonder when Gudmé, head hung in remorse, bowed down.

"What's he doing?" Will peered over the bod's stooped back, confused by its behaviour. "I thought you were a baddie now."

The bod shook its head and clamped its pudgy hands together, begging Will for something.

"You killed Christian," Will said, seeing the wicker's dead body, and then the blood dribbling down Blue's front. He forced the image away in tearful blinks, unable to bear it.

The bod whimpered and sniffled.

"My sister," Dante said. "She put a curse on you, didn't she? To use you as a puppet. To do her bidding."

Nodding, the bod wrapped its arms around her ankle and buried its weeping head into her leg.

She stroked one finger down its hairy back. "Poor little thing."

"So, he never meant to kill Christian? Or fight Esko? Molina made him do it?"

"Bods are loyal to their wickers, Will. I should have known it was Molina's doing. He doesn't have a wicker to be with now. And no one will want him without his twin."

"What happened to him? Badmé, I mean."

"I assume he…" She changed her mind and said kindly, "Maybe he got away."

The bod pointed a finger at the sky. The reaper that had been shadowing Will was now swooping down upon them like a bird of prey on its quarry. Before anyone had chance to react, it came to a soundless, gentle land and slung back its hood to reveal a skull with drooping dead eyes and a permanent toothy smile.

"It's you," Will said with surprise, recognising the reaper he and Dante had asked for help during their search for Adrian's body.

The reaper bowed courteously.

"You're the one who's been following me all this time?" He stood up clumsily, wiping his wet face with the cuff of Cesar's jacket. "Are you going to kill me?"

"Goodness, no." The reaper's slip of a neck made a scratching noise as the bones scraped together. "You are not to die, child. You are to... lith." He grunted, agitated by his disability.

"Why have you been following me then? What do you want?"

"Nothing. I used you to get to Glue." He tilted his head sharply. "Sorry."

Will's lip trembled. "You… You took Blue?"

"Not exactly. The ott is also to lith."

Dante stood up straight, alert. "Wait. What are you…? What are you saying?"

"The energy returned to its source, so the otts couldn't continue as otts, ogiously. Yet they didn't cross to the land o' the dead like they ought."

"What's your point, Jaws?"

The reaper would undoubtedly have scowled at Dante then, had he been able to. Instead, he tucked his chin and glared upward at her. "The otts are no longer otts. They are the itches they started as. That's the oint."

Dante's face fell. "What?"

"No. Itch," the reaper corrected her.

"How? How is this possible? You're telling me they're alive? All of them?"

Hope and excitement bubbled so strong and fast in Will he nearly lost his balance.

"But they were dead," Dante babbled on. "How could they have been brought back to life?"

"They didn't die. Otts are innortal, Dante. Eternal. Their oddies turn to dust athter death, unless they stay soaked, o' course. Their oddies are easily restored out o' the dust. Only no energies, no gens, see? So they're itches again." He shrugged his bony shoulders and froze on hearing the tear of another flap of skin. "Oh… no." His eyes did a squelchy roll in their sockets. "Take heed, child," he said to Will. "I here to tell you, I glad you got through this. You hath greatness ahead o' you. So just… You stay good, okay?"

"Wait!" Will shouted as the reaper began to float away. "Where are they? Where are they all?"

He was certain the reaper was smiling for real now.

"Close," he said with one last nod.

Will didn't watch the reaper leave. Instead, he held onto Dante, that hopeful excitement building until his head felt on the verge of popping like an overblown balloon. "Is he telling the truth?"

The bod hopped like a frog, mimicking Will's excitement, and he pointed again. Will looked in the direction his finger showed them and juddered to an unnatural stop, wilting, overcome by a surge of relief, ecstasy, disbelief.

Blue and Foyer, alive and healthy again, had come to find them.

Will was sobbing again, but this time out of sheer happiness.

Dante squealed with delight and fell into Foyer's open arms. She kissed him firmly on the lips, while he hauled her from her feet and spun her in a couple of circles.

Blue smiled his loveable, lopsided smile at Will and shrugged his shoulders. "Why are you so surprised? Did I not tell you I'd worked it out? Did I not say everything would be okay?"

Will faked a sneer. "Yeah. You did."

"Yes, I did." Blue dragged Will into a quick one-armed hug. "That's because I, my friend, am a genius."

Dyelann trudged up behind them then, a grudgingly pleased expression on his face. "Yeah, right," he said. "Little Blue saved the day. Whoop-de-do. Of course, we're now witches, of all things, and only have about one measly century left to live before we're old and haggard and, well, dead."

Foyer laughed at him. "Better than being dead now, you ungrateful Nnaleyd."

Dyelann raised his eyebrows. "Backwards name. Really? Witches really are the worst."

"I still don't understand how this is possible," Dante said, gazing into Foyer's eyes like she would never look away. "I thought if the powers were returned, you were all dead."

"Tamzin," Foyer said.

"Tamzin?" Dante's face soured. "Tamzin?" she said again, angrier. "You mean to tell me that she saved you all? She actually sent the four powers back to where they'd come from just by shouting it in a loud voice?" She scoffed. "Seriously? If that's all it took, we could have done something ourselves ages ago. I can scream and rhyme as good as the next crazy witch. You know I can."

Foyer chuckled at her. "I think there was a little more to it than that. The Maker's descendant was always going to have more of a sway on the four powers than any other witch. That's why Molina needed her help in the first place. And you saw her. Both of them. All that rage. Anger like that is a natural power boost, but it tends to throw your spells off. It was Tamzin's spell being thrown that made it possible for us to live on as witches. Quite unintentionally, of course."

"How's that?" Dante asked.

"Return here, powers inherent from birth?" Foyer reminded her. "She meant for the four powers to go to her. She didn't realise the words would send the powers back home, or that her spell would apply to everyone in the room." Foyer stroked Dante's arm up and down as he spoke. "We were all given back our powers inherent from birth. We were extraordinarily lucky. Blue only had a couple of heartbeats left in him. Any later, we'd all have been gone for good."

"So, what, we should be thanking Tamzin?"

Foyer grinned at Dante's annoyance. "Like I say, she had no intention of leaving any of us standing. No gratitude necessary."

Dante held him closer. Sadness clouded her eyes. "Molina must have known about Tamzin all along. Tamzin's spell to change everyone's memories couldn't have worked on her. She's been plotting every last detail of this for eleven years."

"Yes. Molina sent the vision to Tamzin in the first place. She believed that only the descendant could bring about the unmaking of the wots. Turns out that was true. In the end."

Will huffed at Blue. "You said you'd figured all this stuff out, but you hadn't at all, had you?"

"I knew exactly what was going to happen," Blue insisted. "I'd absorbed the four energies into my very being. I was all-knowing, all-powerful, all…"

"All talk?" Dyelann gibed.

"Oh, I knew, all right." Blue winced at Will. "At least, I hoped," he admitted.

Will helped Gudmé onto his shoulder and walked alongside Blue as the group slowly began to make tracks. "Blue?" he said.

"Yeah?"

"Thanks. For saving my life."

"That's okay," Blue said. "Thanks for saving mine. I suppose you'll be going home now?"

Will nodded, and Gudmé nodded too. "I suppose."

"I'm really sorry you never got those wishes I promised you."

"That's okay. Did you really mean what you said before? About wishes being worth more if you have to work to make them come true."

Blue laughed out loud. "Not at all! But it's better than nothing, I suppose." He quietened his voice, as though he didn't want the others to overhear. "Hey, Will? If you had one wish now, what would it be?"

That was an easy one. There was only one thing Will wanted.

"I'd wish for you to promise we'll stay friends after I've gone home."

"Really?" Blue said in surprise. Another grin grew on his face, and he gave a satisfied nod. "Good. That's good. That's one wish I'm fairly sure I can still grant."

And Will Morgan didn't stop smiling the entire journey home.

Printed in Great Britain
by Amazon

68367171R00284